DATE DUE

The New York Edition of Henry James

Scribners

THE NOVELS AND TALES OF
HENRY JAMES

———

New York Edition

VOLUME VII

THE TRAGIC MUSE

VOLUME I

HENRY JAMES

NEW YORK

CHARLES SCRIBNER'S SONS

PREFACE

I PROFESS a certain vagueness of remembrance in respect to the origin and growth of " The Tragic Muse," which appeared in the " Atlantic Monthly " again, beginning January 1889 and running on, inordinately, several months beyond its proper twelve. If it be ever of interest and profit to put one's finger on the productive germ of a work of art, and if in fact a lucid account of any such work involves that prime identification, I can but look on the present fiction as a poor fatherless and motherless, a sort of unregistered and unacknowledged birth. I fail to recover my precious first moment of consciousness of the idea to which it was to give form ; to recognise in it — as I like to do in general — the effect of some particular sharp impression or concussion. I call such remembered glimmers always precious, because without them comes no clear vision of what one may have intended, and without that vision no straight measure of what one may have succeeded in doing. What I make out from furthest back is that I must have had from still further back, must in fact practically have always had, the happy thought of some dramatic picture of the " artist-life " and of the difficult terms on which it is at the best secured and enjoyed, the general question of its having to be not altogether easily paid for. To " do something about art " — art, that is, as a human complication and a social stumbling-block — must have been for me early a good deal of a nursed intention, the conflict between art and " the world " striking me thus betimes as one of the half-dozen great primary motives. I remember even having taken for granted with this fond inveteracy that no one of these pregnant themes was likely to prove under the test more full of matter. This being the case, meanwhile, what would all experience have done but enrich one's conviction ? — since if on the one hand I had

v

PREFACE

gained a more and more intimate view of the nature of art and the conditions therewith imposed, so the world was a conception that clearly required, and that would for ever continue to take, any amount of filling-in. The happy and fruitful truth, at all events, was that there was opposition — why there *should* be was another matter — and that the opposition would beget an infinity of situations. What had doubtless occurred in fact, moreover, was that just this question of the essence and the reasons of the opposition had shown itself to demand the light of experience; so that to the growth of experience, truly, the treatment of the subject had yielded. It had waited for that advantage.

Yet I continue to see experience giving me its jog mainly in the form of an invitation from the gentle editor of the " Atlantic," the late Thomas Bailey Aldrich, to contribute to his pages a serial that should run through the year. That friendly appeal becomes thus the most definite statement I can make of the " genesis " of the book; though from the moment of its reaching me everything else in the matter seems to live again. What lives not least, to be quite candid, is the fact that I was to see this production make a virtual end, for the time, as by its sinister effect — though for reasons still obscure to me — of the pleasant old custom of the " running " of the novel. Not for many years was I to feel the practice, for my benefit, confidingly revive. The influence of " The Tragic Muse " was thus exactly other than what I had all earnestly (if of course privately enough) invoked for it, and I remember well the particular chill, at last, of the sense of my having launched it in a great grey void from which no echo or message whatever would come back. None, in the event, ever came, and as I now read the book over I find the circumstance make, in its name, for a special tenderness of charity; even for that finer consideration hanging in the parental breast about the maimed or slighted, the disfigured or defeated, the unlucky or unlikely child — with this hapless small mortal thought of further as somehow " compromising." I am thus able to take the thing as having quite wittingly and undisturbedly existed for itself

vi

alone, and to liken it to some aromatic bag of gathered herbs of which the string has never been loosed; or, better still, to some jar of potpourri, shaped and overfigured and polished, but of which the lid, never lifted, has provided for the intense accumulation of the fragrance within. The consistent, the sustained, preserved *tone* of "The Tragic Muse," its constant and doubtless rather fine-drawn truth to its particular sought pitch and accent, are, critically speaking, its principal merit — the inner harmony that I perhaps presumptuously permit myself to compare to an unevaporated scent.

After which indeed I may well be summoned to say what I mean, in such a business, by an appreciable " tone " and how I can justify my claim to it — a demonstration that will await us later. Suffice it just here that I find the latent historic clue in my hand again with the easy recall of my prompt grasp of such a chance to make a story about art. *There* was my subject this time — all mature with having long waited, and with the blest dignity that my original perception of its value was quite lost in the mists of youth. I must long have carried in my head the notion of a young man who should amid difficulty — the difficulties being the story — have abandoned " public life " for the zealous pursuit of some supposedly minor craft ; just as, evidently, there had hovered before me some possible picture (but all comic and ironic) of one of the most salient London " social " passions, the unappeasable curiosity for the things of the theatre ; for every one of them, that is, except the drama itself, and for the " personality " of the performer (almost any performer quite sufficiently serving) in particular. This latter, verily, had struck me as an aspect appealing mainly to satiric treatment ; the only adequate or effective treatment, I had again and again felt, for most of the distinctively social aspects of London : the general artlessly histrionised air of things caused so many examples to spring from behind any hedge. What came up, however, at once, for my own stretched canvas, was that it would have to be ample, give me really space to turn round, and that a single illustrative case might easily be meagre fare. The young man who should

" chuck " admired politics, and of course some other admired object with them, would be all very well; but he would n't be enough — therefore what should one say to some other young man who would chuck something and somebody else, admired in their way too ?

There need never, at the worst, be any difficulty about the things advantageously chuckable for art; the question is all but of choosing them in the heap. Yet were I to represent a struggle — an interesting one, indispensably — with the passions of the theatre (as a profession, or at least as an absorption) I should have to place the theatre in another light than the satiric. This, however, would by good luck be perfectly possible too — without a sacrifice of truth; and I should doubtless even be able to make my theatric case as important as I might desire it. It seemed clear that I needed big cases — small ones would practically give my central idea away; and I make out now my still labouring under the illusion that the case of the sacrifice for art *can* ever be, with truth, with taste, with discretion involved, apparently and showily " big." I dare say it glimmered upon me even then that the very sharpest difficulty of the victim of the conflict I should seek to represent, and the very highest interest of his predicament, dwell deep in the fact that his repudiation of the great obvious, great moral or functional or useful character, shall just have to consent to resemble a surrender for absolutely nothing. Those characters are all large and expansive, seated and established and endowed; whereas the most charming truth about the preference for art is that to parade abroad so thoroughly inward and so naturally embarrassed a matter is to falsify and vulgarise it; that as a preference attended with the honours of publicity it is indeed nowhere; that in fact, under the rule of its sincerity, its only honours are those of contraction, concentration and a seemingly deplorable indifference to everything but itself. Nothing can well figure as less " big," in an honest thesis, than a marked instance of somebody's willingness to pass mainly for an ass. Of these things I must, I say, have been in strictness aware; what I perhaps failed of was to

PREFACE

note that if a certain romantic glamour (even that of mere eccentricity or of a fine perversity) may be flung over the act of exchange of a " career" for the æsthetic life in general, the prose and the modesty of the matter yet come in with any exhibition of the particular branch of æsthetics selected. Then it is that the attitude of hero or heroine may look too much — for the romantic effect — like a low crouching over proved trifles. Art indeed has in our day taken on so many honours and emoluments that the recognition of its importance is more than a custom, has become on occasion almost a fury : the line is drawn — especially in the English world — only at the importance of heeding what it may mean.

The more I turn my pieces over, at any rate, the more I now see I must have found in them, and I remember how, once well in presence of my three typical examples, my fear of too ample a canvas quite dropped. The only question was that if I had marked my political case, from so far back, for " a story by itself," and then marked my theatrical case for another, the joining together of these interests, originally seen as separate, might, all disgracefully, betray the seam, show for mechanical and superficial. A story was a story, a picture a picture, and I had a mortal horror of two stories, two pictures, in one. The reason of this was the clearest — my subject was immediately, under that disadvantage, so cheated of its indispensable centre as to become of no more use for expressing a main intention than a wheel without a hub is of use for moving a cart. It was a fact, apparently, that one *had* on occasion seen two pictures in one ; were there not for instance certain sublime Tintorettos at Venice, a measureless Crucifixion in especial, which showed without loss of authority half a dozen actions separately taking place ? Yes, that might be, but there had surely been nevertheless a mighty pictorial fusion, so that the virtue of composition had somehow thereby come all mysteriously to its own. Of course the affair would be simple enough if composition could be kept out of the question ; yet by what art or process, what bars and bolts, what unmuzzled dogs and pointed

ix

guns, perform that feat? I had to know myself utterly inapt for any such valour and recognise that, to make it possible, sundry things should have begun for me much further back than I had felt them even in their dawn. A picture without composition slights its most precious chance for beauty, and is moreover not composed at all unless the painter knows *how* that principle of health and safety, working as an absolutely premeditated art, has prevailed. There may in its absence be life, incontestably, as " The Newcomes " has life, as " Les Trois Mousquetaires," as Tolstoi's " Peace and War," have it; but what do such large loose baggy monsters, with their queer elements of the accidental and the arbitrary, artistically *mean?* We have heard it maintained, we well remember, that such things are "superior to art"; but we understand least of all what *that* may mean, and we look in vain for the artist, the divine explanatory genius, who will come to our aid and tell us. There is life and life, and as waste is only life sacrificed and thereby prevented from " counting," I delight in a deep-breathing economy and an organic form. My business was accordingly to " go in " for complete pictorial fusion, some such common interest between my two first notions as would, in spite of their birth under quite different stars, do them no violence at all.

I recall with this confirmed infatuation of retrospect that through the mild perceptions I here glance at there struck for " The Tragic Muse " the first hour of a season of no small subjective felicity; lighted mainly, I seem to see, by a wide west window that, high aloft, looked over near and far London sunsets, a half-grey, half-flushed expanse of London life. The production of the thing, which yet took a good many months, lives for me again all contemporaneously in that full projection, upon my very table, of the good fog-filtered Kensington mornings; which had a way indeed of seeing the sunset in and which at the very last are merged to memory in a different and a sharper pressure, that of an hotel bedroom in Paris during the autumn of 1889, with the Exposition du Centenaire about to end — and my long story, through the usual difficulties, as well. The usual

difficulties — and I fairly cherish the record as some adven-
turer in another line may hug the sense of his inveterate
habit of just saving in time the neck he ever undiscourage-
ably risks — were those bequeathed as a particular vice of
the artistic spirit, against which vigilance had been destined
from the first to exert itself in vain, and the effect of which
was that again and again, perversely, incurably, the centre of
my structure would insist on placing itself *not*, so to speak,
in the middle. It mattered little that the reader with the
idea or the suspicion of a structural centre is the rarest of
friends and of critics — a bird, it would seem, as merely fa-
bled as the phœnix : the terminational terror was none the
less certain to break in and my work threaten to masquerade
for me as an active figure condemned to the disgrace of legs
too short, ever so much too short, for its body. I urge myself to the candid confession that in very few of my productions, to my eye, *has* the organic centre succeeded in getting
into proper position.

Time after time, then, has the precious waistband or
girdle, studded and buckled and placed for brave outward
show, practically worked itself, and in spite of desperate remonstrance, or in other words essential counterplotting, to
a point perilously near the knees — perilously I mean for the
freedom of these parts. In several of my compositions this
displacement has so succeeded, at the crisis, in defying and
resisting me, has appeared so fraught with probable dishonour,
that I still turn upon them, in spite of the greater or less
success of final dissimulation, a rueful and wondering eye.
These productions have in fact, if I may be so bold about
it, specious and spurious centres altogether, to make up for
the failure of the true. As to which in my list they are,
however, that is another business, not on any terms to be
made known. Such at least would seem my resolution so far
as I have thus proceeded. Of any attention ever arrested by
the pages forming the object of this reference that rigour of
discrimination has wholly and consistently failed, I gather,
to constitute a part. In which fact there is perhaps after all
a rough justice — since the infirmity I speak of, for example,

has been always but the direct and immediate fruit of a positive excess of foresight, the overdone desire to provide for future need and lay up heavenly treasure against the demands of my climax. If the art of the drama, as a great French master of it has said, is above all the art of preparations, that is true only to a less extent of the art of the novel, and true exactly in the degree in which the art of the particular novel comes near that of the drama. The first half of a fiction insists ever on figuring to me as the stage or theatre for the second half, and I have in general given so much space to making the theatre propitious that my halves have too often proved strangely unequal. Thereby has arisen with grim regularity the question of artfully, of consummately masking the fault and conferring on the false quantity the brave appearance of the true.

But I am far from pretending that these desperations of ingenuity have not — as through seeming *most* of the very essence of the problem — their exasperated charm ; so far from it that my particular supreme predicament in the Paris hotel, after an undue primary leakage of time, no doubt, over at the great river-spanning museum of the Champ de Mars and the Trocadero, fairly takes on to me now the tender grace of a day that is dead. Re-reading the last chapters of " The Tragic Muse " I catch again the very odour of Paris, which comes up in the rich rumble of the Rue de la Paix — with which my room itself, for that matter, seems impregnated — and which hangs for reminiscence about the embarrassed effort to " finish," not ignobly, within my already exceeded limits ; an effort prolonged each day to those late afternoon hours during which the tone of the terrible city seemed to deepen about one to an effect strangely composed at once of the auspicious and the fatal. The " plot " of Paris thickened at such hours beyond any other plot in the world, I think ; but there one sat meanwhile with another, on one's hands, absolutely requiring precedence. Not the least imperative of one's conditions was thus that one should have really, should have finely and (given one's scale) concisely treated one's subject, in spite of there being so much of the

confounded irreducible quantity still to treat. If I spoke just
now, however, of the "exasperated" charm of supreme
difficulty, that is because the challenge of economic representation so easily becomes, in any of the arts, intensely
interesting to meet. To put all that is possible of one's idea
into a form and compass that will contain and express it
only by delicate adjustments and an exquisite chemistry, so
that there will at the end be neither a drop of one's liquor
left nor a hair's breadth of the rim of one's glass to spare —
every artist will remember how often that sort of necessity
has carried with it its particular inspiration. Therein lies the
secret of the appeal, to his mind, of the successfully *fore-
shortened* thing, where representation is arrived at, as I have
already elsewhere had occasion to urge, not by the addition
of items (a light that has for its attendant shadow a possible
dryness) but by the art of figuring synthetically, a compact-
ness into which the imagination may cut thick, as into the
rich density of wedding-cake. The moral of all which indeed, I fear, is, perhaps too trivially, but that the "thick,"
the false, the dissembling second half of the work before me,
associated throughout with the effort to weight my dramatic
values as heavily as might be, since they had to be so few,
presents that effort as at the very last a quite convulsive, yet
in its way highly agreeable, spasm. Of such mild prodigies
is the "history" of any specific creative effort composed!

But I have got too much out of the "old" Kensington
light of twenty years ago — a lingering oblique ray of which,
to-day surely quite extinct, played for a benediction over my
canvas. From the moment I made out, at my high-perched
west window, my lucky title, that is from the moment
Miriam Rooth herself had given it me, so this young woman
had given me with it her own position in the book, and so
that in turn had given me my precious unity, to which no
more than Miriam was either Nick Dormer or Peter
Sherringham to be sacrificed. Much of the interest of the
matter was immediately therefore in working out the detail
of that unity and — always entrancing range of questions
— the order, the reason, the relation, of presented aspects.

PREFACE

With three *general* aspects, that of Miriam's case, that of Nick's and that of Sherringham's, there was work in plenty cut out; since happy as it might be to say " My several actions beautifully become one," the point of the affair would be in *showing* them beautifully become so — without which showing foul failure hovered and pounced. Well, the pleasure of handling an action (or, otherwise expressed, of a " story ") is at the worst, for a storyteller, immense, and the interest of such a question as for example keeping Nick Dormer's story his and yet making it also and all effectively in a large part Peter Sherringham's, of keeping Sherringham's his and yet making it in its high degree his kinsman's too, and Miriam Rooth's into the bargain ; just as Miriam Rooth's is by the same token quite operatively his and Nick's, and just as that of each of the young men, by an equal logic, very contributively hers — the interest of such a question, I say, is ever so considerably the interest of the system on which the whole thing is done. I see to-day that it was but half a system to say: " Oh Miriam, a case herself, is the *link* between the two other cases " ; that device was to ask for as much help as it gave and to require a good deal more application than it announced on the surface. The sense of a system saves the painter from the baseness of the *arbitrary* stroke, the touch without its reason, but as payment for that service the process insists on being kept impeccably the right one.

These are intimate truths indeed, of which the charm mainly comes out but on experiment and in practice; yet I like to have it well before me here that, after all, " The Tragic Muse " makes it not easy to say which of the situations concerned in it predominates and rules. What has become in that imperfect order, accordingly, of the famous centre of one's subject ? It is surely not in Nick's consciousness — since why, if it be, are we treated to such an intolerable dose of Sherringham's ? It can't be in Sherringham's — we have for that altogether an excess of Nick's. How on the other hand can it be in Miriam's, given that we have no direct exhibition of hers whatever, that we get at it all inferentially and inductively, seeing it only through a more or less bewildered interpretation of it by others. The emphasis is all on an absolutely objective Miriam, and, this affirmed, how — with such an amount of exposed subjectivity all round her — can so dense a medium be a centre? Such questions as those go straight — thanks to which they are, I profess, delightful; going straight they are of the sort that makes answers possible. Miriam *is* central then to analysis, in spite of being objective; central in virtue of the fact that the whole thing has visibly, from the first, to get itself done in dramatic, or at least in scenic conditions — though scenic conditions which are as near an approach to the dramatic as the novel may permit itself and which have this in common with the latter, that they move in the light of *alternation*. This imposes a consistency other than that of the novel at its loosest, and, for one's subject, a different view and a different placing of the centre. The charm of the scenic consistency, the consistency of the multiplication of *aspects*, that of making them amusingly various, had haunted the author of " The Tragic Muse " from far back, and he was in due course to yield to it all luxuriously, too luxuriously perhaps, in " The Awkward Age," as will doubtless with the extension of these remarks be complacently shown.

To put himself at any rate as much as possible under the protection of it had been ever his practice (he had notably done so in " The Princess Casamassima," so frankly panoramic and processional); and in what case could this protection have had more price than in the one before us? No character in a play (any play not a mere monologue) has, for the right expression of the thing, a *usurping* consciousness; the consciousness of others is exhibited exactly in the same way as that of the " hero "; the prodigious consciousness of Hamlet, the most capacious and most crowded, the moral presence the most asserted, in the whole range of fiction, only takes its turn with that of the other agents of the story, no matter how occasional these may be. It is left in other words to answer for itself equally with theirs: wherefore (by a parity of reasoning if not of example) Miriam's might without inconsequence be placed on the same footing ; and all in spite of the fact that the " moral presence " of each of the men most importantly concerned with her — or with the second of whom she at least is importantly concerned — *is* independently answered for. The idea of the book being, as I have said, a picture of some of the personal consequences of the art-appetite raised to intensity, swollen to voracity, the heavy emphasis falls where the symbol of some of the complications so begotten might be made (as I judged, heaven forgive me !) most " amusing " : amusing I mean in the blest very modern sense. I never "go behind" Miriam ; only poor Sherringham goes, a great deal, and Nick Dormer goes a little, and the author, while they so waste wonderment, goes behind *them :* but none the less she is as thoroughly symbolic, as functional, for illustration of the idea, as either of them, while her image had seemed susceptible of a livelier and " prettier " concretion. I had desired for her, I remember, all manageable vividness — so ineluctable had it long appeared to " do the actress," to touch the theatre, to meet that connexion somehow or other, in any free plunge of the speculative fork into the contemporary social salad.

The late R. L. Stevenson was to write to me, I recall — and precisely on the occasion of " The Tragic Muse " — that he was at a loss to conceive how one could find an interest in anything so vulgar or pretend to gather fruit in so scrubby an orchard ; but the view of a creature of the stage, the view of the " histrionic temperament," as suggestive much less, verily, in respect to the poor stage *per se* than in respect to "art" at large, affected me in spite of that as justly tenable. An objection of a more pointed order was forced upon me by an acute friend later on and in another connexion : the challenge of one's right, in any pretended show of social realities, to attach to the image of a " public character," a supposed particular celebrity, a range of interest, of intrinsic distinction, greater than any such display of importance on the part of eminent members of the class as we see them about us. There *was* a nice point if one would — yet only nice enough, after all, to be easily amusing. We shall deal with it later on, however, in a more urgent connexion. What would have worried me much more had it dawned earlier is the light lately thrown by that admirable writer M. Anatole France on the question of any animated view of the histrionic temperament — a light that may well dazzle to distress any ingenuous worker in the same field. In those parts of his brief but inimitable *Histoire Comique* on which he is most to be congratulated — for there are some that prompt to reserves — he has "done the actress," as well as the actor, done above all the mountebank, the mummer and the *cabotin*, and mixed them up with the queer theatric air, in a manner that practically warns all other hands off the material for ever. At the same time I think I saw Miriam, and without a sacrifice of truth, that is of the particular glow of verisimilitude I wished her most to benefit by, in a complexity of relations finer than any that appear possible for the gentry of M. Anatole France.

Her relation to Nick Dormer, for instance, was intended as a superior interest — that of being (while perfectly sincere, sincere for *her*, and therefore perfectly consonant with her impulse perpetually to perform and with her success in performing) the result of a touched imagination, a touched pride for " art," as well as of the charm cast on other sensibilities still. Dormer's relation to herself is a different matter, of which more presently ; but the sympathy she, poor young woman, very generously and intelligently offers him where most people have so stinted it, is disclosed largely at the cost of her egotism and her personal pretensions, even though in fact determined by her sense of their together, Nick and she, postponing the "world" to their conception of other and finer decencies. Nick can't on the whole see — for I have represented him as in his day quite sufficiently troubled and anxious — why he should condemn to ugly feebleness his most prized faculty (most prized, at least, by himself) even in order to keep his seat in Parliament, to inherit Mr. Carteret's blessing and money, to gratify his mother and carry out the mission of his father, to marry Julia Dallow in fine, a beautiful imperative woman with a great many thousands a year. It all comes back in the last analysis to the individual vision of decency, the critical as well as the passionate judgement of it under sharp stress; and Nick's vision and judgement, all on the æsthetic ground, have beautifully coincided, to Miriam's imagination, with a now fully marked, an inspired and impenitent, choice of her own : so that, other considerations powerfully aiding indeed, she is ready to see their interest all splendidly as one. She is in the uplifted state to which sacrifices and submissions loom large, but loom so just because they must write sympathy, write passion, large. Her measure of what she would be capable of for him — capable, that is, of *not* asking of him — will depend on what he shall ask of *her*, but she has no fear of not being able to satisfy him, even to the point of " chucking " for him, if need be, that artistic identity of her own which she has begun to build up. It will all be to the glory therefore of their common infatuation with " art " : she will doubtless be no less willing to serve his than she was eager to serve her own, purged now of the too great shrillness.

This puts her quite on a different level from that of the vivid monsters of M. France, whose artistic identity is the last thing *they* wish to chuck — their only dismissal is of all material and social overdraping. Nick Dormer in point of fact asks of Miriam nothing but that she shall remain " awfully interesting to paint "; but that is *his* relation, which, as I say, is quite a matter by itself. He at any rate, luckily for both of them it may be, doesn't put her to the test : he is so busy with his own case, busy with testing himself and feeling his reality. He has seen himself as giving up precious things for an object, and that object has somehow not been the young woman in question, nor anything very nearly like her. She on the other hand has asked everything of Peter Sherringham, who has asked everything of *her ;* and it is in so doing that she has really most testified for art and invited him to testify. With his professed interest in the theatre — one of those deep subjections that, in men of " taste," the Comédie Française used in old days to conspire for and some such odd and affecting examples of which were to be noted

— he yet offers her his hand and an introduction to the very best society if she will leave the stage. The power — and her having the sense of the power — to " shine " in the world is his highest measure of her, the test applied by him to her beautiful human value ; just as the manner in which she turns on him is the application of her own standard and touchstone. She is perfectly sure of her own ; for — if there were nothing else, and there is much — she has tasted blood, so to speak, in the form of her so prompt and auspicious success with the public, leaving all probations behind (the whole of which, as the book gives it, is too rapid and sudden, though inevitably so : processes, periods, intervals, stages, degrees, connexions, may be easily enough and barely enough named, may be unconvincingly stated, in fiction, to the deep discredit of the writer, but it remains the very deuce to *re-present* them, especially represent them under strong compression and in brief and subordinate terms ; and this even though the novelist who does n't represent, and represent " all the time," is lost, exactly as much lost as the painter who, at his work and given his intention, does n't paint " all the time ").

Turn upon her friend at any rate Miriam does ; and one of my main points is missed if it fails to appear that she does so with absolute sincerity and with the cold passion of the high critic who knows, on sight of them together, the more or less dazzling false from the comparatively grey-coloured true. Sherringham's whole profession has been that he rejoices in her as she is, and that the theatre, the organised theatre, will be, as Matthew Arnold was in those very days pronouncing it, irresistible ; and it is the promptness with which he sheds his pretended faith as soon as it feels in the air the breath of reality, as soon as it asks of him a proof or a sacrifice, it is this that excites her doubtless sufficiently arrogant scorn. Where is the virtue of his high interest if it has verily never *been* an interest to speak of and if all it has suddenly to suggest is that, in face of a serious call, it shall be unblushingly relinquished ? If he and she together, and her great field and future, and the whole cause they had armed and declared for, have not been serious things they have been base make-believes and trivialities — which is what in fact the homage of society to art always turns out so soon as art presumes not to be vulgar and futile. It is immensely the fashion and immensely edifying to listen to, this homage, while it confines its attention to vanities and frauds ; but it knows only terror, feels only horror, the moment that, instead of making all the concessions, art proceeds to ask for a few. Miriam is nothing if not strenuous, and evidently nothing if not " cheeky," where Sherringham is concerned at least : these, in the all-egotistical exhibition to which she is condemned, are the very elements of her figure and the very colours of her portrait. But she is mild and inconsequent for Nick Dormer (who demands of her so little); as if gravely and pityingly embracing the truth that *his* sacrifice, on the right side, is probably to have very little of her sort of recompense. I must have had it well before me that she was all aware of the small strain a great sacrifice to Nick would cost her — by reason of the strong effect on her of his own superior logic, in which the very intensity of concentration was so to find its account.

If the man, however, who holds her personally dear yet holds her extremely personal message to the world cheap, so the man capable of a consistency and, as she regards the matter, of an honesty so much higher than Sherringham's, virtually cares, " really " cares, no straw for his fellow struggler. If Nick Dormer attracts and all-indifferently holds her it is because, like herself and unlike Peter, he puts " art " first ; but the most he thus does for her in the event is to let her see how she may enjoy, in intimacy, the rigour it has taught him and which he cultivates at her expense. This is the situation in which we leave her, though there would be more still to be said about the difference for her of the two relations — that to each of the men — could I fondly suppose as much of the interest of the book " left over " for the reader as for myself. Sherringham for instance offers Miriam marriage, ever so " handsomely " ; but if nothing might lead me on further than the question of what it would have been open to us — us novelists, especially in the old days — to show, " serially," a young man in Nick Dormer's quite different position as offering or a young woman in Miriam's as taking, so for that very reason such an excursion is forbidden me. The trade of the stage-player, and above all of the actress, must have so many detestable sides for the person exercising it that we scarce imagine a full surrender to it without a full surrender, not less, to every immediate compensation, to every freedom and the largest ease within reach : which presentment of the possible case for Miriam would yet have been condemned — and on grounds both various and interesting to trace — to remain very imperfect.

I feel moreover that I might still, with space, abound in remarks about Nick's character and Nick's crisis suggested to my present more reflective vision. It strikes me, alas, that he is not quite so interesting as he was fondly intended to be, and this in spite of the multiplication, within the picture, of his pains and penalties ; so that while I turn this slight anomaly over I come upon a reason that affects me as singularly charming and touching and at which indeed I have already glanced. Any presentation of the artist *in triumph* must be flat in proportion as it really sticks to its subject — it can only smuggle in relief and variety. For, to put the matter in an image, all we then — in his triumph — see of the charm-compeller is the back he turns to us as he bends over his work. " His " triumph, decently, is but the triumph of what he produces, and that is another affair. His romance is the romance he himself projects ; he eats the cake of the very rarest privilege, the most luscious baked in the oven of the gods — therefore he may n't " have " it, in the form of the privilege of the hero, at the same time. The privilege of the hero — that is of the martyr or of the interesting and appealing and comparatively floundering *person* — places him in quite a different category, belongs to him only as to the artist deluded, diverted, frustrated or vanquished ; when the " amateur " in him gains, for our admiration or compassion or whatever, all that the expert has to do without. Therefore I strove in vain, I feel, to embroil and adorn this young man on whom a hundred ingenious touches are thus lavished: he has insisted in the event on looking as simple and flat as some mere brass check or engraved number, the symbol and guarantee of a stored treasure. The better part of him is locked too much away from us, and the part we see has to pass for — well, what it passes for, so lamentedly, among his friends and relatives. No, accordingly, Nick Dormer is n't " the best thing in the book," as I judge I imagined he would be, and it contains nothing better, I make out, than that preserved and achieved unity and quality of tone, a value in itself, which I referred to at the beginning of these remarks. What I mean by this is that the interest created, and the expression of that interest, are things kept, as to kind, genuine and true to themselves. The appeal, the fidelity to the prime motive, is, with no little art, strained clear (even as silver is polished) in a degree answering — at least by intention — to the air of beauty. There is an awkwardness again in having thus belatedly to point such features out; but in that wrought appearance of animation and harmony, that effect of free movement and yet of recurrent and insistent reference, " The Tragic Muse " has struck me again as conscious of a bright advantage.

HENRY JAMES.

THE TRAGIC MUSE

VOLUME I

BOOK FIRST

THE TRAGIC MUSE

I

THE people of France have made it no secret that those of England, as a general thing, are to their perception an inexpressive and speechless race, perpendicular and unsociable, unaddicted to enriching any bareness of contact with verbal or other embroidery. This view might have derived encouragement, a few years ago, in Paris, from the manner in which four persons sat together in silence, one fine day about noon, in the garden, as it is called, of the Palais de l'Industrie — the central court of the great glazed bazaar where, among plants and parterres, gravelled walks and thin fountains, are ranged the figures and groups, the monuments and busts, which form in the annual exhibition of the Salon the department of statuary. The spirit of observation is naturally high at the Salon, quickened by a thousand artful or artless appeals, but it need have put forth no great intensity to take in the characters I mention. As a solicitation of the eye on definite grounds these visitors too constituted a successful plastic fact; and even the most superficial observer would have marked them as products of an insular neighbourhood, representatives of that tweed-and-waterproof class with which, on the recurrent occasions when the English turn out for a holiday — Christmas and Easter,

3

Whitsuntide and the autumn — Paris besprinkles itself at a night's notice. They had about them the indefinable professional look of the British traveller abroad; that air of preparation for exposure, material and moral, which is so oddly combined with the serene revelation of security and of persistence, and which excites, according to individual susceptibility, the ire or the admiration of foreign communities. They were the more unmistakeable as they presented mainly the happier aspects of the energetic race to which they had the honour to belong. The fresh diffused light of the Salon made them clear and important; they were finished creations, in their way, and, ranged there motionless on their green bench, were almost as much on exhibition as if they had been hung on the line.

Three ladies and a young man, they were obviously a family — a mother, two daughters and a son; a circumstance which had the effect at once of making each member of the group doubly typical and of helping to account for their fine taciturnity. They were not, with each other, on terms of ceremony, and also were probably fatigued with their course among the pictures, the rooms on the upper floor. Their attitude, on the part of visitors who had superior features even if they might appear to some passers-by to have neglected a fine opportunity for completing these features with an expression, was after all a kind of tribute to the state of exhaustion, of bewilderment, to which the genius of France is still capable of reducing the proud.

"En v'la des abrutis!" more than one of their fellow gazers might have been heard to exclaim; and certain it is that there was something depressed and discouraged in this interesting group, who sat looking vaguely before them, not noticing the life of the place, somewhat as if each had a private anxiety. It might have been finely guessed, however, that though on many questions they were closely united this present anxiety was not the same for each. If they looked grave, moreover, this was doubtless partly the result of their all being dressed in such mourning as told of a recent bereavement. The eldest of the three ladies had indeed a face of a fine austere mould which would have been moved to gaiety only by some force more insidious than any she was likely to recognise in Paris. Cold, still and considerably worn, it was neither stupid nor hard, — it was firm, narrow and sharp. This competent matron, acquainted evidently with grief but not weakened by it, had a high forehead to which the quality of the skin gave a singular polish — it glittered even when seen at a distance; a nose which achieved a high free curve; and a tendency to throw back her head and carry it well above her, as if to disengage it from the possible entanglements of the rest of her person. If you had seen her walk you would have felt her to tread the earth after a fashion suggesting that in a world where she had long since discovered that one could n't have one's own way one could never tell what annoying aggression might take place, so that it was well, from hour to hour, to save what one could. Lady Agnes saved her head, her white triangular forehead, over which her close-crinkled flaxen hair, reproduced in different shades in her children, made a looped silken canopy like the marquee at a garden-party. Her daughters were as tall as herself — that was visible even as they sat there — and one of them, the younger evidently, altogether pretty; a straight slender grey-eyed English girl of the sort who show " good " figures and fresh complexions. The sister, who was not pretty, was also straight and slender and grey-eyed. But the grey in this case was not so pure, nor were the straightness and the slenderness so maidenly. The brother of these young ladies had taken off his hat as if he felt the air of the summer day heavy in the great pavilion. He was a lean strong clear-faced youth, with a formed nose and thick light-brown hair which lay continuously and profusely back from his forehead, so that to smooth it from the brow to the neck but a single movement of the hand was required. I cannot describe him better than by saying that he was the sort of young Englishman who looks particularly well in strange lands and whose general aspect — his inches, his limbs, his friendly eyes, the modulation of his voice, the cleanness of his flesh-tints and the fashion of his garments — excites on the part of those who encounter him in far countries on the ground of a common speech a delightful sympathy of race. This sympathy may sometimes be qualified by the seen limits of his apprehension, but it almost revels as such horizons recede. We shall see quickly enough how accurate a measure it might have taken of Nicholas Dormer. There was food for suspicion perhaps in the wandering blankness that sat at moments in his eyes, as if he had no attention at all,

6

not the least in the world, at his command; but it is
no more than just to add without delay that this
discouraging symptom was known among those who
liked him by the indulgent name of dreaminess. By
his mother and sisters for instance his dreaminess
was constantly noted. He is the more welcome to the
benefit of such an interpretation as there is always
held to be something engaging in the combination of
the muscular and the musing, the mildness of strength.

After some time, an interval during which these
good people might have appeared to have come, individually, to the Palais de l'Industrie much less to
see the works of art than to think over their domestic
affairs, the young man, rousing himself from his
reverie, addressed one of the girls.

"I say, Biddy, why should we sit moping here all
day? Come and take a turn about with me."

His younger sister, while he got up, leaned forward
a little, looking round her, but she gave for the moment no further sign of complying with his invitation.

"Where shall we find you then if Peter comes?"
asked the other Miss Dormer, making no movement
at all.

"I dare say Peter won't come. He'll leave us here
to cool our heels."

"Oh Nick dear!" Biddy exclaimed in a small
sweet voice of protest. It was plainly her theory that
Peter would come, and even a little her fond fear
that she might miss him should she quit that spot.

"We shall come back in a quarter of an hour.
Really I must look at these things," Nick declared,
turning his face to a marble group which stood near

7

them on the right — a man with the skin of a beast round his loins, tussling with a naked woman in some primitive effort of courtship or capture.

Lady Agnes followed the direction of her son's eyes and then observed: " Everything seems very dreadful. I should think Biddy had better sit still. Has n't she seen enough horrors up above ? "

" I dare say that if Peter comes Julia 'll be with him," the elder girl remarked irrelevantly.

" Well then he can take Julia about. That will be more proper," said Lady Agnes.

" Mother dear, she does n't care a rap about art. It 's a fearful bore looking at fine things with Julia," Nick returned.

" Won't you go with him, Grace ? " — and Biddy appealed to her sister.

" I think she has awfully good taste! " Grace exclaimed, not answering this enquiry.

"*Don't* say nasty things about her!" Lady Agnes broke out solemnly to her son after resting her eyes on him a moment with an air of reluctant reprobation.

"I say nothing but what she 'd say herself," the young man urged. "About some things she has very good taste, but about this kind of thing she has no taste at all."

"That 's better, I think," said Lady Agnes, turning her eyes again to the "kind of thing" her son appeared to designate.

"She 's awfully clever — awfully!" Grace went on with decision.

"Awfully, awfully!" her brother repeated, standing in front of her and smiling down at her.

8

"You *are* nasty, Nick. You know you are," said the young lady, but more in sorrow than in anger.

Biddy got up at this, as if the accusatory tone prompted her to place herself generously at his side. "Might n't you go and order lunch — in that place, you know?" she asked of her mother. "Then we'd come back when it was ready."

"My dear child, I can't order lunch," Lady Agnes replied with a cold impatience which seemed to intimate that she had problems far more important than those of victualling to contend with.

"Then perhaps Peter will if he comes. I'm sure he's up in everything of that sort."

"Oh hang Peter!" Nick exclaimed. "Leave him out of account, and *do* order lunch, mother; but not cold beef and pickles."

"I must say — about *him* — you're not nice," Biddy ventured to remark to her brother, hesitating and even blushing a little.

"You make up for it, my dear," the young man answered, giving her chin — a very charming rotund little chin — a friendly whisk with his forefinger.

"I can't imagine what you've got against him," her ladyship said gravely.

"Dear mother, it's disappointed fondness," Nick argued. "They won't answer one's notes; they won't let one know where they are nor what to expect. 'Hell has no fury like a woman scorned'; nor like a man either."

"Peter has such a tremendous lot to do — it's a very busy time at the embassy; there are sure to be reasons," Biddy explained with her pretty eyes.

9

"Reasons enough, no doubt!" said Lady Agnes — who accompanied these words with an ambiguous sigh, however, as if in Paris even the best reasons would naturally be bad ones.

"Does n't Julia write to you, does n't she answer you the very day?" Grace asked, looking at Nick as if she were the bold one.

He waited, returning her glance with a certain severity. "What do you know about my correspondence? No doubt I ask too much," he went on; "I'm so attached to them. Dear old Peter, dear old Julia!"

"She's younger than you, my dear!" cried the elder girl, still resolute.

"Yes, nineteen days."

"I'm glad you know her birthday."

"She knows yours; she always gives you something," Lady Agnes reminded her son.

"Her taste is good *then*, is n't it, Nick?" Grace Dormer continued.

"She makes charming presents; but, dear mother, it is n't *her* taste. It's her husband's."

"How her husband's?"

"The beautiful objects of which she disposes so freely are the things he collected for years laboriously, devotedly, poor man!"

"She disposes of them to you, but not to others," said Lady Agnes. "But that's all right," she added as if this might have been taken for a complaint of the limitations of Julia's bounty. "She has to select among so many, and that's a proof of taste," her ladyship pursued.

"You can't say she does n't choose lovely ones,"

Grace remarked to her brother in a tone of some triumph.

"My dear, they re all lovely. George Dallow's judgement was so sure, he was incapable of making a mistake," Nicholas Dormer returned.

"I don't see how you can talk of him, he was dreadful," said Lady Agnes.

"My dear, if he was good enough for Julia to marry he's good enough for us to talk of."

"She did him a very great honour."

"I dare say, but he was not unworthy of it. No such enlightened collection of beautiful objects has been made in England in our time."

"You think too much of beautiful objects!" Lady Agnes sighed.

"I thought you were just now lamenting that I think too little."

"It's very nice — his having left Julia so well off," Biddy interposed soothingly, as if she foresaw a tangle.

"He treated her *en grand seigneur*, absolutely," Nick went on.

"He used to look greasy, all the same" — Grace bore on it with a dull weight. "His name ought to have been Tallow."

"You're not saying what Julia would like, if that's what you are trying to say," her brother observed.

"Don't be vulgar, Grace," said Lady Agnes.

"I know Peter Sherringham's birthday!" Biddy broke out innocently, as a pacific diversion. She had passed her hand into Nick's arm, to signify her readiness to go with him, while she scanned the remoter reaches of the garden as if it had occurred to her that to direct their steps in some such sense might after all be the shorter way to get at Peter.

"He's too much older than you, my dear," Grace answered without encouragement.

"That's why I've noticed it — he's thirty-four. Do you call that too old? I don't care for slobbering infants!" Biddy cried.

"Don't be vulgar," Lady Agnes enjoined again.

"Come, Bid, we'll go and be vulgar together; for that's what we are, I'm afraid," her brother said to her. "We'll go and look at all these low works of art."

"Do you really think it's necessary to the child's development?" Lady Agnes demanded as the pair turned away. And then while her son, struck as by a challenge, paused, lingering a moment with his little sister on his arm: "What we've been through this morning in this place, and what you've paraded before our eyes — the murders, the tortures, all kinds of disease and indecency!"

Nick looked at his mother as if this sudden protest surprised him, but as if also there were lurking explanations of it which he quickly guessed. Her resentment had the effect not so much of animating her cold face as of making it colder, less expressive, though visibly prouder. "Ah dear mother, don't do the British matron!" he replied good-humouredly.

"British matron's soon said! I don't know what they're coming to."

"How odd that you should have been struck only with the disagreeable things when, for myself, I've felt it to be most interesting, the most suggestive morning I've passed for ever so many months!"

"Oh Nick, Nick!" Lady Agnes cried with a strange depth of feeling.

"I like them better in London — they're much less unpleasant," said Grace Dormer.

"They're things you can look at," her ladyship went on. "We certainly make the better show."

"The subject does n't matter, it's the treatment, the treatment!" Biddy protested in a voice like the tinkle of a silver bell.

"Poor little Bid!" — her brother broke into a laugh.

"How can I learn to model, mamma dear, if I don't look at things and if I don't study them?" the girl continued.

This question passed unheeded, and Nicholas Dormer said to his mother, more seriously, but with a certain kind explicitness, as if he could make a particular allowance: "This place is an immense stimulus to me; it refreshes me, excites me — it's such an exhibition of artistic life. It's full of ideas, full of refinements; it gives one such an impression of artistic experience. They try everything, they feel everything. While you were looking at the murders, apparently, I observed an immense deal of curious and interesting work. There are too many of them, poor devils; so many who must make their way, who must attract attention. Some of them can only *taper fort*, stand on their heads, turn summersaults or commit deeds of violence, to make people notice them. After that, no doubt, a good many will be quieter. But

13

I don't know; to-day I'm in an appreciative mood
— I feel indulgent even to them: they give me an
impression of intelligence, of eager observation. All
art is one — remember that, Biddy dear," the young
man continued, smiling down from his height. "It's
the same great many-headed effort, and any ground
that's gained by an individual, any spark that's
struck in any province, is of use and of suggestion to
all the others. We're all in the same boat."

"'We,' do you say, my dear? Are you really setting
up for an artist?" Lady Agnes asked.

Nick just hesitated. "I was speaking for Biddy."

"But you *are* one, Nick — you are!" the girl cried.

Lady Agnes looked for an instant as if she were
going to say once more "Don't be vulgar!" But she
suppressed these words, had she intended them, and
uttered sounds, few in number and not completely
articulate, to the effect that she hated talking about
art. While her son spoke she had watched him as
if failing to follow; yet something in the tone of her
exclamation hinted that she had understood him but
too well.

"We're all in the same boat," Biddy repeated with
cheerful zeal.

"Not me, if you please!" Lady Agnes replied.
"It's horrid messy work, your modelling."

"Ah but look at the results!" said the girl eagerly
— glancing about at the monuments in the garden
as if in regard even to them she were, through that
unity of art her brother had just proclaimed, in some
degree an effective cause.

"There's a great deal being done here — a real

vitality," Nicholas Dormer went on to his mother in the same reasonable informing way. "Some of these fellows go very far."

"They do indeed!" said Lady Agnes.

"I'm fond of young schools — like this movement in sculpture," Nick insisted with his slightly provoking serenity.

"They're old enough to know better!"

"May n't I look, mamma? It *is* necessary to my development," Biddy declared.

"You may do as you like," said Lady Agnes with dignity.

"She ought to see good work, you know," the young man went on.

"I leave it to your sense of responsibility." This statement was somewhat majestic, and for a moment evidently it tempted Nick, almost provoked him, or at any rate suggested to him an occasion for some pronouncement he had had on his mind. Apparently, however, he judged the time on the whole not quite right, and his sister Grace interposed with the enquiry —

"Please, mamma, are we *never* going to lunch?"

"Ah mother, mother!" the young man murmured in a troubled way, looking down at her with a deep fold in his forehead.

For Lady Agnes also, as she returned his look, it seemed an occasion; but with this difference that she had no hesitation in taking advantage of it. She was encouraged by his slight embarrassment, for ordinarily Nick was not embarrassed. "You used to have so *much* sense of responsibility," she pursued;

15

"but sometimes I don't know what has become of it — it seems all, *all* gone!"

"Ah mother, mother!" he exclaimed again — as if there were so many things to say that it was impossible to choose. But now he stepped closer, bent over her and in spite of the publicity of their situation gave her a quick expressive kiss. The foreign observer whom I took for granted in beginning to sketch this scene would have had to admit that the rigid English family had after all a capacity for emotion. Grace Dormer indeed looked round her to see if at this moment they were noticed. She judged with satisfaction that they had escaped.

II

Nick Dormer walked away with Biddy, but he had not gone far before he stopped in front of a clever bust, where his mother, in the distance, saw him playing in the air with his hand, carrying out by this gesture, which presumably was applausive, some critical remark he had made to his sister. Lady Agnes raised her glass to her eyes by the long handle to which rather a clanking chain was attached, perceiving that the bust represented an ugly old man with a bald head; at which her ladyship indefinitely sighed, though it was not apparent in what way such an object could be detrimental to her daughter. Nick passed on and quickly paused again; this time, his mother discerned, before the marble image of a strange grimacing woman. Presently she lost sight of him; he wandered behind things, looking at them all round.

"I ought to get plenty of ideas for my modelling, ought n't I, Nick?" his sister put to him after a moment.

"Ah my poor child, what shall I say?"

"Don't you think I've any capacity for ideas?" the girl continued ruefully.

"Lots of them, no doubt. But the capacity for applying them, for putting them into practice — how much of that have you?"

"How can I tell till I try?"

"What do you mean by trying, Biddy dear?"

17

"Why you know — you've seen me."

"Do you call that trying?" her brother amusedly demanded.

"Ah Nick!" she said with sensibility. But then with more spirit: "And please what do you call it?"

"Well, this for instance is a good case." And her companion pointed to another bust—a head of a young man in terra-cotta, at which they had just arrived; a modern young man to whom, with his thick neck, his little cap and his wide ring of dense curls, the artist had given the air of some sturdy Florentine of the time of Lorenzo.

Biddy looked at the image a moment. "Ah that's not trying; that's succeeding."

"Not altogether; it's only trying seriously."

"Well, why shouldn't I be serious?"

"Mother wouldn't like it. She has inherited the fine old superstition that art's pardonable only so long as it's bad — so long as it's done at odd hours, for a little distraction, like a game of tennis or of whist. The only thing that can justify it, the effort to carry it as far as one can (which you can't do without time and singleness of purpose) she regards as just the dangerous, the criminal element. It's the oddest hind-part-before view, the drollest immorality."

"She doesn't want one to be professional," Biddy returned as if she could do justice to every system.

"Better leave it alone then. There are always duffers enough."

"I don't want to be a duffer," Biddy said. "But I thought you encouraged me."

"So I did, my poor child. It was only to encourage myself."

"With your own work — your painting?"

"With my futile, my ill-starred endeavours. Union is strength — so that we might present a wider front, a larger surface of resistance."

Biddy for a while said nothing and they continued their tour of observation. She noticed how he passed over some things quickly, his first glance sufficing to show him if they were worth another, and then recognised in a moment the figures that made some appeal. His tone puzzled but his certainty of eye impressed her, and she felt what a difference there was yet between them—how much longer in every case she would have taken to discriminate. She was aware of how little she could judge of the value of a thing till she had looked at it ten minutes; indeed modest little Biddy was compelled privately to add "And often not even then." She was mystified, as I say—Nick was often mystifying, it was his only fault — but one thing was definite: her brother had high ability. It was the consciousness of this that made her bring out at last: "I don't so much care whether or no I please mamma, if I please you."

"Oh don't lean on me. I'm a wretched broken reed—I'm no use *really!*" he promptly admonished her.

"Do you mean you're a duffer?" Biddy asked in alarm.

"Frightful, frightful!"

"So that you intend to give up your work — to let it alone, as you advise *me?*"

19

"It has never been my work, all that business, Biddy. If it had it would be different. I should stick to it."

"And you *won't* stick to it?" the girl said, standing before him open-eyed.

Her brother looked into her eyes a moment, and she had a compunction; she feared she was indiscreet and was worrying him. "Your questions are much simpler than the elements out of which my answer should come."

"A great talent — what's simpler than that?"

"One excellent thing, dear Biddy: no talent at all!"

"Well, yours is so real you can't help it."

"We shall see, we shall see," said Nick Dormer. "Let us go look at that big group."

"We shall see if your talent's real?" Biddy went on as she accompanied him.

"No; we shall see if, as you say, I can't help it. What nonsense Paris makes one talk!" the young man added as they stopped in front of the composition. This was true perhaps, but not in a sense he could find himself tempted to deplore. The present was far from his first visit to the French capital: he had often quitted England and usually made a point of "putting in," as he called it, a few days there on the outward journey to the Continent or on the return; but at present the feelings, for the most part agreeable, attendant upon a change of air and of scene had been more punctual and more acute than for a long time before, and stronger the sense of novelty, refreshment, amusement, of the hundred appeals from that quarter of thought to which on the whole his attention was apt most frequently, though not most confessedly, to stray. He was fonder of Paris than most of his countrymen, though not so fond perhaps as some other captivated aliens: the place had always had the virtue of quickening in him sensibly the life of reflexion and observation. It was a good while since his impressions had been so favourable to the city by the Seine; a good while at all events since they had ministered so to excitement, to exhilaration, to ambition, even to a restlessness that was not prevented from being agreeable by the excess of agitation in it. Nick could have given the reason of this unwonted glow, but his preference was very much to keep it to himself. Certainly to persons not deeply knowing, or at any rate not deeply curious, in relation to the young man's history the explanation might have seemed to beg the question, consisting as it did of the simple formula that he had at last come to a crisis. Why a crisis—what was it and why had he not come to it before? The reader shall learn these things in time if he cares enough for them.

Our young man had not in any recent year failed to see the Salon, which the general voice this season pronounced not particularly good. None the less it was the present exhibition that, for some cause connected with his "crisis," made him think fast, produced that effect he had spoken of to his mother as a sense of artistic life. The precinct of the marbles and bronzes spoke to him especially to-day; the glazed garden, not florally rich, with its new productions alternating with perfunctory plants and its queer, damp smell, partly the odour of plastic clay, of the

21

studios of sculptors, put forth the voice of old associations, of other visits, of companionships now ended — an insinuating eloquence which was at the same time somehow identical with the general sharp contagion of Paris. There was youth in the air, and a multitudinous newness, for ever reviving, and the diffusion of a hundred talents, ingenuities, experiments. The summer clouds made shadows on the roof of the great building; the white images, hard in their crudity, spotted the place with provocations; the rattle of plates at the restaurant sounded sociable in the distance, and our young man congratulated himself more than ever that he had not missed his chance. He felt how it would help him to settle something. At the moment he made this reflexion his eye fell upon a person who appeared — just in the first glimpse — to carry out the idea of help. He uttered a lively ejaculation, which, however, in its want of finish, Biddy failed to understand; so pertinent, so relevant and congruous, was the other party to this encounter.

The girl's attention followed her brother's, resting with it on a young man who faced them without seeing them, engaged as he was in imparting to two companions his ideas about one of the works exposed to view. What Biddy remarked was that this young man was fair and fat and of the middle stature; he had a round face and a short beard and on his crown a mere reminiscence of hair, as the fact that he carried his hat in his hand permitted to be observed. Bridget Dormer, who was quick, placed him immediately as a gentleman, but as a gentleman unlike any other gentleman she had ever seen. She would have

taken him for very foreign but that the words proceeding from his mouth reached her ear and imposed
themselves as a rare variety of English. It was not
that a foreigner might not have spoken smoothly
enough, nor yet that the speech of this young man
was not smooth. It had in truth a conspicuous and
aggressive perfection, and Biddy was sure no mere
learner would have ventured to play such tricks with
the tongue. He seemed to draw rich effects and wandering airs from it — to modulate and manipulate it
as he would have done a musical instrument. Her
view of the gentleman's companions was less operat-
ive, save for her soon making the reflexion that they
were people whom in any country, from China to
Peru, you would immediately have taken for natives.
One of them was an old lady with a shawl; that was
the most salient way in which she presented herself.
The shawl was an ancient much-used fabric of em-
broidered cashmere, such as many ladies wore forty
years ago in their walks abroad and such as no lady
wears to-day. It had fallen half off the back of the
wearer, but at the moment Biddy permitted herself
to consider her she gave it a violent jerk and brought
it up to her shoulders again, where she continued to
arrange and settle it, with a good deal of jauntiness and
elegance, while she listened to the talk of the gentleman. Biddy guessed that this little transaction took
place very frequently, and was not unaware of its
giving the old lady a droll factitious faded appearance, as if she were singularly out of step with the
age. The other person was very much younger —
she might have been a daughter—and had a pale

face, a low forehead and thick dark hair. What she chiefly had, however, Biddy rapidly discovered, was a pair of largely-gazing eyes. Our young friend was helped to the discovery by the accident of their resting at this moment for a time — it struck Biddy as very long — on her own. Both these ladies were clad in light thin scant gowns, giving an impression of flowered figures and odd transparencies, and in low shoes which showed a great deal of stocking and were ornamented with large rosettes. Biddy's slightly agitated perception travelled directly to their shoes: they suggested to her vaguely that the wearers were dancers — connected possibly with the old-fashioned exhibition of the shawl-dance. By the time she had taken in so much as this the mellifluous young man had perceived and addressed himself to her brother. He came on with an offered hand. Nick greeted him and said it was a happy chance—he was uncommonly glad to see him.

"I never come across you — I don't know why," Nick added while the two, smiling, looked each other up and down like men reunited after a long interval.

"Oh it seems to me there's reason enough: our paths in life are so different." Nick's friend had a great deal of manner, as was evinced by his fashion of saluting Biddy without knowing her.

"Different, yes, but not so different as that. Don't we both live in London, after all, and in the nineteenth century?"

"Ah my dear Dormer, excuse me: I don't live in the nineteenth century. Jamais de la vie!" the gentleman declared.

"Nor in London either?"

"Yes — when I'm not at Samarcand! But surely we've diverged since the old days. I adore what you burn, you burn what I adore." While the stranger spoke he looked cheerfully, hospitably, at Biddy; not because it was she, she easily guessed, but because it was in his nature to desire a second auditor — a kind of sympathetic gallery. Her life was somehow filled with shy people, and she immediately knew she had never encountered any one who seemed so to know his part and recognise his cues.

"How do you know what I adore?" Nicholas Dormer asked.

"I know well enough what you used to."

"That's more than I do myself. There were so many things."

"Yes, there are many things — many, many: that's what makes life so amusing."

"Do you find it amusing?"

"My dear fellow, *c'est à se tordre*. Don't you think so? Ah it was high time I should meet you — I see. I've an idea you need me."

"Upon my word I think I do!" Nick said in a tone which struck his sister and made her wonder still more why, if the gentleman was so important as that, he did n't introduce him.

"There are many gods and this is one of their temples," the mysterious personage went on. "It's a house of strange idols — is n't it? — and of some strange and unnatural sacrifices."

To Biddy as much as to her brother this remark might have been offered; but the girl's eyes turned back to the ladies who for the moment had lost their companion. She felt irresponsive and feared she should pass with this easy cosmopolite for a stiff scared English girl, which was not the type she aimed at; but was n't even ocular commerce overbold so long as she had n't a sign from Nick? The elder of the strange women had turned her back and was looking at some bronze figure, losing her shawl again as she did so; but the other stood where their escort had quitted her, giving all her attention to his sudden sociability with others. Her arms hung at her sides, her head was bent, her face lowered, so that she had an odd appearance of raising her eyes from under her brows; and in this attitude she was striking, though her air was so unconciliatory as almost to seem dangerous. Did it express resentment at having been abandoned for another girl? Biddy, who began to be frightened — there was a moment when the neglected creature resembled a tigress about to spring — was tempted to cry out that she had no wish whatever to appropriate the gentleman. Then she made the discovery that the young lady too had a manner, almost as much as her clever guide, and the rapid induction that it perhaps meant no more than his. She only looked at Biddy from beneath her eyebrows, which were wonderfully arched, but there was ever so much of a manner in the way she did it. Biddy had a momentary sense of being a figure in a ballet, a dramatic ballet — a subordinate motionless figure, to be dashed at to music or strangely capered up to. It would be a very dramatic ballet indeed if this young person were the heroine. She had magnificent hair, the girl reflected; and at the same moment heard Nick say to his interlocutor: "You're not in London — one can't meet you there?"

"I rove, drift, float," was the answer; "my feelings direct me — if such a life as mine may be said to have a direction. Where there's anything to feel I try to be there!" the young man continued with his confiding laugh.

"I should like to get hold of you," Nick returned.

"Well, in that case there would be no doubt the intellectual adventure. Those are the currents — any sort of personal relation — that govern my career."

"I don't want to lose you this time," Nick continued in a tone that excited Biddy's surprise. A moment before, when his friend had said that he tried to be where there was anything to feel, she had wondered how he could endure him.

"Don't lose me, don't lose me!" cried the stranger after a fashion which affected the girl as the highest expression of irresponsibility she had ever seen. "After all why should you? Let us remain together unless I interfere" — and he looked, smiling and interrogative, at Biddy, who still remained blank, only noting again that Nick forbore to make them acquainted. This was an anomaly, since he prized the gentleman so. Still, there could be no anomaly of Nick's that would n't impose itself on his younger sister.

"Certainly, I keep you," he said, "unless on my side I deprive those ladies — !"

"Charming women, but it's not an indissoluble union. We meet, we communicate, we part! They're going — I'm seeing them to the door. I shall come

back." With this Nick's friend rejoined his companions, who moved away with him, the strange fine
eyes of the girl lingering on Biddy's brother as well
as on Biddy herself as they receded.

"Who *is* he — who *are* they?" Biddy instantly
asked.

"He's a gentleman," Nick made answer — insuf-
ficiently, she thought, and even with a shade of hesitation. He spoke as if she might have supposed he was
not one, and if he was really one why did n't he introduce him? But Biddy would n't for the world have
put this question, and he now moved to the nearest
bench and dropped upon it as to await the other's
return. No sooner, however, had his sister seated
herself than he said: "See here, my dear, do you
think you had better stay?"

"Do you want me to go back to mother?" the girl
asked with a lengthening visage.

"Well, what do you think?" He asked it indeed
gaily enough.

"Is your conversation to be about — about private
affairs?"

"No, I can't say that. But I doubt if mother would
think it the sort of thing that 's 'necessary to your
development.'"

This assertion appeared to inspire her with the
eagerness with which she again broke out: "But who
are they—who are they?"

"I know nothing of the ladies. I never saw them
before. The man's a fellow I knew very well at
Oxford. He was thought immense fun there. We 've
diverged, as he says, and I had almost lost sight of

him, but not so much as he thinks, because I've read him — read him with interest. He has written a very clever book."

"What kind of a book?"

"A sort of novel."

"What sort of novel?"

"Well, I don't know — with a lot of good writing." Biddy listened to this so receptively that she thought it perverse her brother should add: "I dare say Peter will have come if you return to mother."

"I don't care if he has. Peter's nothing to me. But I'll go if you wish it."

Nick smiled upon her again and then said: "It does n't signify. We'll all go."

"All?" she echoed.

"He won't hurt us. On the contrary he'll do us good."

This was possible, the girl reflected in silence, but none the less the idea struck her as courageous, of their taking the odd young man back to breakfast with them and with the others, especially if Peter should be there. If Peter was nothing to her it was singular she should have attached such importance to this contingency. The odd young man reappeared, and now that she saw him without his queer female appendages he seemed personally less weird. He struck her moreover as generally a good deal accounted for by the literary character, especially if it were responsible for a lot of good writing. As he took his place on the bench Nick said to him, indicating her, "My sister Bridget," and then mentioned his name, "Mr. Gabriel Nash."

29

"You enjoy Paris — you're happy here?" Mr. Nash enquired, leaning over his friend to speak to the girl.

Though his words belonged to the situation it struck her that his tone did n't, and this made her answer him more dryly than she usually spoke. "Oh yes, it's very nice."

"And French art interests you? You find things here that please?"

"Oh yes, I like some of them."

Mr. Nash considered her kindly. "I hoped you'd say you like the Academy better."

"She would if she did n't think you expected it," said Nicholas Dormer.

"Oh Nick!" Biddy protested.

"Miss Dormer's herself an English picture," their visitor pronounced in the tone of a man whose urbanity was a general solvent.

"That's a compliment if you don't like them!" Biddy exclaimed.

"Ah some of them, some of them; there's a certain sort of thing!" Mr. Nash continued. "We must feel everything, everything that we can. We're here for that."

"You do like English art then?" Nick demanded with a slight accent of surprise.

Mr. Nash indulged his wonder. "My dear Dormer, do you remember the old complaint I used to make of you? You had formulas that were like walking in one's hat. One may see something in a case and one may not."

"Upon my word," said Nick, "I don't know any

one who was fonder of a generalisation than you. You turned them off as the man at the street-corner distributes handbills."

"They were my wild oats. I've sown them all."

"We shall see that!"

"Oh there's nothing of them now: a tame scanty homely growth. My only good generalisations are my actions."

"We shall see *them* then."

"Ah pardon me. You can't see them with the naked eye. Moreover mine are principally negative. People's actions, I know, are for the most part the things they do — but mine are all the things I *don't* do. There are so many of those, so many, but they don't produce any effect. And then all the rest are shades — extremely fine shades."

"Shades of behaviour?" Nick enquired with an interest which surprised his sister, Mr. Nash's discourse striking her mainly as the twaddle of the underworld.

"Shades of impression, of appreciation," said the young man with his explanatory smile. "All my behaviour consists of my feelings."

"Well, don't you show your feelings? You used to!"

"Wasn't it mainly those of disgust?" Nash asked. "Those operate no longer. I've closed that window."

"Do you mean you like everything?"

"Dear me, no! But I look only at what I do like."

"Do you mean that you've lost the noble faculty of disgust?"

"I haven't the least idea. I never try it. My dear fellow," said Gabriel Nash, "we've only one life that

31

we know anything about: fancy taking it up with disagreeable impressions! When then shall we go in for the agreeable?"

"What do you mean by the agreeable?" Nick demanded.

"Oh the happy moments of our consciousness — the multiplication of those moments. We must save as many as possible from the dark gulf."

Nick had excited surprise on the part of his sister, but it was now Biddy's turn to make him open his eyes a little. She raised her sweet voice in appeal to the stranger.

"Don't you think there are any wrongs in the world — any abuses and sufferings?"

"Oh so many, so many! That's why one must choose."

"Choose to stop them, to reform them — is n't that the choice?" Biddy asked. "That's Nick's," she added, blushing and looking at this personage.

"Ah our divergence — yes!" Mr. Nash sighed. "There are all kinds of machinery for that — very complicated and ingenious. Your formulas, my dear Dormer, your formulas!"

"Hang 'em, I have n't got any!" Nick now bravely declared.

"To me personally the simplest ways are those that appeal most," Mr. Nash went on. "We pay too much attention to the ugly; we notice it, we magnify it. The great thing is to leave it alone and encourage the beautiful."

"You must be very sure you get hold of the beautiful," said Nick.

"Ah precisely, and that's just the importance of the faculty of appreciation. We must train our special sense. It's capable of extraordinary extension. Life's none too long for that."

"But what's the good of the extraordinary extension if there is no affirmation of it, if it all goes to the negative, as you say? Where are the fine consequences?" Dormer asked.

"In one's own spirit. One is one's self a fine consequence. That's the most important one we have to do with. *I* am a fine consequence," said Gabriel Nash.

Biddy rose from the bench at this and stepped away a little as to look at a piece of statuary. But she had not gone far before, pausing and turning, she bent her eyes on the speaker with a heightened colour, an air of desperation and the question, after a moment: "Are you then an æsthete?"

"Ah there's one of the formulas! That's walking in one's hat! I've *no* profession, my dear young lady. I've no *état civil*. These things are a part of the complicated ingenious machinery. As I say, I keep to the simplest way. I find that gives one enough to do. Merely to be is such a *métier;* to live such an art; to feel such a career!"

Bridget Dormer turned her back and examined her statue, and her brother said to his old friend: "And to write?"

"To write? Oh I shall never do it again!"

"You've done it almost well enough to be inconsistent. That book of yours is anything but negative; it's complicated and ingenious."

" My dear fellow, I'm extremely ashamed of that book," said Gabriel Nash.

"Ah call yourself a bloated Buddhist and have done with it!" his companion exclaimed.

"Have done with it? I have n't the least desire to have done with it. And why should one call one's self anything? One only deprives other people of their dearest occupation. Let me add that you don't *begin* to have an insight into the art of life till it ceases to be of the smallest consequence to you what you may be called. That's rudimentary."

"But if you go in for shades you must also go in for names. You must distinguish," Nick objected. " The observer's nothing without his categories, his types and varieties."

"Ah trust him to distinguish!" said Gabriel Nash sweetly. "That's for his own convenience; he has, privately, a terminology to meet it. That's one's style. But from the moment it's for the convenience of others the signs have to be grosser, the shades begin to go. That's a deplorable hour! Literature, you see, is for the convenience of others. It requires the most abject concessions. It plays such mischief with one's style that really I've had to give it up."

"And politics?" Nick asked.

"Well, what about them?" was Mr. Nash's reply with a special cadence as he watched his friend's sister, who was still examining her statue. Biddy was divided between irritation and curiosity. She had interposed space, but she had not gone beyond earshot. Nick's question made her curiosity throb as a rejoinder to his friend's words.

34

"That, no doubt you'll say, is still far more for the convenience of others — is still worse for one's style."

Biddy turned round in time to hear Mr. Nash answer: "It has simply nothing in life to do with shades! I can't say worse for it than that."

Biddy stepped nearer at this and drew still further on her courage. "Won't mamma be waiting? Ought n't we to go to luncheon?"

Both the young men looked up at her and Mr. Nash broke out: "You ought to protest! You ought to save him!"

"To save him?" Biddy echoed.

"He *had* a style, upon my word he had! But I've seen it go. I've read his speeches."

"You were capable of that?" Nick laughed.

"For you, yes. But it was like listening to a nightingale in a brass band."

"I think they were beautiful," Biddy declared.

Her brother got up at this tribute, and Mr. Nash, rising too, said with his bright colloquial air: "But, Miss Dormer, he had eyes. He was made to see — to see all over, to see everything. There are so few like that."

"I think he still sees," Biddy returned, wondering a little why Nick did n't defend himself.

"He sees his 'side,' his dreadful 'side,' dear young lady. Poor man, fancy your having a 'side' — you, you — and spending your days and your nights looking at it! I'd as soon pass my life looking at an advertisement on a hoarding."

"You don't see me some day a great statesman?" said Nick.

35

"My dear fellow, it's exactly what I've a terror of."

"Mercy! don't you admire them?" Biddy cried.

"It's a trade like another and a method of making one's way which society certainly condones. But when one can be something better —!"

"Why what in the world *is* better?" Biddy asked.

The young man gasped and Nick, replying for him, said: "Gabriel Nash is better! You must come and lunch with us. I must keep you — I must!" he added.

"We shall save him yet," Mr. Nash kept on easily to Biddy while they went and the girl wondered still more what her mother would make of him.

III

AFTER her companions left her Lady Agnes rested for five minutes in silence with her elder daughter, at the end of which time she observed: "I suppose one must have food at any rate," and, getting up, quitted the place where they had been sitting. "And where are we to go? I hate eating out of doors," she went on.

"Dear me, when one comes to Paris — !" Grace returned in a tone apparently implying that in so rash an adventure one must be prepared for compromises and concessions. The two ladies wandered to where they saw a large sign of "Buffet" suspended in the air, entering a precinct reserved for little white-clothed tables, straw-covered chairs and long-aproned waiters. One of these functionaries approached them with eagerness and with a "Mesdames sont seules?" receiving in return from her ladyship the slightly snappish announcement "Non; nous sommes beaucoup!" He introduced them to a table larger than most of the others, and under his protection they took their places at it and began rather languidly and vaguely to consider the question of the repast. The waiter had placed a *carte* in Lady Agnes's hands and she studied it, through her eyeglass, with a failure of interest, while he enumerated with professional fluency the resources of the establishment and Grace watched the people at the other tables. She was hungry and had already broken a morsel from a long glazed roll.

"Not cold beef and pickles, you know," she observed to her mother. Lady Agnes gave no heed to this profane remark, but dropped her eyeglass and laid down the greasy document. "What does it signify? I dare say it's all nasty," Grace continued; and she added inconsequently: "If Peter comes he's sure to be particular."

" Let him first be particular to come!" her ladyship exclaimed, turning a cold eye upon the waiter.

"Poulet chasseur, filets mignons sauce béarnaise," the man suggested.

"You'll give us what I tell you," said Lady Agnes; and she mentioned with distinctness and authority the dishes of which she desired that the meal should be composed. He interjected three or four more suggestions, but as they produced absolutely no impression on her he became silent and submissive, doing justice apparently to her ideas. For Lady Agnes had ideas, and, though it had suited her humour ten minutes before to profess herself helpless in such a case, the manner in which she imposed them on the waiter as original, practical and economical, showed the high executive woman, the mother of children, the daughter of earls, the consort of an official, the dispenser of hospitality, looking back upon a lifetime of luncheons. She carried many cares, and the feeding of multitudes — she was honourably conscious of having fed them decently, as she had always done everything — had ever been one of them. "Everything's absurdly dear," she remarked to her daughter as the waiter went away.

To this remark Grace made no answer. She had been used for a long time back to hearing that everything was very dear; it was what one always expected. So she found the case herself, but she was silent and inventive about it, and nothing further passed, in the way of conversation with her mother, while they waited for the latter's orders to be executed, till Lady Agnes reflected audibly: "He makes me unhappy, the way he talks about Julia."

"Sometimes I think he does it to torment one. One can't mention her!" Grace responded.

"It's better not to mention her, but to leave it alone."

"Yet he never mentions her of himself."

"In some cases that's supposed to show that people like people — though of course something more's required to prove it," Lady Agnes continued to meditate. "Sometimes I think he's thinking of her, then at others I can't fancy *what* he's thinking of."

"It would be awfully suitable," said Grace, biting her roll.

Her companion had a pause, as if looking for some higher ground to put it upon. Then she appeared to find this loftier level in the observation: "Of course he must like her — he has known her always."

"Nothing can be plainer than that she likes him," Grace opined.

"Poor Julia!" Lady Agnes almost wailed; and her tone suggested that she knew more about that than she was ready to state.

"It isn't as if she wasn't clever and well read," her daughter went on. "If there were nothing else there would be a reason in her being so interested in politics, in everything that he is."

"Ah what Nick is — that's what I sometimes wonder!"

Grace eyed her parent in some despair: "Why, mother, is n't he going to be like papa?" She waited for an answer that did n't come; after which she pursued: "I thought you thought him so like him already."

"Well, I don't," said Lady Agnes quietly.

"Who is then? Certainly Percy is n't."

Lady Agnes was silent a space. "There's no one like your father."

"Dear papa!" Grace handsomely concurred. Then with a rapid transition: "It would be so jolly for all of us — she'd be so nice to us."

"She's that already — in her way," said Lady Agnes conscientiously, having followed the return, quick as it was. "Much good does it do her!" And she reproduced the note of her bitterness of a moment before.

"It does her some good that one should look out for her. I do, and I think she knows it," Grace declared. "One can at any rate keep other women off."

"Don't meddle — you're very clumsy," was her mother's not particularly sympathetic rejoinder. "There are other women who are beautiful, and there are others who are clever and rich."

"Yes, but not all in one: that's what's so nice in Julia. Her fortune would be thrown in; he would n't appear to have married her for it."

"If he does he won't," said Lady Agnes a trifle obscurely.

"Yes, that's what's so charming. And he could do anything then, could n't he?"

"Well, your father had no fortune to speak of."

"Yes, but did n't Uncle Percy help him?"

"His wife helped him," said Lady Agnes.

"Dear mamma!"—the girl was prompt. "There's one thing," she added: "that Mr. Carteret will always help Nick."

"What do you mean by 'always'?"

"Why whether he marries Julia or not."

"Things are n't so easy," Lady Agnes judged. "It will all depend on Nick's behaviour. He can stop it to-morrow."

Grace Dormer stared; she evidently thought Mr. Carteret's beneficence a part of the scheme of nature. "How could he stop it?"

"By not being serious. It is n't so hard to prevent people giving you money."

"Serious?" Grace repeated. "Does he want him to be a prig like Lord Egbert?"

"Yes — that's exactly what he wants. And what he'll do for him he'll do for him only if he marries Julia."

"Has he told you?" Grace enquired. And then, before her mother could answer, "I'm delighted at that!" she cried.

"He has n't told me, but that's the way things happen." Lady Agnes was less optimistic than her daughter, and such optimism as she cultivated was a thin tissue with the sense of things as they are showing through. "If Nick becomes rich Charles Carteret will make him more so. If he does n't he won't give him a shilling."

"Oh mamma!" Grace demurred.

"It's all very well to say that in public life money is n't as necessary as it used to be," her ladyship went on broodingly. "Those who say so don't know anything about it. It's always intensely necessary."

Her daughter, visibly affected by the gloom of her manner, felt impelled to evoke as a corrective a more cheerful idea. "I dare say; but there's the fact — is n't there? — that poor papa had so little."

"Yes, and there's the fact that it killed him!"

These words came out with a strange quick little flare of passion. They startled Grace Dormer, who jumped in her place and gasped "Oh mother!" The next instant, however, she added in a different voice "Oh Peter!" for, with an air of eagerness, a gentleman was walking up to them.

"How d'ye do, Cousin Agnes? How d'ye do, little Grace?" Peter Sherringham laughed and shook hands with them, and three minutes later was settled in his chair at their table, on which the first elements of the meal had been placed. Explanations, on one side and the other, were demanded and produced; from which it appeared that the two parties had been in some degree at cross-purposes. The day before Lady Agnes and her companions travelled to Paris Sherringham had gone to London for forty-eight hours on private business of the ambassador's, arriving, on his return by the night-train, only early that morning. There had accordingly been a delay in his receiving

42

Nick Dormer's two notes. If Nick had come to the embassy in person — he might have done him the honour to call — he would have learned that the second secretary was absent. Lady Agnes was not altogether successful in assigning a motive to her son's neglect of this courteous form; she could but say: "I expected him, I wanted him to go; and indeed, not hearing from you, he would have gone immediately — an hour or two hence, on leaving this place. But we're here so quietly — not to go out, not to seem to appeal to the ambassador. Nick put it so — 'Oh mother, we'll keep out of it; a friendly note will do.' I don't know definitely what he wanted to keep out of, unless anything like gaiety. The embassy isn't gay, I know. But I'm sure his note was friendly, wasn't it? I dare say you'll see for yourself. He's different directly he gets abroad; he doesn't seem to care." Lady Agnes paused a moment, not carrying out this particular elucidation; then she resumed: "He said you'd have seen Julia and that you'd understand everything from her. And when I asked how she'd know he said 'Oh she knows everything!'"

"He never said a word to me about Julia," Peter Sherringham returned. Lady Agnes and her daughter exchanged a glance at this: the latter had already asked three times where Julia was, and her ladyship dropped that they had been hoping she would be able to come with Peter. The young man set forth that she was at the moment at an hotel in the Rue de la Paix, but had only been there since that morning; he had seen her before proceeding to the Champs Elysées. She had come up to Paris by an early train

43

— she had been staying at Versailles, of all places in the world. She had been a week in Paris on her return from Cannes — her stay *there* had been of nearly a month: fancy! — and then had gone out to Versailles to see Mrs. Billinghurst. Perhaps they'd remember her, poor Dallow's sister. She was staying there to teach her daughters French — she had a dozen or two! — and Julia had spent three days with her. She was to return to England about the twenty-fifth. It would make seven weeks she must have been away from town — a rare thing for her; she usually stuck to it so in summer.

"Three days with Mrs. Billinghurst — how very good-natured of her!" Lady Agnes commented.

"Oh they're very nice to her," Sherringham said.

"Well, I hope so!" Grace Dormer exhaled. "Why didn't you make her come here?"

"I proposed it, but she wouldn't." Another eye-beam, at this, passed between the two ladies and Peter went on: "She said you must come and see her at the Hôtel de Hollande."

"Of course we'll do that," Lady Agnes declared. "Nick went to ask about her at the Westminster."

"She gave that up; they wouldn't give her the rooms she wanted, her usual set."

"She's delightfully particular!" Grace said complacently. Then she added: "She *does* like pictures, doesn't she?"

Peter Sherringham stared. "Oh I dare say. But that's not what she has in her head this morning. She has some news from London — she's immensely excited."

44

"What has she in her head?" Lady Agnes asked.

"What's her news from London?" Grace added.

"She wants Nick to stand."

"Nick to stand?" both ladies cried.

"She undertakes to bring him in for Harsh. Mr. Pinks is dead — the fellow, you know, who got the seat at the general election. He dropped down in London — disease of the heart or something of that sort. Julia has her telegram, but I see it was in last night's papers."

"Imagine — Nick never mentioned it!" said Lady Agnes.

"Don't you know, mother? — abroad he only reads foreign papers."

"Oh I know. I've no patience with him," her ladyship continued. "Dear Julia!"

"It's a nasty little place, and Pinks had a tight squeeze — 107 or something of that sort; but if it returned a Liberal a year ago very likely it will do so again. Julia at any rate believes it can be made to — if the man's Nick — and is ready to take the order to put him in."

"I'm sure if she can do it she will," Grace pronounced.

"Dear, dear Julia! And Nick can do something for himself," said the mother of this candidate.

"I've no doubt he can do anything," Peter Sherringham returned good-naturedly. Then, "Do you mean in expenses?" he enquired.

"Ah I'm afraid he can't do much in expenses, poor dear boy! And it's dreadful how little we can look to Percy."

"Well, I dare say you may look to Julia. I think that's her idea."

"Delightful Julia!" Lady Agnes broke out. "If poor Sir Nicholas could have known! Of course he must go straight home," she added.

"He won't like that," said Grace.

"Then he'll have to go without liking it."

"It will rather spoil *your* little excursion, if you've only just come," Peter suggested; "to say nothing of the great Biddy's, if she's enjoying Paris."

"We may stay perhaps — with Julia to protect us," said Lady Agnes.

"Ah she won't stay; she'll go over for her man."

"Her man — ?"

"The fellow who stands, whoever he is — especially if he's Nick." These last words caused the eyes of Peter Sherringham's companions to meet again, and he went on: "She'll go straight down to Harsh."

"Wonderful Julia!" Lady Agnes panted. "Of course Nick must go straight there too."

"Well, I suppose he must see first if they'll have him."

"If they'll have him? Why how can he tell till he tries?"

"I mean the people at headquarters, the fellows who arrange it."

Lady Agnes coloured a little. "My dear Peter, do you suppose there will be the least doubt of their 'having' the son of his father?"

"Of course it's a great name, Cousin Agnes — a very great name."

"One of the greatest, simply," Lady Agnes smiled.

46

"It's the best name in the world!" said Grace more emphatically.

"All the same it did n't prevent his losing his seat."

"By half a dozen votes: it was too odious!" her ladyship cried.

"I remember — I remember. And in such a case as that why did n't they immediately put him in somewhere else?"

"How one sees you live abroad, dear Peter! There happens to have been the most extraordinary lack of openings — I never saw anything like it — for a year. They've had their hand on him, keeping him all ready. I dare say they've telegraphed him."

"And he has n't told you?"

Lady Agnes faltered. "He's so very odd when he's abroad!"

"At home too he lets things go," Grace interposed. "He does so little — takes no trouble." Her mother suffered this statement to pass unchallenged, and she pursued philosophically: "I suppose it's because he knows he's so clever."

"So he is, dear old man. But what does he do, what has he been doing, in a positive way?"

"He has been painting."

"Ah not seriously!" Lady Agnes protested.

"That's the worst way," said Peter Sherringham. "Good things?"

Neither of the ladies made a direct response to this, but Lady Agnes said: "He has spoken repeatedly. They're always calling on him."

"He speaks magnificently," Grace attested.

" That's another of the things I lose, living in far

countries. And he's doing the Salon now with the great Biddy?"

"Just the things in this part. I can't think what keeps them so long," Lady Agnes groaned. "Did you ever see such a dreadful place?"

Sherringham stared. "Are n't the things good? I had an idea —!"

"Good?" cried Lady Agnes. "They're too odious, too wicked."

"Ah," laughed Peter, "that's what people fall into if they live abroad. The French ought n't to live abroad!"

"Here they come," Grace announced at this point; "but they've got a strange man with them."

"That's a bore when we want to talk!" Lady Agnes sighed.

Peter got up in the spirit of welcome and stood a moment watching the others approach. "There will be no difficulty in talking, to judge by the gentleman," he dropped; and while he remains so conspicuous our eyes may briefly rest on him. He was middling high and was visibly a representative of the nervous rather than of the phlegmatic branch of his race. He had an oval face, fine firm features and a complexion that tended to the brown. Brown were his eyes, and women thought them soft; dark brown his hair, in which the same critics sometimes regretted the absence of a little undulation. It was perhaps to conceal this plainness that he wore it very short. His teeth were white, his moustache was pointed, and so was the small beard that adorned the extremity of his chin. His face expressed intelligence and was very much

48

alive; it had the further distinction that it often
struck superficial observers with a certain foreignness
of cast. The deeper sort, however, usually felt it lat-
ently English enough. There was an idea that, having taken up the diplomatic career and gone to live in
strange lands, he cultivated the mask of an alien, an
Italian or a Spaniard; of an alien in time even — one
of the wonderful ubiquitous diplomatic agents of
the sixteenth century. In fact, none the less, it would
have been impossible to be more modern than Peter
Sherringham — more of one's class and one's country. But this did n't prevent several stray persons —
Bridget Dormer for instance — from admiring the
hue of his cheek for its olive richness and his moustache and beard for their resemblance to those of
Charles I. At the same time — she rather jumbled
her comparisons — she thought he recalled a Titian.

IV

PETER's meeting with Nick was of the friendliest on both sides, involving a great many "dear fellows" and "old boys," and his salutation to the younger of the Miss Dormers consisted of the frankest "Delighted to see you, my dear Bid!" There was no kissing, but there was cousinship in the air, of a conscious, living kind, as Gabriel Nash doubtless quickly noted, hovering for a moment outside the group. Biddy said nothing to Peter Sherringham, but there was no flatness in a silence which heaved, as it were, with the fairest physiognomic portents. Nick introduced Gabriel Nash to his mother and to the other two as "a delightful old friend" whom he had just come across, and Sherringham acknowledged the act by saying to Mr. Nash, but as if rather less for his sake than for that of the presenter: "I've seen you very often before."

"Ah repetition — recurrence: we have n't yet, in the study of how to live, abolished that clumsiness, have we?" Mr. Nash genially enquired. "It's a poverty in the supernumeraries of our stage that we don't pass once for all, but come round and cross again like a procession or an army at the theatre. It's a sordid economy that ought to have been managed better. The right thing would be just *one* appearance, and the procession, regardless of expense, for ever and for ever different." The company was occupied

50

in placing itself at table, so that the only disengaged attention for the moment was Grace's, to whom, as her eyes rested on him, the young man addressed these last words with a smile. "Alas, it's a very shabby idea, is n't it? The world is n't got up regardless of expense!"

Grace looked quickly away from him and said to her brother: "Nick, Mr. Pinks is dead."

"Mr. Pinks?" asked Gabriel Nash, appearing to wonder where he should sit.

"The member for Harsh; and Julia wants you to stand," the girl went on.

"Mr. Pinks, the member for Harsh? What names, to be sure!" Gabriel mused cheerfully, still unseated.

"Julia wants me? I'm much obliged to her!" Nick absently said. "Nash, please sit by my mother, with Peter on her other side."

"My dear, it is n't Julia," — Lady Agnes spoke earnestly. "Every one wants you. Have n't you heard from your people? Did n't you know the seat was vacant?"

Nick was looking round the table to see what was on it. "Upon my word I don't remember. What else have you ordered, mother?"

"There's some *bœuf braisé*, my dear, and after-wards some galantine. Here's a dish of eggs with asparagus-tips."

"I advise you to go in for it, Nick," said Peter Sherringham, to whom the preparation in question was presented.

"Into the eggs with asparagus-tips? Donnez m'en

51

s'il vous plaît. My dear fellow, how can I stand? how can I sit? Where's the money to come from?"

"The money? Why from Jul —!" Grace began, but immediately caught her mother's eye.

"Poor Julia, how you do work her!" Nick exclaimed. "Nash, I recommend you the asparagus-tips. Mother, he's my best friend — do look after him."

"I've an impression I've breakfasted — I'm not sure," Nash smiled.

"With those beautiful ladies? Try again — you'll find out."

"The money can be managed; the expenses are very small and the seat's certain," Lady Agnes pursued, not apparently heeding her son's injunction in respect to Nash.

"Rather — if Julia goes down!" her elder daughter exclaimed.

"Perhaps Julia won't go down!" Nick answered humorously.

Biddy was seated next to Mr. Nash, so that she could take occasion to ask "Who are the beautiful ladies?" as if she failed to recognise her brother's allusion. In reality this was an innocent trick: she was more curious than she could have given a suitable reason for about the odd women from whom her neighbour had lately separated.

"Deluded, misguided, infatuated persons!" Mr. Nash replied, understanding that she had asked for a description. "Strange eccentric, almost romantic, types. Predestined victims, simple-minded sacrificial lambs!"

This was copious, yet it was vague, so that Biddy could only respond "Oh all that?" But meanwhile Peter Sherringham said to Nick: "Julia's here, you know. You must go and see her."

Nick looked at him an instant rather hard, as if to say "You too?" But Peter's eyes appeared to answer "No, no, not I"; upon which his cousin rejoined: "Of course I'll go and see her. I'll go immediately. Please to thank her for thinking of me."

"Thinking of you? There are plenty to think of you!" Lady Agnes said. "There are sure to be telegrams at home. We must go back — we must go back!"

"We must go back to England?" Nick Dormer asked; and as his mother made no answer he continued: "Do you mean I must go to Harsh?"

Her ladyship evaded this question, enquiring of Mr. Nash if he would have a morsel of fish; but her gain was small, for this gentleman, struck again by the unhappy name of the bereaved constituency, only broke out: "Ah what a place to represent! How can you — how can you?"

"It's an excellent place," said Lady Agnes coldly. "I imagine you've never been there. It's a very good place indeed. It belongs very largely to my cousin, Mrs. Dallow."

Gabriel partook of the fish, listening with interest. "But I thought we had no more pocket-boroughs."

"It's pockets we rather lack, so many of us. There are plenty of Harshes," Nick Dormer observed.

"I don't know what you mean," Lady Agnes said to Nash with considerable majesty.

53

Peter Sherringham also addressed him with an "Oh it's all right; they come down on you like a shot!" and the young man continued ingenuously — "Do you mean to say you've to pay money to get into that awful place — that it's not *you* who are paid?"

"Into that awful place?" Lady Agnes repeated blankly.

"Into the House of Commons. That you don't get a high salary?"

"My dear Nash, you're delightful: don't leave me — don't leave me!" Nick cried; while his mother looked at him with an eye that demanded "Who in the world's this extraordinary person?"

"What then did you think pocket-boroughs were?" Peter Sherringham asked.

Mr. Nash's facial radiance rested on him. "Why, boroughs that filled your pocket. To do that sort of thing without a bribe — *c'est trop fort!*"

"He lives at Samarcand," Nick Dormer explained to his mother, who flushed perceptibly. "What do you advise me? I'll do whatever you say," he went on to his old acquaintance.

"My dear, my dear — !" Lady Agnes pleaded.

"See Julia first, with all respect to Mr. Nash. She's of excellent counsel," said Peter Sherringham.

Mr. Nash smiled across the table at his host. "The lady first — the lady first! I've not a word to suggest as against any idea of hers."

"We must n't sit here too long, there'll be so much to do," said Lady Agnes anxiously, perceiving a certain slowness in the service of the *bœuf braisé.*

Biddy had been up to this moment mainly occupied in looking, covertly and in snatches, at Peter Sherringham; as was perfectly lawful in a young lady with a handsome cousin whom she had not seen for more than a year. But her sweet voice now took licence to throw in the words: "We know what Mr. Nash thinks of politics: he told us just now he thinks them dreadful."

"No, not dreadful — only inferior," the personage impugned protested. "Everything's relative."

"Inferior to what?" Lady Agnes demanded.

Mr. Nash appeared to consider a moment. "To anything else that may be in question."

"Nothing else *is* in question!" said her ladyship in a tone that would have been triumphant if it had not been so dry.

"Ah then!" And her neighbour shook his head sadly. He turned after this to Biddy. "The ladies whom I was with just now and in whom you were so good as to express an interest?" Biddy gave a sign of assent and he went on: "They're persons theatrical. The younger one's trying to go upon the stage."

"And are you assisting her?" Biddy enquired, pleased she had guessed so nearly right.

"Not in the least — I'm rather choking her off. I consider it the lowest of the arts."

"Lower than politics?" asked Peter Sherringham, who was listening to this.

"Dear no, I won't say that. I think the Théâtre Français a greater institution than the House of Commons."

"I agree with you there!" laughed Sherringham;

"all the more that I don't consider the dramatic art a low one. It seems to me on the contrary to include all the others."

"Yes — that's a view. I think it's the view of my friends."

"Of your friends?"

"Two ladies — old acquaintances — whom I met in Paris a week ago and whom I've just been spending an hour with in this place."

"You should have seen them; they struck me very much," Biddy said to her cousin.

"I should like to see them if they really have anything to say to the theatre."

"It can easily be managed. Do you believe in the theatre?" asked Gabriel Nash.

"Passionately," Sherringham confessed. "Don't you?"

Before Nash had had time to answer Biddy had interposed with a sigh. "How I wish I could go — but in Paris I can't!"

"I'll take you, Biddy — I vow I'll take you."

"But the plays, Peter," the girl objected. "Mamma says they're worse than the pictures."

"Oh we'll arrange that: they shall do one at the Français on purpose for a delightful little yearning English girl."

"Can you make them?"

"I can make them do anything I choose."

"Ah then it's the theatre that believes in *you*," said Mr. Nash.

"It would be ungrateful if it did n't after all I've done for it!" Sherringham gaily opined.

56

Lady Agnes had withdrawn herself from between him and her other guest and, to signify that she at least had finished eating, had gone to sit by her son, whom she held, with some importunity, in conversation. But hearing the theatre talked of she threw across an impersonal challenge to the paradoxical young man. "Pray should you think it better for a gentleman to be an actor?"

"Better than being a politician? Ah, comedian for comedian, is n't the actor more honest?"

Lady Agnes turned to her son and brought forth with spirit: "Think of your great father, Nicholas!"

"He was an honest man," said Nicholas. "That's perhaps why he could n't stand it."

Peter Sherringham judged the colloquy to have taken an uncomfortable twist, though not wholly, as it seemed to him, by the act of Nick's queer comrade. To draw it back to safer ground he said to this personage: "May I ask if the ladies you just spoke of are English — Mrs. and Miss Rooth: is n't that the rather odd name?"

"The very same. Only the daughter, according to her kind, desires to be known by some *nom de guerre* before she has even been able to enlist."

"And what does she call herself?" Bridget Dormer asked.

"Maud Vavasour, or Edith Temple, or Gladys Vane — some rubbish of that sort."

"What then is her own name?"

"Miriam — Miriam Rooth. It would do very well and would give her the benefit of the prepossessing

57

fact that — to the best of my belief at least — she's more than half a Jewess."

"It is as good as Rachel Félix," Sherringham said.

"The name's as good, but not the talent. The girl's splendidly stupid."

"And more than half a Jewess? Don't you believe it!" Sherringham laughed.

"Don't believe she's a Jewess?" Biddy asked, still more interested in Miriam Rooth.

"No, no — that she's stupid, really. If she is she'll be the first."

"Ah you may judge for yourself," Nash rejoined, "if you'll come to-morrow afternoon to Madame Carré, Rue de Constantinople, *à l'entresol.*"

"Madame Carré? Why, I've already a note from her — I found it this morning on my return to Paris — asking me to look in at five o'clock and listen to a *jeune Anglaise.*"

"That's my arrangement — I obtained the favour. The ladies want an opinion, and dear old Carré has consented to see them and to give one. Maud Vavasour will recite, and the venerable artist will pass judgement."

Sherringham remembered he had his note in his pocket and took it out to look it over. "She wishes to make her a little audience — she says she'll do better with that — and she asks me because I'm English. I shall make a point of going."

"And bring Dormer if you can: the audience will be better. Will you come, Dormer?" Mr. Nash continued, appealing to his friend — "will you come with

58

me to hear an English amateur recite and an old French actress pitch into her?"

Nick looked round from his talk with his mother and Grace. "I'll go anywhere with you so that, as I've told you, I may n't lose sight of you — may keep hold of you."

"Poor Mr. Nash, why is he so useful?" Lady Agnes took a cold freedom to enquire.

"He steadies me, mother."

"Oh I wish you'd take *me*, Peter," Biddy broke out wistfully to her cousin.

"To spend an hour with an old French actress? Do *you* want to go upon the stage?" the young man asked.

"No, but I want to see something — to know something."

"Madame Carré's wonderful in her way, but she's hardly company for a little English girl."

"I'm not little, I'm only too big; and *she* goes, the person you speak of."

"For a professional purpose and with her good mother," smiled Mr. Nash. "I think Lady Agnes would hardly venture —!"

"Oh I've seen her good mother!" said Biddy as if she had her impression of what the worth of that protection might be.

"Yes, but you have n't heard her. It's then that you measure her."

Biddy was wistful still. "Is it the famous Honorine Carré, the great celebrity?"

"Honorine in person: the incomparable, the perfect!" said Peter Sherringham. "The first artist of our time, taking her altogether. She and I are old pals; she has been so good as to come and 'say' things — which she does sometimes still *dans le monde* as no one else *can* — in my rooms."

"Make her come then. We can go *there!*"

"One of these days!"

"And the young lady — Miriam, Maud, Gladys — make her come too."

Sherringham looked at Nash and the latter was bland. "Oh you'll have no difficulty. She'll jump at it!"

"Very good. I'll give a little artistic tea — with Julia too of course. And you must come, Mr. Nash." This gentleman promised with an inclination, and Peter continued: "But if, as you say, you're not for helping the young lady, how came you to arrange this interview with the great model?"

"Precisely to stop her short. The great model will find her very bad. Her judgements, as you probably know, are Rhadamanthine."

"Unfortunate creature!" said Biddy. "I think you're cruel."

"Never mind — I'll look after them," Sherringham laughed.

"And how can Madame Carré judge if the girl recites English?"

"She's so intelligent that she could judge if she recited Chinese," Peter declared.

"That's true, but the *jeune Anglaise* recites also in French," said Gabriel Nash.

"Then she isn't stupid."

"And in Italian, and in several more tongues, for aught I know."

60

Sherringham was visibly interested. "Very good — we'll put her through them all."

"She must be *most* clever," Biddy went on yearningly.

" She has spent her life on the Continent; she has wandered about with her mother; she has picked up things."

"And is she a lady?" Biddy asked.

"Oh tremendous! The great ones of the earth on the mother's side. On the father's, on the other hand, I imagine, only a Jew stockbroker in the City."

"Then they're rich — or ought to be," Sherringham suggested.

"Ought to be — ah there's the bitterness! The stockbroker had too short a go — he was carried off in his flower. However, he left his wife a certain property, which she appears to have muddled away, not having the safeguard of being herself a Hebrew. This is what she has lived on till to-day — this and another resource. Her husband, as she has often told me, had the artistic temperament: that's common, as you know, among *ces messieurs*. He made the most of his little opportunities and collected various pictures, tapestries, enamels, porcelains and similar gewgaws. He parted with them also, I gather, at a profit; in short he carried on a neat little business as a *brocanteur*. It was nipped in the bud, but Mrs. Rooth was left with a certain number of these articles in her hands; indeed they must have formed her only capital. She was not a woman of business; she turned them, no doubt, to indifferent account; but she sold them piece by piece, and they kept her going while her daughter grew up. It was to this precarious traffic, conducted with extraordinary mystery and delicacy, that, five years ago, in Florence, I was indebted for my acquaintance with her. In those days I used to collect — heaven help me! — I used to pick up rubbish which I could ill afford. It was a little phase — we have our little phases, have n't we?" Mr. Nash asked with child-like trust — "and I've come out on the other side. Mrs. Rooth had an old green pot and I heard of her old green pot. To hear of it was to long for it, so that I went to see it under cover of night. I bought it and a couple of years ago I overturned and smashed it. It was the last of the little phase. It was not, however, as you've seen, the last of Mrs. Rooth. I met her afterwards in London, and I found her a year or two ago in Venice. She appears to be a great wanderer. She had other old pots, of other colours, red, yellow, black or blue — she could produce them of any com-plexion you liked. I don't know whether she carried them about with her or whether she had little secret stores in the principal cities of Europe. To-day at any rate they seem all gone. On the other hand she has her daughter, who has grown up and who's a precious vase of another kind — less fragile I hope than the rest. May she not be overturned and smashed!"

Peter Sherringham and Biddy Dormer listened with attention to this history, and the girl testified to the interest with which she had followed it by saying when Mr. Nash had ceased speaking: "A Jewish stockbroker, a dealer in curiosities: what an odd person to marry — for a person who was well born! I dare say he was a German."

"His name must have been simply Roth, and the poor lady, to smarten it up, has put in another o," Sherringham ingeniously suggested.

"You're both very clever," said Gabriel, "and Rudolf Roth, as I happen to know, was indeed the designation of Maud Vavasour's papa. But so far as the question of derogation goes one might as well drown as starve — for what connexion is *not* a misalliance when one happens to have the unaccommodating, the crushing honour of being a Neville-Nugent of Castle Nugent ? That's the high lineage of Maud's mamma. I seem to have heard it mentioned that Rudolf Roth was very versatile and, like most of his species, not unacquainted with the practice of music. He had been employed to teach the harmonium to Miss Neville-Nugent and she had profited by his lessons. If his daughter's like him — and she's not like her mother — he was darkly and dangerously handsome. So I venture rapidly to reconstruct the situation."

A silence, for the moment, had fallen on Lady Agnes and her other two children, so that Mr. Nash, with his universal urbanity, practically addressed these last remarks to them as well as to his other auditors. Lady Agnes looked as if she wondered whom he was talking about, and having caught the name of a noble residence she enquired: "Castle Nugent — where in the world's that ?"

"It's a domain of immeasurable extent and almost inconceivable splendour, but I fear not to be found in any prosaic earthly geography!" Lady Agnes rested her eyes on the tablecloth as if she were n't sure a liberty had not been taken with her, or at least with her "order," and while Mr. Nash continued to abound in descriptive suppositions — "It must be on the banks of the Manzanares or the Guadalquivir" — Peter Sherringham, whose imagination had seemingly been kindled by the sketch of Miriam Rooth, took up the argument and reminded him that he had a short time before assigned a low place to the dramatic art and had not yet answered the question as to whether he believed in the theatre. Which gave the speaker a further chance. "I don't know that I understand your question; there are different ways of taking it. Do I think it's important? Is that what you mean? Important certainly to managers and stage-carpenters who want to make money, to ladies and gentlemen who want to produce themselves in public by lime-light, and to other ladies and gentlemen who are bored and stupid and don't know what to do with their evening. It's a commercial and social convenience which may be infinitely worked. But important artistically, intellectually? How *can* it be — so poor, so limited a form?"

"Upon my honour it strikes me as rich and various! Do *you* think it's a poor and limited form, Nick?" Sherringham added, appealing to his kinsman.

"I think whatever Nash thinks. I've no opinion to-day but his."

This answer of the hope of the Dormers drew the eyes of his mother and sisters to him and caused his friend to exclaim that he was n't used to such responsibilities — so few people had ever tested his presence of mind by agreeing with him. "Oh I used to be of your way of feeling," Nash went on to Sherringham. "I understand you perfectly. It's a phase like another. I've been through it — *j'ai été comme ça.*"

"And you went then very often to the Théâtre Français, and it was there I saw you. I place you now."

"I'm afraid I noticed none of the other spectators," Nash explained. "I had no attention but for the great Carré — she was still on the stage. Judge of my infatuation, and how I can allow for yours, when I tell you that I sought her acquaintance, that I could n't rest till I had told her how I hung upon her lips."

"That's just what *I* told her," Sherringham returned.

"She was very kind to me. She said 'Vous me rendez des forces.'"

"That's just what she said to me!"

"And we've remained very good friends."

"So have we!" laughed Sherringham. "And such perfect art as hers — do you mean to say you don't consider *that* important, such a rare dramatic intelligence?"

"I'm afraid you read the feuilletons. You catch their phrases" — Nash spoke with pity. "Dramatic intelligence is never rare; nothing's more common."

"Then why have we so many shocking actors?"

"Have we? I thought they were mostly good; succeeding more easily and more completely in that business than in anything else. What could they do — those people generally — if they did n't do that poor thing? And reflect that the poor thing enables them to succeed! Of course, always, there are numbers of people on the stage who are no actors at all, for it's even easier to our poor humanity to be ineffectively stupid and vulgar than to bring down the house."

"It's not easy, by what I can see, to produce, completely, any artistic effect," Sherringham declared; "and those the actor produces are among the most momentous we know. You'll not persuade me that to watch such an actress as Madame Carré was n't an education of the taste, an enlargement of one's knowledge."

"She did what she could, poor woman, but in what belittling coarsening conditions! She had to interpret a character in a play, and a character in a play — not to say the whole piece: I speak more particularly of modern pieces — is such a wretchedly small peg to hang anything on! The dramatist shows us so little, is so hampered by his audience, is restricted to so poor an analysis."

"I know the complaint. It's all the fashion now. The *raffinés* despise the theatre," said Peter Sherringham in the manner of a man abreast with the culture of his age and not to be captured by a surprise. "*Connu, connu!*"

"It will be known better yet, won't it? when the essentially brutal nature of the modern audience is still more perceived, when it was been properly analysed: the *omnium gatherum* of the population of a big commercial city at the hour of the day when their taste is at its lowest, flocking out of hideous hotels and restaurants, gorged with food, stultified with buying and selling and with all the other sordid preoccupations of the age, squeezed together in a sweltering mass,

66

disappointed in their seats, timing the author, timing
the actor, wishing to get their money back on the spot
— all before eleven o'clock. Fancy putting the exquisite before such a tribunal as that! There's not
even a question of it. The dramatist would n't if
he could, and in nine cases out of ten he could n't
if he would. He has to make the basest concessions.
One of his principal canons is that he must enable
his spectators to catch the suburban trains, which stop
at 11:30. What would you think of any other artist —
the painter or the novelist — whose governing forces
should be the dinner and the suburban trains? The
old dramatists did n't defer to them — not so much
at least — and that's why they're less and less actable.
If they're touched — the large loose men — it's only
to be mutilated and trivialised. Besides, they had
a simpler civilisation to represent — societies in which
the life of man was in action, in passion, in immediate
and violent expression. Those things could be put
upon the playhouse boards with comparatively little
sacrifice of their completeness and their truth. To-day
we're so infinitely more reflective and complicated
and diffuse that it makes all the difference. What can
you do with a character, with an idea, with a feeling,
between dinner and the suburban trains? You can
give a gross rough sketch of them, but how little you
touch them, how bald you leave them! What crudity
compared with what the novelist does!"

"Do you write novels, Mr. Nash?" Peter candidly
asked.

"No, but I read them when they're extraordinarily
good, and I don't go to plays. I read Balzac for

instance — I encounter the admirable portrait of Valérie Marneffe in 'La Cousine Bette.'"

"And you contrast it with the poverty of Emile Augier's Séraphine in 'Les Lionnes Pauvres'? I was awaiting you there. That's the *cheval de bataille* of you fellows."

"What an extraordinary discussion! What dreadful authors!" Lady Agnes murmured to her son. But he was listening so attentively to the other young men that he made no response, and Peter Sherringham went on:

"I've seen Madame Carré in things of the modern repertory, which she has made as vivid to me, caused to abide as ineffaceably in my memory, as Valérie Marneffe. She's the Balzac, as one may say, of actresses."

"The miniaturist, as it were, of whitewashers!" Nash offered as a substitute.

It might have been guessed that Sherringham resented his damned freedom, yet could but emulate his easy form. "You'd be magnanimous if you thought the young lady you've introduced to our old friend would be important."

Mr. Nash lightly weighed it. "She might be much more so than she ever will be."

Lady Agnes, however, got up to terminate the scene and even to signify that enough had been said about people and questions she had never so much as heard of. Every one else rose, the waiter brought Nicholas the receipt of the bill, and Sherringham went on, to his interlocutor: "Perhaps she'll be more so than you think."

68

"Perhaps — if *you* take an interest in her!"

"A mystic voice seems to exhort me to do so, to whisper that though I've never seen her I shall find something in her." On which Peter appealed. "What do you say, Biddy — shall I take an interest in her?"

The girl faltered, coloured a little, felt a certain embarrassment in being publicly treated as an oracle. "If she's not nice I don't advise it."

"And if she *is* nice?"

"You advise it still less!" her brother exclaimed, laughing and putting his arm round her.

Lady Agnes looked sombre — she might have been saying to herself: "Heaven help us, what chance has a girl of mine with a man who's so agog about actresses?" She was disconcerted and distressed; a multitude of incongruous things, all the morning, had been forced upon her attention — displeasing pictures and still more displeasing theories about them, vague portents of perversity on Nick's part and a strange eagerness on Peter's, learned apparently in Paris, to discuss, with a person who had a tone she never had been exposed to, topics irrelevant and uninteresting, almost disgusting, the practical effect of which was to make light of her presence. "Let us leave this — let us leave this!" she grimly said. The party moved together toward the door of departure, and her ruffled spirit was not soothed by hearing her son remark to his terrible friend: "You know you don't escape me; I stick to you!"

At this Lady Agnes broke out and interposed. "Pardon my reminding you that you're going to call on Julia."

"Well, can't Nash also come to call on Julia? That's just what I want — that she should see him."

Peter Sherringham came humanely to his kinswoman's assistance. "A better way perhaps will be for them to meet under my auspices at my 'dramatic tea.' This will enable me to return one favour for another. If Mr. Nash is so good as to introduce me to this aspirant for honours we estimate so differently, I'll introduce him to my sister, a much more positive quantity."

"It's easy to see who'll have the best of it!" Grace Dormer declared; while Nash stood there serenely, impartially, in a graceful detached way which seemed characteristic of him, assenting to any decision that relieved him of the grossness of choice and generally confident that things would turn out well for him. He was cheerfully helpless and sociably indifferent; ready to preside with a smile even at a discussion of his own admissibility.

"Nick will bring you. I've a little corner at the embassy," Sherringham continued.

"You're very kind. You must bring him then to-morrow — Rue de Constantinople."

"At five o'clock — don't be afraid."

"Oh dear!" Biddy wailed as they went on again and Lady Agnes, seizing his arm, marched off more quickly with her son. When they came out into the Champs Elysées Nick Dormer, looking round, saw his friend had disappeared. Biddy had attached herself to Peter, and Grace could n't have encouraged Mr. Nash.

V

LADY AGNES's idea had been that her son should go straight from the Palais de l'Industrie to the Hôtel de Hollande, with or without his mother and his sisters as his humour should seem to recommend. Much as she desired to see their valued Julia, and as she knew her daughters desired it, she was quite ready to put off their visit if this sacrifice should contribute to a speedy confrontation for Nick. She was anxious he should talk with Mrs. Dallow, and anxious he should be anxious himself; but it presently appeared that he was conscious of no pressure of eagerness. His view was that she and the girls should go to their cousin without delay and should, if they liked, spend the rest of the day in her society. He would go later; he would go in the evening. There were lots of things he wanted to do meanwhile.

This question was discussed with some intensity, though not at length, while the little party stood on the edge of the Place de la Concorde, to which they had proceeded on foot; and Lady Agnes noticed that the "lots of things" to which he proposed to give precedence over an urgent duty, a conference with a person who held out full hands to him, were implied somehow in the friendly glance with which he covered the great square, the opposite bank of the Seine, the steep blue roofs of the quay, the bright immensity of Paris. What in the world could be more important than making sure of his seat? — so quickly did the good lady's imagination travel. And now that idea appealed to him less than a ramble in search of old books and prints — since she was sure this was what he had in his head. Julia would be flattered should she know it, but of course she must n't know it. Lady Agnes was already thinking of the least injurious account she could give of the young man's want of precipitation. She would have liked to represent him as tremendously occupied, in his room at their own hotel, in getting off political letters to every one it should concern, and particularly in drawing up his address to the electors of Harsh. Fortunately she was a woman of innumerable discretions, and a part of the worn look that sat in her face came from her having schooled herself for years, in commerce with her husband and her sons, not to insist unduly. She would have liked to insist, nature had formed her to insist, and the self-control had told in more ways than one. Even now it was powerless to prevent her suggesting that before doing anything else Nick should at least repair to the inn and see if there were n't some telegrams.

He freely consented to do as much as this, and, having called a cab that she might go her way with the girls, kissed her again as he had done at the exhibition. This was an attention that could never displease her, but somehow when he kissed her she was really the more worried: she had come to recognise it as a sign that he was slipping away from her, and she wished she might frankly take it as his clutch at her to save him. She drove off with a vague sense that at any rate she and the girls might do something toward keeping the place warm for him. She had been a little vexed that Peter had not administered more of a push toward the Hôtel de Hollande, clear as it had become to her now that there was a foreignness in Peter which was not to be counted on and which made him speak of English affairs and even of English domestic politics as local and even "funny." They were very grandly local, and if one recalled, in public life, an occasional droll incident was n't that, liberally viewed, just the warm human comfort of them? As she left the two young men standing together in the middle of the Place de la Concorde, the grand composition of which Nick, as she looked back, appeared to have paused to admire — as if he had n't seen it a thousand times! — she wished she might have thought of Peter's influence with her son as exerted a little more in favor of localism. She had a fear he would n't abbreviate the boy's ill-timed *flânerie*. However, he had been very nice: he had invited them all to dine with him that evening at a convenient café, promising to bring Julia and one of his colleagues. So much as this he had been willing to do to make sure Nick and his sister should meet. His want of localism moreover was not so great as that if it should turn out that there *was* anything beneath his manner toward Biddy —! The upshot of this reflexion might have been represented by the circumstance of her ladyship's remarking after a minute to her younger daughter, who sat opposite her in the *voiture de place*, that it would do no harm if she should get a new hat and that the search might be instituted that afternoon.

"A French hat, mamma?" said Grace. "Oh do wait till she gets home!"

"I think they're really prettier here, you know," Biddy opined; and Lady Agnes said simply "I dare say they're cheaper." What was in her mind in fact was "I dare say Peter thinks them becoming." It will be seen she had plenty of inward occupation, the sum of which was not lessened by her learning when she reached the top of the Rue de la Paix that Mrs. Dallow had gone out half an hour before and had left no message. She was more disconcerted by this incident than she could have explained or than she thought was right, as she had taken for granted Julia would be in a manner waiting for them. How could she be sure Nick was n't coming? When people were in Paris a few days they did n't mope in the house, but she might have waited a little longer or have left an explanation. Was she then not so much in earnest about Nick's standing? Did n't she recognise the importance of being there to see him about it? Lady Agnes wondered if her behaviour were a sign of her being already tired of the way this young gentleman treated her. Perhaps she had gone out because an instinct told her that the great propriety of their meeting early would make no difference with him — told her he would n't after all come. His mother's heart sank as she glanced at this possibility that their precious friend was already tired, she having on her side an intuition that there were still harder things in store. She had disliked having to tell Mrs. Dallow that Nick would n't see her till the evening, but now she dis-

liked still more her not being there to hear it. She
even resented a little her kinswoman's not having
reasoned that she and the girls would come in any
event, and not thought them worth staying in for. It
came up indeed that she would perhaps have gone
to their hotel, which was a good way up the Rue de
Rivoli, near the Palais Royal — on which the cab-
man was directed to drive to that establishment.

As he jogged along she took in some degree the
measure of what that might mean, Julia's seeking
a little to avoid them. Was she growing to dislike
them? Did she think they kept too sharp an eye on
her, so that the idea of their standing in a still closer
relation would n't be enticing? Her conduct up to
this time had not worn such an appearance, unless
perhaps a little, just a very little, in the matter of her
ways with poor Grace. Lady Agnes knew she was n't
particularly fond of poor Grace, and could even
sufficiently guess the reason — the manner in which
Grace betrayed most how they wanted to make sure
of her. She remembered how long the girl had stayed
the last time she had been at Harsh — going for
an acceptable week and dragging out her visit to
a month. She took a private heroic vow that Grace
should n't go near the place again for a year; not,
that is, unless Nick and Julia were married within
the time. If that were to happen she should n't care.
She recognised that it was n't absolutely everything
Julia should be in love with Nick; it was also better
she should dislike his mother and sisters after a probable pursuit of him than before. Lady Agnes did
justice to the natural rule in virtue of which it

75

usually comes to pass that a woman does n't get on with her husband's female belongings, and was even willing to be sacrificed to it in her disciplined degree. But she desired not to be sacrificed for nothing: if she was to be objected to as a mother-in-law she wished to be the mother-in-law first.

At the hotel in the Rue de Rivoli she had the disappointment of finding that Mrs. Dallow had not called, and also that no telegrams had come. She went in with the girls for half an hour and then straggled out with them again. She was undetermined and dissatisfied and the afternoon was rather a problem; of the kind moreover that she disliked most and was least accustomed to: not a choice between different things to do — her life had been full of that — but a want of anything to do at all. Nick had said to her before they separated "You can knock about with the girls, you know; everything's amusing here." That was easily said while he sauntered and gossiped with Peter Sherringham and perhaps went to see more pictures like those in the Salon. He was usually, on such occasions, very good-natured about spending his time with them; but this episode had taken altogether a perverse profane form. She had no desire whatever to knock about and was far from finding everything in Paris amusing. She had no aptitude for aimlessness and moreover thought it vulgar. If she had found Julia's card at the hotel — the sign of a hope of catching them just as they came back from the Salon — she would have made a second attempt to see her before the evening; but now certainly they would leave her alone. Lady Agnes wandered joylessly with the girls in the Palais Royal and the Rue de Richelieu, and emerged upon the Boulevard, where they continued their frugal prowl, as Biddy rather irritatingly called it. They went into five shops to buy a hat for Biddy, and her lady-ship's presumptions of cheapness were woefully belied.

"Who in the world's your comic friend?" Peter Sherringham was meanwhile asking of his kinsman as they walked together.

"Ah there's something else you lost by going to Cambridge — you lost Gabriel Nash!"

"He sounds like an Elizabethan dramatist," Sherringham said. "But I have n't lost him, since it appears now I shan't be able to have you without him."

"Oh, as for that, wait a little. I'm going to try him again, but I don't know how he wears. What I mean is that you've probably lost his freshness, which was the great thing. I rather fear he's becoming conventional, or at any rate serious."

"Bless me, do you call that serious?"

"He used to be so gay. He had a real genius for playing with ideas. He was a wonderful talker."

"It seems to me he does very well now," said Peter Sherringham.

"Oh this is nothing. He had great flights of old, very great flights; one saw him rise and rise and turn somersaults in the blue — one wondered how far he could go. He's very intelligent, and I should think it might be interesting to find out what it is that prevents the whole man from being as good as his parts. I mean in case he is n't so good."

"I see you more than suspect that. May n't it be simply that he 's too great an ass?"

"That would be the whole — I shall see in time — but it certainly is n't one of the parts. It may be the effect, but it is n't the cause, and it 's for the cause I claim an interest. Do you think him an ass for what he said about the theatre — his pronouncing it a coarse art?"

"To differ from you about him that reason would do," said Sherringham. "The only bad one would be one that should n't preserve our difference. You need n't tell me you agree with him, for frankly I don't care."

"Then your passion still burns?" Nick Dormer asked.

"My passion — ?"

"I don't mean for any individual exponent of the equivocal art: mark the guilty conscience, mark the rising blush, mark the confusion of mind! I mean the old sign one knew you best by: your permanent stall at the Français, your inveterate attendance at *premières*, the way you 'follow' the young talents and the old."

"Yes, it 's still my little hobby, my little folly if you like," Sherringham said. "I don't find I get tired of it. What will you have? Strong predilections are rather a blessing; they 're simplifying. I 'm fond of representation — the representation of life: I like it better, I think, than the real thing. You like it too, you 'd be ready in other conditions to go in for it, in your way — so you 've no right to cast the stone. You like it best done by one vehicle and I by another; and our preference on either side has a deep root in us. There's a fascination to me in the way the actor does it, when his talent — ah he must have that! — has been highly trained. Ah it must *be* that! The things he can do in this effort at representation, with the dramatist to back him, seem to me innumerable — he can carry it to a point! — and I take great pleasure in observing them, in recognising and comparing them. It's an amusement like another — I don't pretend to call it by any exalted name, but in this vale of friction it will serve. One can lose one's self in it, and it has the recommendation — in common I suppose with the study of the other arts — that the further you go in it the more you find. So I go rather far, if you will. But is it the principal sign one knows me by?" Peter abruptly asked.

"Don't be ashamed of it," Nick returned — "else it will be ashamed of you. I ought to discriminate. You're distinguished among my friends and relations by your character of rising young diplomatist; but you know I always want the final touch to the picture, the last fruit of analysis. Therefore I make out that you're conspicuous among rising young diplomatists for the infatuation you describe in such pretty terms."

"You evidently believe it will prevent my ever rising very high. But pastime for pastime is it any idler than yours?"

"Than mine?"

"Why you've half a dozen while I only allow myself the luxury of one. For the theatre's my sole vice, really. Is this more wanton, say, than to devote

79

weeks to the consideration of the particular way in
which your friend Mr. Nash may be most intensely
a twaddler and a bore? That's not my ideal of
choice recreation, but I'd undertake to satisfy you
about him sooner. You're a young statesman —
who happens to be *en disponibilité* for the moment
— but you spend not a little of your time in besmear-
ing canvas with bright-coloured pigments. The idea
of representation fascinates you, but in your case
it's representation in oils — or do you practise water-
colours and pastel too? You even go much further
than I, for I study my art of predilection only in the
works of others. I don't aspire to leave works of
my own. You're a painter, possibly a great one; but
I'm not an actor." Nick Dormer declared he would
certainly become one — he was so well on the way
to it; and Sherringham, without heeding this charge,
went on: "Let me add that, considering you *are*
a painter, your portrait of the complicated Nash is
lamentably dim."

"He's not at all complicated; he's only too simple
to give an account of. Most people have a lot of
attributes and appendages that dress them up and
superscribe them, and what I like Gabriel for is that
he hasn't any at all. It makes him, it keeps him,
so refreshingly cool."

"By Jove, you match him there! Isn't it an ap-
pendage and an attribute to escape kicking? How
does he manage that?" Sherringham asked.

"I haven't the least idea — I don't know that he
doesn't rouse the kicking impulse. Besides, he can
kick back and I don't think any one has ever seen

80

him duck or dodge. His means, his profession, his belongings, have never anything to do with the question. He does n't shade off into other people; he 's as neat as an outline cut out of paper with scissors. I like him therefore because in dealing with him you know what you 've got hold of. With most men you don't: to pick the flower you must break off the whole dusty thorny worldly branch; you find you 're taking up in your grasp all sorts of other people and things, dangling accidents and conditions. Poor Nash has none of those encumbrances: he 's the solitary fragrant blossom."

"My dear fellow, you 'd be better for a little of the same pruning!" Sherringham retorted; and the young men continued their walk and their gossip, jerking each other this way and that, punching each other here and there, with an amicable roughness consequent on their having been boys together. Intimacy had reigned of old between the little Sherringhams and the little Dormers, united in the country by ease of neighbouring and by the fact that there was first cousinship, not neglected, among the parents, Lady Agnes standing in this plastic relation to Lady Windrush, the mother of Peter and Julia as well as of other daughters and of a maturer youth who was to inherit, and who since then had inherited, the ancient barony. Many things had altered later on, but not the good reasons for not explaining. One of our young men had gone to Eton and the other to Harrow — the scattered school on the hill was the tradition of the Dormers — and the divergence had rather taken its course in university years. Bricket, however, had remained accessible to Windrush, and Windrush to Bricket, to which estate Percival Dormer had now succeeded, terminating the interchange a trifle rudely by letting out that pleasant white house in the midlands—its expropriated inhabitants, Lady Agnes and her daughters, adored it — to an American reputed rich, who in the first flush of his sense of contrasts considered that for twelve hundred a year he got it at a bargain. Bricket had come to the late Sir Nicholas from his elder brother, dying wifeless and childless. The new baronet, so different from his father — though recalling at some points the uncle after whom he had been named — that Nick had to make it up by cultivating conformity, roamed about the world, taking shots which excited the enthusiasm of society, when society heard of them, at the few legitimate creatures of the chase the British rifle had up to that time spared. Lady Agnes meanwhile settled with her girls in a gabled latticed house in a mentionable quarter, though it still required a little explaining, of the temperate zone of London. It was not into her lap, poor woman, that the revenues of Bricket were poured. There was no dower-house attached to that moderate property, and the allowance with which the estate was charged on her ladyship's behalf was not an incitement to grandeur.

Nick had a room under his mother's roof, which he mainly used to dress for dinner when dining in Calcutta Gardens, and he had "kept on" his chambers in the Temple; for to a young man in public life an independent address was indispensable.

Moreover he was suspected of having a studio in an out-of-the-way district, the indistinguishable parts of South Kensington, incongruous as such a retreat might seem in the case of a member of Parliament. It was an absurd place to see his constituents unless he wanted to paint their portraits, a kind of "representation" with which they would scarce have been satisfied; and in fact the only question of portraiture had been when the wives and daughters of several of them expressed a wish for the picture of their handsome young member. Nick had not offered to paint it himself, and the studio was taken for granted rather than much looked into by the ladies in Calcutta Gardens. Too express a disposition to regard whims of this sort as extravagance pure and simple was known by them to be open to correction; for they were not oblivious that Mr. Carteret had humours which weighed against them in the shape of convenient cheques nestling between the inside pages of legible letters of advice. Mr. Carteret was Nick's providence, just as Nick was looked to, in a general way, to be that of his mother and sisters, especially since it had become so plain that Percy, who was not subtly selfish, would operate, mainly with a "six-bore," quite out of that sphere. It was not for studios certainly that Mr. Carteret sent cheques; but they were an expression of general confidence in Nick, and a little expansion was natural to a young man enjoying such a luxury as that. It was sufficiently felt in Calcutta Gardens that he could be looked to not to betray such confidence; for Mr. Carteret's behaviour could have no name at all unless one were prepared to call it encouraging. He had never promised anything, but he was one of the delightful persons with whom the redemption precedes or dispenses with the vow. He had been an early and lifelong friend of the late right honourable gentleman, a political follower, a devoted admirer, a stanch supporter in difficult hours. He had never married, espousing nothing more reproductive than Sir Nicholas's views — he used to write letters to the *Times* in favour of them — and had, so far as was known, neither chick nor child; nothing but an amiable little family of eccentricities, the flower of which was his odd taste for living in a small steep clean country town, all green gardens and red walls with a girdle of hedge-rows, all clustered about an immense brown old abbey. When Lady Agnes's imagination rested upon the future of her second son she liked to remember that Mr. Carteret had nothing to "keep up": the inference seemed so direct that he would keep up Nick.

The most important event in the life of this young man had been incomparably his success, under his father's eyes, more than two years before, in the sharp contest for Crockhurst — a victory which his consecrated name, his extreme youth, his ardour in the fray, the marked personal sympathy of the party and the attention excited by the fresh cleverness of his speeches, tinted with young idealism and yet sticking sufficiently to the question — the burning question which has since burned out — had made quite splendid. There had been leaders in the newspapers about it, half in compliment to her husband, who

84

was known to be failing so prematurely — he was almost as young to die, and to die famous, for Lady Agnes regarded it as famous, as his son had been to stand — tributes the boy's mother religiously preserved, cut out and tied together with a ribbon, in the innermost drawer of a favourite cabinet. But it had been a barren, or almost a barren triumph, for in the order of importance in Nick's history another incident had run it, as the phrase is, very close: nothing less than the quick dissolution of the Parliament in which he was so manifestly destined to give symptoms of a future. He had not recovered his seat at the general election, for the second contest was even sharper than the first and the Tories had put forward a loud, vulgar, rattling, bullying, money-spending man. It was to a certain extent a comfort that poor Sir Nicholas, who had been witness of the bright hour, should have passed away before the darkness. He died with all his hopes on his second son's head, unconscious of near disappointment, handing on the torch and the tradition, after a long, supreme interview with Nick at which Lady Agnes had not been present, but which she knew to have been a thorough paternal dedication, an august communication of ideas on the highest national questions (she had reason to believe he had touched on those of external as well as of domestic and of colonial policy) leaving on the boy's nature and manner from that moment the most unmistakeable traces. If his tendency to reverie increased it was because he had so much to think over in what his pale father had said to him in the hushed dim chamber, laying on him the great mission that death had cut short, breathing into him with unforgettable solemnity the very accents — Sir Nicholas's voice had been wonderful for richness — that he was to sound again. It was work cut out for a lifetime, and that "co-ordinating power in relation to detail" which was one of the great characteristics of the lamented statesman's high distinction — the most analytic of the weekly papers was always talking about it — had enabled him to rescue the prospect from any shade of vagueness or of ambiguity.

Five years before Nick Dormer went up to be questioned by the electors of Crockhurst Peter Sherringham had appeared before a board of examiners who let him off much less easily, though there were also some flattering prejudices in his favour; such influences being a part of the copious light unembarrassing baggage with which each of the young men began life. Peter passed, however, passed high, and had his reward in prompt assignment to small subordinate diplomatic duties in Germany. Since then he had had his professional adventures, which need not arrest us, inasmuch as they had all paled in the light of his appointment, nearly three years previous to the moment of our making his acquaintance, to a secretaryship of embassy in Paris. He had done well and had gone fast and for the present could draw his breath at ease. It pleased him better to remain in Paris as a subordinate than to go to Honduras as a principal, and Nick Dormer had not put a false colour on the matter in speaking of his stall at the Théâtre Français as a sedative to his ambition. Nick's inferiority in age to his cousin sat on him more lightly than when they had been in their teens; and indeed no one can very well be much older than a young man who has figured for a year, however imperceptibly, in the House of Commons. Separation and diversity had made them reciprocally strange enough to give a price to what they shared; they were friends without being particular friends; that further degree could always hang before them as a suitable but not oppressive contingency, and they were both conscious that it was in their interest to keep certain differences to "chaff" each other about — so possible was it that they might have quarrelled if they had had everything in common. Peter, as being wide-minded, was a little irritated to find his cousin always so intensely British, while Nick Dormer made him the object of the same compassionate criticism, recognised in him a rare knack with foreign tongues, but reflected, and even with extravagance declared, that it was a pity to have gone so far from home only to remain so homely. Moreover Nick had his ideas about the diplomatic mind, finding in it, for his own sympathy, always the wrong turn. Dry, narrow, barren, poor he pronounced it in familiar conversation with the clever secretary; wanting in imagination, in generosity, in the finest perceptions and the highest courage. This served as well as anything else to keep the peace between them; it was a necessity of their friendly intercourse that they should scuffle a little, and it scarcely mattered what they scuffled about. Nick Dormer's express enjoyment of Paris, the shop-windows on the quays, the old books on the parapet, the gaiety of the river, the grandeur of the Louvre, every fine feature of that prodigious face, struck his companion as a sign of insularity; the appreciation of such things having become with Sherringham an unconscious habit, a contented assimilation. If poor Nick, for the hour, was demonstrative and lyrical, it was because he had no other way of sounding the note of farewell to the independent life of which the term seemed now definitely in sight — the sense so pressed upon him that these were the last moments of his freedom. He would waste time till half-past seven, because half-past seven meant dinner, and dinner meant his mother solemnly attended by the strenuous shade of his father and re-enforced by Julia.

VI

WHEN he arrived with the three members of his family at the restaurant of their choice Peter Sherringham was already seated there by one of the immaculate tables, but Mrs. Dallow was not yet on the scene, and they had time for a sociable settlement — time to take their places and unfold their napkins, crunch their rolls, breathe the savoury air and watch the door, before the usual raising of heads and suspension of forks, the sort of stir that accompanied most of this lady's movements, announced her entrance. The *dame de comptoir* ducked and re-ducked, the people looked round, Peter and Nick got up, there was a shuffling of chairs — Julia had come. Peter was relating how he had stopped at her hotel to bring her with him and had found her, according to her custom, by no means ready; on which, fearing his guests would arrive first at the rendezvous and find no proper welcome, he had come off without her, leaving her to follow. He had not brought a friend, as he intended, having divined that Julia would prefer a pure family party if she wanted to talk about her candidate. Now she stood looking down at the table and her expectant kinsfolk, drawing off her gloves, letting her brother draw off her jacket, lifting her hands for some re-arrangement of her hat. She looked at Nick last, smiling, but only for a moment. She said to Peter " Are we going to dine

89

here? Oh dear, why did n't you have a private
room?"

Nick had not seen her at all for several weeks and
had seen her but little for a year, but her off-hand
cursory manner had not altered in the interval. She
spoke remarkably fast, as if speech were not in itself
a pleasure — to have it over as soon as possible; and
her *brusquerie* was of the dark shade friendly critics
account for by pleading shyness. Shyness had never
appeared to him an ultimate quality or a real explanation of anything; it only explained an effect by another effect, neither with a cause to boast of. What
he suspected in Julia was that her mind was less
pleasing than her person; an ugly, a really blighting
idea, which as yet he had but half-accepted. It was
a case in which she was entitled to the benefit of every
doubt and ought n't to be judged without a complete
trial. Nick meanwhile was afraid of the trial — this
was partly why he had been of late to see her so little
— because he was afraid of the sentence, afraid of
anything that might work to lessen the charm it was
actually in the power of her beauty to shed. There
were people who thought her rude, and he hated rude
women. If he should fasten on that view, or rather if
that view should fasten on him, what could still please
and what he admired in her would lose too much of
its sweetness. If it be thought odd that he had not
yet been able to read the character of a woman he
had known since childhood the answer is that this
character had grown faster than Nick's observation.
The growth was constant, whereas the observation
was but occasional, though it had begun early. If he

had attempted inwardly to phrase the matter, as he probably had not, he might have pronounced the effect she produced upon him too much a compulsion; not the coercion of design, of importunity, nor the vulgar pressure of family expectation, a betrayed desire he should like her enough to marry her, but a mixture of divers urgent things; of the sense that she was imperious and generous — probably more the former than the latter — and of a certain prevision of doom, the influence of the idea that he should come to it, that he was predestined.

This had made him shrink from knowing the worst about her; not the wish to get used to it in time, but what was more characteristic of him, the wish to interpose a temporary illusion. Illusions and realities and hopes and fears, however, fell into confusion whenever he met her after a separation. The separation, so far as seeing her alone or as continuous talk was concerned, had now been tolerably long; had lasted really ever since his failure to regain his seat. An impression had come to him that she judged that failure rather stiffly, had thought, and had somewhat sharply said, that he ought to have done better. This was a part of her imperious way, and a part not *all* to be overlooked on a mere present basis. If he were to marry her he should come to an understanding with her: he should give her his own measure as well as take hers. But the understanding might in the actual case suggest too much that he *was* to marry her. You could quarrel with your wife because there were compensations — for her; but you might n't be prepared to offer these compensations as prepayment for the luxury of quarrelling.

It was not that such a luxury would n't be considerable, our young man none the less thought as Julia Dallow's fine head poised itself before him again; a high spirit was of course better than a mawkish to be mismated with, any day in the year. She had much the same colour as her brother, but as nothing else in her face was the same the resemblance was not striking. Her hair was of so dark a brown that it was commonly regarded as black, and so abundant that a plain arrangement was required to keep it in natural relation to the rest of her person. Her eyes were of a grey sometimes pronounced too light, and were not sunken in her face, but placed well on the surface. Her nose was perfect, but her mouth was too small; and Nick Dormer, and doubtless other persons as well, had sometimes wondered how with such a mouth her face could have expressed decision. Her figure helped it, for she appeared tall — being extremely slender — yet was not; and her head took turns and positions which, though a matter of but half an inch out of the common this way or that, somehow contributed to the air of resolution and temper. If it had not been for her extreme delicacy of line and surface she might have been called bold; but as it was she looked refined and quiet — refined by tradition and quiet for a purpose. And altogether she was beautiful, with the gravity of her elegant head, her hair like the depths of darkness, her eyes like its earlier clearing, her mouth like a rare pink flower.

Peter said he had not taken a private room because he knew Biddy's tastes; she liked to see the world — she had told him so — the curious people, the coming and going of Paris. "Oh anything for Biddy!" Julia replied, smiling at the girl and taking her place. Lady Agnes and her elder daughter exchanged one of their looks, and Nick exclaimed jocosely that he did n't see why the whole party should be sacrificed to a presumptuous child. The presumptuous child blushingly protested she had never expressed any such wish to Peter, upon which Nick, with broader humour, revealed that Peter had served them so out of stinginess: he had pitchforked them together in the public room because he would n't go to the expense of a *cabinet*. He had brought no guest, no foreigner of distinction nor diplomatic swell, to honour them, and now they would see what a paltry dinner he would give them. Peter stabbed him indignantly with a long roll, and Lady Agnes, who seemed to be waiting for some manifestation on Mrs. Dallow's part which did n't come, concluded, with a certain coldness, that they quite sufficed to themselves for privacy as well as for society. Nick called attention to this fine phrase of his mother's and said it was awfully neat, while Grace and Biddy looked harmoniously at Julia's clothes. Nick felt nervous and joked a good deal to carry it off — a levity that did n't prevent Julia's saying to him after a moment: "You might have come to see me to-day, you know. Did n't you get my message from Peter?"

"Scold him, Julia — scold him well. I begged him to go," said Lady Agnes; and to this Grace

added her voice with an "Oh Julia, do give it to him!"
These words, however, had not the effect they suggested, since Mrs. Dallow only threw off for answer,
in her quick curt way, that that would be making
far too much of him. It was one of the things in
her that Nick mentally pronounced ungraceful, the
perversity of pride or of shyness that always made
her disappoint you a little if she saw you expected
a thing. She snubbed effusiveness in a way that yet
gave no interesting hint of any wish to keep it herself in reserve. Effusiveness, however, certainly, was
the last thing of which Lady Agnes would have consented to be accused; and Nick, while he replied to
Julia that he was sure he should n't have found her,
was not unable to perceive the operation on his
mother of that shade of manner. "He ought to have
gone; he owed you that," she went on; "but it's very
true he would have had the same luck as we. I went
with the girls directly after luncheon. I suppose you
got our card."

"He might have come after I came in," said Mrs.
Dallow.

"Dear Julia, I'm going to see you to-night. I've
been waiting for that," Nick returned.

"Of course *we* had no idea when you'd come in,"
said Lady Agnes.

"I'm so sorry. You must come to-morrow. I hate
calls at night," Julia serenely added.

"Well then, will you roam with me? Will you
wander through Paris on my arm?" Nick asked,
smiling. "Will you take a drive with me?"

"Oh that would be perfection!" cried Grace.

94

"I thought we were all going somewhere — to the Hippodrome, Peter," Biddy said.

"Oh not all; just you and me!" laughed Peter.

"I'm going home to my bed. I've earned my rest," Lady Agnes sighed.

"Can't Peter take *us?*" demanded Grace. "Nick can take you home, mamma, if Julia won't receive him, and I can look perfectly after Peter and Biddy."

"Take them to something amusing; please take them," Mrs. Dallow said to her brother. Her voice was kind, but had the expectation of assent in it, and Nick observed both the good nature and the pressure. "You're tired, poor dear," she continued to Lady Agnes. "Fancy your being dragged about so! What did you come over for?"

"My mother came because I brought her," Nick said. "It's I who have dragged her about. I brought her for a little change. I thought it would do her good. I wanted to see the Salon."

"It isn't a bad time. I've a carriage and you must use it; you must use nothing else. It shall take you everywhere. I'll drive you about to-morrow." Julia dropped these words with all her air of being able rather than of wanting; but Nick had already noted, and he noted now afresh and with pleasure, that her lack of unction interfered not a bit with her always acting. It was quite sufficiently manifest to him that for the rest of the time she might be near his mother she would do for her numberless good turns. She would give things to the girls — he had a private adumbration of that; expensive Parisian, perhaps not perfectly useful, things.

Lady Agnes was a woman who measured outlays and returns, but she was both too acute and too just not to recognise the scantest offer from which an advantage could proceed. "Dear Julia!" she exclaimed responsively; and her tone made this brevity of acknowledgement adequate. Julia's own few words were all she wanted. "It's so interesting about Harsh," she added. "We're immensely excited."

"Yes, Nick looks it. Merci, pas de vin. It's just the thing for you, you know," Julia said to him.

"To be sure he knows it. He's immensely grateful. It's really very kind of you."

"You do me a very great honour, Julia," Nick hastened to add.

"Don't be tiresome, please," that lady returned.

"We'll talk about it later. Of course there are lots of points," Nick pursued. "At present let's be purely convivial. Somehow Harsh is such a false note here. *Nous causerons de ça.*"

"My dear fellow, you've caught exactly the tone of Mr. Gabriel Nash," Peter Sherringham declared on this.

"Who's Mr. Gabriel Nash?" Mrs. Dallow asked.

"Nick, *is* he a gentleman? Biddy says so," Grace Dormer interposed before this enquiry was answered.

"It's to be supposed that any one Nick brings to lunch with us — !" Lady Agnes rather coldly sighed.

"Ah Grace, with your tremendous standard!" her son said; while Peter Sherringham explained to his sister that Mr. Nash was Nick's new Mentor or oracle — whom moreover she should see if she would come and have tea with him.

"I have n't the least desire to see him," Julia made answer, "any more than I have to talk about Harsh and bore poor Peter."

"Oh certainly, dear, you 'd bore me," her brother rang out.

"One thing at a time then. Let us by all means be convivial. Only you must show me how," Mrs. Dallow went on to Nick. "What does he mean, Cousin Agnes? Does he want us to drain the wine-cup, to flash with repartee?"

"You 'll do very well," said Nick. "You 're thoroughly charming to-night."

"Do go to Peter's, Julia, if you want something exciting. You 'll see a wonderful girl," Biddy broke in with her smile on Peter.

"Wonderful for what?"

"For thinking she can act when she can't," said the roguish Biddy.

"Dear me, what people you all know! I hate Peter's theatrical people."

"And are n't you going home, Julia?" Lady Agnes enquired.

"Home to the hotel?"

"Dear, no, to Harsh — to see about everything."

"I 'm in the midst of telegrams. I don't know yet."

"I suppose there 's no doubt they 'll have him," Lady Agnes decided to pursue.

"Who 'll have whom?"

"Why, the local people and the party managers. I 'm speaking of the question of my son's standing."

"They 'll have the person I want them to have, I dare say. There are so many people in it, in one

97

way or another — it's dreadful. I like the way you sit there," Julia went on to Nick.

"So do I," he smiled back at her; and he thought she *was* charming now, because she was gay and easy and willing really, though she might plead incompetence, to understand how jocose a dinner in a pothouse in a foreign town might be. She was in good humour or was going to be, and not grand nor stiff nor indifferent nor haughty nor any of the things people who disliked her usually found her and sometimes even a little made him believe her. The spirit of mirth in some cold natures manifests itself not altogether happily, their effort of recreation resembles too much the bath of the hippopotamus; but when Mrs. Dallow put her elbows on the table one felt she could be trusted to get them safely off again.

For a family in mourning the dinner was lively; the more so that before it was half over Julia had arranged that her brother, eschewing the inferior spectacle, should take the girls to the Théâtre Français. It was her idea, and Nick had a chance to observe how an idea was apt to be not successfully controverted when it was Julia's. Even the programme appeared to have been pre-arranged to suit it, just the thing for the cheek of the young person — "Il ne Faut Jurer de Rien" and "Mademoiselle de la Seiglière." Peter was all willingness, but it was Julia who settled it, even to sending for the newspaper — he was by a rare accident unconscious of the evening's bill — and to reassuring Biddy, who was happy but anxious, on the article of their being too late for good places. Peter could always get good places: a word from him and the best box was at his disposal. She made him write the word on a card and saw a messenger dispatched with it to the Rue de Richelieu; and all this without loudness or insistence, parenthetically and authoritatively. The box was bespoken and the carriage, as soon as they had had their coffee, found to be in attendance. Peter drove off in it with the girls, understanding that he was to send it back, and Nick waited for it over the finished repast with the two ladies. After this his mother was escorted to it and conveyed to her apartments, and all the while it had been Julia who governed the succession of events. "Do be nice to her," Lady Agnes breathed to him as he placed her in the vehicle at the door of the café; and he guessed it gave her a comfort to have left him sitting there with Mrs. Dallow.

He had every disposition to be nice to his charming cousin; if things went as she liked them it was the proof of a certain fine force in her — the force of assuming they would. Julia had her differences — some of them were much for the better; and when she was in a mood like this evening's, liberally dominant, he was ready to encourage most of what she took for granted. While they waited for the return of the carriage, which had rolled away with his mother, she sat opposite him with her elbows on the table, playing first with one and then with another of the objects that encumbered it; after five minutes of which she exclaimed "Oh I say, we'll go!" and got up abruptly, asking for her jacket. He said something about the carriage and its order to come back for them, and she replied "Well, it can go away again. I don't

want a carriage," she added: "I want to walk " —
and in a moment she was out of the place, with the
people at the tables turning round again and the
caissière swaying in her high seat. On the pavement
of the boulevard she looked up and down: there were
people at little tables by the door; there were people
all over the broad expanse of the asphalt; there was
a profusion of light and a pervasion of sound; and
everywhere, though the establishment at which they
had been dining was not in the thick of the fray, the
tokens of a great traffic of pleasure, that night-aspect
of Paris which represents it as a huge market for
sensations. Beyond the Boulevard des Capucines it
flared through the warm evening like a vast bazaar,
and opposite the Café Durand the Madeleine rose
theatrical, a high artful *décor* before the footlights of
the Rue Royale. "Where shall we go, what shall we
do ?" Mrs. Dallow asked, looking at her companion
and somewhat to his surprise, as he had supposed
she wanted but to go home.

"Anywhere you like. It's so warm we might
drive instead of going indoors. We might go to the
Bois. That would be agreeable."

"Yes, but it would n't be walking. However,
that does n't matter. It's mild enough for anything
— for sitting out like all these people. And I've
never walked in Paris at night: it would amuse me."

Nick hesitated. "So it might, but it is n't particularly recommended to ladies."

"I don't care for that if it happens to suit me."

"Very well then, we'll walk to the Bastille if you
like."

Julia hesitated, on her side, still looking about. "It's too far; I'm tired; we'll sit here." And she dropped beside an empty table on the "terrace" of M. Durand. "This will do; it's amusing enough and we can look at the Madeleine — that's respectable. If we must have something we'll have a *madère* — is that respectable? Not particularly? So much the better. What are those people having? *Bocks?* Could n't we have bocks? Are they very low? Then I shall have one. I've been so wonderfully good — I've been staying at Versailles: *je me dois bien cela.*"

She insisted, but pronounced the thin liquid in the tall glass very disgusting when it was brought. Nick was amazed, reflecting that it was not for such a discussion as this that his mother had left him with such complacency; and indeed he too had, as she would have had, his share of perplexity, observing that after nearly half an hour his cousin still said nothing of Harsh.

She leaned back against the lighted glass of the café, comfortable and beguiled, watching the passers, the opposite shops, the movement of the square in front of them. She talked about London, about the news sent her in her absence, about Cannes and the people she had seen there, about her poor sister-in-law and her numerous progeny, together with two or three droll things that had happened at Versailles. She discoursed considerably about herself, mentioning matters of importance on her return to town, her plans for the rest of the season. Her carriage came and drew up, and Nick asked if he should send it away; to which she but answered "No, let it stand

a bit." She let it stand a long time and then told
him to dismiss it — they would after all walk home.
She took his arm and they went along the boulevard,
on the right-hand side, to the Rue de la Paix, saying
little to each other during the transit; and then they
passed into the hotel and up to her rooms. All she
had said on the way was that she was very tired of
Paris. There was a shaded lamp in her salon, but
the windows were open and the light of the street,
with its undisturbing murmur, as if everything ran
on india-rubber, came up through the interstices of
the balcony and made a vague glow and a flitting
of shadows on the ceiling. Her maid appeared,
busying herself a moment; and when she had gone
out Julia began suddenly to her companion: "Should
you mind telling me what's the matter with you?"

"The matter with me?"

"Don't you want to stand?"

"I'll do anything to oblige you."

"Why should you oblige me?"

"Well, is n't that the way people treat you?" Nick
demanded.

"They treat me best when they're a little serious."

"My dear Julia, it seems to me I'm serious enough.
Surely it is n't an occasion to be so very solemn, the
idea of going down into a small stodgy country town
and talking a lot of rot."

"Why do you call it rot?"

"Because I can think of no other name that on
the whole describes it so well. You know the sort of
thing. Come! — you've listened to enough of it first
and last. One blushes for it when one sees it in print

in the local papers. The local papers—ah the thought
of them makes me want to stay in Paris."

"If you don't speak well it's your own fault; you
know how to perfectly. And you usually do," Julia
declared.

"I always do," he conceded, "and that's what I'm
ashamed of. I speak beautifully. I've got the cursed
humbugging trick of it. I can turn it on, a fine flood
of it, at the shortest notice. The better it is the worse
it is — the kind's so inferior. It has nothing to
do with the truth or with any search for it; nothing
to do with the effort really to understand or really to
discuss — with intelligence or candour or honesty.
It's an appeal to everything that for one's self one
despises," the young man went on; "to stupidity,
to ignorance, to prejudice, to the love of names and
phrases, the love of hollow idiotic words, of shutting
the eyes tight and making a noise. Do men who
respect each other or themselves talk to each other
that way? They know they'd deserve kicking! A man
would blush to say to himself in the darkness of the
night the things he stands up on a platform in the
garish light of day to stuff into the ears of a multitude whose intelligence he pretends he rates high."
Nick Dormer stood at one of the windows with his
hands in his pockets. He had been looking out, but
as his eloquence flowed faster he turned to his friend,
who had dropped upon a sofa with her face to the
window. She had given her jacket and gloves to her
maid, but had kept on her hat; and she leaned forward a little as she sat, clasping her hands together
in her lap and keeping her eyes on him. The lamp,

in a corner, was so thickly veiled that the room was in tempered obscurity, lighted almost equally from the street and the brilliant shop-fronts opposite. "Therefore why be sapient and solemn about it, like an editorial in a newspaper?" Nick added with a smile.

She continued to look at him after he had spoken, then she said: "If you don't want to stand you've only to say so. You need n't give your reasons."

"It's too kind of you to let me off that! And then I'm a tremendous fellow for reasons; that's my strong point, don't you know? I've a lot more besides those I've mentioned, done up and ready for delivery. The odd thing is that they don't always govern my behaviour. I rather think I do want to stand."

"Then what you said just now was a speech," Julia declared.

"A speech?"

"The 'rot,' the humbug of the hustings."

"No, those great truths remain, and a good many others. But an inner voice tells me I'm in for it. And it will be much more graceful to embrace this opportunity, accepting your co-operation, than to wait for some other and forfeit that advantage."

"I shall be very glad to help you anywhere," she went on.

"Thanks awfully," he returned, still standing there with his hands in his pockets. "You'd do it best in your own place, and I've no right to deny myself such a help."

Julia calmly considered. "I don't do it badly."

"Ah you're so political!"

"Of course I am; it's the only decent thing to be. But I can only help you if you'll help yourself. I can do a good deal, but I can't do everything. If you'll work I'll work with you; but if you're going into it with your hands in your pockets I'll have nothing to do with you." Nick instantly changed the position of these members and sank into a seat with his elbows on his knees. "You're very clever, but you must really take a little trouble. Things don't drop into people's mouths."

"I'll try — I'll try. I've a great incentive," he admitted.

"Of course you have."

"My mother, my poor mother." Julia breathed some vague sound and he went on: "And of course always my father, dear good man. My mother's even more political than you."

"I dare say she is, and quite right!" said Mrs. Dallow.

"And she can't tell me a bit more than you can what she thinks, what she believes, what she wants."

"Pardon me, I can tell you perfectly. There's one thing I always immensely want — to keep out a Tory."

"I see. That's a great philosophy."

"It will do very well. And I desire the good of the country. I'm not ashamed of that."

"And can you give me an idea of what it is — the good of the country?"

"I know perfectly what it isn't. It isn't what the Tories want to do."

"What do they want to do?"

"Oh it would take me long to tell you. All sorts of trash."

"It would take you long, and it would take them longer! All they want to do is to prevent *us* from doing. On our side we want to prevent them from preventing us. That's about as clearly as we all see it. So on both sides it's a beautiful lucid inspiring programme."

"I don't believe in you," Mrs. Dallow replied to this, leaning back on her sofa.

"I hope not, Julia, indeed!" He paused a moment, still with his face toward her and his elbows on his knees; then he pursued: "You're a very accomplished woman and a very zealous one; but you have n't an idea, you know — not to call an idea. What you mainly want is to be at the head of a political salon; to start one, to keep it up, to make it a success."

"Much you know me!" Julia protested; but he could see, through the dimness, that her face spoke differently.

"You'll have it in time, but I won't come to it," Nick went on.

"You can't come less than you do."

"When I say you'll have it I mean you've already got it. That's why I don't come."

"I don't think you know what you mean," said Mrs. Dallow. "I've an idea that's as good as any of yours, any of those you've treated me to this evening, it seems to me — the simple idea that one ought to do something or other for one's country."

"'Something or other' certainly covers all the

ground. There's one thing one can always do for one's country, which is not to be afraid."

"Afraid of what?"

Nick Dormer waited a little, as if his idea amused him, but he presently said "I'll tell you another time. It's very well to talk so glibly of standing," he added; "but it is n't absolutely foreign to the question that I have n't got the cash."

"What did you do before?" she asked.

"The first time my father paid."

"And the other time?"

"Oh Mr. Carteret."

"Your expenses won't be at all large; on the contrary," said Julia.

"They shan't be; I shall look out sharp for that. I shall have the great Hutchby."

"Of course; but you know I want you to do it well." She paused an instant and then: "Of course you can send the bill to me."

"Thanks awfully; you're tremendously kind. I should n't think of that." Nick Dormer got up as he spoke, and walked to the window again, his companion's eyes resting on him while he stood with his back to her. "I shall manage it somehow," he wound up.

"Mr. Carteret will be delighted," said Julia.

"I dare say, but I hate taking people's money."

"That's nonsense — when it's for the country. Is n't it for *them*?"

"When they get it back!" Nick replied, turning round and looking for his hat. "It's startlingly late; you must be tired." Mrs. Dallow made no response to this, and he pursued his quest, successful only when he reached a duskier corner of the room, to which the hat had been relegated by his cousin's maid. "Mr. Carteret will expect so much if he pays. And so would you."

"Yes, I'm bound to say I should! I should expect a great deal — everything." And Mrs. Dallow emphasised this assertion by the way she rose erect. "If you're riding for a fall, if you're only going in to miss it, you had better stay out."

"How can I miss it with *you*?" the young man smiled. She uttered a word, impatiently but indistinguishably, and he continued: "And even if I do it will have been immense fun."

"It *is* immense fun," said Julia. "But the best fun is to win. If you don't —!"

"If I don't?" he repeated as she dropped.

"I'll never speak to you again."

"How much you expect even when you don't pay!"

Mrs. Dallow's rejoinder was a justification of this remark, expressing as it did the fact that should they receive on the morrow information on which she believed herself entitled to count, information tending to show how hard the Conservatives meant to fight, she should look to him to be in the field as early as herself. Sunday was a lost day; she should leave Paris on Monday.

"Oh they'll fight it hard; they'll put up Kingsbury," said Nick, smoothing his hat. "They'll all come down — all that can get away. And Kingsbury has a very handsome wife."

"She's not so handsome as your cousin," Julia smiled.

"Oh dear, no — a cousin sooner than a wife any day!" Nick laughed as soon as he had said this, as if the speech had an awkward side; but the reparation perhaps scarcely mended it, the exaggerated mock-meekness with which he added: "I'll do any blessed thing you tell me."

"Come here to-morrow then — as early as ten." She turned round, moving to the door with him; but before they reached it she brought out: "Pray is n't a gentleman to do anything, to be anything?"

"To be anything — ?"

"If he does n't aspire to serve the State."

"Aspire to make his political fortune, do you mean? Oh bless me, yes, there are other things."

"What other things that can compare with that?"

"Well, I for instance, I'm very fond of the arts."

"Of the arts?" she echoed.

"Did you never hear of them? I'm awfully fond of painting."

At this Julia stopped short, and her fine grey eyes had for a moment the air of being set further forward in her head. "Don't be odious! Good-night," she said, turning away and leaving him to go.

BOOK SECOND

VII

PETER SHERRINGHAM reminded Nick the next day
that he had promised to be present at Madame
Carré's interview with the ladies introduced to her
by Gabriel Nash; and in the afternoon, conformably
to this arrangement, the two men took their way to
the Rue de Constantinople. They found Mr. Nash
and his friends in the small beflounced drawing-room
of the old actress, who, as they learned, had sent in
a request for ten minutes' grace, having been detained
at a lesson — a rehearsal of the *comédie de salon* about
to be given for a charity by a fine lady, at which she
had consented to be present as an adviser. Mrs.
Rooth sat on a black satin sofa with her daughter
beside her while Gabriel Nash, wandering about the
room, looked at the votive offerings which converted
the little panelled box, decorated in sallow white and
gold, into a theatrical museum: the presents, the portraits, the wreaths, the diadems, the letters, framed
and glazed, the trophies and tributes and relics collected by Madame Carré during half a century of
renown. The profusion of this testimony was hardly
more striking than the confession of something missed,
something hushed, which seemed to rise from it all
and make it melancholy, like a reference to clappings
which, in the nature of things, could now only be
present as a silence: so that if the place was full of
history it was the form without the fact, or at the most

113

a redundancy of the one to a pinch of the other — the history of a mask, of a squeak, of a series of vain gestures.

Some of the objects exhibited by the distinguished artist, her early portraits, in lithograph or miniature, represented the costume and embodied the manner of a period so remote that Nick Dormer, as he glanced at them, felt a quickened curiosity to look at the woman who reconciled being alive to-day with having been alive so long ago. Peter Sherringham already knew how she managed this miracle, but every visit he paid her added to his amused, charmed sense that it *was* a miracle and that his extraordinary old friend had seen things he should never, never see. Those were just the things he wanted to see most, and her duration, her survival, cheated him agreeably and helped him a little to guess them. His appreciation of the actor's art was so systematic that it had an antiquarian side, and at the risk of representing him as attached to an absurd futility it must be said that he had as yet hardly known a keener regret for anything than for the loss of that antecedent world, and in particular for his having belatedly missed the great *comédienne*, the light of the French stage in the early years of the century, of whose example and instruction Madame Carré had had the inestimable benefit. She had often described to him her rare predecessor, straight from whose hands she had received her most celebrated parts and of whom her own manner was often a religious imitation; but her descriptions troubled him more than they consoled, only confirming his theory, to which so much of his observation had already ministered, that the actor's art in general was going down and down, descending a slope with abysses of vulgarity at its foot, after having reached its perfection, more than fifty years ago, in the talent of the lady in question. He would have liked to dwell for an hour beneath the meridian.

Gabriel Nash introduced the new-comers to his companions; but the younger of the two ladies gave no sign of lending herself to this transaction. The girl was very white; she huddled there, silent and rigid, frightened to death, staring, expressionless. If Bridget Dormer had seen her at this moment she might have felt avenged for the discomfiture of her own spirit suffered at the Salon, the day before, under the challenging eyes of Maud Vavasour. It was plain at the present hour that Miss Vavasour would have run away had she not regarded the persons present as so many guards and keepers. Her appearance made Nick feel as if the little temple of art in which they were collected had been the waiting-room of a dentist. Sherringham had seen a great many nervous girls tremble before the same ordeal, and he liked to be kind to them, to say things that would help them to do themselves justice. The probability in a given case was almost overwhelmingly in favour of their having any other talent one could think of in a higher degree than the dramatic; but he could rarely refrain from some care that the occasion should n't be, even as against his conscience, too cruel. There were occasions indeed that could scarce be too cruel to punish properly certain examples of presumptuous ineptitude. He remembered what Mr. Nash had said about this blighted maiden, and perceived that though she might be inept she was now anything but presumptuous. Gabriel fell to talking with Nick Dormer while Peter addressed himself to Mrs. Rooth. There was no use as yet for any direct word to the girl, who was too scared even to hear. Mrs. Rooth, with her shawl fluttering about her, nestled against her daughter, putting out her hand to take one of Miriam's soothingly. She had pretty, silly, near-sighted eyes, a long thin nose and an upper lip which projected over the under as an ornamental cornice rests on its support. "So much depends — really everything!" she said in answer to some sociable observation of Sherringham's. "It's either this," and she rolled her eyes expressively about the room, "or it's — I don't know what!"

"Perhaps we're too many," Peter hazarded to her daughter. "But really you'll find, after you fairly begin, that you'll do better with four or five."

Before she answered she turned her head and lifted her fine eyes. The next instant he saw they were full of tears. The words she spoke, however, though uttered as if she had tapped a silver gong, had not the note of sensibility: "Oh I don't care for *you !*" He laughed at this, declared it was very well said and that if she could give Madame Carré such a specimen as that —! The actress came in before he had finished his phrase, and he observed the way the girl ruefully rose to the encounter, hanging her head a little and looking out from under her brows. There was no sentiment in her face — only a vacancy of awe and anguish which had not even the merit of being

fine of its kind, for it spoke of no spring of reaction.
Yet the head was good, he noted at the same moment;
it was strong and salient and made to tell at a distance.
Madame Carré scarcely heeded her at first, greeting
her only in her order among the others and pointing to seats, composing the circle with smiles and
gestures, as if they were all before the prompter's
box. The old actress presented herself to a casual
glance as a red-faced raddled woman in a wig, with
beady eyes, a hooked nose and pretty hands; but
Nick Dormer, who had a sense for the overscored
human surface, soon observed that these comparatively gross marks included a great deal of delicate
detail — an eyebrow, a nostril, a flitting of expressions, as if a multitude of little facial wires were pulled
from within. This accomplished artist had in particular a mouth which was visibly a rare instrument,
a pair of lips whose curves and fine corners spoke of
a lifetime of "points" unerringly made and verses
exquisitely spoken, helping to explain the purity of
the sound that issued from them. Her whole countenance had the look of long service — of a thing
infinitely worn and used, drawn and stretched to
excess, with its elasticity overdone and its springs
relaxed, yet religiously preserved and kept in repair,
even as some valuable old timepiece which might have
quivered and rumbled but could be trusted to strike
the hour. At the first words she spoke Gabriel Nash
exclaimed endearingly "Ah la voix de Célimène!"
Célimène, who wore a big red flower on the summit of her dense wig, had a very grand air, a toss of
the head and sundry little majesties of manner; in

addition to which she was strange, almost grotesque, and to some people would have been even terrifying, capable of reappearing, with her hard eyes, as a queer vision of the darkness. She excused herself for having made the company wait, and mouthed and mimicked in the drollest way, with intonations as fine as a flute, the performance and the pretensions of the *belles dames* to whom she had just been endeavouring to communicate a few of the rudiments. "Mais celles-là, c'est une plaisanterie," she went on to Mrs. Rooth; "whereas you and your daughter, *chère madame* — I'm sure you are quite another matter."

The girl had got rid of her tears, and was gazing at her, and Mrs. Rooth leaned forward and said portentously: "She knows four languages."

Madame Carré gave one of her histrionic stares, throwing back her head. "That's three too many. The thing's to do something proper with one."

"We're very much in earnest," continued Mrs. Rooth, who spoke excellent French.

"I'm glad to hear it — il n'y a que ça. La tête est bien — the head's very good," she said as she looked at the girl. "But let us see, my dear child, what you've got in it!" The young lady was still powerless to speak; she opened her lips, but nothing came. With the failure of this effort she turned her deep sombre eyes to the three men. "Un beau regard — it carries well," Madame Carré further commented. But even as she spoke Miss Rooth's fine gaze was suffused again and the next moment she had definitely begun to weep. Nick Dormer sprung up; he felt embarrassed and intrusive — there was such an indelicacy in sitting there to watch a poor working-girl's struggle with timidity. There was a momentary confusion; Mrs. Rooth's tears were seen also to flow; Mr. Nash took it gaily, addressing, however, at the same time, the friendliest, most familiar encouragement to his companions, and Peter Sherringham offered to retire with Nick on the spot, should their presence incommode the young lady. But the agitation was over in a minute; Madame Carré motioned Mrs. Rooth out of her seat and took her place beside the girl, and Nash explained judiciously to the other men that she'd be worse should they leave her. Her mother begged them to remain, "so that there should be at least some English"; she spoke as if the old actress were an army of Frenchwomen. The young heroine of the occasion quickly came round, and Madame Carré, on the sofa beside her, held her hand and emitted a perfect music of reassurance. "The nerves, the nerves — they're half our affair. Have as many as you like, if you've got something else too. *Voyons* — do you know anything?"

"I know some pieces."

"Some pieces of the *répertoire?*"

Miriam Rooth stared as if she did n't understand. "I know some poetry."

"English, French, Italian, German," said her mother.

Madame Carré gave Mrs. Rooth a look which expressed irritation at the recurrence of this announcement. "Does she wish to act in all those tongues? The phrase-book is n't the comedy!"

"It's only to show you how she has been educated."

"Ah, *chère madame*, there's no education that matters! I mean save the right one. Your daughter must have a particular form of speech, like me, like *ces messieurs*."

"You see if I can speak French," said the girl, smiling dimly at her hostess. She appeared now almost to have collected herself.

"You speak it in perfection."

"And English just as well," said Miss Rooth.

"You ought n't to be an actress — you ought to be a governess."

"Oh don't tell us that: it's to escape from that!" pleaded Mrs. Rooth.

"I'm very sure your daughter will escape from that," Peter Sherringham was moved to interpose.

"Oh if *you* could help her!" said the lady with a world of longing.

"She has certainly all the qualities that strike the eye," Peter returned.

"You're *most* kind, sir!" Mrs. Rooth declared, elegantly draping herself.

"She knows Célimène; I've heard her do Célimène," Gabriel Nash said to Madame Carré.

"And she knows Juliet, she knows Lady Macbeth and Cleopatra," added Mrs. Rooth.

"*Voyons*, my dear child, do you wish to work for the French stage or for the English?" the old actress demanded.

"Ours would have sore need of you, Miss Rooth," Sherringham gallantly threw off.

"Could you speak to any one in London — could you introduce her?" her mother eagerly asked.

"Dear madam, I must hear her first, and hear what Madame Carré says."

"She has a voice of rare beauty, and I understand voices," said Mrs. Rooth.

"Ah then if she has intelligence she has every gift."

"She has a most poetic mind," the old lady went on.

"I should like to paint her portrait; she's made for that," Nick Dormer ventured to observe to Mrs. Rooth; partly because struck with the girl's suitability for sitting, partly to mitigate the crudity of inexpressive spectatorship.

"So all the artists say. I've had three or four heads of her, if you would like to see them: she has been done in several styles. If you were to do her I'm sure it would make her celebrated."

"And me too," Nick easily laughed.

"It would indeed — a member of Parliament!" Nash declared.

"Ah, I have the honour — ?" murmured Mrs. Rooth, looking gratified and mystified.

Nick explained that she had no honour at all, and meanwhile Madame Carré had been questioning the girl. "*Chère madame*, I can do nothing with your daughter: she knows too much!" she broke out. "It's a pity, because I like to catch them wild."

"Oh she's wild enough, if that's all! And that's the very point, the question of where to try," Mrs. Rooth went on. "Into what do I launch her — upon what dangerous stormy sea? I've thought of it so anxiously."

"Try here — try the French public: they're so much the most serious," said Gabriel Nash.

121

"Ah no, try the English: there's such a rare opening!" Sherringham urged in quick opposition.

"Oh it is n't the public, dear gentlemen. It's the private side, the other people — it's the life, it's the moral atmosphere."

"Je ne connais qu'une scène — la nôtre," Madame Carré declared. "I'm assured by every one who knows that there's no other."

"Very correctly assured," said Mr. Nash. "The theatre in our countries is puerile and barbarous."

"There's something to be done for it, and perhaps mademoiselle's the person to do it," Sherringham contentiously suggested.

"Ah but, *en attendant*, what can it do for her?" Madame Carré asked.

"Well, anything I can help to bring about," said Peter Sherringham, more and more struck with the girl's rich type. Miriam Rooth sat in silence while this discussion went on, looking from one speaker to the other with a strange dependent candour.

"Ah, if your part's marked out I congratulate you, mademoiselle!" — and the old actress underlined the words as she had often underlined others on the stage. She smiled with large permissiveness on the young aspirant, who appeared not to understand her. Her tone penetrated, however, to certain depths in the mother's nature, adding another stir to agitated waters.

"I feel the responsibility of what she shall find in the life, the standards, of the theatre," Mrs. Rooth explained. "Where is the purest tone — where are the highest standards? That's what I ask," the good lady continued with a misguided intensity which elicited a peal of unceremonious but sociable laughter from Gabriel Nash.

"The purest tone — qu'est-ce-que-c'est que ça ?" Madame Carré demanded in the finest manner of modern comedy.

"We're very, *very* respectable," Mrs. Rooth went on, but now smiling and achieving lightness too. "What I want is to place my daughter where the conduct — and the picture of conduct in which she should take part — would n't be quite absolutely dreadful. Now, *chère madame*, how about all that; how about *conduct* in the French theatre — all the things she should see, the things she should hear, the things she should learn ?"

Her hostess took it, as Sherringham felt, *de très-haut*. "I don't think I know what you're talking about. They're the things she may see and hear and learn everywhere; only they're better done, they're better said, above all they're better taught. The only conduct that concerns an actress, it seems to me, is her own, and the only way for her to behave herself is not to be a helpless stick. I know no other conduct."

"But there are characters, there are situations, which I don't think I should like to see *her* undertake."

"There are many, no doubt, which she would do well to leave alone!" laughed the Frenchwoman.

"I should n't like to see her represent a very bad woman — a *really* bad one," Mrs. Rooth serenely pursued.

123

"Ah in England then, and in your theatre, every one's immaculately good? Your plays must be even more ingenious than I supposed!"

"We have n't any plays," said Gabriel Nash.

"People will write them for Miss Rooth — it will be a new era," Sherringham threw in with wanton, or at least with combative, optimism.

"Will *you*, sir — will you do something? A sketch of one of our grand English ideals?" the old lady asked engagingly.

"Oh I know what you do with our pieces — to show your superior virtue!" Madame Carré cried before he had time to reply that he wrote nothing but diplomatic memoranda. "Bad women? Je n'ai joué que ça, madame. 'Really' bad? I tried to make them real!"

"I can say 'L'Aventurière,'" Miriam interrupted in a cold voice which seemed to hint at a want of participation in the maternal solicitudes.

"Allow us the pleasure of hearing you then. Madame Carré will give you the *réplique*," said Peter Sherringham.

"Certainly, my child; I can say it without the book," Madame Carré responded. "Put yourself there — move that chair a little away." She patted her young visitor, encouraging her to rise, settling with her the scene they should take, while the three men sprang up to arrange a place for the performance. Miriam left her seat and looked vaguely about her; then having taken off her hat and given it to her mother she stood on the designated spot with her eyes to the ground. Abruptly, however, instead of

beginning the scene, Madame Carré turned to the
elder lady with an air which showed that a rejoinder
to this visitor's remarks of a moment before had been
gathering force in her breast.

"You mix things up, *chère madame*, and I have it
on my heart to tell you so. I believe it's rather the
case with you other English, and I've never been able
to learn that either your morality or your talent is
the gainer by it. To be too respectable to go where
things are done best is in my opinion to be very
vicious indeed; and to do them badly in order to
preserve your virtue is to fall into a grossness more
shocking than any other. To do them well is virtue
enough, and not to make a mess of it the only respectability. That's hard enough to merit Paradise.
Everything else is base humbug! *Voilà, chère madame*, the answer I have for your scruples!"

"It's admirable — admirable; and I am glad my
friend Dormer here has had the great advantage of
hearing you utter it!" Nash exclaimed with a free
designation of Nick.

That young man thought it in effect a speech de-
noting an intelligence of the question, yet he rather
resented the idea that Gabriel should assume it
would strike him as a revelation; and to show his
familiarity with the line of thought it indicated, as
well as to play his part appreciatively in the little
circle, he observed to Mrs. Rooth, as if they might
take many things for granted, "In other words, your
daughter must find her safeguard in the artistic conscience." But he had no sooner spoken than he was
struck with the oddity of their discussing so publicly,

and under the poor girl's handsome nose, the conditions which Miss Rooth might find the best for the preservation of her personal integrity. However, the anomaly was light and unoppressive—the echoes of a public discussion of delicate questions seemed to linger so familiarly in the egotistical little room. Moreover the heroine of the occasion evidently was losing her embarrassment; she was the priestess on the tripod, awaiting the afflatus and thinking only of that. Her bared head, of which she had changed the position, holding it erect, while her arms hung at her sides, was admirable; her eyes gazed straight out of the window and at the houses on the opposite side of the Rue de Constantinople.

Mrs. Rooth had listened to Madame Carré with startled respectful attention, but Nick, considering her, was very sure she had n't at all taken in the great artist's little lesson. Yet this did n't prevent her from exclaiming in answer to himself: "Oh a fine artistic life — what indeed is more beautiful?"

Peter Sherringham had said nothing; he was watching Miriam and her attitude. She wore a black dress which fell in straight folds; her face, under her level brows, was pale and regular — it had a strange strong tragic beauty. "I don't know what's in her," he said to himself; "nothing, it would seem, from her persistent vacancy. But such a face as that, such a head, is a fortune!" Madame Carré brought her to book, giving her the first line of the speech of Clorinde: "Vous ne me fuyez pas, mon enfant, aujourd'hui." But still the girl hesitated and for an instant appeared to make a vain convulsive effort. In this convulsion she frowned portentously; her low forehead overhung her eyes; the eyes themselves, in shadow, stared, splendid and cold, and her hands clinched themselves at her sides. She looked austere and terrible and was during this moment an incarnation the vividness of which drew from Sherringham a stifled cry. "Elle est bien belle — ah ça!" murmured the old actress; and in the pause which still preceded the issue of sound from the girl's lips Peter turned to his kinsman and said in a low tone: "You must paint her just like that."

"Like that?"

"As the Tragic Muse."

She began to speak; a long strong colorless voice quavered in her young throat. She delivered the lines of Clorinde in the admired interview with Célie, the gem of the third act, with a rude monotony, and then, gaining confidence, with an effort at modulation which was not altogether successful and which evidently she felt not to be so. Madame Carré sent back the ball without raising her hand, repeating the speeches of Célie, which her memory possessed from their having so often been addressed to her, and uttering the verses with soft communicative art. So they went on through the scene, which, when it was over, had not precisely been a triumph for Miriam Rooth. Sherringham forbore to look at Gabriel Nash and Madame Carré said: "I think you've a voice, *ma fille*, somewhere or other. We must try and put our hand on it." Then she asked her what instruction she had had, and the girl, lifting her eyebrows, looked at her mother while her mother prompted her.

"Mrs. Delamere in London; she was once an ornament of the English stage. She gives lessons just to a very few; it's a great favour. Such a very nice person! But above all, Signor Ruggieri — I think he taught us most." Mrs. Rooth explained that this gentleman was an Italian tragedian, in Rome, who instructed Miriam in the proper manner of pronouncing his language and also in the art of declaiming and gesticulating.

"Gesticulating I'll warrant!" declared their hostess. "They mimic as for the deaf, they emphasise as for the blind. Mrs. Delamere is doubtless an epitome of all the virtues, but I never heard of her. You travel too much," Madame Carré went on; "that's very amusing, but the way to study is to stay at home, to shut yourself up and hammer at your scales." Mrs. Rooth complained that they had no home to stay at; in reply to which the old actress exclaimed: "Oh you English, you're *d'une légèreté à faire frémir*. If you have n't a home you must make, or at least for decency pretend to, one. In our profession it's the first requisite."

"But where? That's what I ask!" said Mrs. Rooth.

"Why not here?" Sherringham threw out.

"Oh here!" And the good lady shook her head with a world of sad significance.

"Come and live in London and then I shall be able to paint your daughter," Nick Dormer interposed.

"Is that all it will take, my dear fellow?" asked Gabriel Nash.

"Ah, London's full of memories," Mrs. Rooth

went on. "My father had a great house there — we always came up. But all that's over."

"Study here and then go to London to appear," said Peter, feeling frivolous even as he spoke.

"To appear in French?"

"No, in the language of Shakespeare."

"But we can't study that here."

"Mr. Sherringham means that he will give you lessons," Madame Carré explained. "Let me not fail to say it — he's an excellent critic."

"How do you know that — you who're beyond criticism and perfect?" asked Sherringham: an enquiry to which the answer was forestalled by the girl's rousing herself to make it public that she could recite the "Nights" of Alfred de Musset.

"Diable!" said the actress: "that's more than I can! By all means give us a specimen."

The girl again placed herself in position and rolled out a fragment of one of the splendid conversations of Musset's poet with his muse — rolled it loudly and proudly, tossed it and tumbled it about the room. Madame Carré watched her at first, but after a few moments she shut her eyes, though the best part of the business was to take in her young candidate's beauty. Sherringham had supposed Miriam rather abashed by the flatness of her first performance, but he now saw how little she could have been aware of this: she was rather uplifted and emboldened. She made a mush of the divine verses, which in spite of certain sonorities and cadences, an evident effort to imitate a celebrated actress, a comrade of Madame Carré, whom she had heard declaim them, she produced as if she had been dashing blindfold at some playfellow she was to "catch." When she had finished Madame Carré passed no judgement, only dropping "Perhaps you had better say something English." She suggested some little piece of verse — some fable if there were fables in English. She appeared but scantily surprised to hear that there were not — it was a language of which one expected so little. Mrs. Rooth said "She knows her Tennyson by heart. I think he's much deeper than La Fontaine;" and after some deliberation and delay Miriam broke into "The Lotus-Eaters," from which she passed directly, almost breathlessly, to "Edward Gray." Sherringham had by this time heard her make four different attempts, and the only generalisation very present to him was that she uttered these dissimilar compositions in exactly the same tone — a solemn droning dragging measure suggestive of an exhortation from the pulpit and adopted evidently with the "affecting" intention and from a crude idea of "style." It was all funereal, yet was artlessly rough. Sherringham thought her English performance less futile than her French, but he could see that Madame Carré listened to it even with less pleasure. In the way the girl wailed forth some of her Tennysonian lines he detected a faint gleam as of something pearly in deep water. But the further she went the more violently she acted on the nerves of Mr. Gabriel Nash: that also he could discover from the way this gentleman ended by slipping discreetly to the window and leaning there with his head out and his back to the exhibition. He had the art of mute

expression; his attitude said as clearly as possible:
"No, no, you can't call me either ill-mannered or ill-
natured. I'm the showman of the occasion moreover, and I avert myself, leaving you to judge. If
there's a thing in life I hate it's this idiotic new fashion
of the drawing-room recitation and of the insuffer-
able creatures who practise it, who prevent conversation and whom, as they're beneath it, you can't
punish by criticism. Therefore what I'm doing 's
only too magnanimous — bringing these benighted
women here, paying with my person, stifling my just
repugnance."

While Sherringham judged privately that the manner in which Miss Rooth had acquitted herself offered
no element of interest, he yet remained aware that
something surmounted and survived her failure,
something that would perhaps be worth his curiosity.
It was the element of outline and attitude, the way
she stood, the way she turned her eyes, her head,
and moved her limbs. These things held the attention; they had a natural authority and, in spite of
their suggesting too much the school-girl in the *tableau-
vivant*, a "plastic" grandeur. Her face moreover
grew as he watched it; something delicate dawned
in it, a dim promise of variety and a touching plea
for patience, as if it were conscious of being able to
show in time more shades than the simple and striking gloom which had as yet mainly graced it. These
rather rude physical felicities formed in short her
only mark of a vocation. He almost hated to have
to recognise them; he had seen them so often when
they meant nothing at all that he had come at last to

regard them as almost a guarantee of incompetence. He knew Madame Carré valued them singly so little that she counted them out in measuring an histrionic nature; when deprived of the escort of other properties which helped and completed them she almost held them a positive hindrance to success —success of the only kind she esteemed. Far oftener than himself she had sat in judgement on young women for whom hair and eyebrows and a disposition for the statuesque would have worked the miracle of sanctifying their stupidity if the miracle were workable. But that particular miracle never was. The qualities she rated highest were not the gifts but the conquests, the effects the actor had worked hard for, had dug out of the mine by unwearied study. Sherringham remembered to have had in the early part of their acquaintance a friendly dispute with her on this subject, he having been moved at that time to defend doubtless to excess the cause of the gifts. She had gone so far as to say that a serious comedian ought to be ashamed of them — ashamed of resting his case on them; and when Sherringham had cited the great Rachel as a player whose natural endowment was rich and who had owed her highest triumphs to it, she had declared that Rachel was the very instance that proved her point; — a talent assisted by one or two primary aids, a voice and a portentous brow, but essentially formed by work, unremitting and ferocious work. "I don't care a straw for your handsome girls," she said; "but bring me one who's ready to drudge the tenth part of the way Rachel drudged, and I'll forgive her her beauty. Of course, *notez bien*, Rachel was n't a *grosse bête:* that's a gift if you like!"

Mrs. Rooth, who was evidently very proud of the figure her daughter had made — her daughter who for all one could tell affected their hostess precisely as a *grosse bête* — appealed to Madame Carré rashly and serenely for a verdict; but fortunately this lady's voluble *bonne* came rattling in at the same moment with the tea-tray. The old actress busied herself in dispensing this refreshment, an hospitable attention to her English visitors, and under cover of the diversion thus obtained, while the others talked together, Sherringham put her the question. "Well, is there anything in my young friend?"

"Nothing I can see. She's loud and coarse."

"She's very much afraid. You must allow for that."

"Afraid of me, immensely, but not a bit afraid of her authors — nor of you!" Madame Carré smiled.

"Are n't you prejudiced by what that fellow Nash has told you?"

"Why prejudiced? He only told me she was very handsome."

"And don't you think her so?"

"Admirable. But I'm not a photographer nor a dressmaker nor a coiffeur. I can't do anything with 'back hair' nor with a mere big stare."

"The head's very noble," said Peter Sherringham. "And the voice, when she spoke English, had some sweet tones."

"Ah your English — possibly! All I can say is that I listened to her conscientiously, and I did n't

perceive in what she did a single *nuance*, a single inflexion or intention. But not one, *mon cher*. I don't
think she's intelligent."

"But don't they often seem stupid at first?"

"Say always!"

"Then don't some succeed — even when they're
handsome?"

"When they're handsome they always succeed —
in one way or another."

"You don't understand us English," said Peter
Sherringham.

Madame Carré drank her tea; then she replied:
"Marry her, my son, and give her diamonds. Make
her an ambassadress; she'll look very well."

"She interests you so little that you don't care to
do anything for her?"

"To do anything?"

"To give her a few lessons."

The old actress looked at him a moment; after
which, rising from her place near the table on which
the tea had been served, she said to Miriam Rooth:
"My dear child, I give my voice for the *scène anglaise*.
You did the English things best."

"Did I do them well?" asked the girl.

"You've a great deal to learn; but you've rude
force. The main things *sont encore à dégager*, but
they'll come. You must work."

"I think she has ideas," said Mrs. Rooth.

"She gets them from you," Madame Carré replied.

"I must say that if it's to be *our* theatre I'm relieved. I do think ours safer," the good lady continued.

"Ours is dangerous, no doubt."

"You mean you're more severe," said the girl.

"Your mother's right," the actress smiled; "you have ideas."

"But what shall we do then — how shall we proceed?" Mrs. Rooth made this appeal, plaintively and vaguely, to the three gentlemen; but they had collected a few steps off and were so occupied in talk that it failed to reach them.

"Work — work — work!" exclaimed the actress.

"In English I can play Shakespeare. I want to play Shakespeare," Miriam made known.

"That's fortunate, as in English you have n't any one else to play."

"But he's so great — and he's so pure!" said Mrs. Rooth.

"That indeed seems the saving of you," Madame Carré returned.

"You think me actually pretty bad, don't you?" the girl demanded with her serious face.

"Mon Dieu, que vous dirai-je? Of course you're rough; but so was I at your age. And if you find your voice it may carry you far. Besides, what does it matter what I think? How can I judge for your English public?"

"How shall I find my voice?" asked Miriam Rooth.

"By trying. Il n'y a que ça. Work like a horse, night and day. Besides, Mr. Sherringham, as he says, will help you."

That gentleman, hearing his name, turned round and the girl appealed to him. "Will you help me really?"

"To find her voice," said Madame Carré.

"The voice, when it's worth anything, comes from the heart; so I suppose that's where to look for it," Gabriel Nash suggested.

"Much you know; you have n't got any!" Miriam retorted with the first scintillation of gaiety she had shown on this occasion.

"Any voice, my child?" Mr. Nash enquired.

"Any heart — or any manners!"

Peter Sherringham made the secret reflexion that he liked her better lugubrious, as the note of pertness was not totally absent from her mode of emitting these few words. He was irritated moreover, for in the brief conference he had just had with the young lady's introducer he had had to meet the rather difficult call of speaking of her hopefully. Mr. Nash had said with his bland smile "And what impression does my young friend make?" — in respect to which Peter's optimism felt engaged by an awkward logic. He answered that he recognised promise, though he did nothing of the sort;—at the same time that the poor girl, both with the exaggerated "points" of her person and the vanity of her attempt at expression, constituted a kind of challenge, struck him as a subject for enquiry, a problem, an explorable tract. She was too bad to jump at and yet too "taking" — perhaps after all only vulgarly — to overlook, especially when resting her tragic eyes on him with the trust of her deep "Really?" This note affected him as addressed directly to his honour, giving him a chance to brave verisimilitude, to brave ridicule even a little, in order to show in a special case what he had always maintained in general, that the direction of a young person's studies for the stage may be an interest of as high an order as any other artistic appeal.

"Mr. Nash has rendered us the great service of introducing us to Madame Carré, and I'm sure we're immensely indebted to him," Mrs. Rooth said to her daughter with an air affectionately corrective.

"But what good does that do us?" the girl asked, smiling at the actress and gently laying her finger-tips upon her hand. "Madame Carré listens to me with adorable patience, and then sends me about my business — ah in the prettiest way in the world."

"Mademoiselle, you're not so rough; the tone of that's very *juste*. A la bonne heure; work — work!" the actress cried. "There was an inflexion there — or very nearly. Practise it till you've got it."

"Come and practise it to *me*, if your mother will be so kind as to bring you," said Peter Sherringham.

"Do you give lessons — do you understand?" Miriam asked.

"I'm an old play-goer and I've an unbounded belief in my own judgement."

"'Old,' sir, is too much to say," Mrs. Rooth remonstrated. "My daughter knows your high position, but she's very direct. You'll always find her so. Perhaps you'll say there are less honourable faults. We'll come to see you with pleasure. Oh I've been at the embassy when I was her age. Therefore why shouldn't she go to-day? That was in Lord Davenant's time."

"A few people are coming to tea with me to-morrow. Perhaps you'll come then at five o'clock."

"It will remind me of the dear old times," said Mrs. Rooth.

"Thank you; I'll try and do better to-morrow," Miriam professed very sweetly.

"You do better every minute!" Sherringham returned — and he looked at their hostess in support of this declaration.

"She's finding her voice," Madame Carré acknowledged.

"She's finding a friend!" Mrs. Rooth threw in.

"And don't forget, when you come to London, my hope that you'll come and see *me*," Nick Dormer said to the girl. "To try and paint you — that would do me good!"

"She's finding even two," said Madame Carré.

"It's to make up for one I've lost!" And Miriam looked with very good stage-scorn at Gabriel Nash. "It's he who thinks I'm bad."

"You say that to make me drive you home; you know it will," Nash returned.

"We'll all take you home; why not?" Sherringham asked.

Madame Carré looked at the handsome girl, handsomer than ever at this moment, and at the three young men who had taken their hats and stood ready to accompany her. A deeper expression came for an instant into her hard bright eyes. "Ah la jeunesse!" she sighed. "You'd always have that, my child, if you were the greatest goose on earth!"

VIII

AT Peter Sherringham's the next day Miriam had so evidently come with the expectation of "saying" something that it was impossible such a patron of the drama should forbear to invite her, little as the exhibition at Madame Carré's could have contributed to render the invitation prompt. His curiosity had been more appeased than stimulated, but he felt none the less that he had "taken up" the dark-browed girl and her reminiscential mother and must face the immediate consequences of the act. This responsibility weighed upon him during the twenty-four hours that followed the ultimate dispersal of the little party at the door of the Hôtel de la Garonne.

On quitting Madame Carré the two ladies had definitely declined Mr. Nash's offered cab and had taken their way homeward on foot and with the gentlemen in attendance. The streets of Paris at that hour were bright and episodical, and Sherringham trod them good-humouredly enough and not too fast, leaning a little to talk with Miriam as he went. Their pace was regulated by her mother's, who advanced on the arm of Gabriel Nash (Nick Dormer was on her other side) in refined deprecation. Her sloping back was before them, exempt from retentive stiffness in spite of her rigid principles, with the little drama of her lost and recovered shawl perpetually going on.

Sherringham said nothing to the girl about her performance or her powers; their talk was only of her manner of life with her mother — their travels, their *pensions*, their economies, their want of a home, the many cities she knew well, the foreign tongues and the wide view of the world she had acquired. He guessed easily enough the dolorous type of exile of the two ladies, wanderers in search of Continental cheapness, inured to queer contacts and compromises, "remarkably well connected" in England, but going out for their meals. The girl was but indirectly communicative; though seemingly less from any plan of secrecy than from the habit of associating with people whom she did n't honour with her confidence. She was fragmentary and abrupt, as well as not in the least shy, subdued to dread of Madame Carré as she had been for the time. She gave Sherringham a reason for this fear, and he thought her reason innocently pretentious. "She admired a great artist more than anything in the world; and in the presence of art, of *great* art, her heart beat so fast." Her manners were not perfect, and the friction of a varied experience had rather roughened than smoothed her. She said nothing that proved her intelligent, even though he guessed this to be the design of two or three of her remarks; but he parted from her with the suspicion that she was, according to the contemporary French phrase, a "nature."

The Hôtel de la Garonne was in a small unrenovated street in which the cobble-stones of old Paris still flourished, lying between the Avenue de l'Opéra and the Place de la Bourse. Sherringham had occasionally traversed the high dimness, but had never noticed the tall stale *maison meublée*, the aspect of which, that of a third-rate provincial inn, was an illustration of Mrs. Rooth's shrunken standard. "We would ask you to come up, but it's quite at the top and we have n't a sitting-room," the poor lady bravely explained. "We had to receive Mr. Nash at a café."

Nick Dormer declared that he liked cafés, and Miriam, looking at his cousin, dropped with a flash of passion the demand: "Do you wonder I should want to do something—so that we can stop living like pigs?"

Peter recognised the next day that though it might be boring to listen to her it was better to make her recite than to let her do nothing, so effectually did the presence of his sister and that of Lady Agnes, and even of Grace and Biddy, appear, by a strange tacit opposition, to deprive hers, ornamental as it was, of a reason. He had only to see them all together to perceive that she could n't pass for having come to "meet" them—even her mother's insinuating gentility failed to put the occasion on that footing—and that she must therefore be assumed to have been brought to show them something. She was not subdued, not colourless enough to sit there for nothing, or even for conversation—the sort of conversation that was likely to come off—so that it was inevitable to treat her position as connected with the principal place on the carpet, with silence and attention and the pulling together of chairs. Even when so established it struck him at first as precarious, in the light, or the darkness, of the inexpressive

141

faces of the other ladies, seated in couples and rows on sofas — there were several in addition to Julia and the Dormers; mainly the wives, with their husbands, of Sherringham's fellow secretaries — scarcely one of whom he felt he might count upon for a modicum of gush when the girl should have finished.

Miss Rooth gave a representation of Juliet drinking the potion, according to the system, as her mother explained, of the famous Signor Ruggieri — a scene of high fierce sound, of many cries and contortions: she shook her hair (which proved magnificent) half-down before the performance was over. Then she declaimed several short poems by Victor Hugo, selected among many hundred by Mrs. Rooth, as the good lady was careful to make known. After this she jumped to the American lyre, regaling the company with specimens, both familiar and fresh, of Longfellow, Lowell, Whittier, Holmes, and of two or three poetesses now revealed to Sherringham for the first time. She flowed so copiously, keeping the floor and rejoicing visibly in her luck, that her host was mainly occupied with wondering how he could make her leave off. He was surprised at the extent of her repertory, which, in view of the circumstance that she could never have received much encouragement — it must have come mainly from her mother, and he did n't believe in Signor Ruggieri — denoted a very stiff ambition and a blundering energy. It was her mother who checked her at last, and he found himself suspecting that Gabriel Nash had intimated to the old woman that interference was necessary. For himself he was chiefly glad Madame Carré had n't come.

It was present to him that she would have judged
the exhibition, with its badness, its impudence, the
absence of criticism, wholly indecent.

His only new impression of the heroine of the scene
was that of this same high assurance — her coolness,
her complacency, her eagerness to go on. She had
been deadly afraid of the old actress, but was not a bit
afraid of a cluster of *femmes du monde*, of Julia, of
Lady Agnes, of the smart women of the embassy. It
was positively these personages who were rather in
fear; there was certainly a moment when even Julia
was scared for the first time he had ever remarked
it. The space was too small, the cries, the convul-
sions and rushes of the dishevelled girl were too near.
Lady Agnes wore much of the time the countenance
she might have shown at the theatre during a play
in which pistols were fired; and indeed the manner
of the young reciter had become more spasmodic
and more explosive. It appeared, however, that the
company in general thought her very clever and successful; which showed, to Sherringham's sense, how
little they understood the matter. Poor Biddy was
immensely struck; she grew flushed and absorbed
in proportion as Miriam, at her best moments,
became pale and fatal. It was she who spoke to her
first, after it was agreed that they had better not
fatigue her any more; she advanced a few steps,
happening to be nearest — she murmured "Oh thank
you so much. I never saw anything so beautiful, so
grand."

She looked very red and very pretty as she said this,
and Peter Sherringham liked her enough to notice

her more and like her better when she looked prettier than usual. As he turned away he heard Miriam make answer with no great air of appreciation of her tribute: "I've seen you before — two days ago at the Salon with Mr. Dormer. Yes, I know he's your brother. I've made his acquaintance since. He wants to paint my portrait. Do you think he'll do it well?" He was afraid the girl was something of a brute — also somewhat grossly vain. This impression would perhaps have been confirmed if a part of the rest of the short conversation of the two young women had reached his ear. Biddy ventured to observe that she herself had studied modelling a little and that she could understand how any artist would think Miss Rooth a splendid subject. If indeed *she* could attempt her head, that would be a chance indeed.

"Thank you," said Miriam with a laugh as of high comedy. "I think I had rather not *passer par toute la famille!*" Then she added: "If your brother's an artist I don't understand how he's in Parliament."

"Oh he is n't in Parliament now — we only hope he will be."

"Ah I see."

"And he is n't an artist either," Biddy felt herself conscientiously bound to state.

"Then he is n't anything," said Miss Rooth.

"Well — he's immensely clever."

"Ah I see," Miss Rooth again replied. "Mr. Nash has puffed him up so."

"I don't know Mr. Nash," said Biddy, guilty of a little dryness as well as of a little misrepresentation, and feeling rather snubbed.

"Well, you need n't wish to."

Biddy stood with her a moment longer, still looking at her and not knowing what to say next, but not
finding her any less handsome because she had such
odd manners. Biddy had an ingenious little mind,
which always tried as much as possible to keep
different things separate. It was pervaded now by
the reflexion, attended with some relief, that if the
girl spoke to her with such unexpected familiarity
of Nick she said nothing at all about Peter. Two
gentlemen came up, two of Peter's friends, and made
speeches to Miss Rooth of the kind Biddy supposed
people learned to make in Paris. It was also doubtless
in Paris, the girl privately reasoned, that they learned
to listen to them as this striking performer listened.
She received their advances very differently from
the way she had received Biddy's. Sherringham
noticed his young kinswoman turn away, still very
red, to go and sit near her mother again, leaving
Miriam engaged with the two men. It appeared to
have come over her that for a moment she had been
strangely spontaneous and bold, and that she had
paid a little of the penalty. The seat next her mother
was occupied by Mrs. Rooth, toward whom Lady
Agnes's head had inclined itself with a preoccupied
tolerance. He had the conviction Mrs. Rooth was
telling her about the Neville-Nugents of Castle
Nugent and that Lady Agnes was thinking it odd
she never had heard of them. He said to himself that
Biddy was generous. She had urged Julia to come
in order that they might see how bad the strange
young woman would be, but now that the event

had proved dazzling she forgot this calculation and rejoiced in what she innocently supposed to be the performer's triumph. She kept away from Julia, however; she didn't even look at her to invite her also to confess that, in vulgar parlance, they had been sold. He himself spoke to his sister, who was leaning back with a detached air in the corner of a sofa, saying something which led her to remark in reply: "Ah I dare say it's extremely fine, but I don't care for tragedy when it treads on one's toes. She's like a cow who has kicked over the milking-pail. She ought to be tied up."

"My poor Julia, it isn't extremely fine; it isn't fine at all," Sherringham returned with some irritation.

"Pardon me then. I thought that was why you invited us."

"I imagined she was different," Peter said a little foolishly.

"Ah if you don't care for her so much the better. It has always seemed to me you make too awfully much of those people."

"Oh I do care for her too — rather. She's interesting." His sister gave him a momentary mystified glance and he added: "And she's dreadful." He felt stupidly annoyed and was ashamed of his annoyance, as he could have assigned no reason for it. It didn't grow less for the moment from his seeing Gabriel Nash approach Julia, introduced by Nick Dormer. He gave place to the two young men with some alacrity, for he had a sense of being put in the wrong in respect to their specimen by Nash's very

presence. He remembered how it had been a part of
their bargain, as it were, that he should present that
gentleman to his sister. He was not sorry to be relieved of the office by Nick, and he even tacitly and
ironically wished his kinsman's friend joy of a colloquy with Mrs. Dallow. Sherringham's life was spent
with people, he was used to people, and both as host
and as guest he carried the social burden in general
lightly. He could observe, especially in the former
capacity, without uneasiness and take the tempera-
ture without anxiety. But at present his company
oppressed him; he felt worried and that he showed it
— which was the thing in the world he had ever held
least an honour to a gentleman dedicated to diplo-
macy. He was vexed with the levity that had made
him call his roomful together on so poor a pretext,
and yet was vexed with the stupidity that made the
witnesses so evidently find the pretext sufficient. He
inwardly groaned at the delusion under which he
had saddled himself with the Tragic Muse — a tragic
muse who was strident and pert — and yet wished
his visitors would go away and leave him alone with
her.

Nick Dormer said to Mrs. Dallow that he wanted
her to know an old friend of his, one of the cleverest
men he knew; and he added the hope that she would
be gentle and encouraging with him: he was so timid
and so easily disconcerted. Mr. Nash hereupon
dropped into a chair by the arm of her sofa, their
companion went away and Mrs. Dallow turned her
glance upon her new acquaintance without a perceptible change of position. Then she emitted with

rapidity the remark: "It's very awkward when people are told one's clever."

"It's only awkward if one is n't," Gabriel smiled.

"Yes, but so few people are — enough to be talked about."

"Is n't that just the reason why such a matter, such an exception, ought to be mentioned to them ?" he asked. "They might n't find it out for themselves. Of course, however, as you say, there ought to be a certainty; then they're surer to know it. Dormer's a dear fellow, but he's rash and superficial."

Mrs. Dallow, at this incitement, turned her glance a second time on her visitor; but during the rest of the conversation she rarely repeated the movement. If she liked Nick Dormer extremely — and it may without more delay be communicated to the reader that she did — her liking was of a kind that opposed no difficulty whatever to her not liking, in case of such a complication, a person attached or otherwise belonging to him. It was not in her nature to "put up" with others for the sake of an individual she loved: the putting up was usually consumed in the loving, and with nothing left over. If the affection that isolates and simplifies its object may be distinguished from the affection that seeks communications and contacts for it, Julia Dallow's was quite of the encircling, not to say the narrowing sort. She was not so much jealous as essentially exclusive. She desired no experience for the familiar and yet partly unsounded kinsman in whom she took an interest that she would n't have desired for herself; and indeed the cause of her interest in him was partly the vision of his helping her to the particular extensions she did desire — the taste and thrill of great affairs and of public action. To have such ambitions for him appeared to her the highest honour she could do him; her conscience was in it as well as her inclination, and her scheme, to her sense, was noble enough to varnish over any disdain she might feel for forces drawing him another way. She had a prejudice, in general, against his existing connexions, a suspicion of them and a supply of off-hand contempt in waiting. It was a singular circumstance that she was sceptical even when, knowing her as well as he did, he thought them worth recommending to her: the recommendation indeed mostly confirmed the suspicion.

This was a law from which Gabriel Nash was condemned to suffer, if suffering could on any occasion be predicated of Gabriel Nash. His pretension was in truth that he had purged his life of such possibilities of waste, though probably he would have admitted that if that fair vessel should spring a leak the wound in its side would have been dealt by a woman's hand. In dining two evenings before with her brother and with the Dormers Mrs. Dallow had been moved to exclaim that Peter and Nick knew the most extraordinary people. As regards Peter the attitudinising girl and her mother now pointed that moral with sufficient vividness; so that there was little arrogance in taking a similar quality for granted of the conceited man at her elbow, who sat there as if he might be capable from one moment to another of leaning over the arm of her sofa. She had not the slightest wish to talk with him about himself, and

149

was afraid for an instant that he was on the point of passing from the chapter of his cleverness to that of his timidity. It was a false alarm, however, for he only animadverted on the pleasures of the elegant extract hurled — literally *hurlé* in general — from the centre of the room at one's defenceless head. He intimated that in his opinion these pleasures were all for the performers. The auditors had at any rate given Miss Rooth a charming afternoon; that of course was what Mrs. Dallow's kind brother had mainly intended in arranging the little party. (Julia hated to hear him call her brother "kind": the term seemed offensively patronising.) But he himself, he related, was now constantly employed in the same beneficence, listening two thirds of his time to "intonations" and shrieks. She had doubtless observed it herself, how the great current of the age, the adoration of the mime, was almost too strong for any individual; how it swept one along and dashed one against the rocks. As she made no response to this proposition Gabriel Nash asked her if she had n't been struck with the main sign of the time, the preponderance of the mountebank, the glory and renown, the personal favour, he enjoyed. Had n't she noticed what an immense part of the public attention he held in London at least? For in Paris society was not so pervaded with him and the women of the profession, in particular, were not in every drawing-room.

"I don't know what you mean," Mrs. Dallow said. "I know nothing of any such people."

"Are n't they under your feet wherever you turn — their performances, their portraits, their speeches, their autobiographies, their names, their manners, their ugly mugs, as the people say, and their idiotic pretensions ?"

"I dare say it depends on the places one goes to. If they're everywhere" — and she paused a moment — "I don't go everywhere."

"I don't go anywhere, but they mount on my back at home like the Old Man of the Sea. Just observe a little when you return to London," Mr. Nash went on with friendly instructiveness. Julia got up at this — she did n't like receiving directions; but no other corner of the room appeared to offer her any particular reason for crossing to it: she never did such a thing without a great inducement. So she remained standing there as if she were quitting the place in a moment, which indeed she now determined to do; and her interlocutor, rising also, lingered beside her unencouraged but unperturbed. He proceeded to remark that Mr. Sherringham was quite right to offer Miss Rooth an afternoon's sport; she deserved it as a fine brave amiable girl. She was highly educated, knew a dozen languages, was of illustrious lineage and was immensely particular.

"Immensely particular ?" Mrs. Dallow repeated.

"Perhaps I should say rather that her mother's so on her behalf. Particular about the sort of people they meet — the tone, the standard. I'm bound to say they're like *you:* they don't go everywhere. That spirit's not so common in the mob calling itself good society as not to deserve mention."

She said nothing for a moment; she looked vaguely round the room, but not at Miriam Rooth. Neverthe-

151

less she presently dropped as in forced reference to her an impatient shake. "She's dreadfully vulgar."

"Ah don't say that to my friend Dormer!" Mr. Nash laughed.

"Are you and he such great friends?" Mrs. Dallow asked, meeting his eyes.

"Great enough to make me hope we shall be greater."

Again for a little she said nothing, but then went on: "Why should n't I say to him that she's vulgar?"

"Because he admires her so much. He wants to paint her."

"To paint her?"

"To paint her portrait."

"Oh I see. I dare say she'd do for that."

Mr. Nash showed further amusement. "If that's your opinion of her you're not very complimentary to the art he aspires to practise."

"He aspires to practise?" she echoed afresh.

"Have n't you talked with him about it? Ah you must keep him up to it!"

Julia Dallow was conscious for a moment of looking uncomfortable; but it relieved her to be able to demand of her neighbour with a certain manner: "Are you an artist?"

"I try to be," Nash smiled, "but I work in such difficult material."

He spoke this with such a clever suggestion of mysterious things that she was to hear herself once more pay him the attention of taking him up. "Difficult material?"

"I work in life!"

At this she turned away, leaving him the impression that she probably misunderstood his speech, thinking he meant that he drew from the living model or some such platitude: as if there could have been any likelihood he would have dealings with the dead. This indeed would not fully have explained the abruptness with which she dropped their conversation. Gabriel, however, was used to sudden collapses and even to sudden ruptures on the part of those addressed by him, and no man had more the secret of remaining gracefully with his conversational wares on his hands. He saw Mrs. Dallow approach Nick Dormer, who was talking with one of the ladies of the embassy, and apparently signify that she wished to speak to him. He got up and they had a minute's talk, after which he turned and took leave of his fellow visitors. She said a word to her brother, Nick joined her and they then came together to the door. In this movement they had to pass near Nash, and it gave her an opportunity to nod good-bye to him which he was by no means sure she would have done if Nick had n't been with her. The young man just stopped; he said to Nash: "I should like to see you this evening late. You must meet me somewhere."

"We'll take a walk — I should like that," Nash replied. "I shall smoke a cigar at the café on the corner of the Place de l'Opéra — you'll find me there." He prepared to compass his own departure, but before doing so he addressed himself to the duty of a few civil words to Lady Agnes. This effort proved vain, for on one side she was defended by the wall of the room and on the other rendered inaccessible by Miriam's mother, who clung to her with a quickly-rooted fidelity, showing no symptom of desistance. Nash declined perforce upon her daughter Grace, who said to him: "You were talking with my cousin Mrs. Dallow."

"*To* her rather than with her," he smiled.

"Ah she's very charming," Grace said.

"She's very beautiful."

"And very clever," the girl continued.

"Very, very intelligent." His conversation with Miss Dormer went little beyond this, and he presently took leave of Peter Sherringham, remarking to him as they shook hands that he was very sorry for him. But he had courted his fate.

"What do you mean by my fate?" Sherringham asked.

"You've got them for life."

"Why for life, when I now clearly and courageously recognise that she isn't good?"

"Ah but she'll become so," said Gabriel Nash.

"Do you think that?" Sherringham brought out with a candour that made his visitor laugh.

"*You* will — that's more to the purpose!" the latter declared as he went away.

Ten minutes later Lady Agnes substituted a general vague assent for all further particular ones, drawing off from Mrs. Rooth and from the rest of the company with her daughters. Peter had had very little talk with Biddy, but the girl kept her disappointment out of her pretty eyes and said to him: "You told us she didn't know how — but she

154

does!" There was no suggestion of disappointment in this.

Sherringham held her hand a moment. "Ah it's you who know how, dear Biddy!" he answered; and he was conscious that if the occasion had been more private he would have all lawfully kissed her.

Presently three more of his guests took leave, and Mr. Nash's assurance that he had them for life recurred to him as he observed that Mrs. Rooth and her damsel quite failed to profit by so many examples. The Lovicks remained — a colleague and his sociable wife — and Peter gave them a hint that they were not to plant him there only with the two ladies. Miriam quitted Mrs. Lovick, who had attempted, with no great subtlety, to engage her, and came up to her host as if she suspected him of a design of stealing from the room and had the idea of preventing it.

"I want some more tea: will you give me some more? I feel quite faint. You don't seem to suspect how this sort of thing takes it out of one."

Peter apologised extravagantly for not having seen to it that she had proper refreshment, and took her to the round table, in a corner, on which the little collation had been served. He poured out tea for her and pressed bread and butter on her and *petits fours*, of all which she profusely and methodically partook. It was late; the afternoon had faded and a lamp been brought in, the wide shade of which shed a fair glow on the tea-service and the plates of pretty food. The Lovicks sat with Mrs. Rooth at the other end of the room, and the girl stood at the

155

table, drinking her tea and eating her bread and butter. She consumed these articles so freely that he wondered if she had been truly in want of a meal — if they were so poor as to have to count with that sort of privation. This supposition was softening, but still not so much so as to make him ask her to sit down. She appeared indeed to prefer to stand: she looked better so, as if the freedom, the conspicuity of being on her feet and treading a stage were agreeable to her. While Sherringham lingered near her all vaguely, his hands in his pockets and his mind now void of everything but a planned evasion of the theatrical question — there were moments when he was so plentifully tired of it — she broke out abruptly: "Confess you think me intolerably bad!"

"Intolerably — no."

"Only tolerably! I find that worse."

"Every now and then you do something very right," Sherringham said.

"How many such things did I do to-day?"

"Oh three or four. I don't know that I counted very carefully."

She raised her cup to her lips, looking at him over the rim of it — a proceeding that gave her eyes a strange expression. "It bores you and you think it disagreeable," she then said — "I mean a girl always talking about herself." He protested she could never bore him and she added: "Oh I don't want compliments — I want the hard, the precious truth. An actress has to talk about herself. What else can she talk about, poor vain thing?"

"She can talk sometimes about other actresses."

"That comes to the same thing. You won't be serious. I'm awfully serious." There was something that caught his attention in the note of this — a longing half hopeless, half argumentative to be believed in. "If one really wants to do anything one must worry it out; of course everything does n't come the first day," she kept on. "I can't see everything at once; but I can see a little more — step by step — as I go; can't I ? "

"That's the way — that's the way," he gently enough returned. "When you see the things to do the art of doing them will come — if you hammer away. The great point's to see them."

"Yes; and you don't think me clever enough for that."

"Why do you say so when I've asked you to come here on purpose ? "

"You've asked me to come, but I've had no success."

"On the contrary; every one thought you wonderful."

"Oh but they don't know!" said Miriam Rooth. "You've not said a word to me. I don't mind your not having praised me; that would be too *banal*. But if I'm bad — and I know I'm dreadful — I wish you'd talk to me about it."

"It's delightful to talk to you," Peter found himself saying.

"No, it is n't, but it's kind;" and she looked away from him.

Her voice had with this a quality which made

him exclaim: " Every now and then you 'say' something—!"

She turned her eyes back to him and her face had a light. "I don't want it to come by accident." Then she added: "If there's any good to be got from trying, from showing one's self, how can it come unless one hears the simple truth, the truth that turns one inside out? It's all for that — to know what one is, if one's a stick!"

"You've great courage, you've rare qualities," Sherringham risked. She had begun to touch him, to seem different: he was glad she had not gone.

But for a little she made no answer, putting down her empty cup and yearning over the table as for something more to eat. Suddenly she raised her head and broke out with vehemence: "I will, I will, I will!"

"You'll do what you want, evidently."

"I *will* succeed — I *will* be great. Of course I know too little, I've seen too little. But I've always liked it; I've never liked anything else. I used to learn things and do scenes and rant about the room when I was but five years old." She went on, communicative, persuasive, familiar, egotistical (as was necessary) and slightly common, or perhaps only natural; with reminiscences, reasons and anecdotes, an unexpected profusion, and with an air of comradeship, of freedom in any relation, which seemed to plead that she was capable at least of embracing that side of the profession she desired to adopt. He noted that if she had seen very little, as she said, she had also seen a great deal; but both her experience

and her innocence had been accidental and irregular.
She had seen very little acting — the theatre was
always too expensive. If she could only go often
— in Paris for instance every night for six months —
to see the best, the worst, everything, she would
make things out, would observe and learn what to do,
what not to do: it would be a school of schools. But
she could n't without selling the clothes off her back.
It was vile and disgusting to be poor, and if ever she
were to know the bliss of having a few francs in her
pocket she would make up for it — that she could
promise! She had never been acquainted with any
one who could tell her anything — if it was good or
bad or right or wrong — except Mrs. Delamere and
poor Ruggieri. She supposed they had told her a
great deal, but perhaps they had n't, and she was
perfectly willing to give it up if it was bad. Evidently
Madame Carré thought so; she thought it was horrid. Was n't it perfectly divine, the way the old woman had said those verses, those speeches of Célie?
If she would only let her come and listen to her once
in a while like that it was all she would ask. She
had got lots of ideas just from that half-hour; she
had practised them over, over and over again, the
moment she got home. He might ask her mother —
he might ask the people next door. If Madame Carré
did n't think she could work, she might have heard,
could she have listened at the door, something that
would show her. But she did n't think her even good
enough to criticise — since that was n't criticism,
telling her her head was good. Of course her head
was good — she need n't travel up to the *quartiers*

excentriques to find that out. It was her mother, the way she talked, who gave the idea that she wanted to be elegant and moral and a *femme du monde* and all that sort of trash. Of course that put people off, when they were only thinking of the real right way. Did n't *she* know, Miriam herself, that this was the one thing to think of? But any one would be kind to her mother who knew what a dear she was. "She does n't know when anything's right or wrong, but she's a perfect saint," said the girl, obscuring considerably her vindication. "She does n't mind when I say things over by the hour, dinning them into her ears while she sits there and reads. She's a tremendous reader; she's awfully up in literature. She taught me everything herself. I mean all that sort of thing. Of course I'm not so fond of reading; I go in for the book of life." Sherringham wondered if her mother had not at any rate taught her that phrase — he thought it highly probable. "It would give on *my* nerves, the life I lead her," Miriam continued; "but she's really a delicious woman."

The oddity of this epithet made Peter laugh, and altogether, in a few minutes, which is perhaps a sign that he abused his right to be a man of moods, the young lady had produced in him a revolution of curiosity, set his sympathy in motion. Her mixture, as it spread itself before him, was an appeal and a challenge: she was sensitive and dense, she was underbred and fine. Certainly she was very various, and that was rare; quite not at this moment the heavy-eyed frightened creature who had pulled herself together with such an effort at Madame Carré's, nor the elated "phenomenon" who had just been declaiming, nor the rather affected and contradictious young person with whom he had walked home from the Rue de Constantinople. Was this succession of phases a sign she was really a case of the celebrated artistic temperament, the nature that made people provoking and interesting? That Sherringham himself was of this shifting complexion is perhaps proved by his odd capacity for being of two different minds very nearly at the same time. Miriam was pretty now, with felicities and graces, with charming usual eyes. Yes, there were things he could do for her; he had already forgotten the chill of Mr. Nash's irony, of his prophecy. He was even scarce conscious how little in general he liked hints, insinuations, favours asked obliquely and plaintively: that was doubtless also because the girl was suddenly so taking and so fraternising. Perhaps indeed it was unjust to qualify as roundabout the manner in which Miss Rooth conveyed that it was open to him not only to pay for her lessons, but to meet the expense of her nightly attendance with her mother at instructive exhibitions of theatrical art. It was a large order, sending the pair to all the plays; but what Peter now found himself thinking of was not so much its largeness as the possible interest of going with them sometimes and pointing the moral — the technical one — of showing her the things he liked, the things he disapproved. She repeated her declaration that she recognised the fallacy of her mother's view of heroines impossibly virtuous and of the importance of her looking out for such tremendously proper people. "One must let her talk, but of course it creates a prejudice," she said with her eyes on Mr. and Mrs. Lovick, who had got up, terminating their communion with Mrs. Rooth. "It's a great muddle, I know, but she can't bear anything coarse or nasty — and quite right too. I should n't either if I did n't have to. But I don't care a sou where I go if I can get to act, or who they are if they'll help me. I want to act — that's what I want to do; I don't want to meddle in people's affairs. I can look out for myself — *I*'m all right!" the girl exclaimed roundly, frankly, with a ring of honesty which made her crude and pure. "As for doing the bad ones I'm not afraid of that."

"The bad ones?"

"The bad women in the plays — like Madame Carré. I'll do any vile creature."

"I think you'll do best what you are" — and Sherringham laughed for the interest of it. "You're a strange girl."

"Je crois bien! Does n't one have to be, to want to go and exhibit one's self to a loathsome crowd, on a platform, with trumpets and a big drum, for money — to parade one's body and one's soul?"

He looked at her a moment: her face changed constantly; now it had a fine flush and a noble delicacy. "Give it up. You're too good for it," he found himself pleading. "I doubt if you've an idea of what girls have to go through."

"Never, never — never till I'm pelted!" she cried.

"Then stay on here a bit. I'll take you to the theatres."

"Oh you dear!" Miriam delightedly exclaimed. Mr. and Mrs. Lovick, accompanied by Mrs. Rooth, now crossed the room to them, and the girl went on in the same tone: "Mamma dear, he's the best friend we've ever had — he's a great deal nicer than I thought."

"So are you, mademoiselle," said Peter Sherringham.

"Oh, I trust Mr. Sherringham — I trust him infinitely," Mrs. Rooth returned, covering him with her mild respectable wheedling eyes. "The kindness of every one has been beyond everything. Mr. and Mrs. Lovick can't say enough. They make the most obliging offers. They want you to know their brother."

"Oh I say, he's no brother of mine," Mr. Lovick protested good-naturedly.

"They think he'll be so suggestive, he'll put us up to the right things," Mrs. Rooth went on.

"It's just a little brother of mine — such a dear amusing clever boy," Mrs. Lovick explained.

"Do you know she has got nine? Upon my honour she has!" said her husband. "This one is the sixth. Fancy if I had to take them all over!"

"Yes, it makes it rather awkward," Mrs. Lovick amiably conceded. "He has gone on the stage, poor darling — but he acts rather well."

"He tried for the diplomatic service, but he did n't precisely dazzle his examiners," Mr. Lovick further mentioned.

"Edmund's very nasty about him. There are lots of gentlemen on the stage — he's not the first."

"It's such a comfort to hear that," said Mrs. Rooth.

"I'm much obliged to you. Has he got a theatre?" Miriam asked.

"My dear young lady, he hasn't even got an engagement," replied the young man's terrible brother-in-law.

"He hasn't been at it very long, but I'm sure he'll get on. He's immensely in earnest and very good-looking. I just said that if he should come over to see us you might rather like to meet him. He might give you some tips, as my husband says."

"I don't care for his looks, but I *should* like his tips," Miriam liberally smiled.

"And *is* he coming over to see you?" asked Sherringham, to whom, while this exchange of remarks, which he had not lost, was going on, Mrs. Rooth had in lowered accents addressed herself.

"Not if I can help it I think!" But Mr. Lovick was so gaily rude that it wasn't embarrassing.

"Oh sir, I'm sure you're fond of him," Mrs. Rooth remonstrated as the party passed together into the antechamber.

"No, really, I like some of the others — four or five of them; but I don't like Arty."

"We'll make it up to him, then; *we*'ll like him," Miriam answered with spirit; and her voice rang in the staircase — Sherringham attended them a little way — with a charm which her host had rather missed in her loudness of the day before.

IX

NICK DORMER found his friend Nash that evening at the place of their tryst — smoking a cigar, in the warm bright night, on the terrace of the café forming one of the angles of the Place de l'Opéra. He sat down with him, but at the end of five minutes uttered a protest against the crush and confusion, the publicity and vulgarity of the place, the shuffling procession of the crowd, the jostle of fellow customers, the perpetual brush of waiters. "Come away; I want to talk to you and I can't talk here. I don't care where we go. It will be pleasant to walk; we'll stroll away to the *quartiers sérieux*. Each time I come to Paris I at the end of three days take the Boulevard, with its conventional grimace, into greater aversion. I hate even to cross it — I go half a mile round to avoid it."

The young men took their course together down the Rue de la Paix to the Rue de Rivoli, which they crossed, passing beside the gilded rails of the Tuileries. The beauty of the night — the only defect of which was that the immense illumination of Paris kept it from being quite night enough, made it a sort of bedizened rejuvenated day — gave a charm to the quieter streets, drew our friends away to the right, to the river and the bridges, the older, duskier city. The pale ghost of the palace that had perished by fire hung over them a while, and, by the passage now open at all times across the garden of the Tuileries, they came out upon the Seine. They kept on and on, moving slowly, smoking, talking, pausing, stopping to look, to emphasise, to compare. They fell into discussion, into confidence, into enquiry, sympathetic or satiric, and into explanations which needed in turn to be explained. The balmy night, the time for talk, the amusement of Paris, the memory of younger passages, gave a lift to the occasion. Nick had already forgotten his little brush with Julia on his leaving Peter's tea-party at her side, and that he had been almost disconcerted by the asperity with which she denounced the odious man he had taken it into his head to force upon her. Impertinent and fatuous she had called him; and when Nick began to plead that he was really neither of these things, though he could imagine his manner might sometimes suggest them, she had declared that she did n't wish to argue about him or ever to hear of him again. Nick had n't counted on her liking Gabriel Nash, but had thought her not liking him would n't perceptibly matter. He had given himself the diversion, not cruel surely to any one concerned, of seeing what she would make of a type she had never before met. She had made even less than he expected, and her intimation that he had played her a trick had been irritating enough to prevent his reflecting that the offence might have been in some degree with Nash. But he had recovered from his resentment sufficiently to ask this personage, with every possible circumstance of implied consideration for the lady, what had been the impression made by his charming cousin.

"Upon my word, my dear fellow, I don't regard that as a fair question," Gabriel said. "Besides, if you think Mrs. Dallow charming what on earth need it matter to you what I think? The superiority of one man's opinion over another's is never so great as when the opinion's about a woman."

"It was to help me to find out what I think of yourself," Nick returned.

"Oh, that you'll never do. I shall bewilder you to the end. The lady with whom you were so good as to make me acquainted is a beautiful specimen of the English garden-flower, the product of high cultivation and much tending; a tall delicate stem with the head set upon it in a manner which, as a thing seen and remembered, should doubtless count for us as a gift of the gods. She's the perfect type of the object *raised* or bred, and everything about her hangs together and conduces to the effect, from the angle of her elbow to the way she drops that vague conventional dry little 'Oh!' which dispenses with all further performance. That degree of completeness is always satisfying. But I did n't satisfy her, and she did n't understand me. I don't think they usually understand."

"She's no worse than I then."

"Ah she did n't try."

"No, she does n't try. But she probably thought you a monster of conceit, and she would think so still more if she were to hear you talk about her trying."

"Very likely — very likely," said Gabriel Nash. "I've an idea a good many people think that. It strikes me as comic. I suppose it's a result of my little system."

"What little system?"

"Oh nothing more wonderful than the idea of being just the same to every one. People have so bemuddled themselves that the last thing they can conceive is that one should be simple."

"Lord, do you call yourself simple?" Nick ejaculated.

"Absolutely; in the sense of having no interest of my own to push, no nostrum to advertise, no power to conciliate, no axe to grind. I'm not a savage — ah far from it! — but I really think I'm perfectly independent."

"Well, that's always provoking!" Nick knowingly returned.

"So it would appear, to the great majority of one's fellow mortals; and I well remember the pang with which I originally made that discovery. It darkened my spirit at a time when I had no thought of evil. What we like, when we're unregenerate, is that a new-comer should give us a password, come over to our side, join our little camp or religion, get into our little boat, in short, whatever it is, and help us to row it. It's natural enough; we're mostly in different tubs and cockles, paddling for life. Our opinions, our convictions and doctrines and standards, are simply the particular thing that will make the boat go — *our* boat, naturally, for they may very often be just the thing that will sink another. If you won't get in people generally hate you."

168

"Your metaphor's very lame," said Nick. "It's the overcrowded boat that goes to the bottom."

"Oh I'll give it another leg or two! Boats can be big, in the infinite of space, and a doctrine's a raft that floats the better the more passengers it carries. A passenger jumps over from time to time, not so much from fear of sinking as from a want of interest in the course or the company. He swims, he plunges, he dives, he dips down and visits the fishes and the mermaids and the submarine caves; he goes from craft to craft and splashes about, on his own account, in the blue cool water. The regenerate, as I call them, are the passengers who jump over in search of better fun. I jumped over long ago."

"And now of course you're at the head of the regenerate; for, in your turn" — Nick found the figure delightful — "you all form a select school of porpoises."

"Not a bit, and I know nothing about heads — in the sense you mean. I've grown a tail if you will; I'm the merman wandering free. It's the jolliest of trades!"

Before they had gone many steps further Nick Dormer stopped short with a question. "I say, my dear fellow, do you mind mentioning to me whether you're the greatest humbug and charlatan on earth, or a genuine intelligence, one that has sifted things for itself?"

"I do lead your poor British wit a dance — I'm so sorry," Nash replied benignly. "But I'm very sincere. And I *have* tried to straighten out things a bit for myself."

"Then why do you give people such a handle?"

"Such a handle?"

"For thinking you're an — for thinking you're a mere *farceur*."

"I dare say it's my manner: they're so unused to any sort of candour."

"Well then why don't you try another?" Nick asked.

"One has the manner that one can, and mine moreover's a part of my little system."

"Ah if you make so much of your little system you're no better than any one else," Nick returned as they went on.

"I don't pretend to be better, for we're all miserable sinners; I only pretend to be bad in a pleasanter, brighter way — by what I can see. It's the simplest thing in the world; just take for granted our right to be happy and brave. What's essentially kinder and more helpful than that, what's more beneficent? But the tradition of dreariness, of stodginess, of dull dense literal prose, has so sealed people's eyes that they've ended by thinking the most natural of all things the most perverse. Why so keep up the dreariness, in our poor little day? No one can tell me why, and almost every one calls me names for simply asking the question. But I go on, for I believe one can do a little good by it. I want so much to do a little good," Gabriel Nash continued, taking his companion's arm. "My persistence is systematic: don't you see what I mean? I won't be dreary — no, no, no; and I won't recognise the necessity, or even, if there be any way out of it, the accident, of

dreariness in the life that surrounds me. That's
enough to make people stare: they're so damned
stupid!"

"They think you so damned impudent," Nick
freely explained.

At this Nash stopped him short with a small cry,
and, turning his eyes, Nick saw under the lamps of
the quay that he had brought a flush of pain into
his friend's face. "I don't strike *you* that way?"

"Oh 'me!' Was n't it just admitted that I don't
in the least make you out?"

"That's the last thing!" Nash declared, as if he
were thinking the idea over, with an air of genuine
distress. "But with a little patience we'll clear it up
together — if you care enough about it," he added
more cheerfully. Letting his companion proceed
again he continued: "Heaven help us all, what do
people mean by impudence? There are many, I
think, who don't understand its nature or its limits;
and upon my word I've literally seen mere quick-
ness of intelligence or of perception, the jump of a
step or two, a little whirr of the wings of talk, mistaken for it. Yes, I've encountered men and women
who thought you impudent if you were n't simply so
stupid as they. The only impudence is unprovoked,
or even mere dull, aggression, and I indignantly
protest that I'm never guilty of *that* clumsiness. Ah
for what do they take one, with *their* beastly presump-
tion? Even to defend myself sometimes I've to make
believe to myself that I care. I always feel as if I
did n't successfully make others think so. Perhaps
they see impudence in that. But I dare say the

offence is in the things that I take, as I say, for granted; for if one tries to be pleased one passes perhaps inevitably for being pleased above all with one's self. That's really not my case — I find my capacity for pleasure deplorably below the mark I've set. This is why, as I've told you, I cultivate it, I try to bring it up. And I'm actuated by positive benevolence; I've that impudent pretension. That's what I mean by being the same to every one, by having only one manner. If one's conscious and ingenious to that end what's the harm — when one's motives are so pure? By never, *never* making the concession, one may end by becoming a perceptible force for good."

"What concession are you talking about, in God's name?" Nick demanded.

"Why, that we're here all for dreariness. It's impossible to grant it sometimes if you wish to deny it ever."

"And what do you mean then by dreariness? That's modern slang and terribly vague. Many good things are dreary — virtue and decency and charity, and perseverance and courage and honour."

"Say at once that life's dreary, my dear fellow!" Gabriel Nash exclaimed.

"That's on the whole my besetting impression."

"C'est là que je vous attends! I'm precisely engaged in trying what can be done in taking it the other way. It's my little personal experiment. Life consists of the personal experiments of each of us, and the point of an experiment is that it shall succeed. What we contribute is our treatment of the material, our rendering of the text, our style. A sense of the qualities of a style is so rare that many persons should doubtless be forgiven for not being able to read, or at all events to enjoy, us; but is that a reason for giving it up — for not being, in this other sphere, if one possibly can, an Addison, a Ruskin, a Renan? Ah we must write our best; it 's the great thing we can do in the world, on the right side. One has one's form, *que diable*, and a mighty good thing that one has. I 'm not afraid of putting all life into mine, and without unduly squeezing it. I 'm not afraid of putting in honour and courage and charity — without spoiling them: on the contrary I shall only do them good. People may not read you at sight, may not like you, but there 's a chance they 'll come round; and the only way to court the chance is to keep it up — always to keep it up. That 's what I do, my dear man — if you don't think I 've perseverance. If some one 's touched here and there, if you give a little impression of truth and charm, that 's your reward; besides of course the pleasure for yourself."

"Don't you think your style 's a trifle affected?" Nick asked for further amusement.

"That 's always the charge against a personal manner: if you 've any at all people think you 've too much. Perhaps, perhaps — who can say? The lurking unexpressed is infinite, and affectation must have begun, long ago, with the first act of reflective expression — the substitution of the few placed articulate words for the cry or the thump or the hug. Of course one is n't perfect; but that 's the delightful thing about art, that there 's always more to learn

173

and more to do; it grows bigger the more one uses it and meets more questions the more they come up. No doubt I'm rough still, but I'm in the right direction: I make it my business to testify for the fine."

"Ah the fine — there it stands, over there!" said Nick Dormer. "I'm not so sure about yours — I don't know what I've got hold of. But Notre Dame *is* truth; Notre Dame *is* charm; on Notre Dame the distracted mind can rest. Come over with me and look at her!"

They had come abreast of the low island from which the great cathedral, disengaged to-day from her old contacts and adhesions, rises high and fair, with her front of beauty and her majestic mass, darkened at that hour, or at least simplified, under the stars, but only more serene and sublime for her happy union far aloft with the cool distance and the night. Our young men, fantasticating as freely as I leave the reader to estimate, crossed the wide short bridge which made them face toward the monuments of old Paris — the Palais de Justice, the Conciergerie, the holy chapel of Saint Louis. They came out before the church, which looks down on a square where the past, once so thick in the very heart of Paris, has been made rather a blank, pervaded however by the everlasting freshness of the vast cathedral-face. It greeted Nick Dormer and Gabriel Nash with a kindness the long centuries had done nothing to dim. The lamplight of the old city washed its foundations, but the towers and buttresses, the arches, the galleries, the statues, the vast rose-window, the large full composition, seemed to grow

174

clearer while they climbed higher, as if they had a conscious benevolent answer for the upward gaze of men.

"How it straightens things out and blows away one's vapours — anything that's *done!*" said Nick; while his companion exclaimed blandly and affectionately:

"The dear old thing!"

"The great point's to do something, instead of muddling and questioning; and, by Jove, it makes me want to!"

"Want to build a cathedral?" Nash enquired.

"Yes, just that."

"It's you who puzzle *me* then, my dear fellow. You can't build them out of words."

"What is it the great poets do?" asked Nick.

"*Their* words are ideas — their words are images, enchanting collocations and unforgettable signs. But the verbiage of parliamentary speeches —!"

"Well," said Nick with a candid reflective sigh, "you can rear a great structure of many things — not only of stones and timbers and painted glass." They walked round this example of one, pausing, criticising, admiring and discussing; mingling the grave with the gay and paradox with contemplation. Behind and at the sides the huge dusky vessel of the church seemed to dip into the Seine or rise out of it, floating expansively — a ship of stone with its flying buttresses thrown forth like an array of mighty oars. Nick Dormer lingered near it in joy, in soothing content, as if it had been the temple of a faith so dear to him that there was peace and security in its precinct.

And there was comfort too and consolation of the same sort in the company at this moment of Nash's equal appreciation, of his response, by his own signs, to the great effect. He took it all in so and then so gave it all out that Nick was reminded of the radiance his boyish admiration had found in him of old, the easy grasp of everything of that kind. "Everything of that kind" was to Nick's sense the description of a wide and bright domain.

They crossed to the further side of the river, where the influence of the Gothic monument threw a distinction even over the Parisian smartnesses — the municipal rule and measure, the importunate symmetries, the "handsomeness" of everything, the extravagance of gaslight, the perpetual click on the neat bridges. In front of a quiet little café on the left bank Gabriel Nash said "Let's sit down" — he was always ready to sit down. It was a friendly establishment and an unfashionable quarter, far away from the caravan-series; there were the usual little tables and chairs on the quay, the muslin curtains behind the glazed front, the general sense of sawdust and of drippings of watery beer. The place was subdued to stillness, but not extinguished, by the lateness of the hour; no vehicles passed, only now and then a light Parisian foot. Beyond the parapet they could hear the flow of the Seine. Nick Dormer said it made him think of the old Paris, of the great Revolution, of Madame Roland, *quoi!* Gabriel said they could have watery beer but were not obliged to drink it. They sat a long time; they talked a great deal, and the more they said the more the unsaid came up. Presently Nash found occasion to throw out: "I go about my business like any good citizen — that's all."

"And what *is* your business?"

"The spectacle of the world."

Nick laughed out. "And what do you do with that?"

"What does any one do with spectacles? I look at it. I see."

"You're full of contradictions and inconsistencies," Nick however objected. "You described yourself to me half an hour ago as an apostle of beauty."

"Where's the inconsistency? I do it in the broad light of day, whatever I do: that's virtually what I meant. If I look at the spectacle of the world I look in preference at what's charming in it. Sometimes I've to go far to find it — very likely; but that's just what I do. I go far — as far as my means permit me. Last year I heard of such a delightful little spot; a place where a wild fig-tree grows in the south wall, the outer side, of an old Spanish city. I was told it was a deliciously brown corner — the sun making it warm in winter. As soon as I could I went there."

"And what did you do?"

"I lay on the first green grass — I liked it."

"If that sort of thing's all you accomplish you're not encouraging."

"I accomplish my happiness — it seems to me that's something. I have feelings, I have sensations: let me tell you that's not so common. It's rare to have them, and if you chance to have them it's rare not to be ashamed of them. I go after them — when I judge they won't hurt any one."

"You're lucky to have money for your travelling-expenses," said Nick.

"No doubt, no doubt; but I do it very cheap. I take my stand on my nature, on my fortunate character. I'm not ashamed of it, I don't think it's so horrible, my character. But we've so befogged and befouled the whole question of liberty, of spontaneity, of good humour and inclination and enjoyment, that there's nothing that makes people stare so as to see one natural."

"You're always thinking too much of 'people.'"

"They say I think too little," Gabriel smiled.

"Well, I've agreed to stand for Harsh," said Nick with a roundabout transition.

"It's you then who are lucky to have money."

"I haven't," Nick explained. "My expenses are to be paid."

"Then you too must think of 'people.'"

Nick made no answer to this, but after a moment said: "I wish very much you had more to show for it."

"To show for what?"

"Your little system — the æsthetic life."

Nash hesitated, tolerantly, gaily, as he often did, with an air of being embarrassed to choose between several answers, any one of which would be so right. "Oh having something to show's such a poor business. It's a kind of confession of failure."

"Yes, you're more affected than anything else," said Nick impatiently.

"No, my dear boy, I'm more good-natured: don't I prove it? I'm rather disappointed to find you not more accessible to esoteric doctrine. But there is, I confess, another plane of intelligence, honourable, and very honourable, in its way, from which it *may* legitimately appear important to have something to show. If you must confine yourself to that plane I won't refuse you my sympathy. After all that's what *I* have to show! But the degree of my sympathy must of course depend on the nature of the demonstration you wish to make."

"You know it very well — you've guessed it," Nick returned, looking before him in a conscious modest way which would have been called sheepish had he been a few years younger.

"Ah you've broken the scent with telling me you're going back to the House of Commons," said Nash.

"No wonder you don't make it out! My situation's certainly absurd enough. What I really hanker for is to be a painter; and of portraits, on the whole, I think. That's the abject crude ridiculous fact. In this out-of-the-way corner, at the dead of night, in lowered tones, I venture to disclose it to you. Isn't that the æsthetic life?"

"Do you know how to paint?" asked Nash.

"Not in the least. No element of burlesque is therefore wanting to my position."

"That makes no difference. I'm so glad!"

"So glad I don't know how?"

"So glad of it all. Yes, that only makes it better. You're a delightful case, and I like delightful cases. We must see it through. I rejoice I met you again."

"Do you think I can do anything?" Nick enquired.

"Paint good pictures? How can I tell without seeing some of your work? Does n't it come back to me that at Oxford you used to sketch very prettily? But that's the last thing that matters."

"What does matter then?" Nick asked with his eyes on his companion.

"To be on the right side — on the side of the 'fine.'"

"There'll be precious little of the 'fine' if I produce nothing but daubs."

"Ah you cling to the old false measure of success! I must cure you of that. There'll be the beauty of having been disinterested and independent; of having taken the world in the free brave personal way."

"I shall nevertheless paint decently if I can," Nick presently said.

"I'm almost sorry! It will make your case less clear, your example less grand."

"My example will be grand enough, with the fight I shall have to make."

"The fight? With whom?"

"With myself first of all. I'm awfully against it."

"Ah but you'll have me on the other side," Nash smiled.

"Well, you'll have more than a handful to meet — everything, every one that belongs to me, that touches me near or far; my family, my blood, my heredity, my traditions, my promises, my circumstances, my prejudices; my little past — such as it is; my great future — such as it has been supposed it may be."

"I see, I see. It's splendid!" Nash exclaimed. "And Mrs. Dallow into the bargain," he added.

"Yes, Mrs. Dallow if you like."

"Are you in love with her?"

"Not in the least."

"Well, she is with you — so I understood."

"Don't say that," said Nick Dormer with sudden sternness.

"Ah you are, you are!" his companion pronounced, judging apparently from this accent.

"I don't know *what* I am — heaven help me!" Nick broke out, tossing his hat down on his little tin table with vehemence. "I'm a freak of nature and a sport of the mocking gods. Why should they go out of their way to worry me? Why should they do everything so inconsequent, so improbable, so preposterous? It's the vulgarest practical joke. There has never been anything of the sort among us; we're all Philistines to the core, with about as much æsthetic sense as that hat. It's excellent soil — I don't complain of it — but not a soil to grow that flower. From where the devil then has the seed been dropped? I look back from generation to generation; I scour our annals without finding the least little sketching grandmother, any sign of a building or versifying or collecting or even tulip-raising ancestor. They were all as blind as bats, and none the less happy for that. I'm a wanton variation, an unaccountable monster. My dear father, rest his soul, went through life without a suspicion that there's anything in it that can't be boiled into blue-books, and became in that conviction a very distinguished person. He brought me up in the same simplicity and in the hope of the same eminence. It would have been better if I had remained so. I think it's partly your fault that I have n't," Nick went on. "At Oxford you were very bad company for me — my evil genius: you opened my eyes, you communicated the poison. Since then, little by little, it has been working within me; vaguely, covertly, insensibly at first, but during the last year or two with violence, pertinacity, cruelty. I've resorted to every antidote in life; but it's no use — I'm stricken. " *C'est Vénus toute entière à sa proie attachée* — putting Venus for 'art.' It tears me to pieces as I may say."

"I see, I follow you," said Nash, who had listened to this recital with radiant interest and curiosity. "And that's why you are going to stand."

"Precisely — it's an antidote. And at present you're another."

"Another?"

"That's why I jumped at you. A bigger dose of you may disagree with me to that extent that I shall either die or get better."

"I shall control the dilution," said Nash. "Poor fellow — if you're elected!" he added.

"Poor fellow either way. You don't know the atmosphere in which I live, the horror, the scandal my apostasy would provoke, the injury and suffering it would inflict. I believe it would really kill my mother. She thinks my father's watching me from the skies."

"Jolly to make him jump!" Nash suggested.

"He'd jump indeed — come straight down on top of me. And then the grotesqueness of it — to *begin* all of a sudden at my age."

"It's perfect indeed, it's too lovely a case," Nash raved.

"Think how it sounds — a paragraph in the London papers: 'Mr. Nicholas Dormer, M. P. for Harsh and son of the late Right Honourable and so forth and so forth, is about to give up his seat and withdraw from public life in order to devote himself to the practice of portrait-painting — and with the more commendable perseverance by reason of all the dreadful time he has lost. Orders, in view of this, respectfully solicited.'"

"The nineteenth century's a sweeter time than I thought," said Nash. "It's the portrait then that haunts your dreams?"

"I wish you could see. You must of course come immediately to my place in London."

"Perfidious wretch, you're capable of having talent — which of course will spoil everything!" Gabriel wailed.

"No, I'm too old and was too early perverted. It's too late to go through the mill."

"You make *me* young! Don't miss your election at your peril. Think of the edification."

"The edification — ?"

"Of your throwing it all up the next moment."

"That would be pleasant for Mr. Carteret," Nick brooded.

"Mr. Carteret — ?"

183

"A dear old family friend who'll wish to pay my agent's bill."

"Serve him right for such depraved tastes."

"You do me good," said Nick as he rose and turned away.

"Don't call me useless then."

"Ah but not in the way you mean. It's only if I don't get in that I shall perhaps console myself with the brush," Nick returned with humorous edifying elegance while they retraced their steps.

"For the sake of all the muses then don't stand. For you *will* get in."

"Very likely. At any rate I've promised."

"You've promised Mrs. Dallow?"

"It's her place — she'll *put* me in," Nick said.

"Baleful woman! But I'll pull you out!" cried Gabriel Nash.

X

FOR several days Peter Sherringham had business in hand which left him neither time nor freedom of mind to occupy himself actively with the ladies of the Hôtel de la Garonne. There were moments when they brushed across his memory, but their passage was rapid and not lighted with complacent attention; for he shrank from bringing to the proof the question of whether Miriam would be an interest or only a bore. She had left him after their second meeting with a quickened sympathy, but in the course of a few hours that flame had burned dim. Like most other men he was a mixture of impulse and reflexion, but was peculiar in this, that thinking things over almost always made him think less conveniently. He found illusions necessary, so that in order to keep an adequate number going he often forbade himself any excess of that exercise. Mrs. Rooth and her daughter were there and could certainly be trusted to make themselves felt. He was conscious of their anxiety and their calculations as of a frequent oppression, and knew that whatever results might ensue he should have to do the costly thing for them. An idea of tenacity, of worrying feminine duration, associated itself with their presence; he would have assented with a silent nod to the proposition — enunciated by Gabriel Nash — that he was saddled with them. Remedies hovered

185

before him, but these figured also at the same time
as complications; ranging vaguely from the expend-
iture of money to the discovery that he was in love.
This latter accident would be particularly tedious;
he had a full perception of the arts by which the girl's
mother might succeed in making it so. It would n't
be a compensation for trouble, but a trouble which
in itself would require compensations. Would that
balm spring from the spectacle of the young lady's
genius? The genius would have to be very great to
justify a rising young diplomatist in making a fool
of himself.

With the excuse of pressing work he put off Miss
Rooth from day to day, and from day to day he expected to hear her knock at his door. It would be
time enough when they ran him to earth again; and
he was unable to see how after all he could serve
them even then. He had proposed impetuously a
course of the theatres; but that would be a considerable personal effort now that the summer was about
to begin — a free bid for bad air, stale pieces and
tired actors. When however more than a week had
elapsed without a reminder of his neglected promise
it came over him that he must himself in honour give
a sign. There was a delicacy in such unexpected and
such difficult discretion — he was touched by being
let alone. The flurry of work at the embassy was over
and he had time to ask himself what in especial he
should do. He wanted something definite to suggest
before communicating with the Hôtel de la Garonne.

As a consequence of this speculation he went
back to Madame Carré to ask her to reconsider her

stern judgement and give the young English lady —to oblige him—a dozen lessons of the sort she knew so well how to give. He was aware that this request scarcely stood on its feet; for in the first place Madame Carré never reconsidered when once she had got her impression, and in the second never wasted herself on subjects whom nature had not formed to do her honour. He knew his asking her to strain a point to please him would give her a false idea — save that for that matter she had it already — of his relations, actual or prospective, with the girl; but he decided he need n't care for this, since Miriam herself probably would n't care. What he had mainly in mind was to say to the old actress that she had been mistaken — the jeune Anglaise was n't such a *grue*. This would take some courage, but it would also add to the amusement of his visit.

He found her at home, but as soon as he had expressed his conviction she began: "Oh, your jeune Anglaise, I know a great deal more about her than you! She has been back to see me twice; she does n't go the longest way round. She charges me like a grenadier and asks me to give her — guess a little what! — private recitations all to herself. If she does n't succeed it won't be for want of knowing how to thump at doors. The other day when I came in she was waiting for me; she had been there two hours. My private recitations — have you an idea what people pay for them ?"

"Between artists, you know, there are easier conditions," Sherringham laughed.

"How do I know if she 's an artist ? She won't

open her mouth to me; what she wants is to make me say things to *her*. She does make me — I don't know how — and she sits there gaping at me with her big eyes. They look like open pockets!"

"I dare say she'll profit by it," said Sherringham.

"I dare say *you* will! Her face is stupid while she watches me, and when she has tired me out she simply walks away. However, as she comes back —!" Madame Carré paused a moment, listened and then cried "Did n't I tell you?"

Sherringham heard a parley of voices in the little antechamber, and the next moment the door was pushed open and Miriam Rooth bounded into the room. She was flushed and breathless, without a smile, very direct.

"Will you hear me to-day? I know four things," she immediately broke out. Then seeing Sherringham she added in the same brisk earnest tone, as if the matter were of the highest importance, "Oh how d'ye do? I'm very glad you're here." She said nothing else to him than this, appealed to him in no way, made no allusion to his having neglected her, but addressed herself to Madame Carré as if he had not been there; making no excuses and using no flattery; taking rather a tone of equal authority — all as if the famous artist had an obvious duty toward her. This was another variation Peter thought; it differed from each of the attitudes in which he had previously seen her. It came over him suddenly that so far from there being any question of her having the histrionic nature she simply had it in such perfection that she was always acting; that her existence was a series of parts assumed for the moment, each changed for the next, before the perpetual mirror of some curiosity or admiration or wonder — some spectatorship that she perceived or imagined in the people about her. Interested as he had ever been in the profession of which she was potentially an ornament, this idea startled him by its novelty and even lent, on the spot, a formidable, a really appalling character to Miriam Rooth. It struck him abruptly that a woman whose only being was to "make believe," to make believe she had any and every being you might like and that would serve a purpose and produce a certain effect, and whose identity resided in the continuity of her personations, so that she had no moral privacy, as he phrased it to himself, but lived in a high wind of exhibition, of figuration — such a woman was a kind of monster in whom of necessity there would be nothing to "be fond" of, because there would be nothing to take hold of. He felt for a moment how simple he had been not to have achieved before this analysis of the actress. The girl's very face made it vivid to him now — the discovery that she positively had no countenance of her own, but only the countenance of the occasion, a sequence, a variety — capable possibly of becoming immense — of representative movements. She was always trying them, practising them, for her amusement or profit, jumping from one to the other and extending her range; and this would doubtless be her occupation more and more as she acquired ease and confidence. The expression that came nearest belonging to her, as it were, was the one that came

189

nearest being a blank — an air of inanity when she forgot herself in some act of sincere attention. Then her eye was heavy and her mouth betrayed a commonness; though it was perhaps just at such a moment that the fine line of her head told most. She had looked slightly *bête* even when Sherringham, on their first meeting at Madame Carré's, said to Nick Dormer that she was the image of the Tragic Muse.

Now, at any rate, he seemed to see that she might do what she liked with her face. It was an elastic substance, an element of gutta-percha, like the flexibility of the gymnast, the lady at the music-hall who is shot from the mouth of a cannon. He winced a little at this coarser view of the actress; he had somehow always looked more poetically at that priestess of art. Yet what was she, the priestess, when one came to think of it, but a female gymnast, a mountebank at higher wages? She did n't literally hang by her heels from a trapeze and hold a fat man in her teeth, but she made the same use of her tongue, of her eyes, of the imitative trick, that her muscular sister made of leg and jaw. It was an odd circumstance that Miss Rooth's face seemed to him to-day a finer instrument than old Madame Carré's. It was doubtless that the girl's was fresh and strong and had a future in it, while poor Madame Carré's was worn and weary and had only a past.

The old woman said something, half in jest, half in real resentment, about the brutality of youth while Miriam went to a mirror and quickly took off her hat, patting and arranging her hair as a preliminary to making herself heard. Sherringham saw with surprise and amusement that the keen Frenchwoman, who had in her long life exhausted every adroitness, was in a manner helpless and coerced, obliging all in spite of herself. Her young friend had taken but a few days and a couple of visits to become a successful force; she had imposed herself, and Madame Carré, while she laughed — yet looked terrible too, with such high artifices of eye and gesture — was reduced to the last line of defence; that of pronouncing her coarse and clumsy, saying she might knock her down, but that this proved nothing. She spoke jestingly enough not to offend, but her manner betrayed the irritation of an intelligent woman who at an advanced age found herself for the first time failing to understand. What she did n't understand was the kind of social product thus presented to her by Gabriel Nash; and this suggested to Sherringham that the jeune Anglaise was perhaps indeed rare, a new type, as Madame Carré must have seen innumerable varieties. He saw the girl was perfectly prepared to be abused and that her indifference to what might be thought of her discretion was a proof of life, health and spirit, the insolence of conscious resources.

When she had given herself a touch at the glass she turned round, with a rapid *"Ecoutez maintenant!"* and stood leaning a moment — slightly lowered and inclined backward, her hands behind her and supporting her — on the *console* before the mirror. She waited an instant, turning her eyes from one of her companions to the other as to take possession of them

—an eminently conscious intentional proceeding,
which made Sherringham ask himself what had become of her former terror and if that and her tears
had all been a comedy: after which, abruptly straight-
ening herself, she began to repeat a short French
poem, an ingenious thing of the day, that she had
induced Madame Carré to say over to her. She had
learned it, practised it, rehearsed it to her mother,
and had now been childishly eager to show what she
could do with it. What she mainly did was to reproduce with a crude fidelity, but in extraordinary
detail, the intonations, the personal quavers and
cadences of her model.

"How bad you make me seem to myself and if
I were you how much better I should say it!" was
Madame Carré's first criticism.

Miriam allowed her, however, little time to de-
velop it, for she broke out, at the shortest intervals,
with the several other specimens of verse to which
the old actress had handed her the key. They were
all fine lyrics, of tender or ironic intention, by contemporary poets, but depending for effect on taste
and art, a mastery of the rare shade and the right
touch, in the interpreter. Miriam had gobbled them
up, and she gave them forth in the same way as the
first, with close, rude, audacious mimicry. There
was a moment for Sherringham when it might have
been feared their hostess would see in the performance a designed burlesque of her manner, her airs
and graces, her celebrated simpers and grimaces,
so extravagant did it all cause these refinements to
appear. When it was over the old woman said

"Should you like now to hear how *you* do?" and, without waiting for an answer, phrased and trilled the last of the pieces, from beginning to end exactly as her visitor had done, making this imitation of an imitation the drollest thing conceivable. If she had suffered from the sound of the girl's echo it was a perfect revenge. Miriam had dropped on a sofa, exhausted, and she stared at first, flushed and wild; then she frankly gave way to pleasure, to interest and large laughter. She said afterwards, to defend herself, that the verses in question, and indeed all those she had recited, were of the most difficult sort: you had to do them; they did n't do themselves — they were things in which the *gros moyens* were of no avail.

"Ah my poor child your means are all *gros moyens;* you appear to have no others," Madame Carré replied. "You do what you can, but there are people like that; it's the way they're made. They can never come nearer to fine truth, to the just indication; shades don't exist for them, they don't see certain differences. It was to show you a difference that I repeated that thing as you repeat it, as you represent my doing it. If you're struck with the little the two ways have in common so much the better. But you seem to me terribly to *alourdir* everything you touch."

Peter read into this judgement a deep irritation — Miriam clearly set the teeth of her instructress on edge. She acted on her nerves, was made up of roughnesses and thicknesses unknown hitherto to her fine free-playing finger-tips. This exasperation, however, was a degree of flattery; it was neither indifference nor simple contempt; it acknowledged a mystifying

193

reality in the jeune Anglaise and even a shade of importance. The latter remarked, serenely enough, that the things she wanted most to do were just those that were not for the *gros moyens*, the vulgar obvious dodges, the starts and shouts that any one could think of and that the *gros public* liked. She wanted to do what was most difficult, and to plunge into it from the first; and she explained as if it were a discovery of her own that there were two kinds of scenes and speeches: those which acted themselves, of which the treatment was plain, the only way, so that you had just to take it; and those open to interpretation, with which you had to fight every step, rendering, arranging, doing the thing according to your idea. Some of the most effective passages and the most celebrated and admired, like the frenzy of Juliet with her potion, were of the former sort; but it was the others she liked best.

Madame Carré received this revelation good-naturedly enough, considering its want of freshness, and only laughed at the young lady for looking so nobly patronising while she gave it. Her laughter appeared partly addressed to the good faith with which Miriam described herself as preponderantly interested in the subtler problems of her art. Sherringham was charmed with the girl's pluck — if it was pluck and not mere density; the stout patience with which she submitted, for a purpose, to the old woman's rough usage. He wanted to take her away, to give her a friendly caution, to advise her not to become a bore, not to expose herself. But she held up her beautiful head as to show how little she cared

at present for any exposure, and that (it was half
coarseness — Madame Carré was so far right —
and half fortitude) she had no intention of coming
away so long as there was anything to be picked up.
She sat and still she sat, challenging her hostess with
every sort of question — some reasonable, some ingenious, some strangely futile and some highly indiscreet; but all with the effect that, contrary to Peter's
expectation, their distinguished friend warmed to the
work of answering and explaining, became interested,
was content to keep her and to talk. Yes, she took
her ease; she relieved herself, with the rare cynicism
of the artist — all the crudity, the irony and intensity
of a discussion of esoteric things — of personal mysteries, of methods and secrets. It was the oddest
hour our young man had ever spent, even in the
course of investigations which had often led him
into the *cuisine*, the distillery or back shop, of the
admired profession. He got up several times to come
away; then he remained, partly in order not to leave
Miriam alone with her terrible initiatress, partly because he was both amused and edified, and partly
because Madame Carré held him by the appeal of
her sharp confidential old eyes, addressing her talk
to himself, with Miriam but a pretext and subject,
a vile illustration. She undressed this young lady,
as it were, from head to foot, turned her inside out,
weighed and measured and sounded her: it was all,
for Sherringham, a new revelation of the point to
which, in her profession and nation, an intelligence
of the business, a ferocious analysis, had been carried and a special vocabulary developed. What

struck him above all was the way she knew her grounds and reasons, so that everything was sharp and clear in her mind and lay under her hand. If she had rare perceptions she had traced them to their source; she could give an account of what she did; she knew perfectly why, could explain it, defend it, amplify it, fight for it: all of which was an intellectual joy to her, allowing her a chance to abound and insist and discriminate. There was a kind of cruelty, or at least of hardness in it all, to poor Peter's shy English sense, that sense which can never really reconcile itself to any question of method and form, and has extraneous sentiments to "square," to pacify with compromises and superficialities, the general plea for innocence in everything and often the flagrant proof of it. In theory there was nothing he valued more than just such a logical passion as Madame Carré's, but it was apt in fact, when he found himself at close quarters with it, to appear an ado about nothing.

If the old woman was hard it was not that many of her present conclusions about the jeune Anglaise were not indulgent, but that she had a vision of the great manner, of right and wrong, of the just and the false, so high and religious that the individual was nothing before it — a prompt and easy sacrifice. It made our friend uncomfortable, as he had been made uncomfortable by certain feuilletons, reviews of the theatres in the Paris newspapers, which he was committed to thinking important but of which, when they were very good, he was rather ashamed. When they were very good, that is when they were

196

very thorough, they were very personal, as was inevitable in dealing with the most personal of the arts: they went into details; they put the dots on the *i*'s; they discussed impartially the qualities of appearance, the physical gifts of the poor aspirant, finding them in some cases reprehensibly inadequate. Peter could never rid himself of a dislike to these pronouncements; in the case of the actresses especially they struck him as brutal and offensive — unmanly as launched by an ensconced moustachioed critic over a cigar. At the same time he was aware of the dilemma (he hated it; it made him blush still more) in which his objection lodged him. If one was right in caring for the actor's art one ought to have been interested in every honest judgement of it, which, given the peculiar conditions, would be useful in proportion as it should be free. If the criticism that recognised frankly these conditions seemed an inferior or an unholy thing, then what was to be said for the art itself? What an implication, if the criticism was tolerable only so long as it was worthless — so long as it remained vague and timid! This was a knot Peter had never straightened out: he contented himself with feeling that there was no reason a theatrical critic should n't be a gentleman, at the same time that he often dubbed it an odious trade, which no gentleman could possibly follow. The best of the fraternity, so conspicuous in Paris, were those who did n't follow it — those who, while pretending to write about the stage, wrote about everything else.

It was as if Madame Carré, in pursuance of her inflamed sense that the art was everything and the individual nothing save as he happened to serve it, had said: "Well, if she *will* have it she shall; she shall know what she's in for, what I went through, battered and broken in as we all have been — all who are worthy, who have had the honour. She shall know the real point of view." It was as if she were still beset with Mrs. Rooth's twaddle and muddle, her hypocrisy, her idiotic scruples — something she felt all need to belabour, to trample on. Miriam took it all as a bath, a baptism, with shuddering joy and gleeful splashes; staring, wondering, sometimes blushing and failing to follow, but not shrinking nor wounded; laughing, when convicted, at her own expense and feeling evidently that this at last was the high cold air of art, an initiation, a discipline that nothing could undo. Sherringham said he would see her home — he wanted to talk to her and she must walk away with him. "And it's understood then she may come back," he added to Madame Carré. "It's *my* affair of course. You'll take an interest in her for a month or two; she'll sit at your feet."

The old actress had an admirable shrug. "Oh I'll knock her about — she seems stout enough!"

XI

WHEN they had descended to the street Miriam mentioned to Peter that she was thirsty, dying to drink something: upon which he asked her if she should have an objection to going with him to a café.

"Objection? I've spent my life in cafés! They're warm in winter and you get your lamplight for nothing," she explained. "Mamma and I have sat in them for hours, many a time, with a *consommation* of three sous, to save fire and candles at home. We've lived in places we could n't sit in, if you want to know — where there was only really room if we were in bed. Mamma's money's sent out from England and sometimes it use n't to come. Once it did n't come for months — for months and months. I don't know how we lived. There was n't any to come; there was n't any to get home. That is n't amusing when you're away in a foreign town without any friends. Mamma used to borrow, but people would n't always lend. You need n't be afraid — she won't borrow of *you*. We're rather better now — something has been done in England; I don't understand what. It's only fivepence a year, but it has been settled; it comes regularly; it used to come only when we had written and begged and waited. But it made no difference — mamma was always up to her ears in books. They served her for food and drink. When she had nothing to eat she began a novel in ten volumes —

199

the old-fashioned ones; they lasted longest. She knows every *cabinet de lecture* in every town; the little cheap shabby ones, I mean, in the back streets, where they have odd volumes and only ask a sou and the books are so old that they smell like close rooms. She takes them to the cafés — the little cheap shabby cafés too — and she reads there all the evening. That's very well for her, but it does n't feed me. I don't like a diet of dirty old novels. I sit there beside her with nothing to do, not even a stocking to mend; she does n't think that *comme il faut*. I don't know what the people take me for. However, we've never been spoken to: any one can see mamma's a great lady. As for me I dare say I might be anything dreadful. If you're going to be an actress you must get used to being looked at. There were people in England who used to ask us to stay; some of them were our cousins — or mamma says they were. I've never been very clear about our cousins and I don't think they were at all clear about us. Some of them are dead; the others don't ask us any more. You should hear mamma on the subject of our visits in England. It's very convenient when your cousins are dead — that explains everything. Mamma has delightful phrases: 'My family is almost extinct.' Then your family may have been anything you like. Ours of course was magnificent. We did stay in a place once where there was a deer-park, and also private theatricals. I played in them; I was only fifteen years old, but I was very big and I thought I was in heaven. I'll go anywhere you like; you need n't be afraid; we've been in places! I've learned a great deal that way —

sitting beside mamma and watching people, their faces, their types, their movements. There's a great deal goes on in cafés: people come to them to talk things over, their private affairs, their complications; they have important meetings. Oh I've observed scenes between men and women — very quiet, terribly quiet, but awful, pathetic, tragic! Once I saw a woman do something that I'm going to do some day when I'm great — if I can get the situation. I'll tell you what it is sometime —I'll do it for you. Oh it *is* the book of life!"

So Miriam discoursed, familiarly, disconnectedly, as the pair went their way down the Rue de Constantinople; and she continued to abound in anecdote and remark after they were seated face to face at a little marble table in an establishment Peter had selected carefully and where he had caused her, at her request, to be accommodated with *sirop d'orgeat.* "I know what it will come to: Madame Carré will want to keep me." This was one of the felicities she presently threw off.

"To keep you?"

"For the French stage. She won't want to let you have me." She said things of that kind, astounding in self-complacency, the assumption of quick success. She was in earnest, evidently prepared to work, but her imagination flew over preliminaries and probations, took no account of the steps in the process, especially the first tiresome ones, the hard test of honesty. He had done nothing for her as yet, given no substantial pledge of interest; yet she was already talking as if his protection were assured and jealous. Certainly, however, she seemed to belong to him.very much indeed as she sat facing him at the Paris café in her youth, her beauty and her talkative confidence. This degree of possession was highly agreeable to him and he asked nothing more than to make it last and go further. The impulse to draw her out was irresistible, to encourage her to show herself all the way; for if he was really destined to take her career in hand he counted on some good equivalent — such for instance as that she should at least amuse him.

"It's very singular; I know nothing like it," he said — "your equal mastery of two languages."

"Say of half a dozen," Miriam smiled.

"Oh I don't believe in the others to the same degree. I don't imagine that, with all deference to your undeniable facility, you'd be judged fit to address a German or an Italian audience in their own tongue. But you might a French, perfectly, and they're the most particular of all; for their idiom's supersensitive and they're incapable of enduring the *baragouinage* of foreigners, to which we listen with such complacency. In fact your French is better than your English — it's more conventional; there are little queernesses and impurities in your English, as if you had lived abroad too much. Ah you must work that."

"I'll work it with *you*. I like the way you speak."

"You must speak beautifully; you must do something for the standard."

"For the standard?"

"Well, there isn't any after all." Peter had a drop. "It has gone to the dogs."

"Oh I'll bring it back. I know what you mean."

"No one knows, no one cares; the sense is gone — it is n't in the public," he continued, ventilating a grievance he was rarely able to forget, the vision of which now suddenly made a mission full of possible sanctity for his companion. "Purity of speech, on our stage, does n't exist. Every one speaks as he likes and audiences never notice; it's the last thing they think of. The place is given up to abominable dialects and individual tricks, any vulgarity flourishes, and on top of it all the Americans, with every conceivable crudity, come in to make confusion worse confounded. And when one laments it people stare; they don't know what one means."

"Do you mean the grand manner, certain pompous pronunciations, the style of the Kembles?"

"I mean any style that *is* a style, that's a system, a consistency, an art, that contributes a positive beauty to utterance. When I pay ten shillings to hear you speak I want you to know how, *que diable!* Say that to people and they're mostly lost in stupor; only a few, the very intelligent, exclaim: 'Then you want actors to be affected?'"

"And *do* you?" asked Miriam full of interest.

"My poor child, what else under the sun should they be? Is n't their whole art the affectation *par excellence?* The public won't stand that to-day, so one hears it said. If that be true it simply means that the theatre, as I care for it, that is as a personal art, is at an end."

"Never, never, never!" the girl cried in a voice that made a dozen people look round.

"I sometimes think it — that the personal art *is* at an end and that henceforth we shall have only the arts, capable no doubt of immense development in their way — indeed they've already reached it — of the stage-carpenter and the costumer. In London the drama is already smothered in scenery; the interpretation scrambles off as it can. To get the old personal impression, which used to be everything, you must go to the poor countries, and most of all to Italy."

"Oh I've had it; it's very personal!" said Miriam knowingly.

"You've seen the nudity of the stage, the poor painted tattered screen behind, and before that void the histrionic figure, doing everything it knows how, in complete possession. The personality is n't our English personality and it may not always carry us with it; but the direction's right, and it has the superiority that it's a human exhibition, not a mechanical one."

"I can act just like an Italian," Miriam eagerly proclaimed.

"I'd rather you acted like an Englishwoman if an Englishwoman would only act."

"Oh I'll show you!"

"But you're not English," said Peter sociably, his arms on the table.

"I beg your pardon. You should hear mamma about our 'race.'"

"You're a Jewess — I'm sure of that," he went on.

She jumped at this, as he was destined to see later she would ever jump at anything that might make her more interesting or striking; even at things that grotesquely contradicted or excluded each other. "That's always possible if one's clever. I'm very willing, because I want to be the English Rachel."

"Then you must leave Madame Carré as soon as you've got from her what she can give."

"Oh you need n't fear; you shan't lose me," the girl replied with charming gross fatuity. "My name's Jewish," she went on, "but it was that of my grandmother, my father's mother. She was a baroness in Germany. That is she was the daughter of a baron."

Peter accepted this statement with reservations, but he replied: "Put all that together and it makes you very sufficiently of Rachel's tribe."

"I don't care if I'm of her tribe artistically. I'm of the family of the artists — *je me fiche* of any other! I'm in the same style as that woman — I know it."

"You speak as if you had seen her," he said, amused at the way she talked of "that woman."

"Oh I know all about her — I know all about all the great actors. But that won't prevent me from speaking divine English."

"You must learn lots of verse; you must repeat it to me," Sherringham went on. "You must break yourself in till you can say anything. You must learn passages of Milton, passages of Wordsworth."

"Did *they* write plays?"

"Oh it is n't only a matter of plays! You can't speak a part properly till you can speak everything else, anything that comes up, especially in proportion as it's difficult. That gives you authority."

"Oh yes, I'm going in for authority. There's more

205

chance in English," the girl added in the next breath.
"There are not so many others — the terrible competition. There are so many here — not that I'm
afraid," she chattered on. "But we've got America
and they have n't. America's a great place."
"You talk like a theatrical agent. They're lucky
not to have it as we have it. Some of them do go, and
it ruins them."
"Why, it fills their pockets!" Miriam cried.
"Yes, but see what they pay. It's the death of
an actor to play to big populations that don't understand his language. It's nothing then but the *gros
moyens;* all his delicacy perishes. However, they'll
understand *you.*"
"Perhaps I shall be too affected," she said.
"You won't be more so than Garrick or Mrs.
Siddons or John Kemble or Edmund Kean. They
understood Edmund Kean. All reflexion is affectation, and all acting's reflexion."
"I don't know — mine's instinct," Miriam contended.
"My dear young lady, you talk of 'yours'; but
don't be offended if I tell you that yours does n't
exist. Some day it will — if the thing comes off. Madame Carré's does, because she has reflected. The
talent, the desire, the energy are an instinct; but by
the time these things become a performance they're
an instinct put in its place."
"Madame Carré's very philosophic. I shall never
be like her."
"Of course you won't — you'll be original. But
you'll have your own ideas."

"I dare say I shall have a good many of yours" —
and she smiled at him across the table.

They sat a moment looking at each other. "Don't
go in for coquetry," Peter then said. "It's a waste of
time."

"Well, that's civil!" the girl cried.

"Oh I don't mean for me, I mean for yourself.
I want you to be such good faith. I'm bound to
give you stiff advice. You don't strike me as flirta-
tious and that sort of thing, and it's much in your
favour."

"In my favour?"

"It does save time."

"Perhaps it saves too much. Don't you think the
artist ought to have passions?"

Peter had a pause; he thought an examination of
this issue premature. "Flirtations are not passions,"
he replied. "No, you're simple — at least I suspect
you are; for of course with a woman one would be
clever to know."

She asked why he pronounced her simple, but he
judged it best and more consonant with fair play to
defer even a treatment of this branch of the question;
so that to change the subject he said: "Be sure you
don't betray me to your friend Mr. Nash."

"Betray you? Do you mean about your recommending affectation?"

"Dear me, no; he recommends it himself. That
is he practises it, and on a scale!"

"But he makes one hate it."

"He proves what I mean," said Sherringham:
"that the great comedian's the one who raises it to

a science. If we paid ten shillings to listen to Mr. Nash we should think him very fine. But we want to know what it 's supposed to be."

"It 's too odious, the way he talks about *us!*" Miriam cried assentingly.

"About 'us'?"

"Us poor actors."

"It 's the competition he dislikes," Peter laughed.

"However, he 's very good-natured; he lent mamma thirty pounds," the girl added honestly. Our young man, at this information, was not able to repress a certain small twinge noted by his companion and of which she appeared to mistake the meaning. "Of course he 'll get it back," she went on while he looked at her in silence a little. Fortune had not supplied him profusely with money, but his emotion was caused by no foresight of his probably having also to put his hand in his pocket for Mrs. Rooth. It was simply the instinctive recoil of a fastidious nature from the idea of familiar intimacy with people who lived from hand to mouth, together with a sense that this intimacy would have to be defined if it was to go much further. He would wish to know what it was supposed to be, like Nash's histrionics. Miriam after a moment mistook his thought still more completely, and in doing so flashed a portent of the way it was in her to strike from time to time a note exasperatingly, almost consciously vulgar, which one would hate for the reason, along with others, that by that time one would be in love with her. "Well then, he won't — if you don't believe it!" she easily laughed. He was saying to himself that the only possible form was that

208

they should borrow only from him. "You're a funny man. I make you blush," she persisted.

"I must reply with the *tu quoque*, though I've not that effect on you."

"I don't understand," said the girl.

"You're an extraordinary young lady."

"You mean I'm horrid. Well, I dare say I am. But I'm better when you know me."

He made no direct rejoinder to this, but after a moment went on: "Your mother must repay that money. I'll give it her."

"You had better give it *him!*" cried Miriam. "If once mamma has it —!" She interrupted herself and with another and a softer tone, one of her professional transitions, remarked: "I suppose you've never known any one that was poor."

"I'm poor myself. That is I'm very far from rich. But why receive favours —?" And here he in turn checked himself with the sense that he was indeed taking a great deal on his back if he pretended already — he had not seen the pair three times — to regulate their intercourse with the rest of the world. But the girl instantly carried out his thought and more than his thought.

"Favours from Mr. Nash? Oh he doesn't count!"

The way she dropped these words — they would have been admirable on the stage — made him reply with prompt ease: "What I meant just now was that you're not to tell him, after all my swagger, that I consider that you and I are really required to save our theatre."

"Oh if we can save it he shall know it!" She added that she must positively get home; her mother would be in a state: she had really scarce ever been out alone. He might n't think it, but so it was. Her mother's ideas, those awfully proper ones, were not all talk. She *did* keep her! Sherringham accepted this — he had an adequate and indeed an analytic vision of Mrs. Rooth's conservatism; but he observed at the same time that his companion made no motion to rise. He made none either; he only said —

"We're very frivolous, the way we chatter. What you want to do to get your foot in the stirrup is supremely difficult. There's everything to overcome. You've neither an engagement nor the prospect of an engagement."

"Oh you'll get me one!" Her manner presented this as so certain that it was n't worth dilating on; so instead of dilating she enquired abruptly a second time: "Why do you think I'm so simple?"

"I don't then. Did n't I tell you just now that you were extraordinary? That's the term moreover that you applied to yourself when you came to see me —when you said a girl had to be a kind of monster to wish to go on the stage. It remains the right term and your simplicity does n't mitigate it. What's rare in you is that you have — as I suspect at least— no nature of your own." Miriam listened to this as if preparing to argue with it or not, only as it should strike her as a sufficiently brave picture; but as yet, naturally, she failed to understand. "You're always at concert pitch or on your horse; there are no intervals. It's the absence of intervals, of a *fond* or background, that I don't comprehend. You're an embroidery without a canvas."

"Yes — perhaps," the girl replied, her head on one side as if she were looking at the pattern of this rarity. "But I'm very honest."

"You can't be everything, both a consummate actress and a flower of the field. You've got to choose."

She looked at him a moment. "I'm glad you think I'm so wonderful."

"Your feigning may be honest in the sense that your only feeling *is* your feigned one," Peter pursued. "That's what I mean by the absence of a ground or of intervals. It's a kind of thing that's a labyrinth!"

"I know what I am," she said sententiously.

But her companion continued, following his own train. "Were you really so frightened the first day you went to Madame Carré's?"

She stared, then with a flush threw back her head. "Do you think I was pretending?"

"I think you always are. However, your vanity — if you had any! — would be natural."

"I've plenty of that. I'm not a bit ashamed to own it."

"You'd be capable of trying to 'do' the human peacock. But excuse the audacity and the crudity of my speculations — it only proves my interest. What is it that you know you are?"

"Why, an artist. Isn't that a canvas?"

"Yes, an intellectual, but not a moral."

"Ah it's everything! And I'm a good girl too — won't that do?"

"It remains to be seen," Sherringham laughed. "A creature who's absolutely *all* an artist — I'm curious to see that."

"Surely it has been seen — in lots of painters, lots of musicians."

"Yes, but those arts are not personal like yours. I mean not so much so. There's something left for — what shall I call it? — for character."

She stared again with her tragic light. "And do you think I have n't a character?" As he hesitated she pushed back her chair, rising rapidly.

He looked up at her an instant — she seemed so "plastic"; and then rising too answered: "Delightful being, you've a hundred!"

THE summer arrived and the dense air of the Paris theatres became in fact a still more complicated mixture; yet the occasions were not few on which Sherringham, having placed a box near the stage (most often a stuffy dusky *baignoire*) at the disposal of Mrs. Rooth and her daughter, found time just to look in, as he said, to spend a part of the evening with them and point the moral of the performance. The pieces, the successes of the winter, had entered the automatic phase: they went on by the force of the impetus acquired, deriving little fresh life from the interpretation, and in ordinary conditions their strong points, as rendered by the actors, would have been as wearisome to this student as an importunate repetition of a good story. But it was not long before he became aware that the conditions could n't be taken for ordinary. There was a new infusion in his consciousness — an element in his life which altered the relations of things. He was not easy till he had found the right name for it — a name the more satisfactory that it was simple, comprehensive and plausible. A new "distraction," in the French sense, was what he flattered himself he had discovered; he could recognise that as freely as possible without being obliged to classify the agreeable resource as a new entanglement. He was neither too much nor too little diverted; he had all his usual attention to give to his

213

work: he had only an employment for his odd hours which, without being imperative, had over various others the advantage of a certain continuity.

And yet, I hasten to add, he was not so well pleased with it but that among his friends he maintained for the present a rich reserve about it. He had no irresistible impulse to describe generally how he had disinterred a strange handsome girl whom he was bringing up for the theatre. She had been seen by several of his associates at his rooms, but was not soon to be seen there again. His reserve might by the ill-natured have been termed dissimulation, inasmuch as when asked by the ladies of the embassy what had become of the young person who had amused them that day so cleverly he gave it out that her whereabouts was uncertain and her destiny probably obscure; he let it be supposed in a word that his benevolence had scarcely survived an accidental, a charitable occasion. As he went about his customary business, and perhaps even put a little more conscience into the transaction of it, there was nothing to suggest to others that he was engaged in a private speculation of an absorbing kind. It was perhaps his weakness that he carried the apprehension of ridicule too far; but his excuse may have dwelt in his holding it unpardonable for a man publicly enrolled in the service of his country to be markedly ridiculous. It was of course not out of all order that such functionaries, their private situation permitting, should enjoy a personal acquaintance with stars of the dramatic, the lyric or even the choregraphic stage: high diplomatists had indeed not rarely, and not invisibly,

cultivated this privilege without its proving the sepul-
chre of their reputation. That a gentleman who was
not a fool should consent a little to become one for
the sake of a celebrated actress or singer — *cela
s'était vu*, though it was not perhaps to be recommended. It was not a tendency that was encouraged
at headquarters, where even the most rising young
men were not incited to believe they could never fall.
Still, it might pass if kept in its place; and there were
ancient worthies yet in the profession — though not
those whom the tradition had helped to go furthest
— who held that something of the sort was a graceful ornament of the diplomatic character. Sherringham was aware he was very "rising"; but Miriam
Rooth was not yet a celebrated actress. She was only
a young artist in conscientious process of formation
and encumbered with a mother still more conscientious than herself. She was a *jeune Anglaise* — a
"lady" withal — very earnest about artistic, about
remunerative problems. He had accepted the office
of a formative influence; and that was precisely what
might provoke derision. He was a ministering angel
— his patience and good nature really entitled him
to the epithet and his rewards would doubtless some
day define themselves; but meanwhile other promo-
tions were in precarious prospect, for the failure of
which these would not, even in their abundance, be
a compensation. He kept an unembarrassed eye on
Downing Street, and while it may frankly be said
for him that he was neither a pedant nor a prig he
remembered that the last impression he ought to wish
to produce there was that of a futile æstheticism.

215

He felt the case sufficiently important, however, when he sat behind Miriam at the play and looked over her shoulder at the stage; her observation being so keen and her comments so unexpected in their vivacity that his curiosity was refreshed and his attention stretched beyond its wont. If the exhibition before the footlights had now lost much of its annual brilliancy the fashion in which she followed it was perhaps exhibition enough. The attendance of the little party was moreover in most cases at the Théâtre Français; and it has been sufficiently indicated that our friend, though the child of a sceptical age and the votary of a cynical science, was still candid enough to take the serious, the religious view of that establishment — the view of M. Sarcey and of the unregenerate provincial mind. "In the trade I follow we see things too much in the hard light of reason, of calculation," he once remarked to his young charge; "but it's good for the mind to keep up a superstition or two; it leaves a margin — like having a second horse to your brougham for night-work. The arts, the amusements, the æsthetic part of life, are night-work, if I may say so without suggesting that they're illicit. At any rate you want your second horse — your superstition that stays at home when the sun's high — to go your rounds with. The Français is my second horse."

Miriam's appetite for this interest showed him vividly enough how rarely in the past it had been within her reach; and she pleased him at first by liking everything, seeing almost no differences and taking her deep draught undiluted. She leaned on the edge of the box with bright voracity; tasting to the core, yet relishing the surface, watching each movement of each actor, attending to the way each thing was said or done as if it were the most important thing, and emitting from time to time applausive or restrictive sounds. It was a charming show of the critical spirit in ecstasy. Sherringham had his wonder about it, as a part of the attraction exerted by this young lady was that she caused him to have his wonder about everything she did. Was it in fact a conscious show, a line taken for effect, so that at the Comédie her own display should be the most successful of all ? That question danced attendance on the liberal intercourse of these young people and fortunately as yet did little to embitter Sherringham's share of it. His general sense that she was personating had its especial moments of suspense and perplexity, and added variety and even occasionally a degree of excitement to their commerce. At the theatre, for the most part, she was really flushed with eagerness; and with the spectators who turned an admiring eye into the dim compartment of which she pervaded the front she might have passed for a romantic or at least an insatiable young woman from the country.

Mrs. Rooth took a more general view, but attended immensely to the story, in respect to which she manifested a patient good faith which had its surprises and its comicalities for her daughter's patron. She found no play too tedious, no *entr'acte* too long, no *baignoire* too hot, no tissue of incidents too complicated, no situation too unnatural and no sentiments too sublime. She gave him the measure of her power to sit and sit — an accomplishment to which she owed in the struggle for existence such superiority as she might be said to have achieved. She could out-sit everybody and everything; looking as if she had acquired the practice in repeated years of small frugality combined with large leisure — periods when she had nothing but hours and days and years to spend and had learned to calculate in any situation how long she could stay. "Staying" was so often a saving — a saving of candles, of fire and even (as it sometimes implied a scheme for stray refection) of food. Peter saw soon enough how bravely her shreds and patches of gentility and equanimity hung together, with the aid of whatever casual pins and other makeshifts, and if he had been addicted to studying the human mixture in its different combinations would have found in her an interesting compendium of some of the infatuations that survive a hard discipline. He made indeed without difficulty the reflexion that her life might have taught her something of the real, at the same time that he could scarce help thinking it clever of her to have so persistently declined the lesson. She appeared to have put it by with a deprecating ladylike smile — a plea of being too soft and bland for experience.

She took the refined sentimental tender view of the universe, beginning with her own history and feelings. She believed in everything high and pure, disinterested and orthodox, and even at the Hôtel de la Garonne was unconscious of the shabby or the ugly side of the world. She never despaired: otherwise what would have been the use of being a Neville-

Nugent ? Only not to have been one — that would have been discouraging. She delighted in novels, poems, perversions, misrepresentations and evasions, and had a capacity for smooth superfluous falsification which made our young man think her sometimes an amusing and sometimes a tedious inventor. But she was n't dangerous even if you believed her; she was n't even a warning if you did n't. It was harsh to call her a hypocrite, since you never could have resolved her back into her character, there being no reverse at all to her blazonry. She built in the air and was not less amiable than she pretended, only that was a pretension too. She moved altogether in a world of elegant fable and fancy, and Sherringham had to live there with her for Miriam's sake, live there in sociable vulgar assent and despite his feeling it rather a low neighbourhood. He was at a loss how to take what she said — she talked sweetly and discursively of so many things — till he simply noted that he could only take it always for untrue. When Miriam laughed at her he was rather disagreeably affected: "dear mamma's fine stories" was a sufficiently cynical reference to the immemorial infirmity of a parent. But when the girl backed her up, as he phrased it to himself, he liked that even less.

Mrs. Rooth was very fond of a moral and had never lost her taste for edification. She delighted in a beautiful character and was gratified to find so many more than she had supposed represented in the contemporary French drama. She never failed to direct Miriam's attention to them and to remind her that there is nothing in life so grand as a sublime act, above all when sublimely explained. Peter made much of the difference between the mother and the daughter, thinking it singularly marked — the way one took everything for the sense, or behaved as if she did, caring only for the plot and the romance, the triumph or defeat of virtue and the moral comfort of it all, and the way the other was alive but to the manner and the art of it, the intensity of truth to appearances. Mrs. Rooth abounded in impressive evocations, and yet he saw no link between her facile genius and that of which Miriam gave symptoms. The poor lady never could have been accused of successful deceit, whereas the triumph of fraud was exactly what her clever child achieved. She made even the true seem fictive, while Miriam's effort was to make the fictive true. Sherringham thought it an odd unpromising stock (that of the Neville-Nugents) for a dramatic talent to have sprung from, till he reflected that the evolution was after all natural: the figurative impulse in the mother had become conscious, and therefore higher, through finding an aim, which was beauty, in the daughter. Likely enough the Hebraic Mr. Rooth, with his love of old pots and Christian altar-cloths, had supplied in the girl's composition the æsthetic element, the sense of colour and form. In their visits to the theatre there was nothing Mrs. Rooth more insisted on than the unprofitableness of deceit, as shown by the most distinguished authors — the folly and degradation, the corrosive effect on the spirit, of tortuous ways. Their companion soon gave up the futile task of piecing together her incongruous references to her early life and her family in England. He renounced even the doctrine that there was a residuum of truth in her claim of great relationships, since, existent or not, he cared equally little for her ramifications. The principle of this indifference was at bottom a certain desire to disconnect and isolate Miriam; for it was disagreeable not to be independent in dealing with her, and he could be fully so only if she herself were.

The early weeks of that summer — they went on indeed into August — were destined to establish themselves in his memory as a season of pleasant things. The ambassador went away and Peter had to wait for his own holiday, which he did during the hot days contentedly enough — waited in spacious halls and a vast dim bird-haunted garden. The official world and most other worlds withdrew from Paris, and the Place de la Concorde, a larger, whiter desert than ever, became by a reversal of custom explorable with safety. The Champs Elysées were dusty and rural, with little creaking booths and exhibitions that made a noise like grasshoppers; the Arc de Triomphe threw its cool thick shadow for a mile; the Palais de l'Industrie glittered in the light of the long days; the cabmen, in their red waistcoats, dozed inside their boxes, while Sherringham permitted himself a "pot" hat and rarely met a friend. Thus was Miriam as islanded as the chained Andromeda, and thus was it possible to deal with her, even Perseus-like, in deep detachment. The theatres on the boulevard closed for the most part, but the great temple of the Rue de Richelieu, with an æsthetic responsibility, continued imperturbably to dispense examples of style. Madame Carré was going to Vichy, but had not yet taken flight, which was a great advantage for Miriam, who could now solicit her attention with the consciousness that she had no engagements *en ville*.

"I make her listen to me — I make her tell me," said the ardent girl, who was always climbing the slope of the Rue de Constantinople on the shady side, where of July mornings a smell of violets came from the moist flower-stands of fat white-capped *bouquetières* in the angles of doorways. Miriam liked the Paris of the summer mornings, the clever freshness of all the little trades and the open-air life, the cries, the talk from door to door, which reminded her of the south, where, in the multiplicity of her habitations, she had lived; and most of all, the great amusement, or nearly, of her walk, the enviable baskets of the laundress piled up with frilled and fluted whiteness — the certain luxury, she felt while she passed with quick prevision, of her own dawn of glory. The greatest amusement perhaps was to recognise the pretty sentiment of earliness, the particular congruity with the hour, in the studied selected dress of the little tripping women who were taking the day, for important advantages, while it was tender. At any rate she mostly brought with her from her passage through the town good humour enough — with the penny bunch of violets she always stuck in the front of her dress — for whatever awaited her at Madame Carré's. She declared to her friend that her dear mistress was terribly severe, giving her the most difficult, the most exhausting exercises, showing a kind of rage for breaking her in.

"So much the better," Sherringham duly answered; but he asked no questions and was glad to let the preceptress and the pupil fight it out together. He wanted for the moment to know as little as possible about their ways together: he had been over-dosed with that knowledge while attending at their second interview. He would send Madame Carré her money — she was really most obliging — and in the mean time was certain Miriam could take care of herself. Sometimes he remarked to her that she need n't always talk "shop" to him: there were times when he was mortally tired of shop — of hers. Moreover he frankly admitted that he was tired of his own, so that the restriction was not brutal. When she replied, staring, "Why, I thought you considered it as such a beautiful interesting art!" he had no rejoinder more philosophic than "Well, I do; but there are moments when I'm quite sick of it all the same." At other times he put it: "Oh yes, the results, the finished thing, the dish perfectly seasoned and served: not the mess of preparation — at least not always — not the experiments that spoil the material."

"I supposed you to feel just these questions of study, of the artistic education, as you've called it to me, so fascinating," the girl persisted. She was sometimes so flatly lucid.

"Well, after all, I'm not an actor myself," he could but impatiently sigh.

"You might be one if you were serious," she would imperturbably say. To this her friend replied that Mr. Gabriel Nash ought to hear this; which made her promise with a certain grimness that she would settle *him* and his theories some day. Not to seem too inconsistent — for it was cruel to bewilder her when he had taken her up to enlighten — Peter repeated over that for a man like himself the interest of the whole thing depended on its being considered in a large liberal way and with an intelligence that lifted it out of the question of the little tricks of the trade, gave it beauty and elevation. But she hereupon let him know that Madame Carré held there were no *little* tricks, that everything had its importance as a means to a great end, and that if you were not willing to try to *approfondir* the reason why, in a given situation, you should scratch your nose with your left hand rather than with your right, you were not worthy to tread any stage that respected itself.

"That's very well, but if I must go into details read me a little Shelley," groaned the young man in the spirit of a high *raffiné*.

"You're worse than Madame Carré; you don't know what to invent; between you you'll kill me!" the girl declared. "I think there's a secret league between you to spoil my voice, or at least to weaken my *souffle*, before I get it. But *à la guerre comme à la guerre!* How can I read Shelley, however, when I don't understand him?"

"That's just what I want to make you do. It's a part of your general training. You may do without that of course — without culture and taste and perception; but in that case you'll be nothing but a vulgar *cabotine*, and nothing will be of any consequence." He had a theory that the great lyric poets — he induced her to read, and recite as well, long passages of Wordsworth and Swinburne — would teach her many of the secrets of the large utterance, the mysteries of rhythm, the communicableness of style, the latent music of the language and the art of "composing" copious speeches and of retaining her stores of free breath. He held in perfect sincerity that there was a general sense of things, things of the mind, which would be of the highest importance to her and to which it was by good fortune just in his power to contribute. She would do better in proportion as she had more knowledge — even knowledge that might superficially show but a remote connexion with her business. The actor's talent was essentially a gift, a thing by itself, implanted, instinctive, accidental, equally unconnected with intellect and with virtue — Sherringham was completely of that opinion; but it struck him as no *bêtise* to believe at the same time that intellect — leaving virtue for the moment out of the question — might be brought into fruitful relation with it. It would be a bigger thing if a better mind were projected upon it — projected without sacrificing the mind. So he lent his young friend books she never read — she was on almost irreconcileable terms with the printed page save for spouting it — and in the long summer days, when he had leisure, took her to the Louvre to admire the great works of painting and sculpture. Here, as on all occasions, he was struck with the queer jumble of her taste, her mixture of intelligence and puerility. He saw she never read what he gave her, though she sometimes would shamelessly have liked him to suppose so; but in the presence of famous pictures and statues she had remarkable flashes of perception. She felt these things, she liked them, though it was always because she had an idea she could use them. The belief was often presumptuous, but it showed what an eye she had to her business. "I could look just like that if I tried." "That's the dress I mean to wear when I do Portia." Such were the observations apt to drop from her under the suggestion of antique marbles or when she stood before a Titian or a Bronzino.

When she uttered them, and many others besides, the effect was sometimes irritating to her adviser, who had to bethink himself a little that she was no more egotistical than the histrionic conscience required. He wondered if there were necessarily something vulgar in the histrionic conscience — something condemned only to feel the tricky personal question. Was n't it better to be perfectly stupid than to have only one eye open and wear for ever in the great face of the world the expression of a knowing wink? At the theatre, on the numerous July evenings when the Comédie Française exhibited the repertory by the aid of exponents determined the more sparse and provincial audience should have a taste of the tradition, her appreciation was tremendously technical and showed it was not for nothing she was now in and out of Madame Carré's innermost counsels. But there were moments when even her very acuteness seemed to him to drag the matter down, to see it in a small and superficial sense. What he flattered himself he was trying to do for her — and through her for the stage of his time, since she was the instrument, and incon-

testably a fine one, that had come to his hand —
was precisely to lift it up, make it rare, keep it in the
region of distinction and breadth. However, she was
doubtless right and he was wrong, he eventually reasoned: you could afford to be vague only if you had n't
a responsibility. He had fine ideas, but she was to
act them out, that is to apply them, and not he; and
application was of necessity a vulgarisation, a smaller
thing than theory. If she should some day put forth
the great art it was n't purely fanciful to forecast for
her, the matter would doubtless be by that fact
sufficiently transfigured and it would n't signify that
some of the onward steps should have been lame.

This was clear to him on several occasions when
she recited or motioned or even merely looked something for him better than usual; then she quite carried
him away, making him wish to ask no more questions,
but only let her disembroil herself in her own strong
fashion. In these hours she gave him forcibly if fitfully that impression of beauty which was to be her
justification. It was too soon for any general estimate
of her progress; Madame Carré had at last given her
a fine understanding as well as a sore personal, an
almost physical, sense of how bad she was. She had
therefore begun on a new basis, had returned to the
alphabet and the drill. It was a phase of awkwardness,
the splashing of a young swimmer, but buoyancy
would certainly come out of it. For the present there
was mainly no great alteration of the fact that when
she did things according to her own idea they were
not, as yet and seriously judged, worth the devil, as
Madame Carré said, and when she did them accord-

ing to that of her instructress were too apt to be a gross parody of that lady's intention. None the less she gave glimpses, and her glimpses made him feel not only that she was not a fool — this was small relief — but that he himself was not.

He made her stick to her English and read Shakespeare aloud to him. Mrs. Rooth had recognised the importance of apartments in which they should be able to receive so beneficent a visitor, and was now mistress of a small salon with a balcony and a rickety flower-stand — to say nothing of a view of many roofs and chimneys — a very uneven waxed floor, an empire clock, an *armoire à glace*, highly convenient for Miriam's posturings, and several cupboard doors covered over, allowing for treacherous gaps, with the faded magenta paper of the wall. The thing had been easily done, for Sherringham had said: "Oh we must have a sitting-room for our studies, you know, and I'll settle it with the landlady." Mrs. Rooth had liked his "we" — indeed she liked everything about him — and he saw in this way that she heaved with no violence under pecuniary obligations so long as they were distinctly understood to be temporary. That he should have his money back with interest as soon as Miriam was launched was a comfort so deeply implied that it only added to intimacy. The window stood open on the little balcony, and when the sun had left it Peter and Miriam could linger there, leaning on the rail and talking above the great hum of Paris, with nothing but the neighbouring tiles and tall tubes to take account of. Mrs. Rooth, in limp garments much ungirdled, was on the sofa with a novel, making good her frequent assertion that she could put up with any life that would yield her these two conveniences. There were romantic works Peter had never read and as to which he had vaguely wondered to what class they were addressed — the earlier productions of M. Eugène Sue, the once-fashionable compositions of Madame Sophie Gay — with which Mrs. Rooth was familiar and which she was ready to enjoy once more if she could get nothing fresher. She had always a greasy volume tucked under her while her nose was bent upon the pages in hand. She scarcely looked up even when Miriam lifted her voice to show their benefactor what she could do. These tragic or pathetic notes all went out of the window and mingled with the undecipherable concert of Paris, so that no neighbour was disturbed by them. The girl shrieked and wailed when the occasion required it, and Mrs. Rooth only turned her page, showing in this way a great æsthetic as well as a great personal trust.

She rather annoyed their visitor by the serenity of her confidence — for a reason he fully understood only later — save when Miriam caught an effect or a tone so well that she made him in the pleasure of it forget her parent's contiguity. He continued to object to the girl's English, with its foreign patches that might pass in prose but were offensive in the recitation of verse, and he wanted to know why she could n't speak like her mother. He had justly to acknowledge the charm of Mrs. Rooth's voice and tone, which gave a richness even to the foolish things she said. They were of an excellent insular tradition, full both of natural and of cultivated sweetness, and they puzzled him when other indications seemed to betray her — to refer her to more common air. They were like the reverberation of some far-off tutored circle.

The connexion between the development of Miriam's genius and the necessity of an occasional excursion to the country — the charming country that lies in so many directions beyond the Parisian *banlieue* — would not have been immediately apparent to a superficial observer; but a day, and then another, at Versailles, a day at Fontainebleau and a trip, particularly harmonious and happy, to Rambouillet, took their places in our young man's plan as a part of the indirect but contributive culture, an agency in the formation of taste. Intimations of the grand manner for instance would proceed in abundance from the symmetrical palace and gardens of Louis XIV. Peter "adored" Versailles and wandered there more than once with the ladies of the Hôtel de la Garonne. They chose quiet hours, when the fountains were dry; and Mrs. Rooth took an armful of novels and sat on a bench in the park, flanked by clipped hedges and old statues, while her young companions strolled away, walked to the Trianon, explored the long straight vistas of the woods. Rambouillet was vague and vivid and sweet; they felt that they found a hundred wise voices there; and indeed there was an old white château which contained nothing but ghostly sounds. They found at any rate a long luncheon, and in the landscape the very spirit of silvery summer and of the French pictorial brush.

I have said that in these days Sherringham wondered about many things, and by the time his leave
of absence came this practice had produced a particular speculation. He was surprised that he should n't
be in love with Miriam Rooth and considered at
moments of leisure the causes of his exemption. He
had felt from the first that she was a "nature," and
each time she met his eyes it seemed to come to
him straighter that her beauty was rare. You had
to get the good view of her face, but when you did so
it was a splendid mobile mask. And the wearer of
this high ornament had frankness and courage and
variety — no end of the unusual and the unexpected.
She had qualities that seldom went together — im-
pulses and shynesses, audacities and lapses, something coarse, popular and strong all intermingled
with disdains and languors and nerves. And then
above all she was *there*, was accessible, almost belonged to him. He reflected ingeniously that he owed
his escape to a peculiar cause — to the fact that they
had together a positive outside object. Objective,
as it were, was all their communion; not personal
and selfish, but a matter of art and business and discussion. Discussion had saved him and would save
him further, for they would always have something
to quarrel about. Sherringham, who was not a diplomatist for nothing, who had his reasons for steering
straight and wished neither to deprive the British
public of a rising star nor to exchange his actual
situation for that of a yoked *impresario*, blessed
the beneficence, the salubrity, the pure exorcism of
art. At the same time, rather inconsistently and feel-

231

ing that he had a completer vision than before of that oddest of animals the artist who happens to have been born a woman, he felt warned against a serious connexion — he made a great point of the "serious" — with so slippery and ticklish a creature. The two ladies had only to stay in Paris, save their candle-ends and, as Madame Carré had enjoined, practise their scales: there were apparently no autumn visits to English country-houses in prospect for Mrs. Rooth. Peter parted with them on the understanding that in London he would look as thoroughly as possible into the question of an engagement. The day before he began his holiday he went to see Madame Carré, who said to him "Vous devriez bien nous la laisser."

"She *has* something then — ?"

"She has most things. She'll go far. It's the first time in my life of my beginning with a mistake. But don't tell her so. I don't flatter her. She'll be too puffed up."

"Is she very conceited?" Sherringham asked.

"Mauvais sujet!" said Madame Carré.

It was on the journey to London that he indulged in some of those questionings of his state that I have mentioned; but I must add that by the time he reached Charing Cross — he smoked a cigar deferred till after the Channel in a compartment by himself — it had suddenly come over him that they were futile. Now that he had left the girl a subversive unpremeditated heart-beat told him — it made him hold his breath a minute in the carriage — that he had after all not escaped. He *was* in love with her: he had been in love with her from the first hour.

232

BOOK THIRD

XIII

THE drive from Harsh to the Place, as it was called thereabouts, could be achieved by swift horses in less than ten minutes; and if Mrs. Dallow's ponies were capital trotters the general high pitch of the occasion made it all congruous they should show their speed. The occasion was the polling-day an hour after the battle. The ponies had kept pace with other driven forces for the week before, passing and repassing the neat windows of the flat little town — Mrs. Dallow had the complacent belief that there was none in the kingdom in which the flower-stands looked more respectable between the stiff muslin curtains — with their mistress behind them on her all but silver wheels. Very often she was accompanied by the Liberal candidate, but even when she was not the equipage seemed scarce less to represent his easy friendly confidence. It moved in a radiance of ribbons and hand-bills and hand-shakes and smiles; of quickened commerce and sudden intimacy; of sympathy which assumed without presuming and gratitude which promised without soliciting. But under Julia's guidance the ponies pattered now, with no indication of a loss of freshness, along the firm wide avenue which wound and curved, to make up in large effect for not undulating, from the gates opening straight on the town to the Palladian mansion, high, square, grey and clean, which stood among terraces and fountains

235

in the centre of the park. A generous steed had been
sacrificed to bring the good news from Ghent to Aix,
but no such extravagance was after all necessary for
communicating with Lady Agnes.

She had remained at the house, not going to the
Wheatsheaf, the Liberal inn, with the others; prefer-
ring to await in privacy and indeed in solitude the
momentous result of the poll. She had come down
to Harsh with the two girls in the course of the pro-
ceedings. Julia had n't thought they would do much
good, but she was expansive and indulgent now
and had generously asked them. Lady Agnes had not
a nice canvassing manner, effective as she might have
been in the character of the high benignant affable
mother — looking sweet participation but not interfering — of the young and handsome, the shining,
convincing, wonderfully clever and certainly irresistible aspirant. Grace Dormer had zeal without
art, and Lady Agnes, who during her husband's
lifetime had seen their affairs follow the satisfactory
principle of a tendency to defer to supreme merit,
had never really learned the lesson that voting goes
by favour. However, she could pray God if she
could n't make love to the cheesemonger, and Nick
felt she had stayed at home to pray for him. I must
add that Julia Dallow was too happy now, flicking
her whip in the bright summer air, to say anything
so ungracious even to herself as that her companion
had been returned in spite of his nearest female relatives. Besides, Biddy *had* been a rosy help: she had
looked persuasively pretty, in white and blue, on
platforms and in recurrent carriages, out of which

she had tossed, blushing and making people feel they would remember her eyes, several words that were telling for their very simplicity.

Mrs. Dallow was really too glad for any definite reflexion, even for personal exultation, the vanity of recognising her own large share of the work. Nick was in and was now beside her, tired, silent, vague, beflowered and beribboned, and he had been splendid from beginning to end, beautifully good-humoured and at the same time beautifully clever — still cleverer than she had supposed he could be. The sense of her having quickened his cleverness and been repaid by it or by his gratitude — it came to the same thing — in a way she appreciated was not assertive and jealous: it was lost for the present in the general happy break of the long tension. So nothing passed between them in their progress to the house; there was no sound in the park but the pleasant rustle of summer — it seemed an applausive murmur — and the swift roll of the vehicle.

Lady Agnes already knew, for as soon as the result was declared Nick had dispatched a mounted man to her, carrying the figures on a scrawled card. He himself had been far from getting away at once, having to respond to the hubbub of acclamation, to speak yet again, to thank his electors individually and collectively, to chaff the Tories without cheap elation, to be carried hither and yon, and above all to pretend that the interest of the business was now greater for him than ever. If he had said never a word after putting himself in Julia's hands to go home it was partly perhaps because the consciousness had begun

237

to glimmer within him, on the contrary, of some sudden shrinkage of that interest. He wanted to see his mother because he knew she wanted to fold him close in her arms. They had been open there for this purpose the last half-hour, and her expectancy, now no longer an ache of suspense, was the reason of Julia's round pace. Yet this very impatience in her somehow made Nick wince a little. Meeting his mother was like being elected over again.

The others had not yet come back, and Lady Agnes was alone in the large bright drawing-room. When Nick went in with Julia he saw her at the further end; she had evidently been walking up and down the whole length of it, and her tall upright black figure seemed in possession of the fair vastness after the manner of an exclamation-point at the bottom of a blank page. The room, rich and simple, was a place of perfection as well as of splendour in delicate tints, with precious specimens of French furniture of the last century ranged against walls of pale brocade, and here and there a small almost priceless picture. George Dallow had made it, caring for these things and liking to talk about them — scarce ever about anything else; so that it appeared to represent him still, what was best in his kindly, limited nature, his friendly competent tiresome insistence on harmony — on identity of "period." Nick could hear him yet, and could see him, too fat and with a congenital thickness in his speech, lounging there in loose clothes with his eternal cigarette. "Now my dear fellow, *that*'s what I call form: I don't know what you call it" — that was the way he used to begin.

All round were flowers in rare vases, but it looked a place of which the beauty would have smelt sweet even without them.

Lady Agnes had taken a white rose from one of the clusters and was holding it to her face, which was turned to the door as Nick crossed the threshold. The expression of her figure instantly told him — he saw the creased card he had sent her lying on one of the beautiful bare tables — how she had been sailing up and down in a majesty of satisfaction. The inflation of her long plain dress and the brightened dimness of her proud face were still in the air. In a moment he had kissed her and was being kissed, not in quick repetition, but in tender prolongation, with which the perfume of the white rose was mixed. But there was something else too — her sweet smothered words in his ear: "Oh my boy, my boy — oh your father, your father!" Neither the sense of pleasure nor that of pain, with Lady Agnes — as indeed with most of the persons with whom this history is concerned — was a liberation of chatter; so that for a minute all she said again was "I think of Sir Nicholas and wish he were here;" addressing the words to Julia, who had wandered forward without looking at the mother and son.

"Poor Sir Nicholas!" said Mrs. Dallow vaguely.

"Did you make another speech?" Lady Agnes asked.

"I don't know. Did I?" Nick appealed.

"I don't know!"— and Julia spoke with her back turned, doing something to her hat before the glass.

"Oh of course the confusion, the bewilderment!"

said Lady Agnes in a tone rich in political reminiscence.

"It was really immense fun," Mrs. Dallow went
so far as to drop.

"Dearest Julia!" Lady Agnes deeply breathed.
Then she added: "It was you who made it sure."

"There are a lot of people coming to dinner," said
Julia.

"Perhaps you'll have to speak again," Lady Agnes
smiled at her son.

"Thank you; I like the way you talk about it!"
cried Nick. "I'm like Iago: 'from this time forth
I never will speak word!'"

"Don't say that, Nick," said his mother gravely.

"Don't be afraid — he'll jabber like a magpie!"
And Julia went out of the room.

Nick had flung himself on a sofa with an air of
weariness, though not of completely extinct cheer;
and Lady Agnes stood fingering her rose and looking
down at him. His eyes kept away from her; they
seemed fixed on something she could n't see. "I hope
you've thanked Julia handsomely," she presently
remarked.

"Why of course, mother."

"She has done as much as if you had n't been
sure."

"I was n't in the least sure — and she has done
everything."

"She has been too good — but we've done something. I hope you don't leave out your father," Lady
Agnes amplified as Nick's glance appeared for a moment to question her "we."

"Never, never!" Nick uttered these words perhaps a little mechanically, but the next minute he added as if suddenly moved to think what he could say that would give his mother most pleasure: "Of course his name has worked for me. Gone as he is he's still a living force." He felt a good deal of a hypocrite, but one did n't win such a seat every day in the year. Probably indeed he should never win another.

"He hears you, he watches you, he rejoices in you," Lady Agnes opined.

This idea was oppressive to Nick — that of the rejoicing almost as much as of the watching. He had made his concession, but, with a certain impulse to divert his mother from following up her advantage, he broke out: "Julia's a tremendously effective woman."

"Of course she is!" said Lady Agnes knowingly.

"Her charming appearance is half the battle" — Nick explained a little coldly what he meant. But he felt his coldness an inadequate protection to him when he heard his companion observe with something of the same sapience —

"A woman's always effective when she likes a person so much."

It discomposed him to be described as a person liked, and so much, and by a woman; and he simply said abruptly: "When are you going away?"

"The first moment that's civil — to-morrow morning. *You*'ll stay on I hope."

"Stay on? What shall I stay on for?"

"Why you might stay to express your appreciation."

241

Nick considered. "I've everything to do."

"I thought everything was done," said Lady Agnes.

"Well, that's just why," her son replied, not very lucidly. "I want to do other things — quite other things. I should like to take the next train." And he looked at his watch.

"When there are people coming to dinner to meet you?"

"They'll meet *you* — that's better."

"I'm sorry any one's coming," Lady Agnes said in a tone unencouraging to a deviation from the reality of things. "I wish we were alone — just as a family. It would please Julia to-day to feel that we *are* one. Do stay with her to-morrow."

"How will that do — when she's alone?"

"She won't be alone, with Mrs. Gresham."

"Mrs. Gresham does n't count."

"That's precisely why I want you to stop. And her cousin, almost her brother: what an idea that it won't do! Have n't you stayed here before when there has been no one?"

"I've never stayed much, and there have always been people. At any rate it's now different."

"It's just because it's different. Besides, it is n't different and it never was," said Lady Agnes, more incoherent in her earnestness than it often happened to her to be. "She always liked you and she likes you now more than ever — if you call *that* different!" Nick got up at this and, without meeting her eyes, walked to one of the windows, where he stood with his back turned and looked out on the great greenness. She watched him a moment and she might well have been wishing, while he appeared to gaze with intentness, that it would come to him with the same force as it had come to herself — very often before, but during these last days more than ever — that the level lands of Harsh, stretching away before the window, the French garden with its symmetry, its screens and its statues, and a great many more things of which these were the superficial token, were Julia's very own to do with exactly as she liked. No word of appreciation or envy, however, dropped from the young man's lips, and his mother presently went on: "What could be more natural than that after your triumphant contest you and she should have lots to settle and to talk about — no end of practical questions, no end of urgent business? Are n't you her member, and can't her member pass a day with her, and she a great proprietor?"

Nick turned round at this with an odd expression. "*Her* member — am I hers?"

Lady Agnes had a pause — she had need of all her tact. "Well, if the place is hers and you represent the place —!" she began. But she went no further, for Nick had interrupted her with a laugh.

"What a droll thing to 'represent,' when one thinks of it! And what does *it* represent, poor stupid little borough with its strong, though I admit clean, smell of meal and its curiously fat-faced inhabitants? Did you ever see such a collection of fat faces turned up at the hustings? They looked like an enormous sofa, with the cheeks for the gathers and the eyes for the buttons."

"Oh well, the next time you shall have a great

243

town," Lady Agnes returned, smiling and feeling that she *was* tactful.

"It will only be a bigger sofa! I'm joking, of course," Nick pursued, "and I ought to be ashamed of myself. They've done me the honour to elect me and I shall never say a word that's not civil about them, poor dears. But even a new member may blaspheme to his mother."

"I wish you'd be serious to your mother" —and she went nearer him.

"The difficulty is that I'm two men; it's the strangest thing that ever was," Nick professed with his bright face on her. "I'm two quite distinct human beings, who have scarcely a point in common; not even the memory, on the part of one, of the achievements or the adventures of the other. One man wins the seat but it's the other fellow who sits in it."

"Oh Nick, don't spoil your victory by your perversity!" she cried as she clasped her hands to him.

"I went through it with great glee—I won't deny that: it excited me, interested me, amused me. When once I was in it I liked it. But now that I'm out of it again —!"

"Out of it?" His mother stared. "Isn't the whole point that you're in?"

"Ah *now* I'm only in the House of Commons."

For an instant she seemed not to understand and to be on the point of laying her finger quickly to her lips with a "Hush!" —as if the late Sir Nicholas might have heard the "only." Then while a comprehension of the young man's words promptly superseded that impulse she replied with force:

"You'll be in the Lords the day you determine to get there."

This futile remark made Nick laugh afresh, and not only laugh, but kiss her, which was always an intenser form of mystification for poor Lady Agnes and apparently the one he liked best to inflict; after which he said: "The odd thing is, you know, that Harsh has no wants. At least it's not sharply, not articulately conscious of them. We all pretended to talk them over together, and I promised to carry them in my heart of hearts. But upon my honour I can't remember one of them. Julia says the wants of Harsh are simply the national wants — rather a pretty phrase for Julia. She means *she* does everything for the place; *she*'s really their member and this house in which we stand their legislative chamber. Therefore the *lacunae* I've undertaken to fill out are the national wants. It will be rather a job to rectify some of them, won't it? I don't represent the appetites of Harsh — Harsh is gorged. I represent the ideas of my party. That's what Julia says."

"Oh never mind what Julia says!" Lady Agnes broke out impatiently. This impatience made it singular that the very next word she uttered should be: "My dearest son, I wish to heaven you'd marry her. It would be so fitting now!" she added.

"Why now?" Nick frowned.

"She has shown you such sympathy, such devotion."

"Is it for that she has shown it?"

"Ah you might *feel* — I can't tell you!" said Lady Agnes reproachfully.

He blushed at this, as if what he did feel was the reproach. "Must I marry her because you like her?"

"I? Why we're *all* as fond of her as we can be."

"Dear mother, I hope that any woman I ever may marry will be a person agreeable not only to you, but also, since you make a point of it, to Grace and Biddy. But I must tell you this — that I shall marry no woman I'm not unmistakeably in love with."

"And why are you not in love with Julia — charming, clever, generous as she is?" Lady Agnes laid her hands on him — she held him tight. "Dearest Nick, if you care anything in the world to make me happy you'll stay over here to-morrow and be nice to her."

He waited an instant. "Do you mean propose to her?"

"With a single word, with the glance of an eye, the movement of your little finger" — and she paused, looking intensely, imploringly up into his face — "in less time than it takes me to say what I say now, you may have it all." As he made no answer, only meeting her eyes, she added insistently: "You know she's a fine creature — you know she is!"

"Dearest mother, what I seem to know better than anything else in the world is that I love my freedom. I set it far above everything."

"Your freedom? What freedom is there in being poor?" Lady Agnes fiercely demanded. "Talk of that when Julia puts everything she possesses at your feet!"

"I can't talk of it, mother — it's too terrible an idea. And I can't talk of *her*, nor of what I think of her. You must leave that to me. I do her perfect justice."

"You don't or you'd marry her to-morrow," she passionately argued. "You'd feel the opportunity so beautifully rare, with everything in the world to make it perfect. Your father would have valued it for you beyond everything. Think a little what would have given *him* pleasure. That's what I meant when I spoke just now of us all. It wasn't of Grace and Biddy I was thinking — fancy! — it was of him. He's with you always; he takes with you, at your side, every step you take yourself. He'd bless devoutly your marriage to Julia; he'd feel what it would be for you and for us all. I ask for no sacrifice and he'd ask for none. We only ask that you don't commit the crime —!"

Nick Dormer stopped her with another kiss; he murmured "Mother, mother, mother!" as he bent over her. He wished her not to go on, to let him off; but the deep deprecation in his voice didn't prevent her saying:

"You know it — you know it perfectly. All and more than all that I can tell you you know." He drew her closer, kissed her again, held her as he would have held a child in a paroxysm, soothing her silently till it could abate. Her vehemence had brought with it tears; she dried them as she disengaged herself. The next moment, however, she resumed, attacking him again: "For a public man she'd be the perfect companion. She's made for public life — she's made to shine, to be concerned in great things, to occupy a high position and to help him on. She'd back you

up in everything as she has backed you in this. Together there's nothing you could n't do. You can
have the first house in England — yes, the very first!
What freedom *is* there in being poor? How can you
do anything without money, and what money can
you make for yourself — what money will ever come
to you? That's the crime — to throw away such an
instrument of power, such a blessed instrument of
good."

"It is n't everything to be rich, mother," said Nick,
looking at the floor with a particular patience — that
is with a provisional docility and his hands in his
pockets. "And it is n't so fearful to be poor."

"It's vile — it's abject. Don't I know?"

"Are you in such acute want?" he smiled.

"Ah don't make me explain what you've only
to look at to see!" his mother returned as if with
a richness of allusion to dark elements in her fate.

"Besides," he easily went on, "there's other money
in the world than Julia's. I might come by some of
that."

"Do you mean Mr. Carteret's?" The question
made him laugh as her feeble reference five minutes
before to the House of Lords had done. But she
pursued, too full of her idea to take account of such
a poor substitute for an answer: "Let me tell you one
thing, for I've known Charles Carteret much longer
than you and I understand him better. There's
nothing you could do that would do you more good
with him than to marry Julia. I know the way he
looks at things and I know exactly how that would
strike him. It would please him, it would charm him;

it would be the thing that would most prove to him that you're in earnest. You need, you know, to do something of that sort," she said as for plain speaking.

"Have n't I come in for Harsh ?" asked Nick.

"Oh he's very canny. He likes to see people rich. *Then* he believes in them — then he's likely to believe more. He's kind to you because you're your father's son; but I'm sure your being poor takes just so much off."

"He can remedy that so easily," said Nick, smiling still. "Is my being kept by Julia what you call my making an effort for myself ?"

Lady Agnes hesitated; then "You need n't insult Julia!" she replied.

"Moreover if I've *her* money I shan't want his," Nick unheedingly remarked.

Again his mother waited before answering; after which she produced : "And pray would n't you wish to be independent ?"

"You're delightful, dear mother — you're very delightful! I particularly like your conception of independence. Does n't it occur to you that at a pinch I might improve my fortune by some other means than by making a mercenary marriage or by currying favour with a rich old gentleman ? Does n't it occur to you that I might work ?"

"Work at politics ? How does that make money, honourably ?"

"I don't mean at politics."

"What do you mean then ?" — and she seemed to challenge him to phrase it if he dared. This demonstration of her face and voice might have affected him, for he remained silent and she continued: "Are you elected or not?"

"It seems a dream," he rather flatly returned.

"If you are, act accordingly and don't mix up things that are as wide asunder as the poles!" She spoke with sternness and his silence appeared again to represent an admission that her sternness counted for him. Possibly she was touched by it; after a few moments, at any rate, during which nothing more passed between them, she appealed to him in a gentler and more anxious key, which had this virtue to touch him that he knew it was absolutely the first time in her life she had really begged for anything. She had never been obliged to beg; she had got on without it and most things had come to her. He might judge therefore in what a light she regarded this boon for which in her bereft old age she humbled herself to be a suitor. There was such a pride in her that he could feel what it cost her to go on her knees even to her son. He did judge how it was in his power to gratify her; and as he was generous and imaginative he was stirred and shaken as it came over him in a wave of figurative suggestion that he might make up to her for many things. He scarcely needed to hear her ask with a pleading wail that was almost tragic: "Don't you see how things have turned out for us? Don't you know how unhappy I am, don't you know what a bitterness — ?" She stopped with a sob in her voice and he recognised vividly this last tribulation, the unhealed wound of her change of life and her lapse from eminence to flatness. "You know what Percival is and the comfort I have of him. You know the property and what he's doing with it and what comfort I get from *that!* Everything's dreary but what you can do for us. Everything's odious, down to living in a hole with one's girls who don't marry. Grace is impossible — I don't know what's the matter with her; no one will look at her, and she's so conceited with it — sometimes I feel as if I could beat her! And Biddy will never marry, and we're three dismal women in a filthy house; and what are three dismal women, more or less, in London?"

So with an unexpected rage of self-exposure she poured out her disappointments and troubles, tore away the veil from her sadness and soreness. It almost scared him to see how she hated her life, though at another time it might have been amusing to note how she despised her gardenless house. Of course it wasn't a country-house, and she couldn't get used to that. Better than he could do — for it was the sort of thing into which in any case a woman enters more than a man — she felt what a lift into brighter air, what a regilding of his sisters' possibilities, his marriage to Julia would effect for them. He couldn't trace the difference, but his mother saw it all as a shining picture. She hung the bright vision before him now — she stood there like a poor woman crying for a kindness. What was filial in him, all the piety he owed, especially to the revived spirit of his father, more than ever present on a day of such public pledges, became from one moment to the other as the very handle to the door of the chamber of concessions. He had the impulse, so embarrassing when it is a question of consistent action, to see in a touching, an interesting light any forcibly presented side of the life of another: such things effected a union with something in *his* life, and in the recognition of them was no soreness of sacrifice and no consciousness of merit.

Rapidly, at present, this change of scene took place before his spiritual eye. He found himself believing, because his mother communicated the belief, that it depended but on his own conduct richly to alter the social outlook of the three women who clung to him and who declared themselves forlorn. This was not the highest kind of motive, but it contained a spring, it touched into life again old injunctions and appeals. Julia's wide kingdom opened out round him and seemed somehow to wear the face of his own possible future. His mother and sisters floated in the rosy element as if he had breathed it about them. "The first house in England" she had called it; but it might be the first house in Europe, the first in the world, by the fine air and the high humanities that should fill it. Everything beautiful in his actual, his material view seemed to proclaim its value as never before; the house rose over his head as a museum of exquisite rewards, and the image of poor George Dallow hovered there obsequious, expressing that he had only been the modest tasteful organiser, or even upholsterer, appointed to set it all in order and punctually retire. Lady Agnes's tone in fine penetrated further than it had done yet when she brought out with intensity: "Don't desert us — don't desert us."

"Don't desert you — ?"

"Be great — be great. I'm old, I've lived, I've

seen. Go in for a great material position. That will simplify everything else."

"I'll do what I can for you — anything, everything I can. Trust me — leave me alone," Nick went on.

"And you'll stay over — you'll spend the day with her?"

"I'll stay till she turns me out!"

His mother had hold of his hand again now: she raised it to her lips and kissed it. "My dearest son, my only joy!" Then "I don't see how you can resist her," she added.

"No more do I!"

She looked about — there was so much to look at — with a deep exhalation. "If you're so fond of art, what art is equal to all this? The joy of living in the midst of it — of seeing the finest works every day! You'll have everything the world can give."

"That's exactly what was just passing in my own mind. It's too much," Nick reasoned.

"Don't be selfish!"

"Selfish?" he echoed.

"Unselfish then. You'll share it with us."

"And with Julia a little I hope," he said.

"God bless you!" cried his mother, looking up at him. Her eyes were detained by the sudden sense of something in his own that was not clear to her; but before she could challenge it he asked abruptly:

"Why do you talk so of poor Biddy? Why won't she marry?"

"You had better ask Peter Sherringham," said Lady Agnes.

"What has he to do with it?"

"How odd of you not to know — when it's so plain how she thinks of him that it's a matter of common gossip."

"Yes, if you will — we've made it so, and she takes it as an angel. But Peter likes her."

"Does he? Then it's the more shame to him to behave as he does. He had better leave his wretched actresses alone. That's the love of art too!" mocked Lady Agnes.

But Nick glossed it all over. "Biddy's so charming she'll easily marry some one else."

"Never, if she loves him. However, Julia will bring it about — Julia will help her," his mother pursued more cheerfully. "That's what you'll do for us — that *she*'ll do everything!"

"Why then more than now?" he asked.

"Because we shall be yours."

"You're mine already."

"Yes, but she is n't. However, she's as good!" Lady Agnes exulted.

"She'll turn me out of the house," said Nick.

"Come and tell me when she does! But there she is — go to her!" And she gave him a push toward one of the windows that stood open to the terrace. Their hostess had become visible outside; she passed slowly along the terrace with her long shadow. "Go to her," his mother repeated — "she's waiting for you."

Nick went out with the air of a man as ready to pass that way as another, and at the same moment his two sisters, still flushed with participation, appeared in a different quarter.

254

"We go home to-morrow, but Nick will stay a day or two," Lady Agnes said to them.

"Dear old Nick!" Grace ejaculated, looking at her with intensity.

"He's going to speak," she went on. "But don't mention it."

"Don't mention it?" Biddy asked with a milder stare. "Has n't he spoken enough, poor fellow?"

"I mean to Julia," Lady Agnes replied.

"Don't you understand, you goose?" — and Grace turned on her sister.

XIV

THE next morning brought the young man many letters and telegrams, and his coffee was placed beside him in his room, where he remained until noon answering these communications. When he came out he learned that his mother and sisters had left the house. This information was given him by Mrs. Gresham, whom he found dealing with her own voluminous budget at one of the tables in the library. She was a lady who received thirty letters a day, the subject-matter of which, as well as of her punctual answers in a hand that would have been "ladylike" in a manageress, was a puzzle to those who observed her.

She told Nick that Lady Agnes had not been willing to disturb him at his work to say good-bye, knowing she should see him in a day or two in town. He was amused at the way his mother had stolen off —as if she feared further conversation might weaken the spell she believed herself to have wrought. The place was cleared moreover of its other visitors, so that, as Mrs. Gresham said, the fun was at an end. This lady expressed the idea that the fun was after all rather a bore. At any rate now they could rest, Mrs. Dallow and Nick and she, and she was glad Nick was going to stay for a little quiet. She liked Harsh best when it was not *en fête:* then one could see what a sympathetic old place it was. She hoped Nick was not

dreadfully fagged — she feared Julia was completely
done up. Julia, however, had transported her exhaustion to the grounds — she was wandering about
somewhere. She thought more people would be coming to the house, people from the town, people from
the country, and had gone out so as not to have to
see them. She had not gone far — Nick could easily
find her. Nick intimated that he himself was not eager
for more people, whereupon Mrs. Gresham rather
archly smiled. "And of course you hate *me* for being
here." He made some protest and she added: "But
I'm almost part of the house, you know — I'm
one of the chairs or tables." Nick declared that he
had never seen a house so well furnished, and Mrs.
Gresham said: "I believe there *are* to be some
people to dinner; rather an interference, is n't it?
Julia lives so in public. But it's all for you." And
after a moment she added: "It's a wonderful constitution." Nick at first failed to seize her allusion —
he thought it a retarded political reference, a sudden
tribute to the great unwritten instrument by which
they were all governed and under the happy operation
of which his fight had been so successful. He was
on the point of saying "The British? Wonderful!"
when he gathered that the intention of his companion
had been simply to praise Mrs. Dallow's fine robust-
ness. "The surface so delicate, the action so easy, yet
the frame of steel."

He left Mrs. Gresham to her correspondence and
went out of the house; wondering as he walked if she
wanted him to do the same thing his mother wanted,
so that her words had been intended for a prick —

whether even the two ladies had talked over their desire together. Mrs. Gresham was a married woman who was usually taken for a widow, mainly because she was perpetually "sent for" by her friends, who in no event sent for Mr. Gresham. She came in every case, with her air of being *répandue* at the expense of dingier belongings. Her figure was admired — that is it was sometimes mentioned — and she dressed as if it was expected of her to be smart, like a young woman in a shop or a servant much in view. She slipped in and out, accompanied at the piano, talked to the neglected visitors, walked in the rain, and after the arrival of the post usually had conferences with her hostess, during which she stroked her chin and looked familiarly responsible. It was her peculiarity that people were always saying things to her in a lowered voice. She had all sorts of acquaintances and in small establishments sometimes wrote the *menus*. Great ones, on the other hand, had no terrors for her — she had seen too many. No one had ever discovered whether any one else paid her. People only knew what *they* did.

If Lady Agnes had in the minor key discussed with her the propriety of a union between the mistress of Harsh and the hope of the Dormers this last personage could take the circumstance for granted without irritation and even with cursory indulgence; for he was not unhappy now and his spirit was light and clear. The summer day was splendid and the world, as he looked at it from the terrace, offered no more worrying ambiguity than a vault of airy blue arching over a lap of solid green. The wide still trees in the park appeared to be waiting for some daily inspection, and the rich fields, with their official frill of hedges, to rejoice in the light that smiled upon them as named and numbered acres. Nick felt himself catch the smile and all the reasons of it: they made up a charm to which he had perhaps not hitherto done justice — something of the impression he had received when younger from showy "views" of fine country-seats that had pressed and patted nature, as by the fat hands of "benches" of magistrates and landlords, into supreme respectability and comfort. There were a couple of peacocks on the terrace, and his eye was caught by the gleam of the swans on a distant lake, where was also a little temple on an island; and these objects fell in with his humour, which at another time might have been ruffled by them as aggressive triumphs of the conventional.

It was certainly a proof of youth and health on his part that his spirits had risen as the plot thickened and that after he had taken his jump into the turbid waters of a contested election he had been able to tumble and splash not only without a sense of awkwardness but with a considerable capacity for the frolic. Tepid as we saw him in Paris he had found his relation to his opportunity surprisingly altered by his little journey across the Channel, had seen things in a new perspective and breathed an air that set him and kept him in motion. There had been something in it that went to his head — an element that his mother and his sisters, his father from beyond the grave, Julia Dallow, the Liberal party and a hundred friends, were both secretly and overtly occupied in

pumping into it. If he but half-believed in victory
he at least liked the wind of the onset in his ears, and
he had a general sense that when one was "stuck"
there was always the nearest thing at which one must
pull. The embarrassment, that is the revival of scep-
ticism, which might produce an inconsistency shame-
ful to exhibit and yet difficult to conceal, was safe
enough to come later. Indeed at the risk of present-
ing our young man as too whimsical a personage I
may hint that some such sickly glow had even now
begun to tinge one quarter of his inward horizon.

I am afraid moreover that I have no better excuse
for him than the one he had touched on in that momentous conversation with his mother which I have
thought it useful to reproduce in full. He was conscious of a double nature; there were two men in
him, quite separate, whose leading features had little
in common and each of whom insisted on having an
independent turn at life. Meanwhile then, if he was
adequately aware that the bed of his moral existence
would need a good deal of making over if he was to
lie upon it without unseemly tossing, he was also
alive to the propriety of not parading his inconsistencies, not letting his unregulated passions become a
spectacle to the vulgar. He had none of that wish to
appear deep which is at the bottom of most forms of
fatuity; he was perfectly willing to pass for decently
superficial; he only aspired to be decently continuous.
When you were not suitably shallow this presented
difficulties; but he would have assented to the proposition that you must be as subtle as you can and that
a high use of subtlety is in consuming the smoke of

your inner fire. The fire was the great thing, not the chimney. He had no view of life that counted out the need of learning; it was teaching rather as to which he was conscious of no particular mission. He enjoyed life, enjoyed it immensely, and was ready to pursue it with patience through as many channels as possible. He was on his guard, however, against making an ass of himself, that is against not thinking out his experiments before trying them in public. It was because, as yet, he liked life in general better than it was clear to him he liked particular possibilities that, on the occasion of a constituency's holding out a cordial hand to him while it extended another in a different direction, a certain bloom of boyhood that was on him had not paled at the idea of a match.

He had risen to the fray as he had risen to matches at school, for his boyishness could still take a pleasure in an inconsiderate show of agility. He could meet electors and conciliate bores and compliment women and answer questions and roll off speeches and chaff adversaries — he could do these things because it was amusing and slightly dangerous, like playing football or ascending an Alp, pastimes for which nature had conferred on him an aptitude not so very different in kind from a due volubility on platforms. There were two voices to admonish him that all this was not really action at all, but only a pusillanimous imitation of it: one of them fitfully audible in the depths of his own spirit and the other speaking, in the equivocal accents of a very crabbed hand, from a letter of four pages by Gabriel Nash. However, Nick carried the imitation as far as possible, and the flood of sound floated him. What more could a working faith have done ? He had not broken with the axiom that in a case of doubt one should hold off, for this applied to choice, and he had not at present the slightest pretension to choosing. He knew he was lifted along, that what he was doing was not first-rate, that nothing was settled by it and that if there was a hard knot in his life it would only grow harder with keeping. Doing one's sum to-morrow instead of to-day does n't make the sum easier, but at least makes to-day so.

Sometimes in the course of the following fort-night it seemed to him he had gone in for Harsh because he was sure he should lose ; sometimes he foresaw that he should win precisely to punish him for having tried and for his want of candour; and when presently he did win he was almost scared at his success. Then it appeared to him he had done something even worse than not choose — he had let others choose for him. The beauty of it was that they had chosen with only their own object in their eye, for what did they know about his strange alter-native ? He was rattled about so for a fortnight — Julia taking care of this — that he had no time to think save when he tried to remember a quotation or an American story, and all his life became an over-flow of verbiage. Thought could n't hear itself for the noise, which had to be pleasant and persuasive, had to hang more or less together, without its aid. Nick was surprised at the airs he could play, and often when, the last thing at night, he shut the door of his room, found himself privately exclaim-

ing that he had had no idea he was such a mountebank.

I must add that if this reflexion did n't occupy him
long, and if no meditation, after his return from
Paris, held him for many moments, there was a reason better even than that he was tired, that he was
busy, that he appreciated the coincidence of the hit
and the hurrah, the hurrah and the hit. That reason
was simply Mrs. Dallow, who had suddenly become
a still larger fact in his consciousness than his having
turned actively political. She *was* indeed his being
so — in the sense that if the politics were his, how
little soever, the activity was hers. She had better
ways of showing she was clever than merely saying
clever things — which in general only prove at the
most that one would be clever if one could. The
accomplished fact itself was almost always the
demonstration that Mrs. Dallow could; and when
Nick came to his senses after the proclamation of the
victor and the drop of the uproar her figure was, of
the whole violent dance of shadows, the only thing
that came back, that stayed. She had been there
at each of the moments, passing, repassing, returning, before him, beside him, behind him. She had
made the business infinitely prettier than it would
have been without her, added music and flowers
and ices, a finer charm, converting it into a kind of
heroic "function," the form of sport most dangerous. It had been a garden-party, say, with one's life
at stake from pressure of the crowd. The concluded
affair had bequeathed him thus not only a seat in
the House of Commons, but a perception of what

may come of women in high embodiments and an abyss of intimacy with one woman in particular.

She had wrapped him up in something, he did n't know what — a sense of facility, an overpowering fragrance — and they had moved together in an immense fraternity. There had been no love-making, no contact that was only personal, no vulgarity of flirtation: the hurry of the days and the sharpness with which they both tended to an outside object had made all that irrelevant. It was as if she had been too near for him to see her separate from himself; but none the less, when he now drew breath and looked back, what had happened met his eyes as a composed picture — a picture of which the subject was inveterately Julia and her ponies: Julia wonderfully fair and fine, waving her whip, cleaving the crowd, holding her head as if it had been a banner, smiling up into second-storey windows, carrying him beside her, carrying him to his doom. He had not reckoned at the time, in the few days, how much he had driven about with her; but the image of it was there, in his consulted conscience, as well as in a personal glow not yet chilled: it looked large as it rose before him. The things his mother had said to him made a rich enough frame for it all, and the whole impression had that night kept him much awake.

XV

WHILE, after leaving Mrs. Gresham, he was hesitating which way to go and was on the point of hailing a gardener to ask if Mrs. Dallow had been seen, he noticed, as a spot of colour in an expanse of shrubbery, a far-away parasol moving in the direction of the lake. He took his course toward it across the park, and as the bearer of the parasol strolled slowly it was not five minutes before he had joined her. He went to her soundlessly, on the grass — he had been whistling at first, but as he got nearer stopped — and it was not till he was at hand that she looked round. He had watched her go as if she were turning things over in her mind, while she brushed the smooth walks and the clean turf with her dress, slowly made her parasol revolve on her shoulder and carried in the other hand a book which he perceived to be a monthly review.

"I came out to get away," she said when he had begun to walk with her.

"Away from me?"

"Ah that's impossible." Then she added: "The day's so very nice."

"Lovely weather," Nick dropped. "You want to get away from Mrs. Gresham, I suppose."

She had a pause. "From everything!"

"Well, I want to get away too."

"It has been such a racket. Listen to the dear birds."

"Yes, our noise is n't so good as theirs," said Nick. "I feel as if I had been married and had shoes and rice thrown after me," he went on. "But not to you, Julia — nothing so good as that."

Julia made no reply; she only turned her eyes on the ornamental water stretching away at their right. In a moment she exclaimed "How nasty the lake looks!" and Nick recognised in her tone a sign of that odd shyness — a perverse stiffness at a moment when she probably but wanted to be soft — which, taken in combination with her other qualities, was so far from being displeasing to him that it represented her nearest approach to extreme charm. *He* was not shy now, for he considered this morning that he saw things very straight and in a sense altogether superior and delightful. This enabled him to be generously sorry for his companion — if he were the reason of her being in any degree uncomfortable, and yet left him to enjoy some of the motions, not in themselves without grace, by which her discomfort was revealed. He would n't insist on anything yet: so he observed that her standard in lakes was too high, and then talked a little about his mother and the girls, their having gone home, his not having seen them that morning, Lady Agnes's deep satisfaction in his victory and the fact that she would be obliged to "do something" for the autumn — take a house or something or other.

"I 'll lend her a house," said Mrs. Dallow.

"Oh Julia, Julia!" Nick half groaned.

But she paid no attention to his sound; she only held up her review and said: "See what I 've brought with me to read — Mr. Hoppus's article."

"That's right; then *I* shan't have to. You'll tell me about it." He uttered this without believing she had meant or wished to read the article, which was entitled "The Revision of the British Constitution," in spite of her having encumbered herself with the stiff fresh magazine. He was deeply aware she was not in want of such inward occupation as periodical literature could supply. They walked along and he added: "But is that what we're in for, reading Mr. Hoppus? Is it the sort of thing constituents expect? Or, even worse, pretending to have read him when one hasn't? Oh what a tangled web we weave!"

"People are talking about it. One has to know. It's the article of the month."

Nick looked at her askance. "You say things every now and then for which I could really kill you. 'The article of the month' for instance: I could kill you for that."

"Well, kill me!" Mrs. Dallow returned.

"Let me carry your book," he went on irrelevantly. The hand in which she held it was on the side of her on which he was walking, and he put out his own hand to take it. But for a couple of minutes she forbore to give it up, so that they held it together, swinging it a little. Before she surrendered it he asked where she was going.

"To the island," she answered.

"Well, I'll go with you — and I'll kill you there."

"The things I say are the right things," Julia declared.

"It's just the right things that are wrong. It's be-cause you're so political," Nick too lightly explained. "It's your horrible ambition. The woman who has a salon should have read the article of the month. See how one dreadful thing leads to another."

"There are some things that lead to nothing," said Mrs. Dallow.

"No doubt — no doubt. And how are you going to get over to your island?"

"I don't know."

"Isn't there a boat?"

"I don't know."

Nick had paused to look round for the boat, but his hostess walked on without turning her head. "Can you row?" he then asked.

"Don't you know I can do everything?"

"Yes, to be sure. That's why I want to kill you. There's the boat."

"Shall you drown me?" she asked.

"Oh let me perish with you!" Nick answered with a sigh. The boat had been hidden from them by the bole of a great tree which rose from the grass at the water's edge. It was moored to a small place of embarkation and was large enough to hold as many persons as were likely to wish to visit at once the little temple in the middle of the lake, which Nick liked be-cause it was absurd and which Mrs. Dallow had never had a particular esteem for. The lake, fed by a nat-ural spring, was a liberal sheet of water, measured by the scale of park scenery; and though its principal merit was that, taken at a distance, it gave a gleam of abstraction to the concrete verdure, doing the office of an open eye in a dull face, it could also be approached without derision on a sweet summer morning when it made a lapping sound and reflected candidly various things that were probably finer than itself — the sky, the great trees, the flight of birds. A man of taste, coming back from Rome a hundred years before, had caused a small ornamental structure to be raised, from artificial foundations, on its bosom, and had endeavoured to make this architectural pleasantry as nearly as possible a reminiscence of the small ruined rotunda which stands on the bank of the Tiber and is pronounced by *ciceroni* once sacred to Vesta. It was circular, roofed with old tiles, surrounded by white columns and considerably dilapidated. George Dallow had taken an interest in it — it reminded him not in the least of Rome, but of other things he liked — and had amused himself with restoring it. "Give me your hand — sit there and I'll ferry you," Nick said.

Julia complied, placing herself opposite him in the boat; but as he took up the paddles she declared that she preferred to remain on the water — there was too much malice prepense in the temple. He asked her what she meant by that, and she said it was ridiculous to withdraw to an island a few feet square on purpose to meditate. She had nothing to meditate about that required so much scenery and attitude.

"On the contrary, it would be just to change the scene and the *pose*. It's what we have been doing for a week that's attitude; and to be for half an hour where nobody's looking and one has n't to keep it

269

up is just what I wanted to put in an idle irresponsible day for. I'm not keeping it up now — I suppose you've noticed," Nick went on as they floated and he scarcely dipped the oars.

"I don't understand you " — and Julia leaned back in the boat.

He gave no further explanation than to ask in a minute: "Have you people to dinner to-night?"

"I believe there are three or four, but I'll put them off if you like."

"Must you *always* live in public, Julia?" he continued.

She looked at him a moment and he could see how she coloured. "We'll go home — I'll put them off."

"Ah no, don't go home; it's too jolly here. Let them come, let them come, poor wretches!"

"How little you know me," Julia presently broke out, "when, ever so many times, I've lived here for months without a creature!"

"Except Mrs. Gresham, I suppose."

"I have had to have the house going, I admit."

"You're perfect, you're admirable, and I don't criticise you."

" I don't understand you!" she tossed back.

"That only adds to the generosity of what you've done for me," Nick returned, beginning to pull faster. He bent over the oars and sent the boat forward, keeping this up for a succession of minutes during which they both remained silent. His companion, in her place, motionless, reclining — the seat in the stern was most comfortable — looked only at the water, the sky, the trees. At last he

270

headed for the little temple, saying first, however, "Shan't we visit the ruin?"

"If you like. I don't mind seeing how they keep it."

They reached the white steps leading up to it. He held the boat and his companion got out; then, when he had made it fast, they mounted together to the open door. "They keep the place very well," Nick said looking round. "It's a capital place to give up everything in."

"It might do at least for you to explain what you mean." And Julia sat down.

"I mean to pretend for half an hour that I don't represent the burgesses of Harsh. It's charming — it's very delicate work. Surely it has been retouched."

The interior of the pavilion, lighted by windows which the circle of columns was supposed outside and at a distance to conceal, had a vaulted ceiling and was occupied by a few pieces of last-century furniture, spare and faded, of which the colours matched with the decoration of the walls. These and the ceiling, tinted and not exempt from indications of damp, were covered with fine mouldings and medallions. It all made a very elegant little tea-house, the mistress of which sat on the edge of a sofa rolling her parasol and remarking "You ought to read Mr. Hoppus's article to me."

"Why, is *this* your salon?" Nick smiled.

"What makes you always talk of that? My salon's an invention of your own."

"But isn't it the idea you're most working for?"

Suddenly, nervously, she put up her parasol and sat under it as if not quite sensible of what she was doing.

"How much you know me! I'm not 'working' for anything — that you'll ever guess."

Nick wandered about the room and looked at various things it contained — the odd volumes on the tables, the bits of quaint china on the shelves. "They do keep it very well. You've got charming things."

"They're supposed to come over every day and look after them."

"They must come over in force."

"Oh no one knows."

"It's spick and span. How well you have everything done!"

"I think you've some reason to say so," said Mrs. Dallow. Her parasol was now down and she was again rolling it tight.

"But you're right about my not knowing you. Why were you so ready to do so much for me?"

He stopped in front of her and she looked up at him. Her eyes rested long on his own; then she broke out: "Why do you hate me so?"

"Was it because you like me personally?" Nick pursued as if he hadn't heard her. "You may think that an odd or positively an odious question; but isn't it natural, my wanting to know?"

"Oh if you don't know!" Julia quite desperately sighed.

"It's a question of being sure."

"Well then if you're not sure —!"

"Was it done for me as a friend, as a man?"

"You're not a man — you're a child," his hostess declared with a face that was cold, though she had been smiling the moment before.

"After all I was a good candidate," Nick went on.

"What do I care for candidates?"

"You're the most delightful woman, Julia," he said as he sat down beside her, "and I can't imagine what you mean by my hating you."

"If you have n't discovered that I like you, you might as well."

"Might as well discover it?"

She was grave — he had never seen her so pale and never so beautiful. She had stopped rolling her parasol; her hands were folded in her lap and her eyes bent on them. Nick sat looking at them as well — a trifle awkwardly. "Might as well have hated me," she said.

"We've got on so beautifully together all these days: why should n't we get on as well for ever and ever?" he brought out. She made no answer, and suddenly he said: "Ah Julia, I don't know what you've done to me, but you've done it. You've done it by strange ways, but it will serve. Yes, I hate you," he added in a different tone and with his face all nearer.

"Dear Nick, dear Nick —!" she began. But she stopped, feeling his nearness and its intensity, a nearness now so great that his arm was round her, that he was really in possession of her. She closed her eyes but heard him ask again "Why should n't it be for ever, for ever?" in a voice that had for her ear a vibration none had ever had.

"You've done it, you've done it," Nick repeated.

"What do you want of me?" she appealed.

"To stay with me — this way — always."

273

"Ah not this way," she answered softly, but as if in pain and making an effort, with a certain force, to detach herself.

"This way then — or this!" He took such pressing advantage of her that he had kissed her with repetition. She rose while he insisted, but he held her yet, and as he did so his tenderness turned to beautiful words. "If you'll marry me, why should n't it be so simple, so right and good?" He drew her closer again, too close for her to answer. But her struggle ceased and she rested on him a minute; she buried her face in his breast.

"You're hard, and it's cruel!" she then exclaimed, shaking herself free.

"Hard — cruel?"

"You do it with so little!" And with this, unexpectedly to Nick, Julia burst straight into tears. Before he could stop her she was at the door of the pavilion as if she wished to get immediately away. There, however, he stayed her, bending over her while she sobbed, unspeakably gentle with her.

"So little? It's with everything — with everything I have."

"I've done it, you say? What do you accuse me of doing?" Her tears were already over.

"Of making me yours; of being so precious, Julia, so exactly what a man wants, as it seems to me. I did n't know you could," he went on, smiling down at her. "I did n't — no, I did n't."

"It's what I say — that you've always hated me."

"I'll make it up to you!" he laughed.

She leaned on the doorway with her forehead against the lintel. "You don't even deny it."

"Contradict you *now?* I'll admit it, though it's rubbish, on purpose to live it down."

"It does n't matter," she said slowly; "for however much you might have liked me you'd never have done so half as much as I've cared for you."

"Oh I'm so poor!" Nick murmured cheerfully.

With her eyes looking at him as in a new light she slowly shook her head. Then she declared: "You never can live it down."

"I like that! Have n't I asked you to marry me? When did you ever ask me?"

"Every day of my life! As I say, it's hard — for a proud woman."

"Yes, you're too proud even to answer me."

"We must think of it, we must talk of it."

"Think of it? I've thought of it ever so much."

"I mean together. There are many things in such a question."

"The principal thing is beautifully to give me your word."

She looked at him afresh all strangely; then she threw off "I wish I did n't adore you!" She went straight down the steps.

"You don't adore me at all, you know, if you leave me now. Why do you go? It's so charming here and we're so delightfully alone."

"Untie the boat; we'll go on the water," Julia said.

Nick was at the top of the steps, looking down at her. "Ah stay a little — *do* stay!" he pleaded.

275

"I'll get in myself, I'll put off," she simply answered.

At this he came down and bent a little to undo the rope. He was close to her and as he raised his head he felt it caught; she had seized it in her hands and she pressed her lips, as he had never felt lips pressed, to the first place they encountered. The next instant she was in the boat.

This time he dipped the oars very slowly indeed; and, while for a period that was longer than it seemed to them they floated vaguely, they mainly sat and glowed at each other as if everything had been settled. There were reasons enough why Nick should be happy; but it is a singular fact that the leading one was the sense of his having escaped a great and ugly mistake. The final result of his mother's appeal to him the day before had been the idea that he must act with unimpeachable honour. He was capable of taking it as an assurance that Julia had placed him under an obligation a gentleman could regard but in one way. If she herself had understood it so, putting the vision, or at any rate the appreciation, of a closer tie into everything she had done for him, the case was conspicuously simple and his course unmistakeably plain. That is why he had been gay when he came out of the house to look for her: he could be gay when his course was plain. He could be all the gayer, naturally, I must add, that, in turning things over as he had done half the night, what he had turned up oftenest was the recognition that Julia now had a new personal power with him. It was not for nothing that she had thrown herself personally into his life.

276

She had by her act made him live twice as intensely, and such an office, such a service, if a man had accepted and deeply tasted it, was certainly a thing to put him on his honour. He took it as distinct that there was nothing he could do in preference that would n't be spoiled for him by any deflexion from that point. His mother had made him uncomfortable by bringing it so heavily up that Julia was in love with him — he did n't like in general to be told such things; but the responsibility seemed easier to carry and he was less shy about it when once he was away from other eyes, with only Julia's own to express that truth and with indifferent nature all about. Besides, what discovery had he made this morning but that he also was in love?

"You've got to be a very great man, you know," she said to him in the middle of the lake. "I don't know what you mean about my salon, but I *am* ambitious."

"We must look at life in a large bold way," he concurred while he rested his oars.

"That's what I mean. If I did n't think you could I would n't look at you."

"I could what?"

"Do everything you ought — everything I imagine, I dream of. You *are* clever: you can never make me believe the contrary after your speech on Tuesday. Don't speak to me! I've seen, I've heard, and I know what's in you. I shall hold you to it. You're everything you pretend not to be."

Nick looked at the water while she talked. "Will it always be so amusing?" he asked.

"Will what always be?"

"Why my career."

"Shan't I make it so?"

"Then it will be yours — it won't be mine," said Nick.

"Ah don't say that — don't make me out that sort of woman! If they should say it's me I'd drown myself."

"If they should say what's you?"

"Why your getting on. If they should say I push you and do things for you. Things I mean that you can't do yourself."

"Well, won't you do them? It's just what I count on."

"Don't be dreadful," Julia said. "It would be loathsome if I were thought the cleverest. That's not the sort of man I want to marry."

"Oh I shall make you work, my dear!"

"Ah *that* —!" she sounded in a tone that might come back to a man after years.

"You'll do the great thing, you'll make my life the best life," Nick brought out as if he had been touched to deep conviction. "I dare say that will keep me in heart."

"In heart? Why should n't you be in heart?" And her eyes, lingering on him, searching him, seemed to question him still more than her lips.

"Oh it will be all right!" he made answer.

"You'll like success as well as any one else. Don't tell me — you're not so ethereal!"

"Yes, I shall like success."

"So shall I! And of course I'm glad you'll now

be able to do things," Julia went on. "I'm glad you'll have things. I'm glad I'm not poor."

"Ah don't speak of that," Nick murmured. "Only be nice to my mother. We shall make her supremely happy."

"It wouldn't be for your mother I'd do it — yet I'm glad I like your people," Mrs. Dallow rectified. "Leave them to me!"

"You're generous — you're noble," he stammered.

"Your mother must live at Broadwood; she must have it for life. It's not at all bad."

"Ah Julia," her companion replied, "it's well I love you!"

"Why should n't you?" she laughed; and after this no more was said between them till the boat touched shore. When she had got out she recalled that it was time for luncheon; but they took no action in consequence, strolling in a direction which was not that of the house. There was a vista that drew them on, a grassy path skirting the foundations of scattered beeches and leading to a stile from which the charmed wanderer might drop into another division of Mrs. Dallow's property. She said something about their going as far as the stile, then the next instant exclaimed: "How stupid of you — you've forgotten Mr. Hoppus!"

Nick wondered. "We left him in the temple of Vesta. Darling, I had other things to think of there."

"I'll send for him," said Julia.

"Lord, can you think of him now?" he asked.

"Of course I can — more than ever."

"Shall we go back for him?" — and he pulled up.

She made no direct answer, but continued to walk, saying they would go as far as the stile. "Of course I know you're fearfully vague," she presently resumed.

"I was n't vague at all. But you were in such a hurry to get away."

"It does n't signify. I 've another at home."

"Another summer-house?" he more lightly suggested.

"A copy of Mr. Hoppus."

"Mercy, how you go in for him! Fancy having two!"

"He sent me the number of the magazine, and the other's the one that comes every month."

"Every month; I see" — but his manner justified considerably her charge of vagueness. They had reached the stile and he leaned over it, looking at a great mild meadow and at the browsing beasts in the distance.

"Did you suppose they come every day?" Julia went on.

"Dear no, thank God!" They remained there a little; he continued to look at the animals and before long added: "Delightful English pastoral scene. Why do they say it won't paint?"

"Who says it won't?"

"I don't know — some of them. It will in France; but somehow it won't here."

"What are you talking about?" Mrs. Dallow demanded.

He appeared unable to satisfy her on this point; instead of answering her directly he at any rate said: "Is Broadwood very charming?"

"Have you never been there? It shows how you've treated me. We used to go there in August. George had ideas about it," she added. She had never affected not to speak of her late husband, especially with Nick, whose kinsman he had in a manner been and who had liked him better than some others did.

"George had ideas about a great many things."

Yet she appeared conscious it would be rather odd on such an occasion to take this up. It was even odd in Nick to have said it. "Broadwood's just right," she returned at last. "It's neither too small nor too big, and it takes care of itself. There's nothing to be done: you can't spend a penny."

"And don't you want to use it?"

"We can go and stay with *them*," said Julia.

"They'll think I bring them an angel." And Nick covered her white hand, which was resting on the stile, with his own large one.

"As they regard you yourself as an angel they'll take it as natural of you to associate with your kind."

"Oh *my* kind!" he quite wailed, looking at the cows.

But his very extravagance perhaps saved it, and she turned away from him as if starting homeward, while he began to retrace his steps with her. Suddenly she said: "What did you mean that night in Paris?"

"That night — ?"

"When you came to the hotel with me after we had all dined at that place with Peter."

"What did I mean — ?"

"About your caring so much for the fine arts. You seemed to want to frighten me."

"Why should you have been frightened? I can't imagine what I had in my head: not now."

"You *are* vague," said Julia with a little flush.

"Not about the great thing."

"The great thing?"

"That I owe you everything an honest man has to offer. How can I care about the fine arts now?"

She stopped with lighted eyes on him. "Is it because you think you *owe* it — " and she paused, still with the heightened colour in her cheek, then went on — "that you've spoken to me as you did there?" She tossed her head toward the lake.

"I think I spoke to you because I could n't help it."

"You *are* vague!" And she walked on again.

"You affect me differently from any other woman."

"Oh other women — ! Why should n't you care about the fine arts now?" she added.

"There'll be no time. All my days and my years will be none too much for what you expect of me."

"I don't expect you to give up anything. I only expect you to do more."

"To do more I must do less. I've no talent."

"No talent?"

"I mean for painting."

Julia pulled up again. "That's odious! You *have* — you must."

He burst out laughing. "You're altogether delightful. But how little you know about it — about the honourable practice of any art!"

"What do you call practice? You'll have all our things — you'll live in the midst of them."

"Certainly I shall enjoy looking at them, being so near them."

"Don't say I've taken you away then."

"Taken me away — ?"

"From the love of art. I like them myself now, poor George's treasures. I did n't of old so much, because it seemed to me he made too much of them — he was always talking."

"Well, I won't always talk," said Nick.

"You may do as you like — they're yours."

"Give them to the nation," Nick went on.

"I like that! When we've done with them."

"We shall have done with them when your Vandykes and Moronis have cured me of the delusion that I may be of *their* family. Surely that won't take long."

"You shall paint *me*," said Julia.

"Never, never, never!" He spoke in a tone that made his companion stare — then seemed slightly embarrassed at this result of his emphasis. To relieve himself he said, as they had come back to the place beside the lake where the boat was moored, "Shan't we really go and fetch Mr. Hoppus?"

She hesitated. "You may go; I won't, please."

"That's not what I want."

"Oblige me by going. I'll wait here." With which she sat down on the bench attached to the little landing.

Nick, at this, got into the boat and put off; he smiled at her as she sat there watching him. He made his short journey, disembarked and went into the

283

pavilion; but when he came out with the object of his errand he saw she had quitted her station, had returned to the house without him. He rowed back quickly, sprang ashore and followed her with long steps. Apparently she had gone fast; she had almost reached the door when he overtook her.

"Why did you basely desert me?" he asked, tenderly stopping her there.

"I don't know. Because I'm so happy."

"May I tell mother then?"

"You may tell her she shall have Broadwood."

XVI

He lost no time in going down to see Mr. Carteret, to whom he had written immediately after the election and who had answered him in twelve revised pages of historical parallel. He used often to envy Mr. Carteret's leisure, a sense of which came to him now afresh, in the summer evening, as he walked up the hill toward the quiet house where enjoyment had ever been mingled for him with a vague oppression. He was a little boy again, under Mr. Carteret's roof — a little boy on whom it had been duly impressed that in the wide plain peaceful rooms he was not to "touch." When he paid a visit to his father's old friend there were in fact many things — many topics — from which he instinctively kept his hands. Even Mr. Chayter, the immemorial blank butler, who was so like his master that he might have been a twin brother, helped to remind him that he must be good. Mr. Carteret seemed to Nick a very grave person, but he had the sense that Chayter thought him rather frivolous.

Our young man always came on foot from the station, leaving his portmanteau to be carried: the direct way was steep and he liked the slow approach, which gave him a chance to look about the place and smell the new-mown hay. At this season the air was full of it — the fields were so near that it was in the clean still streets. Nick would never have thought

of rattling up to Mr. Carteret's door, which had on
an old brass plate the proprietor's name, as if he had
been the principal surgeon. The house was in the
high part, and the neat roofs of other houses, lower
down the hill, made an immediate prospect for it,
scarcely counting, however, since the green country
was just below these, familiar and interpenetrating,
in the shape of small but thick-tufted gardens. Free
garden-growths flourished in all the intervals, but
the only disorder of the place was that there were
sometimes oats on the pavements. A crooked lane,
with postern doors and cobblestones, opened near
Mr. Carteret's house and wandered toward the old
abbey; for the abbey was the secondary fact of Beauclere — it came after Mr. Carteret. Mr. Carteret
sometimes went away and the abbey never did; yet
somehow what was most of the essence of the place
was that it could boast of the resident in the squarest
of the square red houses, the one with the finest of
the arched hall-windows, in three divisions, over the
widest of the last-century doorways. You saw the
great church from the doorstep, beyond gardens of
course, and in the stillness you could hear the flutter
of the birds that circled round its huge short towers.
The towers had been finished only as time finishes
things, by lending assurances to their lapses. There
is something right in old monuments that have been
wrong for centuries: some such moral as that was
usually in Nick's mind as an emanation of Beauclere when he saw the grand line of the roof ride the
sky and draw out its length.

When the door with the brass plate was opened

and Mr. Chayter appeared in the middle distance — he always advanced just to the same spot, as a prime minister receives an ambassador — Nick felt anew that he would be wonderfully like Mr. Carteret if he had had an expression. He denied himself this freedom, never giving a sign of recognition, often as the young man had been at the house. He was most attentive to the visitor's wants, but apparently feared that if he allowed a familiarity it might go too far. There was always the same question to be asked — had Mr. Carteret finished his nap? He usually had not finished it, and this left Nick what he liked — time to smoke a cigarette in the garden or even to take before dinner a turn about the place. He observed now, every time he came, that Mr. Carteret's nap lasted a little longer. There was each year a little more strength to be gathered for the ceremony of dinner: this was the principal symptom — almost the only one — that the clear-cheeked old gentleman gave of not being so fresh as of yore. He was still wonderful for his age. To-day he was particularly careful: Chayter went so far as to mention to Nick that four gentlemen were expected to dinner — an exuberance perhaps partly explained by the circumstance that Lord Bottomley was one of them.

The prospect of Lord Bottomley was somehow not stirring; it only made the young man say to himself with a quick thin sigh "This time I *am* in for it!" And he immediately had the unpolitical sense again that there was nothing so pleasant as the way the quiet bachelor house had its best rooms on the big garden, which seemed to advance into them

through their wide windows and ruralise their dull-
ness.

"I expect it will be a lateish eight, sir," said Mr.
Chayter, superintending in the library the production of tea on a large scale. Everything at Mr. Carteret's seemed to Nick on a larger scale than anywhere else — the tea-cups, the knives and forks, the
door-handles, the chair-backs, the legs of mutton,
the candles and the lumps of coal: they represented
and apparently exhausted the master's sense of pleasing effect, for the house was not otherwise decorated.
Nick thought it really hideous, but he was capable at
any time of extracting a degree of amusement from
anything strongly characteristic, and Mr. Carteret's
interior expressed a whole view of life. Our young
man was generous enough to find in it a hundred
instructive intimations even while it came over him —
as it always did at Beauclere — that this was the view
he himself was expected to take. Nowhere were the
boiled eggs at breakfast so big or in such big recepta-
cles; his own shoes, arranged in his room, looked to
him vaster there than at home. He went out into the
garden and remembered what enormous strawber-
ries they should have for dinner. In the house was
a great deal of Landseer, of oilcloth, of woodwork
painted and "grained."

Finding there would be time before the evening
meal or before Mr. Carteret was likely to see him he
quitted the house and took a stroll toward the abbey.
It covered acres of ground on the summit of the hill,
and there were aspects in which its vast bulk reminded
him of the ark left high and dry upon Ararat. It was

the image at least of a great wreck, of the indestructible vessel of a faith, washed up there by a storm centuries before. The injury of time added to this appearance — the infirmities round which, as he knew, the battle of restoration had begun to be fought. The cry had been raised to save the splendid pile, and the counter-cry by the purists, the sentimentalists, whatever they were, to save it from being saved. They were all exchanging compliments in the morning papers.

Nick sauntered about the church — it took a good while; he leaned against low things and looked up at it while he smoked another cigarette. It struck him as a great pity such a pile should be touched: so much of the past was buried there that it was like desecrating, like digging up a grave. Since the years were letting it down so gently why jostle the elbow of slow-fingering time ? The fading afternoon was exquisitely pure; the place was empty; he heard nothing but the cries of several children, which sounded sweet, who were playing on the flatness of the very old tombs. He knew this would inevitably be one of the topics at dinner, the restoration of the abbey; it would give rise to a considerable deal of orderly debate. Lord Bottomley, oddly enough, would probably oppose the expensive project, but on grounds that would be characteristic of him even if the attitude were not. Nick's nerves always knew on this spot what it was to be soothed; but he shifted his position with a slight impatience as the vision came over him of Lord Bottomley's treating a question of æsthetics. It was enough to make one want to take the other side, the idea of having the same taste as his lordship: one would have it for such different reasons.

Dear Mr. Carteret would be deliberate and fair all round and would, like his noble friend, exhibit much more architectural knowledge than he, Nick, possessed: which would not make it a whit less droll to our young man that an artistic idea, so little really assimilated, should be broached at that table and in that air. It would remain so outside of their minds and their minds would remain so outside of it. It would be dropped at last, however, after half an hour's gentle worrying, and the conversation would incline itself to public affairs. Mr. Carteret would find his natural level — the production of anecdote in regard to the formation of early ministries. He knew more than any one else about the personages of whom certain cabinets would have consisted if they had not consisted of others. His favourite exercise was to illustrate how different everything might have been from what it was, and how the reason of the difference had always been somebody's inability to "see his way" to accept the view of somebody else — a view usually at the time discussed in strict confidence with Mr. Carteret, who surrounded his actual violation of that confidence thirty years later with many precautions against scandal. In this retrospective vein, at the head of his table, the old gentleman enjoyed a hearing, or at any rate commanded a silence, often intense. Every one left it to some one else to ask another question; and when by chance some one else did so every one was struck

with admiration at any one's being able to say anything. Nick knew the moment when he himself would
take a glass of a particular port and, surreptitiously
looking at his watch, perceive it was ten o'clock. That
timepiece might as well mark 1830.

All this would be a part of the suggestion of leisure
that invariably descended upon him at Beauclere —
the image of a sloping shore where the tide of time
broke with a ripple too faint to be a warning. But
there was another admonition almost equally sure
to descend upon his spirit during a stroll in a summer
hour about the grand abbey; to sink into it as the
light lingered on the rough red walls and the local
accent of the children sounded soft in the church-
yard. It was simply the sense of England — a sort
of apprehended revelation of his country. The dim
annals of the place were sensibly, heavily in the air —
foundations bafflingly early, a great monastic life,
wars of the Roses, with battles and blood in the streets,
and then the long quietude of the respectable centuries, all corn-fields and magistrates and vicars — and
these things were connected with an emotion that
arose from the green country, the rich land so infinitely lived in, and laid on him a hand that was too
ghostly to press and yet somehow too urgent to be
light. It produced a throb he could n't have spoken
of, it was so deep, and that was half imagination
and half responsibility. These impressions melted
together and made a general appeal, of which, with
his new honours as a legislator, he was the sentient
subject. If he had a love for that particular scene
of life might n't it have a love for him and expect

something of him? What fate could be so high as to grow old in a national affection? What a fine sort of reciprocity, making mere soreness of all the balms of indifference!

The great church was still open and he turned into it and wandered a little in the twilight that had gathered earlier there. The whole structure, with its immensity of height and distance, seemed to rest on tremendous facts — facts of achievement and endurance — and the huge Norman pillars to loom through the dimness like the ghosts of heroes. Nick was more struck with its thick earthly than with its fine spiritual reference, and he felt the oppression of his conscience as he walked slowly about. It was in his mind that nothing in life was really clear, all things were mingled and charged, and that patriotism might be an uplifting passion even if it had to allow for Lord Bottomley and for Mr. Carteret's blindness on certain sides. He presently noticed that half-past seven was about to strike, and as he went back to his old friend's he could n't have said if he walked in gladness or in gloom.

"Mr. Carteret will be in the drawing-room at a quarter to eight, sir," Chayter mentioned, and Nick as he went to dress asked himself what was the use of being a member of Parliament if one was still sensitive to an intimation on the part of such a functionary that one ought already to have begun that business. Chayter's words but meant that Mr. Carteret would expect to have a little comfortable conversation with him before dinner. Nick's usual rapidity in dressing was, however, quite adequate

292

to the occasion, so that his host had not appeared when he went down. There were flowers in the unfeminine saloon, which contained several paintings in addition to the engravings of pictures of animals; but nothing could prevent its reminding Nick of a comfortable committee-room.

Mr. Carteret presently came in with his gold-headed stick, a laugh like a series of little warning coughs and the air of embarrassment that our young man always perceived in him at first. He was almost eighty but was still shy — he laughed a great deal, faintly and vaguely, at nothing, as if to make up for the seriousness with which he took some jokes. He always began by looking away from his interlocutor, and it was only little by little that his eyes came round; after which their limpid and benevolent blue made you wonder why they should ever be circumspect. He was clean-shaven and had a long upper lip. When he had seated himself he talked of "majorities" and showed a disposition to converse on the general subject of the fluctuation of Liberal gains. He had an extraordinary memory for facts of this sort, and could mention the figures relating to the returns from innumerable places in particular years. To many of these facts he attached great importance, in his simple kindly presupposing way; correcting himself five minutes later if he had said that in 1857 some one had had 6014 instead of 6004.

Nick always felt a great hypocrite as he listened to him, in spite of the old man's courtesy — a thing so charming in itself that it would have been grossness to speak of him as a bore. The difficulty was that he took for granted all kinds of positive assent, and Nick, in such company, found himself steeped in an element of tacit pledges which constituted the very medium of intercourse and yet made him draw his breath a little in pain when for a moment he measured them. There would have been no hypocrisy at all if he could have regarded Mr. Carteret as a mere sweet spectacle, the last or almost the last illustration of a departing tradition of manners. But he represented something more than manners; he represented what he believed to be morals and ideas, ideas as regards which he took your personal deference — not discovering how natural that was — for participation. Nick liked to think that his father, though ten years younger, had found it congruous to make his best friend of the owner of so nice a nature: it gave a softness to his feeling for that memory to be reminded that Sir Nicholas had been of the same general type — a type so pure, so disinterested, so concerned for the public good. Just so it endeared Mr. Carteret to him to perceive that he considered his father had done a definite work, prematurely interrupted, which had been an absolute benefit to the people of England. The oddity was, however, that though both Mr. Carteret's aspect and his appreciation were still so fresh this relation of his to his late distinguished friend made the latter appear to Nick even more irrecoverably dead. The good old man had almost a vocabulary of his own, made up of old-fashioned political phrases and quite untainted with the new terms, mostly borrowed from America; indeed his language and his tone made those of almost any one

who might be talking with him sound by contrast
rather American. He was, at least nowadays, never
severe nor denunciatory; but sometimes in telling an
anecdote he dropped such an expression as "the
rascal said to me" or such an epithet as "the vulgar
dog."

Nick was always struck with the rare simplicity —
it came out in his countenance — of one who had
lived so long and seen so much of affairs that draw
forth the passions and perversities of men. It often
made him say to himself that Mr. Carteret must have
had many odd parts to have been able to achieve
with his means so many things requiring cleverness.
It was as if experience, though coming to him in
abundance, had dealt with him so clean-handedly
as to leave no stain, and had moreover never provoked him to any general reflexion. He had never
proceeded in any ironic way from the particular to
the general; certainly he had never made a reflexion
upon anything so unparliamentary as Life. He would
have questioned the taste of such an extravagance
and if he had encountered it on the part of another
have regarded it as an imported foreign toy with
the uses of which he was unacquainted. Life, for
him, was a purely practical function, not a question
of more or less showy phrasing. It must be added
that he had to Nick's perception his variations — his
back windows opening into grounds more private.
That was visible from the way his eye grew cold and
his whole polite face rather austere when he listened
to something he did n't agree with or perhaps even
understand; as if his modesty did n't in strictness

forbid the suspicion that a thing he did n't understand would have a probability against it. At such times there was something rather deadly in the silence in which he simply waited with a lapse in his face, not helping his interlocutor out. Nick would have been very sorry to attempt to communicate to him a matter he would n't be likely to understand. This cut off of course a multitude of subjects.

The evening passed exactly as he had foreseen, even to the markedly prompt dispersal of the guests, two of whom were "local" men, earnest and distinct, though not particularly distinguished. The third was a young slim uninitiated gentleman whom Lord Bottomley brought with him and concerning whom Nick was informed beforehand that he was engaged to be married to the Honourable Jane, his lordship's second daughter. There were recurrent allusions to Nick's victory, as to which he had the fear that he might appear to exhibit less interest in it than the company did. He took energetic precautions against this and felt repeatedly a little spent with them, for the subject always came up once more. Yet it was not as his but as theirs that they liked the triumph. Mr. Carteret took leave of him for the night directly after the other guests had gone, using at this moment the words he had often used before:

"You may sit up to any hour you like. I only ask that you don't read in bed."

XVII

NICK's little visit was to terminate immediately after luncheon the following day: much as the old man enjoyed his being there he would n't have dreamed of asking for more of his time now that it had such great public uses. He liked infinitely better that his young friend should be occupied with parliamentary work than only occupied in talking it over with him. Talking it over, however, was the next best thing, as on the morrow, after breakfast, Mr. Carteret showed Nick he considered. They sat in the garden, the morning being warm, and the old man had a table beside him covered with the letters and newspapers the post had poured forth. He was proud of his correspondence, which was altogether on public affairs, and proud in a manner of the fact that he now dictated almost everything. That had more in it of the statesman in retirement, a character indeed not consciously assumed by Mr. Carteret, but always tacitly attributed to him by Nick, who took it rather from the pictorial point of view — remembering on each occasion only afterwards that though he was in retirement he had not exactly been a statesman. A young man, a very sharp handy young man, came every morning at ten o'clock and wrote for him till luncheon. The young man had a holiday to-day in honour of Nick's visit — a fact the mention of which led Nick to make some not particularly sincere

speech about *his* being ready to write anything if
Mr. Carteret were at all pressed.

"Ah but your own budget — what will become of
that?" the old gentleman objected, glancing at Nick's
pockets as if rather surprised not to see them stuffed
out with documents in split envelopes. His visitor
had to confess that he had not directed his letters
to meet him at Beauclere: he should find them in
town that afternoon. This led to a little homily from
Mr. Carteret which made him feel quite guilty; there
was such an implication of neglected duty in the way
the old man said "You won't do them justice — you
won't do them justice." He talked for ten minutes,
in his rich simple urbane way, about the fatal consequences of getting behind. It was his favourite doctrine that one should always be a little before, and
his own eminently regular respiration seemed to
illustrate the idea. A man was certainly before who
had so much in his rear.

This led to the bestowal of a good deal of general
advice on the mistakes to avoid at the beginning of
a parliamentary career — as to which Mr. Carteret
spoke with the experience of one who had sat for fifty
years in the House of Commons. Nick was amused,
but also mystified and even a little irritated, by his
talk: it was founded on the idea of observation and
yet our young man could n't at all regard him as an
observer. "He does n't observe *me*," he said to himself; "if he did he would see, he would n't think —!"
The end of this private cogitation was a vague impatience of all the things his venerable host took for
granted. He did n't see any of the things Nick saw.

Some of these latter were the light touches the summer morning scattered through the sweet old garden. The time passed there a good deal as if it were sitting still with a plaid under its feet while Mr. Carteret distilled a little more of the wisdom he had laid up in his fifty years. This immense term had something fabulous and monstrous for Nick, who wondered whether it were the sort of thing his companion supposed *he* had gone in for. It was not strange Mr. Carteret should be different; he might originally have been more — well, to himself Nick was not obliged to phrase it : what our young man meant was more of what it was perceptible to him that his old friend was not. Should even he, Nick, be like that at the end of fifty years ? What Mr. Carteret was so good as to expect for him was that he should be much more distinguished; and would n't this exactly mean much more like that ? Of course Nick heard some things he had heard before; as for instance the circumstances that had originally led the old man to settle at Beauclere. He had been returned for that borough — it was his second seat — in years far remote, and had come to live there because he then had a conscientious conviction, modified indeed by later experience, that a member should be constantly resident. He spoke of this now, smiling rosily, as he might have spoken of some wild aberration of his youth; yet he called Nick's attention to the fact that he still so far clung to his conviction as to hold — though of what might be urged on the other side he was perfectly aware — that a representative should at least be as resident as possible. This gave

Nick an opening for something that had been on and off his lips all the morning.

"According to that I ought to take up my abode at Harsh."

"In the measure of the convenient I should n't be sorry to see you do it."

"It ought to be rather convenient," Nick largely smiled. "I 've got a piece of news for you which I 've kept, as one keeps that sort of thing — for it 's very good — till the last." He waited a little to see if Mr. Carteret would guess, and at first thought nothing would come of this. But after resting his young-looking eyes on him for a moment the old man said —

"I should indeed be very happy to hear that you 've arranged to take a wife."

"Mrs. Dallow has been so good as to say she 'll marry me," Nick returned.

"That 's very suitable. I should think it would answer."

"It 's very jolly," said Nick. It was well Mr. Carteret was not what his guest called observant, or he might have found a lower pitch in the sound of this sentence than in the sense.

"Your dear father would have liked it."

"So my mother says."

"And *she* must be delighted."

"Mrs. Dallow, do you mean?" Nick asked.

"I was thinking of your mother. But I don't exclude the charming lady. I remember her as a little girl. I must have seen her at Windrush. Now I understand the fine spirit with which she threw herself into your canvass."

"It was her they elected," said Nick.

"I don't know," his host went on, "that I've ever been an enthusiast for political women, but there's no doubt that in approaching the mass of electors a graceful affable manner, the manner of the real English lady, is a force not to be despised."

"Julia's a real English lady and at the same time a very political woman," Nick remarked.

"Isn't it rather in the family? I remember once going to see her mother in town and finding the leaders of both parties sitting with her."

"My principal friend, of the others, is her brother Peter. I don't think he troubles himself much about that sort of thing," said Nick.

"What does he trouble himself about?" Mr. Carteret asked with a certain gravity.

"He's in the diplomatic service; he's a secretary in Paris."

"That may be serious," said the old man.

"He takes a great interest in the theatre. I suppose you'll say that may be serious too," Nick laughed.

"Oh!" — and Mr. Carteret looked as if he scarcely understood. Then he continued: "Well, it can't hurt you."

"It can't hurt me?"

"If Mrs. Dallow takes an interest in your interests."

"When a man's in my situation he feels as if nothing could hurt him."

"I'm very glad you're happy," said Mr. Carteret. He rested his mild eyes on our young man, who had a sense of seeing in them for a moment the faint

301

ghost of an old story, the last strange flicker, as from cold ashes, of a flame that had become the memory of a memory. This glimmer of wonder and envy, the revelation of a life intensely celibate, was for an instant infinitely touching. Nick had harboured a theory, suggested by a vague allusion from his father, who had been discreet, that their benevolent friend had had in his youth an unhappy love-affair which had led him to forswear for ever the commerce of woman. What remained in him of conscious renunciation gave a throb as he looked at his bright companion, who proposed to take the matter so much the other way. "It's good to marry and I think it's right. I've not done right, I know that. If she's a good woman it's the best thing," Mr. Carteret went on. "It's what I've been hoping for you. Sometimes I've thought of speaking to you."

"She's a very good woman," said Nick.

"And I hope she's not poor." Mr. Carteret spoke exactly with the same blandness.

"No indeed, she's rich. Her husband, whom I knew and liked, left her a large fortune."

"And on what terms does she enjoy it?"

"I have n't the least idea," said Nick.

Mr. Carteret considered. "I see. It does n't concern you. It need n't concern you," he added in a moment.

Nick thought of his mother at this, but he returned: "I dare say she can do what she likes with her money."

"So can I, my dear young friend," said Mr. Carteret.

Nick tried not to look conscious, for he felt a significance in the old man's face. He turned his own everywhere but toward it, thinking again of his mother. "That must be very pleasant, if one has any."

"I wish you had a little more."

"I don't particularly care," said Nick.

"Your marriage will assist you ; you can't help that," Mr. Carteret declared. "But I should like you to be under obligations not quite so heavy."

"Oh I'm so obliged to her for caring for me —!"

"That the rest does n't count ? Certainly it's nice of her to like you. But why should n't she ? Other people do."

"Some of them make me feel as if I abused it," said Nick, looking at his host. "That is they don't make me, but I feel it," he corrected.

"I've no son" — and Mr. Carteret spoke as if his companion might n't have been sure. "Shan't you be very kind to her ?" he pursued. "You'll gratify her ambition."

"Oh she thinks me cleverer than I am."

"That's because she's in love," the old gentleman hinted as if this were very subtle. "However, you must be as clever as we think you. If you don't prove so —!" And he paused with his folded hands.

"Well, if I don't ?" asked Nick.

"Oh it won't do — it won't do," said Mr. Carteret in a tone his companion was destined to remember afterwards. "I say I've no son," he continued; "but if I had had one he should have risen high."

"It's well for me such a person does n't exist. I should n't easily have found a wife."

"He would have gone to the altar with a little money in his pocket."

"That would have been the least of his advantages, sir," Nick declared.

"When are you to be married?" Mr. Carteret asked.

"Ah that's the question. Julia won't yet say."

"Well," said the old man without the least flourish, "you may consider that when it comes off I'll make you a settlement."

"I feel your kindness more than I can express," Nick replied; "but that will probably be the moment when I shall be least conscious of wanting anything."

"You'll appreciate it later — you'll appreciate it very soon. I shall like you to appreciate it," Mr. Carteret went on as if he had a just vision of the way a young man of a proper spirit should feel. Then he added: "Your father would have liked you to appreciate it."

"Poor father!" Nick exclaimed vaguely, rather embarrassed, reflecting on the oddity of a position in which the ground for holding up his head as the husband of a rich woman would be that he had accepted a present of money from another source. It was plain he was not fated to go in for independence; the most that he could treat himself to would be dependence that was duly grateful. "How much do you expect of me?" he enquired with a grave face.

"Well, Nicholas, only what your father did. He so often spoke of you, I remember, at the last, just after you had been with him alone — you know I saw him then. He was greatly moved by his interview with you, and so was I by what he told me of it. He said he should live on in you — he should work in you. It has always given me a special feeling, if I may use the expression, about you."

"The feelings are indeed not usual, dear Mr. Carteret, which take so munificent a form. But you do — oh you do — expect too much," Nick brought himself to say.

"I expect you to repay me!" the old man returned gaily. "As for the form, I have it in my mind."

"The form of repayment?"

"The form of repayment!"

"Ah don't talk of that now," said Nick, "for, you see, nothing else is settled. No one has been told except my mother. She has only consented to my telling you."

"Lady Agnes, do you mean?"

"Ah no; dear mother would like to publish it on the house-tops. She's so glad — she wants us to have it over to-morrow. But Julia herself," Nick explained, "wishes to wait. Therefore kindly mention it for the present to no one."

"My dear boy, there's at this rate nothing to mention! What does Julia want to wait for?"

"Till I like her better — that's what she says."

"It's the way to make you like her worse," Mr. Carteret knowingly declared. "Has n't she your affection?"

"So much so that her delay makes me exceedingly unhappy."

Mr. Carteret looked at his young friend as if he did n't strike him as quite wretched; but he put the question: "Then what more does she want?" Nick laughed out at this, though perceiving his host had n't meant it as an epigram; while the latter resumed: "I don't understand. You're engaged or you're not engaged."

"She is, but I'm not. That's what she says about it. The trouble is she does n't believe in me."

Mr. Carteret shone with his candour. "Does n't she love you then?"

"That's what I ask her. Her answer is that she loves me only too well. She's so afraid of being a burden to me that she gives me my freedom till I've taken another year to think."

"I like the way you talk about other years!" Mr. Carteret cried. "You had better do it while I'm here to bless you."

"She thinks I proposed to her because she got me in for Harsh," said Nick.

"Well, I'm sure it would be a very pretty return."

"Ah she does n't believe in me," the young man repeated.

"Then I don't believe in *her*."

"Don't say that — don't say that. She's a very rare creature. But she's proud, shy, suspicious."

"Suspicious of what?"

"Of everything. She thinks I'm not persistent."

"Oh, oh!" — Nick's host deprecated such freedom.

"She can't believe I shall arrive at true eminence."

306

"A good wife should believe what her husband believes," said Mr. Carteret.

"Ah unfortunately" — and Nick took the words at a run — "I don't believe it either."

Mr. Carteret, who might have been watching an odd physical rush, spoke with a certain dryness. "Your dear father did."

"I think of that — I think of that," Nick replied. "Certainly it will help me. If I say we're engaged," he went on, "it's because I consider it so. She gives me my liberty, but I don't take it."

"Does she expect you to take back your word?"

"That's what I ask her. *She* never will. Therefore we're as good as tied."

"I don't like it," said Mr. Carteret after a moment. "I don't like ambiguous uncertain situations. They please me much better when they're definite and clear." The retreat of expression had been sounded in his face — the aspect it wore when he wished not to be encouraging. But after an instant he added in a tone more personal: "Don't disappoint me, dear boy."

"Ah not willingly!" his visitor protested.

"I've told you what I should like to do for you. See that the conditions come about promptly in which I *may* do it. Are you sure you do everything to satisfy Mrs. Dallow?" Mr. Carteret continued.

"I think I'm very nice to her," Nick declared. "But she's so ambitious. Frankly speaking, it's a pity for her that she likes me."

"She can't help that!" the old man charmingly said.

"Possibly. But is n't it a reason for taking me as I am? What she wants to do is to take me as I may be a year hence."

"I don't understand — since you tell me that even then she won't take back her word," said Mr. Carteret.

"If she does n't marry me I think she 'll never marry again at all."

"What then does she gain by delay?"

"Simply this, as I make it out" said Nick — "that she 'll feel she has been very magnanimous. She won't have to reproach herself with not having given me a chance to change."

"To change? What does she think you liable to do?"

Nick had a pause. "I don't know!" he then said — not at all candidly.

"Everything has altered: young people in my day looked at these questions more naturally," Mr. Carteret observed. "A woman in love has no need to be magnanimous. If she plays too fair she is n't in love," he added shrewdly.

"Oh, Julia's safe — she 's safe," Nick smiled.

"If it were a question between you and another gentleman one might comprehend. But what does it mean, between you and nothing?"

"I 'm much obliged to you, sir," Nick returned. "The trouble is that she does n't know what she has got hold of."

"Ah, if you can't make it clear to her!" — and his friend showed the note of impatience.

"I 'm such a humbug," said the young man. And

while his companion stared he continued: "I deceive people without in the least intending it."

"What on earth do you mean? Are you deceiving me?"

"I don't know — it depends on what you think."

"I think you're flighty," said Mr. Carteret, with the nearest approach to sternness Nick had ever observed in him. "I never thought so before."

"Forgive me; it's all right. I'm not frivolous; that I promise you I'm not."

"You *have* deceived me if you are."

"It's all right," Nick stammered with a blush.

"Remember your name — carry it high."

"I will — as high as possible."

"You've no excuse. Don't tell me, after your speeches at Harsh!" Nick was on the point of declaring again that he was a humbug, so vivid was his inner sense of what *he* thought of his factitious public utterances, which had the cursed property of creating dreadful responsibilities and importunate credulities for him. If *he* was "clever" (ah the idiotic "clever"!) what fools many other people were! He repressed his impulse and Mr. Carteret pursued. "If, as you express it, Mrs. Dallow does n't know what she has got hold of, won't it clear the matter up a little by informing her that the day before your marriage is definitely settled to take place you'll come into something comfortable?"

A quick vision of what Mr. Carteret would be likely to regard as something comfortable flitted before Nick, but it did n't prevent his replying: "Oh I'm afraid that won't do any good. It would make her like you better, but it would n't make her like me. I 'm afraid she won't care for any benefit that comes to me from another hand than hers. Her affection's a very jealous sentiment."

"It's a very peculiar one!" sighed Mr. Carteret. "Mine's a jealous sentiment too. However, if she takes it that way don't tell her."

"I 'll let you know as soon as she comes round," said Nick.

"And you 'll tell your mother," Mr. Carteret returned. "I shall like *her* to know."

"It will be delightful news to her. But she's keen enough already."

"I know that. I may mention now that she has written to me," the old man added.

"So I suspected."

"We 've — a — corresponded on the subject," Mr. Carteret continued to confess. "My view of the advantageous character of such an alliance has entirely coincided with hers."

"It was very good-natured of you then to leave me to speak first," said Nick.

"I should have been disappointed if you had n't. I don't like all you 've told me. But don't disappoint me now."

"Dear Mr. Carteret!" Nick vaguely and richly sounded.

"I won't disappoint *you*," that gentleman went on with a finer point while he looked at his big old-fashioned watch.

BOOK FOURTH

XVIII

AT first Peter Sherringham thought of asking to be transferred to another post and went so far, in London, as to take what he believed good advice on the subject. The advice perhaps struck him as the better for consisting of a strong recommendation to do nothing so foolish. Two or three reasons were mentioned to him why such a request would not, in the particular circumstances, raise him in the esteem of his superiors, and he promptly recognised their force. He next became aware that it might help him — not with his superiors but with himself — to apply for an extension of leave, and then on further reflexion made out that, though there are some dangers before which it is perfectly consistent with honour to flee, it was better for every one concerned that he should fight this especial battle on the spot. During his holiday his plan of campaign gave him plenty of occupation. He refurbished his arms, rubbed up his strategy, laid down his lines of defence.

There was only one thing in life his mind had been much made up to, but on this question he had never wavered: he would get on, to the utmost, in his profession. That was a point on which it was perfectly lawful to be unamiable to others — to be vigilant, eager, suspicious, selfish. He had not in fact been unamiable to others, for his affairs had not required it: he had got on well enough without hardening his heart. Fortune had been kind to him and he had passed so many competitors on the way that he could forswear jealousy and be generous. But he had always flattered himself his hand would n't falter on the day he should find it necessary to drop bitterness into his cup. This day would be sure to dawn, since no career could be all clear water to the end; and then the sacrifice would find him ready. His mind was familiar with the thought of a sacrifice: it is true that no great plainness invested beforehand the occasion, the object or the victim. All that particularly stood out was that the propitiatory offering would have to be some cherished enjoyment. Very likely indeed this enjoyment would be associated with the charms of another person — a probability pregnant with the idea that such charms would have to be dashed out of sight. At any rate it never had occurred to Sherringham that he himself might be the sacrifice. You had to pay to get on, but at least you borrowed from others to do it. When you could n't borrow you did n't get on, for what was the situation in life in which you met the whole requisition yourself?

Least of all had it occurred to our friend that the wrench might come through his interest in that branch of art on which Nick Dormer had rallied him. The beauty of a love of the theatre was precisely in its being a passion exercised on the easiest terms. This was not the region of responsibility. It was sniffed at, to its discredit, by the austere; but if it was not, as such people said, a serious field, was not the compensation just that you could n't be seriously entangled in it? Sherringham's great advantage, as he regarded the matter, was that he had always kept his taste for the drama quite in its place. His facetious cousin was free to pretend that it sprawled through his life; but this was nonsense, as any unprejudiced observer of that life would unhesitatingly attest. There had not been the least sprawling, and his interest in the art of Garrick had never, he was sure, made him in any degree ridiculous. It had never drawn down from above anything approaching a reprimand, a remonstrance, a remark. Sherringham was positively proud of his discretion, for he was not a little proud of what he did know about the stage. Trifling for trifling, there were plenty of his fellows who had in their lives infatuations less edifying and less confessable. Had n't he known men who collected old invitation-cards and were ready to commit *bassesses* for those of the eighteenth century? had n't he known others who had a secret passion for shuffleboard? His little weaknesses were intellectual — they were a part of the life of the mind. All the same, on the day they showed a symptom of interfering they should be plucked off with a turn of the wrist.

Sherringham scented interference now, and interference in rather an invidious form. It might be a bore, from the point of view of the profession, to find one's self, as a critic of the stage, in love with a *coquine;* but it was a much greater bore to find one's self in love with a young woman whose character remained to be estimated. Miriam Rooth was neither fish nor flesh: one had with her neither the guarantees of one's own class nor the immunities of hers. What

315

was hers if one came to that? A rare ambiguity on this point was part of the fascination she had ended by throwing over him. Poor Peter's scheme for getting on had contained no proviso against his falling in love, but it had embodied an important clause on the subject of surprises. It was always a surprise to fall in love, especially if one was looking out for it; so this contingency had not been worth official paper. But it became a man who respected the service he had undertaken for the State to be on his guard against predicaments from which the only issue was the rigour of matrimony. Ambition, in the career, was probably consistent with marrying — but only with opening one's eyes very wide to do it. That was the fatal surprise — to be led to the altar in a dream. Sherringham's view of the proprieties attached to such a step was high and strict; and if he held that a man in his position was, above all as the position improved, essentially a representative of the greatness of his country, he considered that the wife of such a personage would exercise in her degree — for instance at a foreign court — a function no less symbolic. She would in short always be a very important quantity, and the scene was strewn with illustrations of this general truth. She might be such a help and might be such a blight that common prudence required some test of her in advance. Sherringham had seen women in the career, who were stupid or vulgar, make such a mess of things as would wring your heart. Then he had his positive idea of the perfect ambassadress, the full-blown lily of the future; and with this idea Miriam Rooth presented no analogy whatever.

The girl had described herself with characteristic directness as "all right"; and so she might be, so she assuredly was: only all right for what? He had made out she was not sentimental — that whatever capacity she might have for responding to a devotion or for desiring it was at any rate not in the direction of vague philandering. With him certainly she had no disposition to philander. Sherringham almost feared to dwell on this, lest it should beget in him a rage convertible mainly into caring for her more. Rage or no rage it would be charming to be in love with her if there were no complications; but the complications were just what was clearest in the prospect. He was perhaps cold-blooded to think of them, but it must be remembered that they were the particular thing his training had equipped him for dealing with. He was at all events not too cold-blooded to have, for the two months of his holiday, very little inner vision of anything more abstract than Miriam's face. The desire to see it again was as pressing as thirst, but he tried to practise the endurance of the traveller in the desert. He kept the Channel between them, but his spirit consumed every day an inch of the interval, until — and it was not long — there were no more inches left. The last thing he expected the future ambassadress to have been was a *fille de théâtre*. The answer to this objection was of course that Miriam was not yet so much of one but that he could easily, by a handsome "worldly" offer, arrest her development. Then came worrying retorts to that, chief among which was the sense that to his artistic conscience arresting her development would be a

317

plan combining on his part fatuity, not to say imbecility, with baseness. It was exactly to her development the poor girl had the greatest right, and he should n't really alter anything by depriving her of it. Was n't she the artist to the tips of her tresses — the ambassadress never in the world — and would n't she take it out in something else if one were to make her deviate ? So certain was that demonic gift to insist ever on its own.

Besides, *could* one make her deviate ? If she had no disposition to philander what was his warrant for supposing she could be corrupted into respectability ? How could the career — his career — speak to a nature that had glimpses as vivid as they were crude of such a different range and for which success meant quite another sauce to the dish ? Would the brilliancy of marrying Peter Sherringham be such a bribe to relinquishment ? How could he think so without pretensions of the sort he pretended exactly not to flaunt ? — how could he put himself forward as so high a prize ? Relinquishment of the opportunity to exercise a rare talent was not, in the nature of things, an easy effort to a young lady who was herself presumptuous as well as ambitious. Besides, she might eat her cake and have it — might make her fortune both on the stage and in the world. Successful actresses had ended by marrying dukes, and was not that better than remaining obscure and marrying a commoner ? There were moments when he tried to pronounce the girl's "gift" not a force to reckon with; there was so little to show for it as yet that the caprice of believing in it would perhaps sud-

denly leave him. But his conviction that it was real
was too uneasy to make such an experiment peaceful, and he came back moreover to his deepest impression — that of her being of the inward mould
for which the only consistency is the play of genius.
Had n't Madame Carré declared at the last that
she could "do anything"? It was true that if
Madame Carré had been mistaken in the first place
she might also be mistaken in the second. But in
this latter case she would be mistaken with *him* — and
such an error would be too like a truth.

How, further, shall we exactly measure for him —
Sherringham felt the discomfort of the advantage
Miriam had of him — the advantage of her present-
ing herself in a light that rendered any passion he
might entertain an implication of duty as well as of
pleasure? Why there should have been this implication was more than he could say; sometimes he held
himself rather abject, or at least absurdly supersti-
tious, for seeing it. He did n't know, he could scarcely
conceive, of another case of the same general type
in which he would have recognised it. In foreign
countries there were very few ladies of Miss Rooth's
intended profession who would not have regarded it
as too strong an order that, to console them for not
being admitted into drawing-rooms, they should have
no offset but the exercise of a virtue in which no one
would believe. This was because in foreign countries
actresses were not admitted into drawing-rooms: that
was a pure English drollery, ministering equally little
to real histrionics and to the higher tone of these
resorts. Did the oppressive sanctity which made it

a burden to have to reckon with his young friend come then from her being English? Peter could recall cases in which that privilege operated as little as possible as a restriction. It came a great deal from Mrs. Rooth, in whom he apprehended depths of calculation as to what she might achieve for her daughter by "working" the idea of a life blameless amid dire obsessions. Her romantic turn of mind would n't in the least prevent her regarding that idea as a substantial capital, to be laid out to the best worldly advantage. Miriam's essential irreverence was capable, on a pretext, of making mince-meat of it — that he was sure of; for the only capital she recognised was the talent which some day managers and agents would outbid each other in paying for. Yet as a creature easy at so many points she was fond of her mother, would do anything to oblige — that might work in all sorts of ways — and would probably like the loose slippers of blamelessness quite as well as having to meet some of the queer high standards of the opposite camp.

Sherringham, I may add, had no desire that she should indulge a different preference: it was distasteful to him to compute the probabilities of a young lady's misbehaving for his advantage — that seemed to him definitely base — and he would have thought himself a blackguard if, even when a prey to his desire, he had not wished the thing that was best for the object of it. The thing best for Miriam might be to become the wife of the man to whose suit she should incline her ear. That this would be the best thing for the gentleman in question

by no means, however, equally followed, and Sherringham's final conviction was that it would never
do for him to act the part of that hypothetic personage. He asked for no removal and no extension of
leave, and he proved to himself how well he knew
what he was about by never addressing a line, during
his absence, to the Hôtel de la Garonne. He would
simply go straight, inflicting as little injury on Peter
Sherringham as on any one else. He remained away
to the last hour of his privilege and continued to act
lucidly in having nothing to do with the mother and
daughter for several days after his return to Paris.

It was when this discipline came to an end one
afternoon after a week had passed that he felt most
the force of the reference we have just made to Mrs.
Rooth's private calculations. He found her at home,
alone, writing a letter under the lamp, and as soon
as he came in she cried out that he was the very person to whom the letter was addressed. She could bear
it no longer; she had permitted herself to reproach
him with his terrible silence — to ask why he had
quite forsaken them. It was an illustration of the
way in which her visitor had come to regard her that
he put rather less than more faith into this description of the crumpled papers lying on the table. He
was not even sure he quite believed Miriam to have
just gone out. He told her mother how busy he had
been all the while he was away and how much time
above all he had had to give in London to seeing on
her daughter's behalf the people connected with the
theatres.

"Ah if you pity me tell me you've got her an

engagement!" Mrs. Rooth cried while she clasped her hands.

"I took a great deal of trouble; I wrote ever so many notes, sought introductions, talked with people — such impossible people some of them. In short I knocked at every door, I went into the question exhaustively." And he enumerated the things he had done, reported on some of the knowledge he had gathered. The difficulties were immense, and even with the influence he could command, such as it was, there was very little to be achieved in face of them. Still he had gained ground: two or three approachable fellows, men with inferior theatres, had listened to him better than the others, and there was one in particular whom he had a hope he really might have interested. From him he had extracted benevolent assurances: this person would see Miriam, would listen to her, would do for her what he could. The trouble was that no one would lift a finger for a girl unless she were known, and yet that she never could become known till innumerable fingers had been lifted. You could n't go into the water unless you could swim, and you could n't swim until you had been in the water.

"But new performers appear; they get theatres, they get audiences, they get notices in the newspapers," Mrs. Rooth objected. "I know of these things only what Miriam tells me. It's no knowledge that I was born to."

"It's perfectly true. It's all done with money."

"And how do they come by money?" Mrs. Rooth candidly asked.

322

"When they're women people give it to them."

"Well, what people now?"

"People who believe in them."

"As you believe in Miriam?"

Peter had a pause. "No, rather differently. A poor man doesn't believe in anything the same way that a rich man does."

"Ah don't call yourself poor!" groaned Mrs. Rooth.

"What good would it do me to be rich?"

"Why you could take a theatre. You could do it all yourself."

"And what good would that do me?"

"Ah don't you delight in her genius?" demanded Mrs. Rooth.

"I delight in her mother. You think me more disinterested than I am," Sherringham added with a certain soreness of irritation.

"I know why you didn't write!" Mrs. Rooth declared archly.

"You must go to London," Peter said without heeding this remark.

"Ah if we could only get there it would be a relief. I should draw a long breath. There at least I know where I am and what people are. But here one lives on hollow ground!"

"The sooner you get away the better," our young man went on.

"I know why you say that."

"It's just what I'm explaining."

"I couldn't have held out if I hadn't been so sure of Miriam," said Mrs. Rooth.

"Well, you need n't hold out any longer."

"Don't *you* trust her?" asked Sherringham's hostess.

"Trust her?"

"You don't trust yourself. That's why you were silent, why we might have thought you were dead, why we might have perished ourselves."

"I don't think I understand you; I don't know what you 're talking about," Peter returned. "But it does n't matter."

"Does n't it? Let yourself go. Why should you struggle?" the old woman agreeably enquired.

Her unexpected insistence annoyed her visitor, and he was silent again, meeting her eyes with reserve and on the point of telling her that he did n't like her tone. But he had his tongue under such control that he was able presently to say instead of this — and it was a relief to him to give audible voice to the reflexion — "It's a great mistake, either way, for a man to be in love with an actress. Either it means nothing serious, and what's the use of that? or it means everything, and that's still more delusive."

"Delusive?"

"Idle, unprofitable."

"Surely a pure affection is its own beautiful reward," Mrs. Rooth pleaded with soft reasonableness.

"In such a case how can it be pure?"

"I thought you were talking of an English gentleman," she replied.

"Call the poor fellow whatever you like: a man with his life to lead, his way to make, his work, his duties, his career to attend to. If it means nothing, as I say, the thing it means least of all is marriage."

"Oh my own Miriam!" Mrs. Rooth wailed.

"Fancy on the other hand the complication when such a man marries a woman who's on the stage."

Mrs. Rooth looked as if she were trying to follow. "Miriam is n't on the stage yet."

"Go to London and she soon will be."

"Yes, and then you'll have your excuse."

"My excuse?"

"For deserting us altogether."

He broke into laughter at this, the logic was so droll. Then he went on: "Show me some good acting and I won't desert you."

"Good acting? Ah what's the best acting compared with the position of a true English lady? If you'll take her as she is you may have her," Mrs. Rooth suddenly added.

"As she is, with all her ambitions unassuaged?"

"To marry *you* — might not that be an ambition?"

"A very paltry one. Don't answer for her, don't attempt that," said Peter. "You can do much better."

"Do you think *you* can?" smiled Mrs. Rooth.

"I don't want to; I only want to let it alone. She's an artist; you must give her her head," the young man pursued. "You must always give an artist his head."

"But I've known great ladies who were artists. In English society there's always a field."

"Don't talk to me of English society! Thank goodness, in the first place, I don't live in it. Do you want her to give up her genius?" he demanded.

325

"I thought you did n't care for it."

"She'd say 'No I thank you, dear mamma.'"

"My wonderful child!" Mrs. Rooth almost comprehendingly murmured.

"Have you ever proposed it to her?"

"Proposed it?"

"That she should give up trying."

Mrs. Rooth hesitated, looking down. "Not for the reason you mean. We don't talk about love," she simpered.

"Then it's so much less time wasted. Don't stretch out your hand to the worse when it may some day grasp the better," Peter continued. Mrs. Rooth raised her eyes at him as if recognising the force there might be in that, and he added: "Let her blaze out, let her look about her. Then you may talk to me if you like."

"It's very puzzling!" the old woman artlessly sighed.

He laughed again and then said: "Now don't tell me I'm not a good friend."

"You are indeed — you're a very noble gentleman. That's just why a quiet life with you —"

"It would n't be quiet for *me!*" he broke in. "And that's not what Miriam was made for."

"*Don't say that* for my precious one!" Mrs. Rooth quavered.

"Go to London — go to London," her visitor repeated.

Thoughtfully, after an instant, she extended her hand and took from the table the letter on the composition of which he had found her engaged. Then

326

with a quick movement she tore it up. "That's what Mr. Dashwood says."

"Mr. Dashwood?"

"I forgot you don't know him. He's the brother of that lady we met the day you were so good as to receive us; the one who was so kind to us — Mrs. Lovick."

"I never heard of him."

"Don't you remember how she spoke of him and that Mr. Lovick didn't seem very nice about him? She told us that if he were to meet us — and she was so good as to intimate that it would be a pleasure to him to do so — he might give us, as she said, a tip."

Peter achieved the effort to recollect. "Yes, he comes back to me. He's an actor."

"He's a gentleman too," said Mrs. Rooth.

"And you've met him, and he *has* given you a tip?"

"As I say, he wants us to go to London."

"I see, but even I can tell you that."

"Oh yes," said Mrs. Rooth; "but *he* says he can help us."

"Keep hold of him then, if he's in the business." Peter was all for that.

"He's a perfect gentleman," said Mrs. Rooth. "He's immensely struck with Miriam."

"Better and better. Keep hold of him."

"Well, I'm glad you don't object," she grimaced.

"Why should I object?"

"You don't regard us as *all* your own?"

"My own? Why, I regard you as the public's — the world's."

She gave a little shudder. "There's a sort of chill

in that. It's grand, but it's cold. However, I need n't hesitate then to tell you that it's with Mr. Dashwood Miriam has gone out."

"Why hesitate, gracious heaven?" But in the next breath Sherringham asked: "Where have they gone?"

"You don't like it!" his hostess laughed.

"Why should it be a thing to be enthusiastic about?"

"Well, he's charming and *I* trust him."

"So do I," said Sherringham.

"They 've gone to see Madame Carré."

"She has come back then?"

"She was expected back last week. Miriam wants to show her how she has improved."

"And *has* she improved?"

"How can I tell — with my mother's heart?" asked Mrs. Rooth. "I don't judge; I only wait and pray. But Mr. Dashwood thinks she 's wonderful."

"That's a blessing. And when did he turn up?"

"About a fortnight ago. We met Mrs. Lovick at the English church, and she was so good as to recognise us and speak to us. She said she had been away with her children — otherwise she 'd have come to see us. She had just returned to Paris."

"Yes, I 've not yet seen her. I see Lovick," Peter added, "but he does n't talk of his brother-in-law."

"I did n't, that day, like his tone about him," Mrs. Rooth observed. "We walked a little way with Mrs. Lovick after church and she asked Miriam about her prospects and if she were working. Miriam said she had no prospects."

"That was n't very nice to me," Sherringham commented.

"But when you had left us in black darkness what *were* our prospects ?"

"I see. It's all right. Go on."

"Then Mrs. Lovick said her brother was to be in Paris a few days and she would tell him to come and see us. He arrived, she told him and he came. *Voilà!*" said Mrs. Rooth.

"So that now — so far as *he* is concerned — Miss Rooth has prospects ?"

"He is n't a manager unfortunately," she qualified.

"Where does he act ?"

"He is n't acting just now; he has been abroad. He has been to Italy, I believe, and is just stopping here on his way to London."

"I see; he *is* a perfect gentleman," said Sherringham.

"Ah you're jealous of him!"

"No, but you're trying to make me so. The more competitors there are for the glory of bringing her out the better for her."

"Mr. Dashwood wants to take a theatre," said Mrs. Rooth.

"Then perhaps he's our man."

"Oh if you'd help him!" she richly cried.

"Help him ?"

"Help him to help us."

"We'll all work together; it will be very jolly," said Sherringham gaily. "It's a sacred cause, the love of art, and we shall be a happy band. Dashwood's his name?" he added in a moment. "Mrs. Lovick was n't a Dashwood."

"It's his *nom de théâtre* — Basil Dashwood. Do you like it?" Mrs. Rooth wonderfully enquired.

"You say that as Miriam might. Her talent's catching!"

"She's always practising — always saying things over and over to seize the tone. I've her voice in my ears. He wants *her* not to have any."

"Not to have any what?"

"Any *nom de théâtre*. He wants her to use her own; he likes it so much. He says it will do so well — you can't better it."

"He's a capital adviser," said Sherringham, getting up. "I'll come back to-morrow."

"I won't ask you to wait for them — they may be so long," his hostess returned.

"Will he come back with her?" Peter asked while he smoothed his hat.

"I hope so, at this hour. With my child in the streets I tremble. We don't live in cabs, as you may easily suppose."

"Did they go on foot?" Sherringham continued.

"Oh yes; they started in high spirits."

"And is Mr. Basil Dashwood acquainted with Madame Carré?"

"Ah no, but he longed to be introduced to her; he persuaded Miriam to take him. Naturally she wishes to oblige him. She's very nice to him — if he can do anything."

"Quite right; that's the way!" Peter cheerfully rang out.

"And she also wanted him to see what she can do for the great critic," Mrs. Rooth added — "that terrible old woman in the red wig."

"That's what I should like to see too," Peter permitted himself to acknowledge.

"Oh she has gone ahead; she's pleased with herself. 'Work, work, work,' said Madame Carré. Well, she has worked, worked, worked. That's what Mr. Dashwood is pleased with even more than with other things."

"What do you mean by other things?"

"Oh her genius and her fine appearance."

"He approves of her fine appearance? I ask because you think he knows what will take."

"I know why you ask!" Mrs. Rooth bravely mocked. "He says it will be worth hundreds of thousands to her."

"That's the sort of thing I like to hear," Peter returned. "I'll come in to-morrow," he repeated.

"And shall you mind if Mr. Dashwood's here?"

"Does he come every day?"

"Oh they're always at it."

"At it — ?" He was vague.

"Why she acts to him — every sort of thing — and he says if it will do."

"How many days has he been here then?"

Mrs. Rooth reflected. "Oh I don't know! Since he turned up they've passed so quickly."

"So far from 'minding' it I'm eager to see him," Sherringham declared; "and I can imagine nothing better than what you describe — if he is n't an awful ass."

"Dear me, if he is n't clever you must tell us: we can't afford to be deceived!" Mrs. Rooth innocently wailed. "What do we know — how can we judge?" she appealed.

He had a pause, his hand on the latch. "Oh, I'll tell you frankly what I think of him!"

XIX

WHEN he got into the street he looked about him for a cab, but was obliged to walk some distance before encountering one. In this little interval he saw no reason to modify the determination he had formed in descending the steep staircase of the Hôtel de la Garonne; indeed the desire prompting it only quickened his pace. He had an hour to spare and would also go to see Madame Carré. If Miriam and her companion had proceeded to the Rue de Constantinople on foot he would probably reach the house as soon as they. It was all quite logical: he was eager to see Miriam — that was natural enough; and he had admitted to Mrs. Rooth that he was keen on the subject of Mrs. Lovick's theatrical brother, in whom such effective aid might perhaps reside. To catch Miriam really revealing herself to the old actress after the jump she believed herself to have taken — since that was her errand — would be a very happy stroke, the thought of which made her benefactor impatient. He presently found his cab and, as he bounded in, bade the coachman drive fast. He learned from Madame Carré's portress that her illustrious *locataire* was at home and that a lady and a gentleman had gone up some time before.

In the little antechamber, after his admission, he heard a high voice come from the salon and, stopping a moment to listen, noted that Miriam was already launched in a recitation. He was able to make out the words, all the more that before he could prevent the movement the maid-servant who had let him in had already opened the door of the room — one of the leaves of it, there being, as in most French doors, two of these — before which, within, a heavy curtain was suspended. Miriam was in the act of rolling out some speech from the English poetic drama —

> " For I am sick and capable of fears,
> Oppressed with wrongs and therefore full of fears."

He recognised one of the great tirades of Shakespeare's Constance and saw she had just begun the magnificent scene at the beginning of the third act of "King John," in which the passionate injured mother and widow sweeps in wild organ-tones the entire scale of her irony and wrath. The curtain concealed him and he lurked three minutes after he had motioned to the *femme de chambre* to retire on tiptoe. The trio in the salon, absorbed in the performance, had apparently not heard his entrance or the opening of the door, which was covered by the girl's splendid declamation. Peter listened intently, arrested by the spirit with which she attacked her formidable verses. He had needed to hear her set afloat but a dozen of them to measure the long stride she had taken in his absence; they assured him she had leaped into possession of her means. He remained where he was till she arrived at

> "Then speak again; not all thy former tale,
> But this one word, whether thy tale be true."

This apostrophe, briefly responded to in another voice, gave him time quickly to raise the curtain and show himself, passing into the room with a "Go on, go on!" and a gesture earnestly deprecating a stop.

Miriam, in the full swing of her part, paused but for an instant and let herself ring out again, while Peter sank into the nearest chair and she fixed him with her illumined eyes, that is with those of the raving Constance. Madame Carré, buried in a chair, kissed her hand to him, and a young man who, near the girl, stood giving the cue, stared at him over the top of a little book. "Admirable, magnificent, go on," Sherringham repeated — "go on to the end of the scene, do it all!" Miriam's colour rose, yet he as quickly felt that she had no personal emotion in seeing him again; the cold passion of art had perched on her banner and she listened to herself with an ear as vigilant as if she had been a Paganini drawing a fiddle-bow. This effect deepened as she went on, rising and rising to the great occasion, moving with extraordinary ease and in the largest clearest style at the dizzy height of her idea. That she had an idea was visible enough, and that the whole thing was very different from all Sherringham had hitherto heard her attempt. It belonged quite to another class of effort; she was now the finished statue lifted from the ground to its pedestal. It was as if the sun of her talent had risen above the hills and she knew she was moving and would always move in its guiding light. This conviction was the one artless thing that glimmered like a young joy through the tragic mask of Constance, and Sherringham's heart beat faster as he caught it in her face. It only showed her as more intelligent, and yet there had been a time when he thought her stupid! Masterful the whole spirit in which she carried the scene, making him cry to himself from point to point "How she feels it, sees it and really 'renders' it!"

He looked now and again at Madame Carré and saw she had in her lap an open book, apparently a French prose version, brought by her visitors, of the play; but she never either glanced at him or at the volume: she only sat screwing into the girl her hard bright eyes, polished by experience like fine old brasses. The young man uttering the lines of the other speakers was attentive in another degree; he followed Miriam, in his own copy, to keep sure of the cue; but he was elated and expressive, was evidently even surprised; he coloured and smiled, and when he extended his hand to assist Constance to rise, after the performer, acting out her text, had seated herself grandly on "the huge firm earth," he bowed over her as obsequiously as if she had been his veritable sovereign. He was a good-looking young man, tall, well-proportioned, straight-featured and fair, of whom manifestly the first thing to be said on any occasion was that he had remarkably the stamp of a gentleman. He carried this appearance, which proved inveterate and importunate, to a point that was almost a denial of its spirit: so prompt the question of whether it could be in good taste to wear any character, even that particular one, so much on one's sleeve. It was literally on his sleeve that this young man partly wore his own; for it resided considerably in his garments, and in especial in a certain close-fitting dark blue frock-coat, a miracle of a fit, which moulded his juvenility just enough and not too much, and constituted, as Sherringham was destined to perceive later, his perpetual uniform or badge. It was not till afterwards that Peter began to feel exasperated by Basil Dashwood's "type" — the young stranger was of course Basil Dashwood — and even by his blue frock-coat, the recurrent unvarying imperturbable good form of his aspect. This unprofessional air ended by striking the observer as the very profession he had adopted, and was indeed, so far as had as yet been indicated, his mimetic capital, his main qualification for the stage.

The ample and powerful manner in which Miriam handled her scene produced its full impression, the art with which she surmounted its difficulties, the liberality with which she met its great demand upon the voice, and the variety of expression that she threw into a torrent of objurgation. It was a real composition, studded with passages that called a suppressed tribute to the lips and seeming to show that a talent capable of such an exhibition was capable of anything.

> "But thou art fair, and at thy birth, dear boy,
> Nature and Fortune join'd to make thee great:
> Of Nature's gifts thou mayst with lilies boast,
> And with the half-blown rose."

As the girl turned to her imagined child with this exquisite apostrophe — she addressed Mr. Dashwood as if he were playing Arthur, and he lowered his book, dropped his head and his eyes and looked handsome and ingenuous — she opened at a stroke to Sherringham's vision a prospect that they would yet see her express tenderness better even than anything else. Her voice was enchanting in these lines, and the beauty of her performance was that though she uttered the full fury of the part she missed none of its poetry.

"Where did she get hold of that — where did she get hold of that?" Peter wondered while his whole sense vibrated. "She had n't got hold of it when I went away." And the assurance flowed over him again that she had found the key to her box of treasures. In the summer, during their weeks of frequent meeting, she had only fumbled with the lock. One October day, while he was away, the key had slipped in, had fitted, or her finger at last had touched the right spring and the capricious casket had flown open.

It was during the present solemnity that, excited by the way she came out and with a hundred stirred ideas about her wheeling through his mind, he was for the first time and most vividly visited by a perception that ended by becoming frequent with him — that of the perfect presence of mind, unconfused, unhurried by emotion, that any artistic performance requires and that all, whatever the instrument, require in exactly the same degree: the application, in other words, clear and calculated, crystal-firm as it were, of the idea conceived in the glow of experience, of suffering, of joy. He was afterwards often to talk of this with Miriam, who, however, was never to be able to present him with a neat theory of the subject. She had no knowledge that it was publicly discussed; she only

338

ranged herself in practice on the side of those who hold that at the moment of production the artist can't too much have his wits about him. When Peter named to her the opinion of those maintaining that at such a crisis the office of attention ceases to be filled she stared with surprise and then broke out: "Ah the poor idiots!" She eventually became, in her judgements, in impatience and the expression of contempt, very free and absolutely irreverent.

"What a splendid scolding!" the new visitor exclaimed when, on the entrance of the Pope's legate, her companion closed the book on the scene. Peter pressed his lips to Madame Carré's finger-tips; the old actress got up and held out her arms to Miriam. The girl never took her eyes off Sherringham while she passed into that lady's embrace and remained there. They were full of their usual sombre fire, and it was always the case that they expressed too much anything they could express at all; but they were not defiant nor even triumphant now — they were only deeply explicative. They seemed to say "That's the sort of thing I meant; that's what I had in mind when I asked you to try to do something for me." Madame Carré folded her pupil to her bosom, holding her there as the old marquise in a *comédie de mœurs* might in the last scene have held her god-daughter the *ingénue*.

"Have you got me an engagement?" — the young woman then appealed eagerly to her friend. "Yes, he has done something splendid for me," she went on to Madame Carré, resting her hand caressingly on one of the actress's while the old woman discoursed with Mr. Dashwood, who was telling her in very pretty

339

French that he was tremendously excited about Miss Rooth. Madame Carré looked at him as if she wondered how he appeared when he was calm and how, as a dramatic artist, he expressed that condition.

"Yes, yes, something splendid, for a beginning," Peter answered radiantly, recklessly; feeling now only that he would say anything and do anything to please her. He spent on the spot, in imagination, his last penny.

"It's such a pity you could n't follow it; you'd have liked it so much better," Mr. Dashwood observed to their hostess.

"Could n't follow it? Do you take me for *une sotte?*" the celebrated artist cried. "I suspect I followed it *de plus près que vous, monsieur!*"

"Ah you see the language is so awfully fine," Basil Dashwood replied, looking at his shoes.

"The language? Why she rails like a fish-wife. Is that what you call language? Ours is another business."

"If you understood, if you understood, you'd see all the greatness of it," Miriam declared. And then in another tone: "Such delicious expressions!"

"On dit que c'est très-fort. But who can tell if you really say it?" Madame Carré demanded.

"Ah, *par exemple*, I can!" Sherringham answered.

"Oh you — you're a Frenchman."

"Could n't he make it out if he were n't?" asked Basil Dashwood.

The old woman shrugged her shoulders. "He would n't know."

"That's flattering to me."

340

"Oh you — don't you pretend to complain," Madame Carré said. "I prefer *our* imprecations — those of Camille," she went on. "They have the beauty *des plus belles choses*."

"I can say them too," Miriam broke in.

"*Insolente!*" smiled Madame Carré. "Camille does n't squat down on the floor in the middle of them.

"'For grief is proud and makes his owner stoop.
    To me and to the state of my great grief
    Let kings assemble,'"

Miriam quickly declaimed. "Ah if you don't feel the way she makes a throne of it!"

"It's really tremendously fine, *chère madame*," Sherringham said. "There's nothing like it."

"Vous êtes insupportables," the old woman answered. "Stay with us. I'll teach you Phèdre."

"Ah Phædra, Phædra!" Basil Dashwood vaguely ejaculated, looking more gentlemanly than ever.

"You've learned all I've taught you, but where the devil have you learned what I have n't?" Madame Carré went on.

"I've worked — I have; you'd call it work — all through the bright late summer, all through the hot dull empty days. I've battered down the door — I did hear it crash one day. But I'm not so very good yet. I'm only in the right direction."

"Malicieuse!" growled Madame Carré.

"Oh I can beat that," the girl went on.

"Did you wake up one morning and find you had grown a pair of wings?" Peter asked. "Because that's what the difference amounts to — you really soar. Moreover you're an angel," he added, charmed with her unexpectedness, the good nature of her forbearance to reproach him for not having written to her. And it seemed to him privately that she *was* angelic when in answer to this she said ever so blandly:

"You know you read 'King John' with me before you went away. I thought over immensely what you said. I did n't understand it much at the time — I was so stupid. But it all came to me later."

"I wish you could see yourself," Peter returned.

"My dear fellow, I do. What sort of a dunce do you take me for? I did n't miss a vibration of my voice, a fold of my robe."

"Well, I did n't see you troubling about it," Peter handsomely insisted.

"No one ever will. Do you think I 'd ever show it?"

"Ars celare artem," Basil Dashwood jocosely dropped.

"You must first have the art to hide," said Sherringham, wondering a little why Miriam did n't introduce her young friend to him. She was, however, both then and later perfectly neglectful of such cares, never thinking, never minding how other people got on together. When she found they did n't get on she jeered at them: that was the nearest she came to arranging for them. Our young man noted in her from the moment she felt her strength an immense increase of this good-humoured inattention to detail — all detail save that of her work, to which she was ready to sacrifice holocausts of feelings when the

342

feelings were other people's. This conferred on her a large profanity, an absence of ceremony as to her social relations, which was both amusing because it suggested that she would take what she gave, and formidable because it was inconvenient and you might n't care to give what she, would take.

"If you have n't any art it's not quite the same as if you did n't hide it, is it?" Basil Dashwood ingeniously threw out.

"That's right — say one of your clever things!" Miriam sweetly responded.

"You're always acting," he declared in English and with a simple-minded laugh, while Sherringham remained struck with his expressing just what he himself had felt weeks before.

"And when you've shown them your fish-wife, to your public *de là-bas*, what will you do next?" asked Madame Carré.

"I'll do Juliet — I'll do Cleopatra."

"Rather a big bill, is n't it?" Mr. Dashwood volunteered to Sherringham in a friendly but discriminating manner.

"Constance and Juliet — take care you don't mix them," said Sherringham.

"I want to be various. You once told me I had a hundred characters," Miriam returned.

"Ah, *vous-en-êtes là?*" cried the old actress. "You may have a hundred characters, but you've only three plays. I'm told that's all there are in English."

Miriam, admirably indifferent to this charge, appealed to Peter. "What arrangements have you made? What do the people want?"

"The people at the theatre?"

"I'm afraid they don't want 'King John,' and I don't believe they hunger for 'Antony and Cleopatra,'" Basil Dashwood suggested. "Ships and sieges and armies and pyramids, you know: we must n't be too heavy."

"Oh I hate scenery!" the girl sighed.

"Elle est superbe," said Madame Carré. "You must put those pieces on the stage: how will you do it?"

"Oh we know how to get up a play in London, Madame Carré" — Mr. Dashwood was all geniality. "They put money on it, you know."

"On it? But what do they put *in* it? Who'll interpret them? Who'll manage a style like that — the style of which the rhapsodies she has just repeated are a specimen? Whom have you got that one has ever heard of?"

"Oh you'll hear of a good deal when once she gets started," Dashwood cheerfully contended.

Madame Carré looked at him a moment; then, "I feel that you'll become very bad," she said to Miriam. "I'm glad I shan't see it."

"People will do things for me — I'll make them," the girl declared. "I'll stir them up so that they'll have ideas."

"What people, pray?"

"Ah terrible woman!" Peter theatrically groaned.

"We translate your pieces — there will be plenty of parts," Basil Dashwood said.

"Why then go out of the door to come in at the window? — especially if you smash it! An English

344

arrangement of a French piece is a pretty woman with her back turned."

"Do you really want to keep her?" Sherringham asked of Madame Carré — quite as if thinking for a moment that this after all might be possible.

She bent her strange eyes on him. "No, you're all too queer together. We could n't be bothered with you and you 're not worth it."

"I 'm glad it 's 'together' that we 're queer then — we can console each other."

"If you only would; but you don't seem to! In short I don't understand you — I give you up. But it does n't matter," said the old woman wearily, "for the theatre's dead and even you, *ma toute-belle*, won't bring it to life. Everything's going from bad to worse, and I don't care what becomes of you. You would n't understand us here and they won't understand you there, and everything's impossible, and no one's a whit the wiser, and it 's not of the least consequence. Only when you raise your arms lift them just a little higher," Madame Carré added.

"My mother will be happier *chez nous*," said Miriam, throwing her arms straight up and giving them a noble tragic movement.

"You won't be in the least in the right path till your mother's in despair."

"Well, perhaps we can bring that about even in London," Sherringham patiently laughed.

"Dear Mrs. Rooth — she 's great fun," Mr. Dashwood as imperturbably dropped.

Miriam transferred the dark weight of her gaze to him as if she were practising. "*You* won't upset her, at any rate." Then she stood with her beautiful and fatal mask before her hostess. "I want to do the modern too. I want to do *le drame*, with intense realistic effects."

"And do you want to look like the portico of the Madeleine when it's draped for a funeral?" her instructress mocked. "Never, never. I don't believe you're various: that's not the way I see you. You're pure tragedy, with *de grands éclats de voix* in the great style, or you're nothing."

"Be beautiful — be only that," Peter urged with high interest. "Be only what you can be so well — something that one may turn to for a glimpse of perfection, to lift one out of all the vulgarities of the day."

Thus apostrophised the girl broke out with one of the speeches of Racine's Phædra, hushing her companions on the instant. "You'll be the English Rachel," said Basil Dashwood when she stopped.

"Acting in French!" Madame Carré amended. "I don't believe in an English Rachel."

"I shall have to work it out, what I shall be," Miriam concluded with a rich pensive effect.

"You're in wonderfully good form to-day," Sherringham said to her; his appreciation revealing a personal subjection he was unable to conceal from his companions, much as he wished it.

"I really mean to do everything."

"Very well; after all Garrick did."

"Then I shall be the Garrick of my sex."

"There's a very clever author doing something for me; I should like you to see it," said Basil Dashwood, addressing himself equally to Miriam and to her diplomatic friend.

"Ah if you 've very clever authors — !" And Madame Carré spun the sound to the finest satiric thread.

"I shall be very happy to see it," Peter returned.

This response was so benevolent that Basil Dashwood presently began: "May I ask you at what theatre you 've made arrangements ?"

Sherringham looked at him a moment. "Come and see me at the embassy and I 'll tell you." Then he added: "I know your sister, Mrs. Lovick."

"So I supposed: that 's why I took the liberty of asking such a question."

"It 's no liberty, but Mr. Sherringham does n't appear to be able to tell you," said Miriam.

"Well, you know, it 's a very curious world, all those theatrical people over there," Peter conceded.

"Ah don't say anything against them when I 'm one of them," Basil Dashwood laughed.

"I might plead the absence of information," Peter returned, "as Miss Rooth has neglected to make us acquainted."

Miriam vaguely smiled. "I know you both so little." But she presented them with a great stately air to each other, and the two men shook hands while Madame Carré observed them.

"*Tiens!* you gentlemen meet here for the first time ? You do right to become friends — that 's the best thing. Live together in peace and mutual confidence. C'est de beaucoup le plus sage."

"Certainly, for yoke-fellows," said Sherringham.

347

He began the next moment to repeat to his new acquaintance some of the things he had been told in London; but their hostess stopped him off, waving the talk away with charming overdone stage horror and the young hands of the heroines of Marivaux. "Ah wait till you go — for that! Do you suppose I care for news of your mountebanks' booths?"

XX

As many people know, there are not, in the famous
Théâtre Français, more than a dozen good seats
accessible to ladies.[1] The stalls are forbidden them,
the boxes are a quarter of a mile from the stage
and the balcony is a delusion save for a few chairs
at either end of its vast horseshoe. But there are
two excellent *baignoires d'avant-scène*, which indeed
are by no means always to be had. It was, however,
into one of them that, immediately after his return
to Paris, Sherringham ushered Mrs. Rooth and her
daughter, with the further escort of Basil Dashwood.
He had chosen the evening of the reappearance of
the celebrated Mademoiselle Voisin — she had been
enjoying a *congé* of three months — an actress whom
Miriam had seen several times before and for whose
method she professed a high though somewhat critical
esteem. It was only for the return of this charming
performer that Peter had been waiting to respond to
Miriam's most ardent wish — that of spending an
hour in the *foyer des artistes* of the great theatre. She
was the person whom he knew best in the house of
Moliére; he could count on her to do them the honours some night when she was in the "bill," and to
make the occasion sociable. Miriam had been impatient for it — she was so convinced that her eyes
would be opened in the holy of holies; but wishing
as particularly as he did to participate in her impres-

[1] 1890.

sion he had made her promise she would n't taste
of this experience without him — not let Madame
Carré, for instance, take her in his absence. There
were questions the girl wished to put to Mademoiselle Voisin — questions which, having admired her
from the balcony, she felt she was exactly the person
to answer. She was more "in it" now, after all, than
Madame Carré, in spite of her slenderer talent: she
was younger, fresher, more modern and — Miriam
found the word — less academic. She was in fine less
"vieux jeu." Peter perfectly foresaw the day when
his young friend would make indulgent allowances
for poor Madame Carré, patronising her as an old
woman of good intentions.

The play to-night was six months old, a large serious successful comedy by the most distinguished
of authors, with a thesis, a chorus embodied in one
character, a *scène à faire* and a part full of opportunities for Mademoiselle Voisin. There were things to
be said about this artist, strictures to be dropped as
to the general quality of her art, and Miriam leaned
back now, making her comments as if they cost her
less; but the actress had knowledge and distinction
and pathos, and our young lady repeated several
times: "How quiet she is, how wonderfully quiet!
Scarcely anything moves but her face and her voice.
Le geste rare, but really expressive when it comes. I
like that economy; it's the only way to make the
gesture significant."

"I don't admire the way she holds her arms,"
Basil Dashwood said: "like a *demoiselle de magasin*
trying on a jacket."

"Well, she holds them at any rate. I dare say it's more than you do with yours."

"Oh yes, she holds them; there's no mistake about that. 'I hold them, I hope, *hein?*' she seems to say to all the house." The young English professional laughed good-humouredly, and Sherringham was struck with the pleasant familiarity he had established with their brave companion. He was knowing and ready and he said in the first *entr'acte* — they were waiting for the second to go behind — amusing perceptive things. "They teach them to be ladylike and Voisin's always trying to show that. 'See how I walk, see how I sit, see how quiet I am and how I have *le geste rare*. Now can you say I ain't a lady?' She does it all as if she had a class."

"Well, to-night I'm her class," said Miriam.

"Oh I don't mean of actresses, but of *femmes du monde*. She shows them how to act in society."

"You had better take a few lessons," Miriam retorted.

"Ah you should see Voisin in society," Peter interposed.

"Does she go into it?" Mrs. Rooth demanded with interest.

Her friend hesitated. "She receives a great many people."

"Why shouldn't they when they're nice?" Mrs. Rooth frankly wanted to know.

"When the people are nice?" Miriam asked.

"Now don't tell me *she's* not what one would wish," said Mrs. Rooth to Sherringham.

"It depends on what that is," he darkly smiled.

351

"What I should wish if she were my daughter," the old woman rejoined blandly.

"Ah wish your daughter to act as well as that and you'll do the handsome thing for her!"

"Well, she *seems* to feel what she says," Mrs. Rooth piously risked.

"She has some stiff things to say. I mean about her past," Basil Dashwood remarked. "The past — the dreadful past — on the stage!"

"Wait till the end, to see how she comes out. We must all be merciful!" sighed Mrs. Rooth.

"We've seen it before; you know what happens," Miriam observed to her mother.

"I've seen so many I get them mixed."

"Yes, they're all in queer predicaments. Poor old mother — what we show you!" laughed the girl.

"Ah it will be what *you* show me — something noble and wise!"

"I want to do this; it's a magnificent part," said Miriam.

"You couldn't put it on in London — they wouldn't swallow it," Basil Dashwood declared.

"Aren't there things they do there to get over the difficulties?" the girl enquired.

"You can't get over what *she* did!" — her companion had a rueful grimace.

"Yes, we must pay, we must expiate!" Mrs. Rooth moaned as the curtain rose again.

When the second act was over our friends passed out of their *baignoire* into those corridors of tribulation where the bristling *ouvreuse*, like a pawnbroker driving a roaring trade, mounts guard upon piles of heterogeneous clothing, and, gaining the top of the fine staircase which forms the state entrance and connects the statued vestibule of the basement with the grand tier of boxes, opened an ambiguous door composed of little mirrors and found themselves in the society of the initiated. The janitors were courteous folk who greeted Sherringham as an acquaintance, and he had no difficulty in marshalling his little troop toward the foyer. They traversed a low, curving lobby, hung with pictures and furnished with velvet-covered benches where several unrecognised persons of both sexes looked at them without hostility, and arrived at an opening, on the right, from which, by a short flight of steps, there was a descent to one of the wings of the stage. Here Miriam paused, in silent excitement, like a young warrior arrested by a glimpse of the battle-field. Her vision was carried off through a lane of light to the point of vantage from which the actor held the house; but there was a hushed guard over the place and curiosity could only glance and pass.

Then she came with her companions to a sort of parlour with a polished floor, not large and rather vacant, where her attention flew delightedly to a coat-tree, in a corner, from which three or four dresses were suspended — dresses she immediately perceived to be costumes in that night's play — accompanied by a saucer of something and a much-worn powder-puff casually left on a sofa. This was a familiar note in the general impression of high decorum which had begun at the threshold — a sense of majesty in the place. Miriam rushed at the powder-

353

puff — there was no one in the room — snatched it up and gazed at it with droll veneration, then stood rapt a moment before the charming petticoats ("That's Dunoyer's first underskirt," she said to her mother) while Sherringham explained that in this apartment an actress traditionally changed her gown when the transaction was simple enough to save the long ascent to her *loge*. He felt himself a cicerone showing a church to a party of provincials; and indeed there was a grave hospitality in the air, mingled with something academic and important, the tone of an institution, a temple, which made them all, out of respect and delicacy, hold their breath a little and tread the shining floors with discretion.

These precautions increased — Mrs. Rooth crept about like a friendly but undomesticated cat — after they entered the foyer itself, a square spacious saloon covered with pictures and relics and draped in official green velvet, where the *genius loci* holds a reception every night in the year. The effect was freshly charming to Peter; he was fond of the place, always saw it again with pleasure, enjoyed its honourable look and the way, among the portraits and scrolls, the records of a splendid history, the green velvet and the waxed floors, the *genius loci* seemed to be "at home" in the quiet lamplight. At the end of the room, in an ample chimney, blazed a fire of logs. Miriam said nothing; they looked about, noting that most of the portraits and pictures were "old-fashioned," and Basil Dashwood expressed disappointment at the absence of all the people they wanted most to see. Three or four gentlemen in evening dress circulated slowly, looking, like themselves, at the pictures, and another gentleman stood before a lady, with whom he was in conversation, seated against the wall. The foyer resembled in these conditions a ball-room, cleared for the dance, before the guests or the music had arrived.

"Oh it's enough to see *this;* it makes my heart beat," said Miriam. "It's full of the vanished past, it makes me cry. I feel them here, all, the great artists I shall never see. Think of Rachel — look at her grand portrait there! — and how she stood on these very boards and trailed over them the robes of Hermione and Phèdre." The girl broke out theatrically, as on the spot was right, not a bit afraid of her voice as soon as it rolled through the room; appealing to her companions as they stood under the chandelier and making the other persons present, who had already given her some attention, turn round to stare at so unusual a specimen of the English miss. She laughed, musically, when she noticed this, and her mother, scandalised, begged her to lower her tone. "It's all right. I produce an effect," said Miriam: "it shan't be said that I too have n't had my little success in the maison de Molière." And Sherringham repeated that it was all right — the place was familiar with mirth and passion, there was often wonderful talk there, and it was only the setting that was still and solemn. It happened that this evening — there was no knowing in advance — the scene was not characteristically brilliant; but to confirm his assertion, at the moment he spoke, Mademoiselle Dunoyer, who was also in the play, came into the room attended by a pair of gentle-men.

She was the celebrated, the perpetual, the neces-sary *ingénue*, who with all her talent could n't have represented a woman of her actual age. She had the gliding, hopping movement of a small bird, the same air of having nothing to do with time, and the clear sure piercing note, a miracle of exact vocalisation. She chaffed her companions, she chaffed the room; she might have been a very clever little girl trying to personate a more innocent big one. She scattered her amiability about — showing Miriam how the child-ren of Molière took their ease — and it quickly placed her in the friendliest communication with Peter Sherringham, who already enjoyed her acquaint-ance and who now extended it to his companions and in particular to the young lady *sur le point d'entrer au théâtre.*

"You deserve a happier lot," said the actress, looking up at Miriam brightly, as if to a great height, and taking her in; upon which Sherringham left them together a little and led Mrs. Rooth and young Dashwood to consider further some of the pictures.

"Most delightful, most curious," the old woman murmured about everything; while Basil Dashwood exclaimed in the presence of most of the portraits: "But their ugliness — their ugliness: did you ever see such a collection of hideous people? And those who were supposed to be good-looking — the beauties of the past — they're worse than the others. Ah you may say what you will, *nous sommes mieux que ça!*" Sherringham suspected him of irritation, of not liking the theatre of the great rival nation to be thrust down his throat. They returned to Miriam and Mademoiselle Dunoyer, and Peter asked the actress a question about one of the portraits to which there was no name attached. She replied, like a child who had only played about the room, that she was *toute honteuse* not to be able to tell him the original: she had forgotten, she had never asked — "Vous allez me trouver bien légère!" She appealed to the other persons present, who formed a gallery for her, and laughed in delightful ripples at their suggestions, which she covered with ridicule. She bestirred herself; she declared she would ascertain, she should n't be happy till she did, and swam out of the room, with the prettiest paddles, to obtain the information, leaving behind her a perfume of delicate kindness and gaiety. She seemed above all things obliging, and Peter pronounced her almost as natural off the stage as on. She did n't come back.

XXI

WHETHER he had prearranged it is more than I can say, but Mademoiselle Voisin delayed so long to show herself that Mrs. Rooth, who wished to see the rest of the play, though she had sat it out on another occasion, expressed a returning relish for her corner of the *baignoire* and gave her conductor the best pretext he could have desired for asking Basil Dashwood to be so good as to escort her back. When the young actor, of whose personal preference Peter was quite aware, had led Mrs. Rooth away with an absence of moroseness which showed that his striking resemblance to a gentleman was not kept for the footlights, the two others sat on a divan in the part of the room furthest from the entrance, so that it gave them a degree of privacy, and Miriam watched the coming and going of their fellow visitors and the indefinite people, attached to the theatre, hanging about, while her companion gave a name to some of the figures, Parisian celebrities.

"Fancy poor Dashwood cooped up there with mamma!" the girl exclaimed whimsically.

"You're awfully cruel to him; but that's of course," said Sherringham.

"It seems to me I'm as kind as you; you sent him off."

"That was for your mother; she was tired."

358

"Oh gammon! And why, if I *were* cruel, should it be of course?"

"Because you must destroy and torment and wear out — that's your nature. But you can't help your type, can you?"

"My type?" she echoed.

"It's bad, perverse, dangerous. It's essentially insolent."

"And pray what's yours when you talk like that? Would you say such things if you did n't know the depths of my good nature?"

"Your good nature all comes back to that," said Sherringham. "It's an abyss of ruin — for others. You've no respect. I'm speaking of the artistic character — in the direction and in the plentitude in which you have it. It's unscrupulous, nervous, capricious, wanton."

"I don't know about respect. One can be good," Miriam mused and reasoned.

"It does n't matter so long as one's powerful," he returned. "We can't have everything, and surely we ought to understand that we must pay for things. A splendid organisation for a special end, like yours, is so rare and rich and fine that we ought n't to grudge it its conditions."

"What do you call its conditions?" Miriam asked as she turned and looked at him.

"Oh the need to take its ease, to take up space, to make itself at home in the world, to square its elbows and knock others about. That's large and free; it's the good nature you speak of. You must forage and ravage and leave a track behind you; you

359

must live upon the country you traverse. And you give such delight that, after all, you're welcome — you're infinitely welcome!"

"I don't know what you mean. I only care for the idea," the girl said.

"That's exactly what I pretend — and we must all help you to it. You use us, you push us about, you break us up. We're your tables and chairs, the simple furniture of your life."

"Whom do you mean by 'we'?"

Peter gave an ironic laugh. "Oh don't be afraid — there will be plenty of others!"

She made no return to this, but after a moment broke out again. "Poor Dashwood immured with mamma — he's like a lame chair that one has put into the corner."

"Don't break him up before he has served. I really believe something will come out of him," her companion went on. "However, you'll break me up first," he added, "and him probably never at all."

"And why shall I honour you so much more?"

"Because I'm a better article and you'll feel that."

"You've the superiority of modesty — I see."

"I'm better than a young mountebank — I've vanity enough to say that."

She turned on him with a flush in her cheek and a splendid dramatic face. "How you hate us! Yes, at bottom, below your little cold taste, you *hate* us!" she repeated.

He coloured too, met her eyes, looked into them

a minute, seemed to accept the imputation and then said quickly: "Give it up: come away with me."

"Come away with you?"

"Leave this place. Give it up."

"You brought me here, you insisted it should be only you, and now you must stay," she declared with a head-shake and a high manner. "You should know what you want, dear Mr. Sherringham."

"I do — I know now. Come away before you see her."

"Before — ?" she seemed to wonder.

"She's success, this wonderful Voisin, she's triumph, she's full accomplishment: the hard brilliant realisation of what I want to avert for you." Miriam looked at him in silence, the cold light still in her face, and he repeated: "Give it up — give it up."

Her eyes softened after a little; she smiled and then said: "Yes, you're better than poor Dashwood."

"Give it up and we'll live for ourselves, *in* ourselves, in something that can have a sanctity."

"All the same you do hate us," the girl went on.

"I don't want to be conceited, but I mean that I'm sufficiently fine and complicated to tempt you. I'm an expensive modern watch with a wonderful escapement — therefore you'll smash me if you can."

"Never — never!" she said as she got up. "You tell me the hour too well." She quitted her companion and stood looking at Gérôme's fine portrait of the pale Rachel invested with the antique attributes of tragedy. The rise of the curtain had drawn away most of the company. Peter, from his bench, watched his friend a little, turning his eyes from her to the vivid image of the dead actress and thinking how little she suffered by the juxtaposition. Presently he came over and joined her again and she resumed: "I wonder if that's what your cousin had in his mind."

"My cousin — ?"

"What was his name? Mr. Dormer; that first day at Madame Carré's. He offered to paint my portrait."

"I remember. I put him up to it."

"Was he thinking of this?"

"I doubt if he has ever seen it. I dare say *I* was."

"Well, when we go to London he must do it," said Miriam.

"Oh there's no hurry," Peter was moved to reply.

"Don't you want my picture?" asked the girl with one of her successful touches.

"I'm not sure I want it from *him*. I don't know quite what he'd make of you."

"He looked so clever — I liked him. I saw him again at your party."

"He's a jolly good fellow; but what's one to say," Peter put to her, "of a painter who goes for his inspiration to the House of Commons?"

"To the House of Commons?" she echoed.

"He has lately got himself elected."

"Dear me, what a pity! I wanted to sit for him. But perhaps he won't have me — as I'm not a member of Parliament."

"It's my sister, rather, who has got him in."

"Your sister who was at your house that day? What has she to do with it?" Miriam asked.

"Why she's his cousin just as I am. And in addition," Sherringham went on, "she's to be married to him."

"Married — really?" She had a pause, but she continued. "So he paints *her*, I suppose?"

"Not much, probably. His talent in that line isn't what she esteems in him most."

"It isn't great then?"

"I haven't the least idea."

"And in the political line?" the girl persisted.

"I scarcely can tell. He's very clever."

"He does paint decently, then?"

"I dare say."

Miriam looked once more at Gérôme's picture. "Fancy his going into the House of Commons! And your sister put him there?"

"She worked, she canvassed."

"Ah you're a queer family!" she sighed, turning round at the sound of a step.

"We're lost — here's Mademoiselle Voisin," said Sherringham.

This celebrity presented herself smiling and addressing Miriam. "I acted for *you* to-night — I did my best."

"What a pleasure to speak to you, to thank you!" the girl murmured admiringly. She was startled and dazzled.

"I couldn't come to you before, but now I've got a rest — for half an hour," the actress went on.

Gracious and passive, as if a little spent, she let Sherringham, without looking at him, take her hand and raise it to his lips. "I'm sorry I make you lose the others — they're so good in this act," she added.

"We've seen them before and there's nothing so good as you," Miriam promptly returned.

"I like my part," said Mademoiselle Voisin gently, smiling still at our young lady with clear charming eyes. "One's always better in that case."

"She's so bad sometimes, you know!" Peter jested to Miriam; leading the actress thus to glance at him, kindly and vaguely, in a short silence which you couldn't call on her part embarrassment, but which was still less affectation.

"And it's so interesting to be here — *so* interesting!" Miriam protested.

"Ah you like our old house? Yes, we're very proud of it." And Mademoiselle Voisin smiled again at Sherringham all good-humoredly, but as if to say: "Well, here I am, and what do you want of me? Don't ask me to invent it myself, but if you'll tell me I'll do it." Miriam admired the note of discreet interrogation in her voice — the slight suggestion of surprise at their "old house" being liked. This performer was an astonishment from her seeming still more perfect on a nearer view — which was not, the girl had an idea, what performers usually did. This was very encouraging to her — it widened the programme of a young lady about to embrace the scenic career. To have so much to show before the footlights and yet to have so much left when you came off — that was really wonderful. Mademoiselle Voisin's eyes, as one looked into them, were still more agreeable than the distant spectator would have supposed; and there was in her appearance an extreme finish which instantly suggested to Miriam that she herself, in comparison, was big and rough and coarse.

"You're lovely to-night — you're particularly lovely," Sherringham said very frankly, translating Miriam's own impression and at the same time giving her an illustration of the way that, in Paris at least, gentlemen expressed themselves to the stars of the drama. She thought she knew her companion very well and had been witness of the degree to which, in such general conditions, his familiarity could increase; but his address to the slim distinguished harmonious woman before them had a different quality, the note of a special usage. If Miriam had had an apprehension that such directness might be taken as excessive it was removed by the manner in which Mademoiselle Voisin returned —

"Oh one's always well enough when one's made up; one's always exactly the same." That served as an example of the good taste with which a star of the drama could receive homage that was wanting in originality. Miriam determined on the spot that this should be the way *she* would ever receive it. The grace of her new acquaintance was the greater as the becoming bloom to which she alluded as artificial was the result of a science so consummate that it had none of the grossness of a mask. The perception of all this was exciting to our young aspirant, and her excitement relieved itself in the enquiry, which struck her as rude as soon as she had uttered it —

"You acted for 'me'? How did you know? What am I to you?"

"Monsieur Sherringham has told me about you. He says we're nothing beside you — that you're to be the great star of the future. I'm proud that you've seen me."

"That of course is what I tell every one," Peter acknowledged a trifle awkwardly to Miriam.

"I can believe it when I see you. Je vous ai bien observée," the actress continued in her sweet conciliatory tone.

Miriam looked from one of her interlocutors to the other as if there were joy for her in this report of Sherringham's remarks — joy accompanied and partly mitigated, however, by a quicker vision of what might have passed between a secretary of embassy and a creature so exquisite as Mademoiselle Voisin. "Ah you're wonderful people — a most interesting impression!" she yearningly sighed.

"I was looking for you; he had prepared me. We're such old friends!" said the actress in a tone courteously exempt from intention: upon which Sherringham, again taking her hand, raised it to his lips with a tenderness which her whole appearance seemed to bespeak for her, a sort of practical consideration and carefulness of touch, as if she were an object precious and frail, an instrument for producing rare sounds, to be handled, like a legendary violin, with a recognition of its value.

"Your dressing-room is so pretty — show her your dressing-room," he went on.

"Willingly, if she'll come up. Vous savez que c'est une montée."

"It's a shame to inflict it on *you*," Miriam objected.

"Comment donc? If it will interest you in the least!" They exchanged civilities, almost caresses, trying which could have the nicest manner to the other. It was the actress's manner that struck Miriam most; it denoted such a training, so much taste, expressed such a ripe conception of urbanity.

"No wonder she acts well when she has that tact — feels, perceives, is so remarkable, *mon Dieu, mon Dieu!*" the girl said to herself as they followed their conductress into another corridor and up a wide plain staircase. The staircase was spacious and long and this part of the establishment sombre and still, with the gravity of a college or a convent. They reached another passage lined with little doors, on each of which the name of a comedian was painted, and here the aspect became still more monastic, like that of a row of solitary cells. Mademoiselle Voisin led the way to her own door all obligingly and as if wishing to be hospitable; she dropped little subdued friendly attempts at explanation on the way. At her threshold the monasticism stopped — Miriam found herself in a wonderfully upholstered nook, a nest of lamplight and delicate cretonne. Save for its pair of long glasses it might have been a tiny boudoir, with a water-colour drawing of value in each of its panels of stretched

367

stuff, with its crackling fire and its charming order. It was intensely bright and extremely hot, singularly pretty and exempt from litter. Nothing lay about, but a small draped doorway led into an inner sanctuary. To Miriam it seemed royal; it immediately made the art of the comedian the most distinguished thing in the world. It was just such a place as they *should* have for their intervals if they were expected to be great artists. It was a result of the same evolution as Mademoiselle Voisin herself — not that our young lady found this particular term at hand to express her idea. But her mind was flooded with an impression of style, of refinement, of the long continuity of a tradition. The actress said "*Voilà, c'est tout!*" as if it were little enough and there were even something clumsy in her having brought them so far for nothing, and in their all sitting there waiting and looking at each other till it was time for her to change her dress. But to Miriam it was occupation enough to note what she did and said: these things and her whole person and carriage struck our young woman as exquisite in their adaptation to the particular occasion. She had had an idea that foreign actresses were rather of the *cabotin* order, but her hostess suggested to her much more a princess than a *cabotine*. She would do things as she liked and do them straight off: Miriam could n't fancy her in the gropings and humiliations of rehearsal. Everything in her had been sifted and formed, her tone was perfect, her amiability complete, and she might have been the charming young wife of a secretary of state receiving a pair of strangers of distinction. The girl observed all her movements. And then, as Sherringham had said, she was particularly lovely. But she suddenly told this gentleman that she must put him *à la porte* — she wanted to change her dress. He retired and returned to the foyer, where Miriam was to rejoin him after remaining the few minutes more with Mademoiselle Voisin and coming down with her. He waited for his companion, walking up and down and making up his mind; and when she presently came in he said to her:

"Please don't go back for the rest of the play. Stay here." They now had the foyer virtually to themselves.

"I want to stay here. I like it better." She moved back to the chimney-piece, from above which the cold portrait of Rachel looked down, and as he accompanied her he went on:

"I meant what I said just now."

"What you said to Voisin?"

"No, no; to you. Give it up and live with *me*."

"Give it up?" She turned her stage face on him.

"Give it up and I'll marry you to-morrow."

"This is a happy time to ask it!" she said with superior amusement. "And this is a good place!"

"Very good indeed, and that's why I speak: it's a place to make one choose — it puts it all before one."

"To make *you* choose, you mean. I'm much obliged, but that's not my choice," laughed Miriam.

"You shall be anything you like except this."

"Except what I most want to be? I *am* much obliged."

"Don't you care for me? Have n't you any gratitude?" Sherringham insisted.

"Gratitude for kindly removing the blest cup from my lips? I want to be what *she* is — I want it more than ever."

"Ah what she is — !" He took it impatiently.

"Do you mean I can't? We'll see if I can't. Tell me more about her — tell me everything."

"Have n't you seen for yourself and, knowing things as you do, can't you judge?"

"She's strange, she's mysterious," Miriam allowed, looking at the fire. "She showed us nothing — nothing of her real self."

"So much the better, all things considered."

"Are there all sorts of other things in her life? That's what I believe," the girl went on, raising her eyes to him.

"I can't tell you what there is in the life of such a woman."

"Imagine — when she's so perfect!" she exclaimed thoughtfully. "Ah she kept me off — she kept me off! Her charming manner is in itself a kind of contempt. It's an abyss — it's the wall of China. She has a hard polish, an inimitable surface, like some wonderful porcelain that costs more than you'd think."

"Do you want to become like that?" Sherringham asked.

"If I could I should be enchanted. One can always try."

"You must act better than she," he went on.

"Better? I thought you wanted me to give it up."

370

"Ah I don't know what I want," he cried, "and you torment me and turn me inside out! What I want is you yourself."

"Oh don't worry," said Miriam — now all kindly. Then she added that Mademoiselle Voisin had invited her to "call"; to which Sherringham replied with a certain dryness that she would probably not find that necessary. This made the girl stare and she asked: "Do you mean it won't do on account of mamma's prejudices?"

"Say this time on account of mine."

"Do you mean because she has lovers?"

"Her lovers are none of our business."

"None of mine, I see. So you've been one of them?"

"No such luck!"

"What a pity!" she richly wailed. "I should have liked to see that. One must see everything — to be able to do everything." And as he pressed for what in particular she had wished to see she replied: "The way a woman like that receives one of the old ones."

Peter gave a groan at this, which was at the same time partly a laugh, and, turning away to drop on a bench, ejaculated: "You'll do — you'll do!"

He sat there some minutes with his elbows on his knees and his face in his hands. His friend remained looking at the portrait of Rachel, after which she put to him: "Does n't such a woman as that receive — receive every one?"

"Every one who goes to see her, no doubt."

"And who goes?"

"Lots of men — clever men, eminent men."

371

"Ah what a charming life! Then does n't she go out?"

"Not what we Philistines mean by that — not into society, never. She never enters a lady's drawing-room."

"How strange, when one's as distinguished as that; except that she must escape a lot of stupidities and *corvées*. Then where does she learn such manners?"

"She teaches manners, *à ses heures:* she does n't need to learn them."

"Oh she has given me ideas! But in London actresses go into society," Miriam continued.

"Oh into ours, such as it is. In London *nous mêlons les genres.*"

"And shan't I go — I mean if I want?"

"You'll have every facility to bore yourself. Don't doubt it."

"And does n't she feel excluded?" Miriam asked.

"Excluded from what? She has the fullest life."

"The fullest?"

"An intense artistic life. The cleverest men in Paris talk over her work with her; the principal authors of plays discuss with her subjects and characters and questions of treatment. She lives in the world of art."

"Ah the world of art — how I envy her! And you offer me Dashwood!"

Sherringham rose in his emotion. "I ' offer ' you — ? "

Miriam burst out laughing. "You look so droll! You offer me yourself then, instead of all these things."

"My dear child, I also am a very clever man," he said, trying to sink his consciousness of having for a moment stood gaping.

"You are — you are; I delight in you. No ladies at all — no *femmes comme il faut?*" she began again.

"Ah what do *they* matter? Your business is the artistic life!" he broke out with inconsequence, irritated moreover at hearing her sound that trivial note again.

"You're a dear — your charming good sense comes back to you! What do you want of me then?"

"I want you for myself — not for others; and now, in time, before anything's done."

"Why then did you bring me here? Everything's done — I feel it to-night."

"I know the way you should look at it — if you do look at it at all," Sherringham conceded.

"That's so easy! I thought you liked the stage so," Miriam artfully added.

"Don't you want me to be a great swell?"

"And don't you want *me* to be?"

"You *will* be — you'll share my glory."

"So will you share mine."

"The husband of an actress? Yes, I see myself that!" Peter cried with a frank ring of disgust.

"It's a silly position, no doubt. But if you're too good for it why talk about it? Don't you think I'm important?" she demanded. Her companion met her eyes and she suddenly said in a different tone: "Ah why should we quarrel when you've been so kind, so generous? Can't we always be friends — the truest friends?"

373

Her voice sank to the sweetest cadence and her eyes were grateful and good as they rested on him. She sometimes said things with such perfection that they seemed dishonest, but in this case he was stirred to an expressive response. Just as he was making it, however, he was moved to utter other words — "Take care, here's Dashwood!" Mrs. Rooth's tried attendant was in the doorway. He had come back to say that they really must relieve him.

END OF VOLUME I